SEVEN SEALS

A HAND OF ADONAI NOVEL

AARON GANSKY

Brimstone Fiction

THE SEVEN SEALS, A Hand of Adonai Novel by Aaron D. Gansky

Published by Brimstone Fiction

1440 W. Taylor Street, Suite 449, Chicago, IL 60607

ISBN: Papberback: 978-1-946758-25-5

Ebook: 978-1-946758-24-8

Copyright © 2019 by Aaron D. Gansky

Cover design by Elaina Lee www.forthemusedesign.com

Interior design by Meaghan Burnett: www.meaghanburnett.com

Available in print and ebook from your local bookstore, online, or from the publisher at: www.brimstonefiction.com

For more information on this book and the author visit: www.aarongansky.com

Brought to you by the creative team at Brimstone Fiction.com:

Bethany R. Kaczmarek, Jessie Andersen, Rowena Kuo, and Meaghan Burnett.

Library of Congress Cataloging-in-Publication Data

Gansky, Aaron D.

The Seven Seals, a Hand of Adonai Novel / Aaron D. Gansky 1st ed.

PRAISE FOR THE SEVEN SEALS

The Seven Seals, book three in the Hand of Adoni series, does not fail to surprise and delight. Once again, readers will experience Gansky's well-crafted fiction jam-packed with tension, suspense, and emotion. Be prepared to catapult into uncharted territory as each character faces new and challenging dilemmas, including questions about reality and loyalty and a hero's true destiny. Under Gansky's masterful hand, the reader experiences, in exquisite detail, the rifts between North Chester and Alrujah, until the lines between fantasy and reality blur in unsettling and delightful ways. Follow this band of reluctant heroes as they fight and struggle and cry and love and in doing so learn the abominations they've been facing in Alrujah are indeed not the worst evil. As Shedoah's chains have been loosed, the true evil of Alrujah is about to rise. The characters we've grown to love are in for the fight of their lives, and the reader will not be able to put this book down until the very last page.

~Dennis Fulgoni
Author of *At the Broken Places*, *Thunder*, and *Dead Man's Nail*

Fans of *The Hand of Adonai* series will not be disappointed! *The Seven*

Seals continues its journey in this wondrously original epic fantasy. With a truly remarkable cast of characters, this enchantingly beautiful and magical tale is thrilling and poignant in equal measure. A brilliant combination of realistic fiction and epic fantasy, readers will have trouble leaving behind this wondrous world that enchants from the first sentence to the last.

~Heather Luby,
Author of *Laws of Motion, The Boys Were Watching,* and *Shine.*

Aaron Gansky just keeps getting better and better. *The Seven Seals,* the newest in *The Hand of Adonai* series, is a masterful tale that once again follows a band of teens into the role-playing, video-game world of Alrujah. The teens have encountered danger there in the past, but now they are about to come face to face with pure evil. *The Seven Seals* is a story of faith and unbelief, of decisions and their consequences, of love and loyalty. Above all, this is a tale that breathes new life and a fresh vibrancy into the age-old story of good versus evil.

~ Ann Tatlock,
novelist, editor, and blogger

Book three in the Hand of Adonai series, The Seven Seals is a masterfully woven gaming-crossover fantasy that delivers an enchanting blend of non-stop action and character dilemmas readers can relate to. The characters are enduring and their trials are relatable, and the ending delivers a punch readers won't forget.

~Lauricia Matuska,
Author of *The Healer's Rune* and *The Guardian Prince*

Aaron Gansky continues to up the stakes and the pacing in this continuation of the Hand of Adonai series. With unsuspected twists and cliffhanger chapters, Gansky sucks the reader into the story and then takes them on a roller coaster ride from one world to another and back again.

~Ralene Burke,
~author of the *Sacred Armor trilogy* and Marketing Director for Realm Makers

To Stephen McLain and Dennis Fulgoni

For your guidance, encouragement, and help throughout this series.
Most of all, for your friendships.

ACKNOWLEDGMENTS

So here's the thing: no book ever happens as the work of a single writer. Over the course of drafts, edits, and revisions, several people work together, and their efforts culminate over time into something that, ideally, is more than the sum of its parts. I've dedicated this book to Steve McLain and Dennis Fulgoni, my two "Alpha Readers." They took every step with me as I drafted this series from the ground up. They kept me on the right track, saved me a ton of time, and helped me avoid some rather embarrassing mistakes along the way. The second book in this series was dedicated to my wife, who patiently listened to all my not-so-wonderful ideas as they occurred to me and refrained from mocking me as those ideas changed shape countless times. It takes a special kind of person to not laugh out loud at some of my ideas. The first book was dedicated to Bailey Renee Gray, my niece—who helped give me the idea for the character who shares her name. I hope, at this point, you love Bailey as much as I do.

Along the way, there have been several others who have contributed to this series, and their efforts have improved the story immeasurably. My mother, Becky Gansky, lent her keen editorial eye as well as her loving support on this journey. Colleague and friend, Dr. Gale George, demonstrated her mastery of line edits and global edits alike. She is, undoubtedly, the master of identifying my missed commas. Comma master, some might say. Friend and former co-author Cindy Sproles, mom #2, also gave some great guidance along the way. Additionally, several of my students (and former students) contributed their artistic skills (which can be seen on the Facebook page as well as the blog). Among these are Katie Campbell, Dana Song, Sherri Sanderson, and Kristen Brittner. Additionally, a great big thank you to Caleb Kaczmarek (the map you see at the front of each book was made possible by his efforts).

Special thanks to Sharon Schlegel, former boss and joyful proof-reader. Also, a big thanks to Pops for giving me my love of writing.

Lastly, I'd be remiss if I didn't mention the efforts of the Brimstone team. Rowena Kuo, Meghan Burnett, and Bethany Kaczmarek. They make the often-tedious process of publication a joy. Bethany's fingerprints are all over Alrujah and North Chester. They have made it what it is. Send them a thank you note when you get some time.

Thanks again to each of you, and thank you especially, to my readers. May Alrujah persist in your minds and hearts.

Blessings of Adonai,

Aaron Gansky

CHARACTERS

Lauren Knowles/Indigo: Daughter of Becca Knowles. For years, she's dreamed of the land of Alrujah, and she's put every detail into her journals for her friend Oliver to program into the role-playing game they'd been working on together since junior high school. When she wakes up in Alrujah, she takes the role of Princess Indigo, daughter of King Ribillius, and sets out to find *The Book of Sealed Magic* so she and her friends can get home.

Oliver Shaw/Vicmorn the Devout: The boy genius behind the Alrujah video game. He designed his own programming language to make the game more realistic. In Alrujah, he takes on the role of Vicmorn, a Father of the Monks of the Cerulean Order.

Erica Hall/Lakia: A gothic teenager with few friends in high school, Erica has long been admired by Oliver. When she wakes up in the game, she sees it as an opportunity to escape her tragic life.

Aiden Price/Jaurru: New to North Chester High School this year, Aiden Price found a home on the football team, though not without some conflict getting there. He's had his eye on Lauren, and will do whatever it takes to protect her in the dangerous world of Alrujah, where he has become Jaurru, King Ribillius's personal guard.

Ullwen of Varuth: A former Varuthian Infiltrator and current

Varuthian Elite, Ullwen of Varuth fell in love with Princess Indigo. Now, he accompanies Lakia in her quest to free her parents from the dungeons of Alrujah.

Bailey Renee Knowles: Lauren's little sister. Bailey is very smart, athletically gifted, and wracked with guilt over the disappearance of Lauren from North Chester. She has been pulled into the game, too, but as an angel of Adonai.

Becca Knowles: Overcome with grief over the disappearances of her daughters Lauren and Bailey, she has nowhere left to turn but Detective Joseph Parker.

Detective Joseph Parker: Detective Parker works missing persons cases for the North Chester PD. He's taken a special interest in the disappearance of the five teens.

Pacha el Nai: A mighty angel who speaks for Adonai.

Abaddon: A fearsome angel who, centuries ago, helped King Solous defeat the elves and retake the throne of Alrujah for men.

King Solous: the long dead King of Alrujah who, with the help of seven angels, overthrew the elves from the throne of Alrujah.

King Ribillius: the murdered king and direct descendent of Solous who reigned over Alrujah in a time of turmoil.

King Korodeth: Former Captain of the Guard of Alrujah and trusted advisor for King Ribillius. His devotion to Shedoah convinced him to murder King Ribillius and take the crown for himself.

Yarborough: Fierce warrior. Half-dwarf. The nameless heir, prophesied to lead his people back to prominence in Alrujah.

Langley: Arrogant half-elf, ruthlessly dedicated to the cause of his people. He holds the Blood Sword, an ancient, cursed blade of incredible power.

Council of Yeval: A body of leaders gathered from throughout Alrujah, representing all three species: human, dwarf, and elf. They rule the land from the Heart of Yeval, a fiercely protected forest where they govern from the shadows.

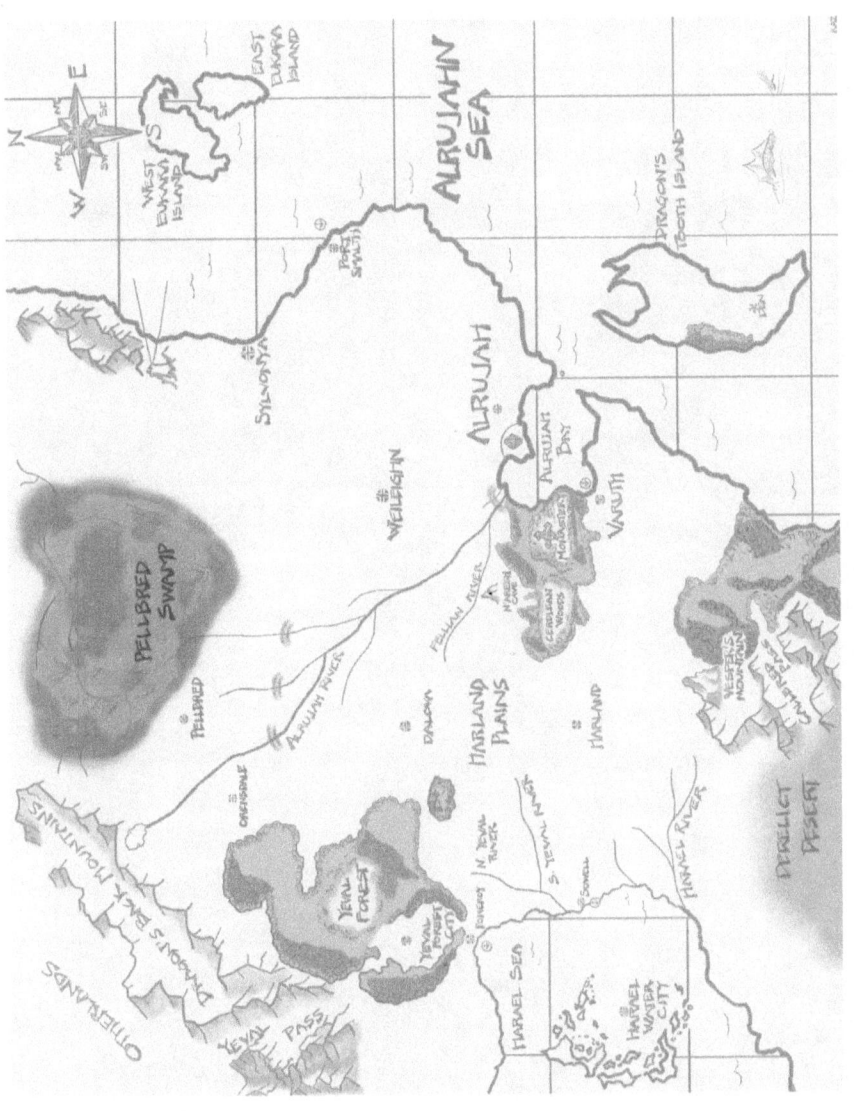

PROLOGUE

With a touch, I will call Adonai's servants to my cause. I will open their eyes, transform their bodies, give them power unimagined. And so shall the Hand of Shedoah have six fingers, with which he will crush the deceiver Adonai.
—The Shedoahn Prophecies

THE VOICES of the devout demanded an answer. Abaddon curled his lip and brought his massive two-handed sword arcing over his head. With a twist of his bony wrist, the air before him shifted, tore like fabric pulled too tight.

"Hear us," the voices said. "Reveal yourself to us."

He stepped from the warm nether of the spiritual realm into the aggressive chill of the Dragon's Back Mountains and cocooned himself with his scaly wings.

When had he lost his feathers?

The wind shifted. A pungent stench clouded the crisp mountain air.

Griffins. Pacha el Nai was here, and he would not be pleased with Abaddon's plan.

Abaddon wrinkled his lip and turned around. "Save your rhetoric. I will not stay."

Pacha el Nai, Adonai's favored angel, stood between his griffins. His gold armor shimmered in the sunset, and his feathers glowed like opals.

Such beauty, such majesty soured Abaddon's stomach. "Why must you always stand in my way?"

"Your heart has made its choice."

Abaddon raised his sword, leaning back into a cat's crouch. "You've grown weak these hundred years. You cannot stand against me."

The black griffin sat on its haunches and shrieked. The tawny griffin lifted into the air with a commanding thrust of its golden wings. Its claws flashed pearl in the dimming light. But Pacha el Nai put his hand on its paw, and it dropped back to the mountainside. "Adonai wishes you to repent and return to Him. You've been gone too long."

Denied his excuse to fight, Abaddon frowned. It'd been too long since he'd felt the thrill of battle, since he'd left elf and dwarf and man cowering in abject terror. "I've been watching the swamp dwellers as commanded by King Solous. Has Adonai forgotten His directives? Has He changed His mind?"

Pacha spoke with the voice of trees exploding in winter. "Their worship has poisoned your mind."

Abaddon's voice buzzed. "I happen to like poison."

"And disease, and pestilence, and insects. Your heart has accepted the worship of Pellbred. Shedoah's touch has tainted you, though you've not fallen too far for Adonai to save. Come back with me."

Carried on the wind, the stench of rotting meat eclipsed the scent of griffins. Three dead animals—a diseased serpent, a crocodile, and an egret—rotted on Abaddon's altar. He inhaled deeply. "Adonai fears what I've become."

"Adonai only fears for you. If you heed the call of these fallen people, so too will you be truly fallen, and Adonai will stretch out His Hand against you."

Abaddon sheathed his sword in the bone casing between his wings. Pacha would not fight. He'd have to find something else to kill. "Where was His Hand when I sat alone, watching over a destitute swampland? Where was His Hand when those people cried out to me, begged me for favor, pled me to keep disease from their livestock, to keep the insects from their crops?"

Pacha el Nai's mouth fell to a frown. "Maewen turned her heart from Adonai, and I buried her. You are my brother, Abaddon. We've fought beside each other. Adonai had no fiercer warrior than you. Do not turn your heart from Him."

Voices swirled on the wind. "Heed our call, oh great Abaddon. Protect us from disease."

"Hear them, Pacha. They do not call for Adonai. He has turned a deaf ear to them for fifty years. My people suffer, and you ask me not to aid them?"

The black griffin shrieked again. Abaddon wished it would fly at him.

"Look at yourself. Your armor is bone. Each day you become more insect and less angel. Shedoah poisons you. You must resist his taint."

"Shedoah gives me power. He hears my calls."

"You've spoken to him?"

A grin curled Abaddon's lips. "Did Adonai not tell you?"

Pacha folded his arms, wrapping his wings around his shoulders. "He tells me what He wills."

"He wills to tell you little. Do you not hear the call of the humans, brother?" Abaddon stepped closer and stretched out his hand. His gauntlets had fused to his skin.

The wind swirled snow near their ankles into tiny tornados. "I do."

"Do you not hear the voice of Shedoah? Can you not feel his touch?"

Pacha took a step back. "It is a spear in my chest. Each day, I must shield myself against it, as should you."

When had Pacha gotten so small? When had he abandoned his will so completely? Abaddon would not be weak like Pacha. He stretched his wings. "My people summon me. I must go."

"Expect His Hand, Abaddon. He will crush you with it."

"Let him try." He leapt toward the silvery moon, spread his wings like a shadow, and glided to his people.

THE BLOOD of his best friend slicked Korodeth's boots. He stepped from the puddle, his heart heavy. Had there been any other way, he would not have had to kill him. But the glorious burden of preparing the way for Shedoah fell squarely on Korodeth's shoulders, and he could not accomplish the task without the crown on his head.

He had no desire to wear it. He knew it would be heavy with responsibility. Alrujah was a kingdom in turmoil, and now it would be a kingdom divided. Still, he lifted the crown with the midnight sapphire and placed it on his head.

Dybarian crashed through the doors to the throne room. His eyes found the body of the fallen king. He knelt, his fist over heart. "Your grace. The crown is yours. My men will have the usurpers in custody soon."

"No," Korodeth said. He sat in the throne, unwilling to join the fray. He could easily end it. With a snap of his fingers, he could freeze Lakia and Ullwen and the others where they stood, but that would be overplaying his hand. They must escape. They must spread dissent among the cities. Such was the price of the coming of Shedoah.

For how could his god restore peace if there was no war? How could he bring healing without disease? How could he bring sustenance without famine? These were the birthpangs that heralded the glorious return of Shedoah. "Where is Indigo?"

A voice came in a rasp. "Harael."

"The Seers?"

"They stand, but not for long. A razorbeak arrived earlier from my men in the island city. Langley of Erul stands against Neldohr. Blood will spill."

He gestured to the room. "It already has. Belphegor and Moloch and now the Seers. The seals are breaking more rapidly than I'd anticipated. Bring Indigo back."

"Alive?"

"I can't crown a corpse. Not everyone will accept my rule. Dalova and Weileigh and Port Smalth will rebel. Blood will mark my short reign. I'd like to minimize it as much as I can. If Indigo wears the crown when Shedoah returns, so be it. It is his honor to remove her if he sees fit. It is not my place to crown kings in his name, only to prepare the way for him."

Dybarian stood. "We need not bring her back to Alrujah by force. She is a princess in the line of Ribillius. She shares his temper. When she hears her father is dead, she will return to Alrujah on her own, but she will lead an army."

The hallway rang with the sounds of battle—metal on metal, the whisping of arrows through the air. How many soldiers would die today, trying to stop the Hand of Adonai? How much blood would his servants have to scrub clean tomorrow morning? This was not the way he wanted his reign to begin.

Korodeth stood. "We must be ready."

1

The prophet shall come from the line of Pentavus. His life will mark the coming of the Hand of Adonai. By his devotion, he shall become the agent of Adonai; he shall call forth the Hand of Adonai.
—The Book of Things to Come

IN THE LATE AFTERNOON, Detective Joseph Parker found Ms. Knowles in her pajamas, ankle deep in the snow, a foot away from the edge of the steep cliff overlooking North Chester. She wore a nightgown better suited for California summers, not Minnesota winters. She folded her arms and shivered. Wind circled her and rippled her gown like a flag. The tops of her slippers peeked through a skeletal layer of ice and snow.

Parker shoved his hands in the pockets of his overcoat and felt around until he found a cigarette. He pulled it out, inspected it, shoved it back in. "Hypothermia doesn't take long to set in."

"Couldn't sleep," she said.

Parker checked his watch. "It's only five."

A full, silver moon hung in a cloudless indigo sky. Ms. Knowles stepped closer to the edge. "Lauren was standing here the day before she disappeared. Bailey used to come out here, too, after Lauren disappeared. They're both gone now."

Parker took off his wool overcoat and slipped it around her shoulders. His suit jacket did little to shield him from the stabbing cold of the air. Goosebumps ridged Ms. Knowles's fair skin.

He should say something, but nothing would comfort her. The loss of a child was bad enough. The loss of two was unimaginable. He caught himself thinking of his own daughter and reminded himself that her disappearance wasn't his fault.

Hard not to imagine his ex-wife Wendy when he looked at Becca Knowles—the suffering Wendy felt when Cindy vanished. He wrapped an arm around Becca's shoulder.

Immediately, her shoulders shook, and she turned into him. She put her head in his chest and wept.

He shouldn't be holding her, shouldn't allow her to cry in his arms. It wasn't professional. She'd grow attached to him. But he shared her pain. He'd come to care deeply for Bailey Renee. If his daughter had survived, she'd be about her age. The line of her jaw, the set of her ears, reminded him of Cindy, of the life she should have had.

Holding Becca hurt his heart, but he couldn't turn her loose. He needed to grieve again, to let her sorrow pull at him.

Lavender wafted up from her neck. Her hands grabbed the back of his suit jacket. He pulled her chin up. Her gray eyes met his. "I'm going to crack this case. I'm going to get them back. You got my word."

Ms. Knowles said nothing, but her body steadied.

Keeping an arm around her, he guided her toward the house. "Let's get you inside where it's warm."

She pulled away from him and turned back to the edge, taking a few slow steps, her toes inching closer to the precipice. "I tried to nap, but I couldn't get this cliff out of my head. There's something about this place."

Parker grabbed her elbow. "You're too close."

"I can feel the girls," she whispered, the trail of tears turning to ice on her cheeks.

"Guess I'll take you in myself." He lifted her, carrying her toward her front door.

"Put me back." She put up little fight. Her arms wrapped around him, and she hugged him. It surprised him at first, and he wanted to put her down. Another part of him, the lonely three-year bachelor, wanted to hold her closer.

He opened the door and set her down inside the warm foyer. She didn't let go. Parker needed a smoke, but he resisted the urge to fish the cigarette from his pocket. "Okay," he said, pulling away gently.

She didn't let go. "Stay. Please."

"I wanted to ask you a few questions, but I'm not sure you're up for it."

She held on to him with a quiet desperation. "Please. I'll make you something to eat."

Parker took a deep breath. If he left, she'd head right out to the cliff again; maybe slip off the cliff or into hypothermia. "Already ate. But I'd take some coffee."

"Tea okay?"

"Perfect."

∽

LAUREN STOOD among the rubble of the crumbled statues of the Seers. Torap's marble head lay at her feet; the empty star-shaped hole of his missing left eye stared up at her. White marble, cracked into chunks of jagged stone, lay strewn across the entirety of the island. As far as the opposite side, near the water's edge beyond the mass of dilapidated homes, among the huts of the poorest of elves, chips of marble lay like stone snowflakes.

Her legs weakened as the surge of adrenaline bled from her, replaced instead by an intense, burning pain. She leaned on Oliver's staff. Even when he was gone, Oliver held her up. She missed him, his encouragement, his unwavering faith. Why had she argued with him about the stupid details of this game? She'd been petty. In Oliver's absence, such silliness became trivial. She wanted to slip back in time, to take him in her arms and hug him once more, to tell him he was right all along; Adonai was real; God was real.

But he'd been swept away in the chaos of the battle. She turned her eyes from the destruction surrounding her. The suns sank toward the sea. He'd been gone too long.

"You okay?" Aiden asked. He dug an armored foot under Torap's head and kicked it down the hill until it rolled into the green waters of the Harael Sea.

"Thinking," she said.

"About Oliver?"

Bailey Renee, who'd flown around the island several times, dropped back to the earth. Folding her feathered wings around her, she shivered in the chilled air. "I can't find him anywhere. I've searched miles in all directions." Her angelic voice cracked as she spoke.

Lauren took Bailey Renee in her arms. How long had it been since they'd hugged? Even in North Chester, they hardly glanced at each other. But here, now, in Alrujah, with Bailey Renee's wings encircling her, Lauren lost control. Her chest heaved, and hot tears stung her eyes. "I've missed you so bad," she said.

The half-dwarf Yarborough, still holding his wounded shoulder with a bloodied hand, joined the group. Slowly, he raised his hand toward the sea. Closing his eyes, he intoned in a deep, resonant voice, "May Adonai grant you easy passage to Delosoph, Vicmorn the Devout."

From their squalid hovels, the elves of Torap Island made their way toward the carnage and chaos of the blood-stained battlefield. Their eyes locked on the half-elf Langley with wonderment and fear. Lauren's heart broke even more.

More elves—better dressed, better fed—tentatively peered out from the capitol building. A white, marbled dust covered their robes of fine, blue silk.

The body of Neldohr lay in a crumpled heap near the entrance.

His blood trailed down the steps of the capitol building, a crimson, viscous sludge. Elf blood ran thick.

The elves squinted, faces swimming with elation, loathing, confusion. The Blood Sword stirred awe in every elvish eye.

Langley surveyed the blood-stained battle field before him. Were those tears in his eyes? Holding the Blood Sword upside down by the hilt, he scooped his hands into the air, as if cupping water from a river. The green waters of the Harael Sea shot up in a column.

Lauren spun around as water bubbled and popped, as if something rose from it, some sort of sea serpent or water dragon. But nothing showed itself. The column of water ascended into the indigo sky. The moon, rising in the early dusk, shone around the column, embedding it with diamond-shaped silver reflections. Its beauty awed her. Its power terrified her.

"What's he doing?" Aiden asked, sword firm in his hand.

"He's angry," Yarborough said.

Lauren stared up at the column, her neck crimping back. The spray of water foamed and frothed at the top, six stories above.

"An awesome anger," Yarborough whispered, his neck bent back.

The column split in two as Langley worked his hands in alternating patterns, like a weaver looming an intricate carpet. The two became four, the four eight, until the columns surrounded Torap Island—like prisons bars. "Should we do something?" Aiden asked.

Lauren held Bailey's hand in hers, Oliver's staff in the other. "What can we do?"

All at once, the hundred columns of water rained in, splashing around each shattered shard of the fallen stone Seers. They encased each remnant of the marble monsters, the fangands and the beresus, every splinter, every sliver, and simultaneously lifted them into the air. Like whips, the watery columns flung the final vestiges of the Seers deep into the sea.

The hushed whispers of awed elves carried over the sound and the spray of water. Not even King Neldohr, the most prolific practitioner of the elvish arcane arts, could have accomplished such a feat. Finally, the columns receded into the sea. Langley's chest heaved with heavy breaths. His arms shook. Sweat sat in beads across his brow and his angular cheeks.

Langley of Erul, half-elf, ambassador to Harland, leaned on the Blood Sword. He opened his mouth as if to say something but clenched it shut soon after. He cleared his throat and spoke. "Your gods," he said to the assembled elves, both the starving families beyond the capitol building and the well-dressed politicians gathered in front of him, "are dead."

Lauren touched Aiden's arm. It twitched; his muscles tensed for battle and sent his armor trembling.

Langley held the Blood Sword high. At this, the elves ceased their whispering. "The sword in my hand is the Blood Sword, which I took from the pit of Moloch, from the ruins of Fort Norgren. I wrested the blade from Moloch's dead hand. The cursed blade is cursed no more, and by its strength I shall return the elves to power. We will be a strong nation, a just nation! There will be no room for selfish greed. Neldohr has paid for his sins with his blood, and his tyranny lies dead at my feet!"

From somewhere in the midst of the terrified, huddled elves, a shout erupted, a lone voice stirring hundreds of echoes in turn. "All hail Langley god-slayer!"

Aiden hunched his shoulders and moved forward through the crowd of elves, all taller than him by a head. He maneuvered through their thin bodies like a pinball bouncing down a table past traps and flippers. "Hold up a sec, bro. You weren't the only one fighting."

Langley's eyes cut to Aiden. "Still your tongue, human. Your kind has no say in the business of elves."

Bailey said, "In case you missed it, we were all up in your elf business five minutes ago. Your elf business nearly got us killed."

Langley leveled the Blood Sword toward Bailey's chest. The assembled elves stared at her. "This is not the time, winged one."

Lauren touched Aiden's shoulder. She'd seen something in Langley's face, something beyond the mere façade of anger. Langley's eyes pleaded with hers. "I'm getting a bad feeling about this. We may want to let him have his moment."

Yarborough stood next to her and spoke sternly to Langley, as a father would to a son. "How dare you take credit for the work of Adonai? His Hand lay the Seers waste, not you. Remember your place."

Langley stepped over the slain body of Neldohr. He made his way down the steps, through the blood of the fallen elf-king, until he stood inches from Lauren and Aiden, Yarborough and Bailey Renee. "This is my home. You have no business here, outsiders. My grace alone allows you to stay."

"Bro, you better back it up." Aiden raised his sword and pointed it at Langley.

Langley wouldn't let Aiden's act of aggression go unpunished. Lauren tried to push Aiden's arm back down, but it wouldn't budge.

With a sneer, Langley said, "You are all banished from Harael. By my grace, you may leave peacefully. Leave immediately, or I will kill you."

Aiden grinned. "Come at me, bro."

Irritation and fear crashed over Lauren. How dare Aiden goad Langley into a fight, especially one they may not be able to win? So long as Langley held the Blood Sword, he'd have access to power like none they'd ever seen. "Don't do this," she whispered.

Langley leapt backward with all the grace of a jungle cat. In one fluid motion, he parried Aiden's attack and lunged at the armored knight. Moving swiftly to the side, Aiden deflected the sword, but as his golden dwarven blade met the Blood Sword, the dwarven blade fell in two.

Holding the hilt, Aiden said, "You kidding me?"

Langley lunged again, this time firing a ray of intense light toward Bailey Renee. She spun out of the way. "Not cool," she said, and took to the air.

Lauren's blood ran cold, and she launched a volley of ice shards toward Langley.

The half-elf made a wall of fire, melting them before they got close.

He must be the Mage Lord. Since he took the formerly cursed

blade, his power had increased exponentially, as had his attitude, his disrespect toward Adonai, his pride, and vanity.

Langley rushed Aiden, the Blood Sword angling toward Aiden's chest. Aiden dodged. The blade narrowly missed him. He staggered backward. Langley shifted his attention to Bailey, launching a piercing light from his palm. Bailey barrel-rolled and dove toward Langley. She swung her blade at him, but he ducked, grabbed her wrist, and threw her to the ground. She rolled, gasping and crying.

Yarborough sprinted toward Langley, but the other elves had armed themselves. The well-dressed city elves surrounded the half-dwarf. They brandished sharp blades, long bows, and arrows. With his shoulder wounded already, he'd have little chance against so many.

How had it come to this? Moments earlier, Langley had fought on their side. He'd helped topple the Seers. She'd assumed he'd had a change of heart, assumed he'd relinquished his worship of the Seers and embraced Adonai as the true God. Now, it seemed he'd done it for his own selfish means. He wanted the throne. And what better way to establish oneself as a leader than by destroying deities?

She had to do something, to find a way to get them out before Langley killed them. They'd used too much of their energy against the Seers. They were tired and wounded, but the Blood Sword filled Langley with a terrible power. His pallid skin glowed with it.

White-hot light seared her face as a beam shot past her cheek. She reeled away and touched her still-burning skin.

Aiden helped Bailey up. Together, they flanked Langley. A swarm of elves interposed themselves. Aiden extended his shield in front of him and bowled through them. Bailey Renee flew low over their heads, brandishing her flaming sword.

With Yarborough's one good arm, he'd crushed enough legs and arms to dissuade the elves from pressing in on him. A blast of fire erupted toward the half-dwarf and knocked him back. He howled in pain.

Aiden leapt in front of the column of flame, raised his shield, and the flame split in two. The maneuver gave Yarborough an opportunity to find safer ground.

Langley fired a bolt of light toward Lauren with one hand. With the other, he leveled the Blood Sword toward Bailey, and an equally piercing light shot toward her.

Lauren waved Oliver's staff in front of her, and a blue semi-transparent mirror appeared before her. The light bounced off the mirror toward Langley, but he simply absorbed the beam with the blade of the Blood Sword. An unearthly brightness emanated from the whites of his eyes. "It's only a matter of time before you fall to me as Neldohr did." When he opened his mouth, light poured out like he'd swallowed the lesser sun.

Such power. Such strength. Already, Lauren's magic reserves ran on empty. If not for Oliver's staff, she'd be powerless, crippled with fatigue. They had to get away.

My staff, a voice said within her. *Raise my staff.*

She did.

A violent pulling sensation gripped her, as if she were a page ripped from a book. Blackness blinked over Harael, replaced seconds later by a wall of massive trees.

ERICA LOWERED her head as the armored horse beneath her galloped through the flaming city gates of Alrujah. Her wolf, Sparky, balanced in front of her, howling into the night. Thick black smoke stung her eyes and lungs. She nudged the horse west, toward the Fellian River, and glanced behind her, her heart exploding. A man in black leather erupted through the dense smoke riding a silver armored horse. Ullwen. He made it. She exhaled acrid smoke and remembered the smell of her last foster mother's cigarettes.

She'd survived a sasquatch attack, rescued her parents, watched Sparky heal from the brink of death, and fallen in love, all on the same trip. But Ribillius was dead. Korodeth murdered him—stabbed the king he'd claimed to serve for years.

Two more figures shot from the smoke. Four more came on their heels, all on heavily armored horses. They would soon outpace Erica's and Ullwen's mounts. Not good. "They're coming," she shouted.

"Shoot them!" Ullwen called.

She reached into the quiver on her back and pulled her hand back fast. Her arrows had gathered the flames as they rode through the burning city. Fire burned the fletching of her arrows, the tips of the shafts. Her horse galloped fast, its sides expanding and contracting with each breath, its muscles straining under the armor. Feet in stirrups, she stood, pulled the quiver off and dropped it in the river. "We need another plan!"

Ullwen rode his horse closer, his breath heaving in his chest. "Have you fought on horseback before?"

Her legs ached; her back throbbed; pain split her head. "I'm not about to learn now. We can lose them in the woods."

"It will slow us, and they will overtake us." He took a few shallow breaths and checked over his shoulder. "Those are Alrujah's finest cavalry, skilled both on their mounts and off. You have no weapon. The woods are a bad idea."

No. The woods were a great idea. Specifically, the pack of fangands she'd call once she got there.

Hoof falls echoed like machine-gun fire. Her breath quickened as they raced over the bridge spanning the Fellian River. In the silvery moonlight, the waters reflected the smoke from the gates of Alrujah. Something in the hoary water pulled her ... called to her. She cleared her throat and glanced over her shoulder.

Ullwen's horse galloped beside hers. The Alrujahn soldiers rode fast and closed the gap. Above them, a bird-like silhouette crossed the moon, casting a shadow over her and Ullwen. Pacha el Nai had her parents still, and they were well on their way to the nar'esh cave. She had to make it back to them. She had an idea, even better than the fangands. "Keep going. I'll meet you at the cave," she said.

Ullwen said, "What are you doing?"

She spoke to her horse and to Sparky. "I'll catch up in the woods.

Wait for me." Drawing in a lungful of air, she dismounted and plunged into the river. The cold of the water bit her bone deep, but she pushed the pain from her mind. She had one thought, one idea. It would be immediate, swift. She pinched her vocal cords and hummed, closing her eyes and holding herself under the surface of the water.

The sound resonated from her throat and carried through the water. Distant sounds of galloping horses punched through the river. She thought of the water dragons in the Alrujahn Bay, of the parial-barbed vi-fish, of Ullwen's kiss.

She moaned like a whale with laryngitis.

She felt it coming before she saw it, the rush of water pressing against her like a tornado snapping light poles into toothpicks. At the edge of her vision, as the Alrujahn soldiers' horses hit the bridge, a slender neck rose out of the water. A gaping maw swallowed one soldier, horse and all, before the muscular neck, thick as a Roman column, crashed down on the bridge. The other soldiers, flailing, arms wielding swords and pole arms, splashed into the chilling waters of the Fellian River.

Terrified, the soldiers struggled against the weight of their armor. The horses splashed as they sank deeper. Erica closed her eyes. The knotting hunger of the river beast twisted her stomach.

Eat well.

2

The seals that barred Shedoah, the Deceiver of Old, from Alrujah will weaken. Thus, he will abandon his prison and flee to Alrujah and will rain destruction and fear and death upon the land.
—The Book of Things to Come

Ms. Knowles's microwave droned while a too-large mug of herbal tea spun around on a rotating plate. Parker hung his overcoat on the rack beside the door. His hands fumbled with the unlit cigarette in his pockets. He wanted to light it before he told her Bailey was gone —really gone. No good would come from the news. She already thought Bailey disappeared days ago, instead of hours. If he told Ms. Knowles Bailey had only recently gone missing—truly missing—he'd have to tell Ms. Knowles he'd known Bailey snuck out of the hospital and stayed at Franky's house.

Ms. Knowles took a canister of sugar from the pantry. "Any news?"

Her voice held a resigned hope, something he heard often in his line of work—a cautious, dubious longing for good news. He didn't like crushing hopes, but he had few options. "We're looking into a few things."

"What kinds of things?" The microwave beeped, and she took the mug from it. She dunked the tea bag a few times before throwing it away in the pantry trash. She stirred in two spoonfuls of sugar and handed Parker the cup.

He'd sound insane if he answered truthfully. *Look, Ms. Knowles, I think your daughters were somehow pulled into a different world, some sort of alternate reality tied to the video game Lauren designed.* Yeah—she'd buy that. Instead, he said, "We're hoping we find more clues in Oliver's game. We've got a guy running the code. Complex stuff, but if there's something there, our guy will find it." He sipped the tea. Too sweet.

"You think they planned this? Like to run away?"

Parker shrugged. "Hard to say. We've exhausted all the scarier options. We can find runaways. Kidnappings and disappearances are tougher. Running away is planned, so they'd have brought what they needed to survive. They're probably staying with friends or family."

Ms. Knowles put a mug of tea in for herself—decaf jasmine and chamomile—and said, "They didn't take anything. Not even their cell phones."

"That we know of." Parker sipped the tea, and his stomach tightened. Over-sweetened tea always irritated his ulcer. He took the unlit cigarette from his pocket and put it between his lips. He pantomimed lighting it and took an imaginary drag. It amazed him how much the simple ritual of pretending to smoke settled him, soothed him. Already, his stomach eased.

Ms. Knowles held the tea in both hands and blew on it.

"They may have stashed some cash and clothes and the like."

"Bailey vanished from a hospital. She wouldn't have had time to plan anything."

"Bailey Renee's bright; for her, sneaking out would be cake." Saying the name made his stomach roil. He took another imaginary drag on the unlit cigarette.

Ms. Knowles sat next to Parker. She stirred her tea for a moment and took a deep, uneven breath.

Parker recognized the ragged inhalation—the surge of a coming storm. Wouldn't be long before tears broke. "Hey," he said, as if leading into a profound or comforting word, but he had no idea what to say next. He took her hands in his. He'd never been a comforter. He brought others along to ensure hope while he investigated clues. Now, with the department so strapped for cash, he had no partner to handle the encouragement.

But he wanted to encourage her, to ease her suffering. He drew stock phrases from past partners, good detectives who didn't fake smoke. "Hey now, it'll be fine. It'll work out. Finding runaways is a matter of time."

"You don't understand."

"I do. You want to believe they ran away because it gives you hope they're alive. But you don't want to believe they ran away because it'd mean you'd screwed up as a parent, right?"

Her slick gray eyes met his. "I'm a failure," she whispered.

"You're not. Teenagers are tough. Nearly impossible when you're working alone. Kids need to find their own way. They'll come back and tell you how much they love you. I've seen it hundreds of times."

Her hands shook in his. She closed her eyes, and her chest trembled with half-heaves.

He wanted to believe what he said, but he knew too much. She didn't, and as long as she had hope, hollow as it may be, she had something to hold onto. He stood up, pulled her into his arms.

She sank into his embrace. "I can't lose them. I can't be alone." She sobbed into his chest. "My babies."

He held her tight, a desperate hug, offering her what he needed: comfort. "You won't be alone," he said.

～

"OKAY. WHAT HAPPENED?" Bailey asked. She stood beside Lauren, her neck bent back to examine the trees surrounding them.

Aiden whispered, "Where are we? And how'd we get here?"

Yarborough leaned against a tree, hand pressed hard to his shoulder. "This looks like the Bleeding Grounds, Yeval Forest, but it does not smell right."

Lauren knelt and examined the soil. Rich and dark, identical to how she'd described it in her journal, to the dreams she'd had in North Chester so many years ago. They must be in Yeval Forest—nearly a week's journey on horseback from Harael. "Rapture," she said. No other logical explanation.

"What's that?" Bailey asked.

Yarborough stared at Lauren. In a voice lined equally with wonder and fear, he said, "Rapture is a sealed spell. How do you come to know it?"

"I designed it, remember?"

Bailey sheathed her sword and examined the thick-trunked trees before them and the thinner, shorter trees behind her. "Still lost."

Lauren walked forward, toward the dark earth of the forest. "Rapture is a spell from *The Book of Sealed Magic*. Hundreds of years ago, after the War of the Suns, King Solous sealed away Alrujah's most powerful spells to prevent the destruction and death that followed the bloodiest war in Alrujahn history. Since then, no human, dwarf, or elf has been able to cast the spells."

Yarborough favored his shoulder as he followed Lauren. "The book is an ancient tome, one with great power, and not for its spells alone. The book itself is fortified with enchantments. Whoever holds it is near invincible."

"Hold up," Aiden said. "You telling me Solous had a book that'd make him invincible, and he got rid of it?"

Lauren said, "It was too dangerous to keep. Temptation would have overwhelmed him. He might have become a tyrant."

Yarborough harrumphed. "Like the Mage Lord. Imagine if Langley held the book. Neither man nor dwarf could stand against him."

"What makes you think Langley doesn't already have the book?"

Bailey asked. She ran her fingers along the bark of the tree, her wings folding around her. "Seemed pretty tyrannical to me."

Lauren studied the trees. Somehow, they made her uneasy, as if something about them had changed. They grew in dense clusters, thick around the group like blood clotting. She touched the cold, stiff bark, analyzing each crevice, each grain with the tips of her fingers. The lumbering pines smelled familiar. She'd never been to Yeval Forest but remembered designing it. Pine grew alongside rognak, before the species died out. But here, spruce trees and larch trees also grew. They gave the forest a mellow, sharp scent. She'd smelled this before.

"She's not wrong," Aiden said. "Dude slung some pretty killer spells. Wasn't even tired from fighting the Seers."

"Something's not right," Lauren said.

"A lot of things aren't right." Bailey stood next to Lauren and touched the same tree. "I don't know what kind of trees they have in Alrujah, but this one looks familiar."

"Pine," Aiden said.

"Quiet," Yarborough said in a hushed whisper. "I hear something." He readied his hammer in his good hand.

The four stilled for a moment. Eyes closed, Lauren listened carefully: wind through trees, the sibilance of feet through dead needles, her chest expanding with air, her slow exhalations, a faint and distant rustling.

Yeval had come to be called The Bleeding Grounds for a reason. Arachands, fangands, sasquatch, beresus, and griffins all made homes here.

More rustling. Too loud to be fangands. Sasquatch and beresus didn't care much about being silent. They overwhelmed with brute strength. If it were sasquatch or beresus, it would have attacked already.

Arachands? She craned her neck back, searching the branches for the monstrous spidery creatures. "Watch the trees," she whispered, her fingertips glowing red.

"Bro, you're not hearing monsters." Aiden pointed ahead of them.

In the waning sunlight, near two hundred yards away, the vague outline of a tent trembled in the breeze. A thin trickle of smoke rose from in front of it. Red and orange sparks leapt up, engulfed a pile of dried needles, and a minute later, a campfire sparkled in the early evening. A man knelt in front of it, dressed in jeans and a bright orange goose down coat.

The bearded man squinted at them. "Hello?" he called. "Who are you?"

Lauren's heart froze as the mystery of the trees became abundantly clear. "This isn't Alrujah," she whispered. "It's North Chester."

Riding a horse in soaking wet clothes proved to be difficult and insufferably uncomfortable. Erica's skin pulled into goose bumps. She tried hard to keep her teeth from chattering and held Sparky close to her chest for warmth as she rode toward the nar'esh cave. The smell of smoke diminished, overwhelmed by the scent of wet wolf.

Ullwen stood in the stirrups and stretched his back. He'd slowed their break-neck pace when they entered the Cerulean Woods. "Not much further." His eyes rested on her an uncomfortably long time.

"What? Do I have a booger?" she asked.

"A what?"

"Never mind. Watch where you're going. Stare at me any longer, and you'll ride right into a tree."

He smiled. "These are war horses. They know not to do anything so foolish. You must be cold."

"Chattering teeth give me away?" She adjusted herself in the saddle. Water ran off her and streaked down the silver horse armor. Moonlight lit the streams with glitter. Her dress stuck to her like plastic wrap. No wonder he leered at her. She grinned but put the thought out of her mind. They had a mission. They had to get back to her parents.

The woods thinned, and the familiar black cliff face spread out before her. Another ten minutes of riding and they'd come to the worn stone path ascending the cliffs to the ledge above that led to the nar'esh cave.

She heeled her horse, eager to get out of the breeze. The minute she got to the cave, she'd kick everyone out of the central chamber, pull her wet dress off, and dry it by the fire. She'd sit near the warming flames, but not too close.

Sparky howled. "I know," she said.

Ullwen rode ahead of her. His whimsy vanished, replaced instead by a chilling determination.

"What's up? Why the hurry?"

"Did you not see them?"

"Who?" She spurred her horse to ride faster. It matched the pace of Ullwen's horse. Sparky worked to keep his balance as Erica stood in the stirrups. She held him, clinging to his warm fur.

He pointed up, between the canopy of the trees. "Pacha el Nai flew by. He's wounded and carrying your parents."

How good were his eyes, exactly? "What? How bad are they?"

"I'm unsure."

They rode swiftly up the uneven black stone path until they'd reached the mouth of the nar'esh cave. Pacha el Nai lay on the ground, wings stretched out, bloodied but breathing. Sores opened on his neck and shoulders. His formerly radiant skin had dimmed to a hollow pallor. Erica didn't know what to say.

Ullwen dismounted and untied a leather pouch from his belt. From it, he took several dried leaves. "Can you eat?" he asked the angel.

Pacha el Nai did not respond. Ullwen put a gentle hand on his back, and Pacha's wings twitched under his touch. "A good sign." He crumpled the leaves until they became dried powder in his hand and funneled it into a small canteen of water strapped to the horse's saddle. "Open his mouth."

Erica dismounted, ignoring the biting chill in the air, the soaked clothes holding her uncomfortably. Sparky leapt down and began sniffing the ledge. He followed his nose into the nar'esh cave. Erica tilted Pacha's head to the side. The muscles of his neck strained against her tender turning. Ullwen squeezed Pacha's cheeks and dribbled the water into his mouth. Then Ullwen snapped Pacha's jaw shut and waited for the angel to swallow.

"Will it help?"

"I can't tell. I am well versed in aid for soldiers, but not for angels."

Erica knelt next to him, ran her fingers over his wings. Blood matted the white feathers together. The ridge of the wings ran crooked. Broken. Crimson blood leaked from his body. He'd taken several arrows as he flew over Alrujah, and, by the sores on his neck, had tangled with the nar'esh upon his arrival. They shouldn't be this close to the entrance. Hadn't she helped drive them back to Margwar?

"Go inside," Ullwen said. "Check your parents. I'll stay with Pacha."

"He needs the mushroom thingy and nar'esh blood. Oliver used those to heal Lauren."

"I have no mushrooms."

"I can get some."

"Hurry."

Erica sprinted into the cave. Her parents, Norby and Breniveer, lay in the stables, bleeding. Their eyes were closed, their skin pale. Erica's breath caught in her throat. "Mom? Dad?"

Norby opened an eye. He tilted his neck to examine Breniveer, who lay beside him. "Lakia? You've made it safely." He moved to sit up, but Erica pushed him back down. "You're hurt. Don't even think about moving."

"It's my arm," he said. He took Breniveer's hand in his. "Her leg."

Inches above Breniveer's knee, a jagged tear in her flesh seeped blood. Norby's left arm sustained a similar wound. "Arrows," Norby said. "Pacha was filled with them, but he made it here somehow."

"Not the arrows," Breniveer whispered. "The sickness. And the lightning."

Erica furrowed her brow. "What do you mean?"

"On the flight over. We took a few hits before Pacha flew up out of their range, but once we were higher, the lightning came. And the sores."

Erica shook her head. "From where?"

"It wasn't natural," Norby said. "It was strong magic."

"Korodeth," Erica whispered. She took a measured breath that cracked the ice freezing her lungs. "Ullwen! I need you!"

SOMEWHERE AROUND EIGHT, after his third cup of nauseating tea and several hundred imaginary drags on an unlit cigarette, Parker gave Ms. Knowles, who insisted he call her Becca, a quick hug and tipped his hat to her. "I'll be in touch," he said.

"Please do." She walked him to the door, her face showing scarce splotching from her earlier sobbing.

Of course she'd sobbed. Losing Cindy had unmade Parker, had destroyed his marriage. Losing two girls must be devastating.

He slid into his car. Becca stood at the front door, one arm on the opposite elbow, housecoat pulled tightly around her waist. Leaning against the door, she waited in the cold for him to start his car and let it idle to warm.

He flipped on the dome light, fumbled in the glove box for a new pack of smokes. The one behind his ear had grown soggy. He wondered how long she'd stay outside waiting for him. She had to be freezing.

He backed down the inclined drive, waved at her before he cranked the wheel to the left, and drove down the street. The lights of his car lit the snow-covered shoulders of the road in silver sparkles. The full moon shone so brightly, he doubted he even needed headlights.

He'd feel better if Becca had a husband to help her through the turmoil. But, like him, she had to face it alone. If he'd been as good a husband as he was a cop, he'd still have a wife to go home to, someone to share his emotional burden with. His marriage would have lasted more than six years.

But he hadn't been a good husband, and so he'd go back to his empty house and leave Becca in hers. A depressing thought for a depressing evening.

Maybe he'd do a few sketches when he made it home. Nothing like a charcoal pencil scratching across a cotton fiber page to still his nerves and distract him from his persistently lonely existence. Maybe another portrait to keep him company on lonely nights.

The road flattened out, and he increased his speed. He couldn't sketch when he had work to do. Could never calm his mind enough. When he got home, he'd search for more clues about Bailey Renee, maybe flip through Lauren's journal again. It changed each time he read it, so it might have new clues. He'd put in a call to the computer guy, but he doubted he'd find anything useful.

Something massive moved in the woods to his right. He took his foot off the gas, strained his eyes to find it in the corner of his head-lights. Deer? No, walked upright. Too big to be a man. The shadow lurched and leapt in front of his car.

Seconds before impact, Parker caught a glimpse of the beast— angry wolfish face, snarling fangs, hairy torso. A werewolf?

The front of his car crumpled. The seatbelt caught against his shoulder; his head whipped forward; the airbag exploded into his face. Glass shattered and peppered his cheek and neck and ears. Cold air rushed from the outside in, surfing on the sounds of metal folding in shrieking howls.

He cursed and checked his neck and ear for blood. His hand came back red and wet. His door wouldn't budge. He put his shoulder into it. Pain rippled up his arm, neck, and back. Injured, but he'd manage. Thank God he hadn't been driving faster. The door creaked open, and he stepped into the chilling Minnesota night. His head-lights pointed in different directions. He checked the body.

Any doubt he'd had vanished when he glimpsed the hairy crea-ture. He'd not imagined it; he hit a werewolf. Or, rather, a man dressed as a werewolf. Had to be.

The furry thing moved, howled. Its elbow twisted the wrong way, and bones stuck from its lower legs. This wasn't a man. Hollywood couldn't make a costume this real. Anatomy was all wrong. Parker drew his Berretta and pointed the business end toward the beast. "Freeze," he said. Maybe he should have tried "sit."

The thing twitched.

Blood running down his face, Parker fired three quick rounds into its chest.

Something moved in the woods. Instinctively, Parker spun around behind his car, ignoring the stabbing pain in his spine and neck. Something leapt over his car, another over the hood. Two more.

This completed his descent into the Twilight Zone.

He leveled his Beretta, fired eight rounds, four at each. The bullets took the hairy animals in their chests. The recoil of the gun punched his shoulder with pain. The beasts staggered forward. "Like a bad episode of X-files," he muttered, firing off his last seven rounds. They made no attempt to avoid the bullets. He landed all seven shots in the left beast, five in the body, two in the head. The werewolf collapsed, but the other pressed forward slowly, thick black blood spurting from its chest.

"Not happening," he whispered, sliding back into his car and closing the door. He had to get another clip. He dropped the glove box open and fumbled around in the dark until his hand grabbed the smooth rectangle of ammunition.

Finally.

He checked the window. The last werewolf reached for him. Parker pushed himself back to the passenger seat out of its reach. Blood ran down its arms and claws; its fingers shook.

Parker pushed the clip in the Beretta and fired. The werewolf howled and staggered back. It collapsed, still staring at Parker. In the moonlight, at the edge of the forest, two more shapes loomed. He grabbed the radio, praying it still worked. "This is Detective Parker, requesting backup. I'm on North Piedmont Road. Shots fired."

The werewolves leapt to his car. They grabbed it near the wheels and lifted.

3

With His Hand, Adonai set the worlds in motion, placed the stars and suns in the sky. By His Hand he established order in the worlds, and by His Hand order is kept within these worlds. Though some strike at His Hand, His Hand is strong. And none shall wrest the worlds from the grip of His Hand.
—The Book of Things to Come

LAUREN RAN nervous hands over her stomach and hips.

Still skinny, thank Adonai.

She exhaled in relief before realizing what skinny meant: she didn't belong in this world.

The hunter stared at them from behind the campfire. "Who's there?"

"Let's go." Lauren walked away from the man in the tent. No way to explain why they walked the woods in the dead of night in such strange costumes.

Aiden followed her fast. "Wait. What are you talking about? We're home. Isn't this what we wanted?"

"Look at yourself," she said in a whisper. "You think you belong in this world looking like that?"

"You some of those crazy LARPers?" the hunter shouted. "You guys are a bunch of freaks. Get a life!"

"I'm so confused right now," Bailey said, keeping pace with the group. "If we're home, why do I still have wings?"

An unsettling anxiety roiled in Lauren's belly. "We have to move."

Yarborough huffed with each step. "Where?"

Aiden told Bailey, "Put those wings to use and scope out the area. We need to know where we are to know where to go. We'll meet you ahead, due north."

"I'm on it." Bailey leapt high, and with a powerful downward thrust of her wings, she ascended above the tree line and vanished.

Lauren kept walking, kept moving away from the campfire.

Yarborough walked beside her. The half-dwarf rested his war hammer over his good shoulder and grimaced with each step. Aiden led the way, pressing back brittle branches with his shield for Lauren and Yarborough to pass through. She needed to find a way to heal Yarborough. She considered checking themselves into the ER, but it'd be a difficult to explain how they'd been injured. They'd have to fill out a police report. And what did doctors know of dwarf anatomy?

"Do we have a plan?" Yarborough asked between heavy breaths.

"Keep walking," Lauren said.

The clanking of Aiden's armor mixed with the sounds of owls, of pine needles swishing under their steps. "Here's what we do," he said. "We go home, yours or mine, doesn't matter. Whichever's closer. We get normal clothes, tell our families we're okay. We find out if Oliver and Erica made it back. If so, we find a way to get Yarborough home. Then we relax. Take a few days off from school before we worry about getting back to normal life."

"You can't be serious." Lauren winced at how much she sounded like her mother.

"Why not?"

With broad sweeps of her arm, Lauren motioned to her sister, the angel, flying around somewhere above the trees on massive, white-feathered wings. "Hello? Angel? Dwarf? How's a change of clothes going to help Bailey or Yarborough? How do we explain them?"

"Explain me to whom?" Yarborough asked.

"To anyone." She took a deep breath and tried to calm herself, but fatigue and irritation overwhelmed her.

Aiden frowned. "Babe. I'm trying to help."

"I know." She shook her head. "Sorry I snapped."

Bailey dropped in front of them suddenly. "Good news, bad news. We're close to home. Piedmont Road is over there, about a half mile. Bad news is we aren't the only visitors from Alrujah. There's a pack of fangands attacking a car not far from here."

"I got this," Aiden said. Shield firm on his left hand, he ran in the direction Bailey pointed.

WHEN ULLWEN DIDN'T COME RUNNING, Erica ran to him. Darkness had settled over the entrance of the nar'esh cave. Ullwen bandaged the wounds and sores on Pacha but didn't look optimistic. The angel's chest rose slowly; his eyes dimmed.

"Work faster," Erica said. "My parents are dying."

"He ails," Ullwen said. "If I leave now, he will die."

"So will they," Erica said.

Pacha's head tilted toward her. "The seals are breaking."

Ullwen frowned. "What seals?"

Pacha's breath slowed. "My time is near. Adonai is calling."

"Shut up," Erica snapped. "You're not going anywhere, and neither are my parents. Tell us what seals. Will it help my parents?"

"I cannot stop them," the angel whispered. "They are breaking. They will break. You must stop."

"Stop what?" Ullwen asked.

"The seals. Breaking." His head dropped forward.

"No," Erica said, kneeling. "You're an angel. Angels don't die."

Pacha el Nai's massive chest constricted.

Erica waited for it to fill again, for his lungs to expand with air, but it stayed still. "Breathe," she whispered.

"He is dead."

Erica shook her head. "No chance. He saved my parents. I'm not going to let him die. Get his armor off."

"Erica, my sweet."

She struggled with the weight of the armor. "Lift his arms. Do something."

With a sigh, Ullwen did as Erica said. She worried they didn't move fast enough. Once the armor had been removed, she breathed into Pacha's mouth. "Push on his chest. Hard. Like this." She put one hand on top of the other, pressed in the center of his chest with stiff arms. "You're stronger than me. Push hard. Fast."

Ullwen shook his head but complied. He pushed hard, with his shoulders, compressing the angel's chest.

"Keep going." She breathed into Pacha again. "Faster. Keep the beat steady. Faster." In her mind, she heard *Staying Alive* by the Bee Gees. At least she'd learned one thing in health class last year. She smacked the rhythm on her thigh. "Match my hand."

"Why are we doing this?" He compressed with each slap. "He is dead."

"You got a lot to learn," she said, wiping the tears from her eyes and breathing into Pacha again. "Where I come from, we don't let death win so easy. He wants to grab Pacha, he's going to have to pry him out of our hands."

Ullwen pressed harder, faster.

Erica breathed, waited, breathed.

They worked for ten minutes straight. "My arms are tired," Ullwen said. "I can't do this much longer."

Erica shook her head. "Please," she said. "Please Pacha. I need you. I need you to help me get my parents help."

Nothing happened.

Ullwen stopped pressing and sat down. "I'm sorry."

Erica stopped breathing into Pacha. "Angels aren't supposed to die."

Ullwen shook his head. "There is much of Adonai we don't know."

"How will we get help for my parents?"

"The monks," Ullwen said. "We are not far from the monastery."

"Moving them might hurt them more."

Ullwen stood and rubbed his shoulders. "If we don't find help for them soon, they may perish here."

She wished Ullwen wouldn't sound so steady. Did he always have to be so brave, so stoic? She wanted his voice to crack with emotion the way hers did. She wanted him to care for her parents, for Pacha, as much as she did. She put the thoughts aside and focused on the task at hand—how to get her parents into the heart of the Cerulean Woods to the Monastery.

"How'd you bring me and Sparky to Varuth?" she asked.

Ullwen knelt next to the angel. He ran his hands over the broken ridges of the wings. "I carried you," he said. "I put Sparky on your chest and walked you to the edge of the Woods. Relina met me and smuggled us in on one of her carts."

"You carried us?"

"Aye."

"Could you carry my parents?"

"No. I shouldn't have moved you the way I did. I probably did more harm than good. Only Adonai's grace kept you from dying. They're bleeding savagely. Any unsteady movement will hasten their deaths."

She thought harder, longer. They had two horses, but her parents couldn't ride in their condition. Something else? Another animal? Something that could carry them, cradle them. Something big, strong.

Beresus wouldn't work—gait was too choppy. Fangands were too fast, too rough. But sasquatch walked like people, had thick feet to disperse their weight. Hardly left a footprint. For such ruthless beasts, they moved gracefully. Hardly two weeks ago, a single sasquatch had attacked them. It left Erica and Sparky near death. Only Ullwen's keen aim kept him alive long enough to bring her and Sparky to

Varuth. She didn't like the idea, but she had few options. "Sasquatch," she said.

Ullwen stood up and took her hands in his—he'd been much freer with physical contact since they'd kissed under thirty feet of water in the Alrujahn Bay. "You speak their tongue?"

She grunted and howled, a sound somewhere between a gorilla and a wolf. The golden Ma'att'tal bracelets, the ones she'd found on her first venture into the nar'esh cave, warmed her wrists, and her voice carried over the plains and the woods. The bracelets carried her calls further, a skill she needed desperately now. "They'll be here soon," she whispered. "I need to check their bandages." She kissed his lips softly. "Come with me?"

Ullwen took her hand. "Always."

HIS CAR LIFTED from the ground and tilted back toward the woods. Parker dropped the radio and steadied himself as fast as his shoulder and back would allow. The car flipped, rolled onto the hood and stopped. Metal twisted, screeched. He fumbled in the wreckage for his gun. Dispatch radioed in. "We're en route."

At least the radio worked. Get here fast, he prayed.

He found his gun on the ceiling next to the dome light and scrambled toward the shattered window. If he had any chance of surviving this, he'd need to be able to move, run. Sitting in the car meant death for sure. He ducked through the window and rolled to his back, gun lifted, searching the night for the deranged animals. They stood on top of his car, ripping the underside apart. He stood up slowly, hoping his car would provide enough distraction for him to sneak away into the woods and hide.

But they flicked their ears up and turned their heads. With another howl, more shapes appeared in the woods.

Should have brought more clips.

He'd have to make each of his fourteen shots count, hit them in the head and hope. He fired a round. The bullet shot a pointed ear off one of the beasts on the car. It leapt toward him, and Parker fell back.

The thing stretched out in the air, obscuring the moon from view. Parker fell under its shadow, leveled his gun, and prayed again. He fired once. But instead of falling forward and landing on him, the beast suddenly crashed to the earth, as if a meteorite landed on its head.

Parker blinked.

An angel stood over the animal, a flaming sword shoved through the werewolf's back. Her skin glowed, shimmered in the light of the moon, of the sword.

Another of the beasts exploded in a massive fireball. A young woman, dressed in all white, emerged from the woods, fire dancing from her fingertips like candles. In one hand, she held a rugged staff.

A tragically short man with a hammer the size of a Volvo leapt into the fray. He smashed his hammer into the skull of a werewolf and stumbled forward.

A knight in silver, spiked armor fought a werewolf with his bloody shield. Each time they killed a werewolf, another took its place.

The angel walked toward him. Parker struggled to his feet, leveled his gun at her chest. "Who are you?" he asked, his voice cracked with fear.

"Don't be afraid, Parker. It's me. Bailey."

Parker's breath heaved. "But, how? Your wings."

"Are you okay?" she asked.

He stared at the chaos spilling from Piedmont Road to the woods beyond. "No," he said. "I've lost my mind."

4

King Solous confined the elves to the city of Harael. There, they flourished.
Other men cried out to Solous to strike them while they were weak, but
Solous gave the reluctant race back to Adonai. "It is not for me to end a race
forged by the Almighty Hand of Adonai," he said. "Adonai created them,
and only He may destroy them."
—The Book of the Ancients

AFTER ANOTHER HOUR OF RIDING, Erica and Ullwen came upon the
Cerulean Monastery under thin, silver moonlight. Remarkably, the
monks had nearly finished rebuilding it after Korodeth ordered it
burned to the ground. They'd reformed walls from the charred
stones and new, gray mortar. How quickly they worked, how fear-
lessly. Korodeth killed a king with impunity; killing the monks of the
Cerulean Order would be a much easier task. If anyone gave such a
command, it'd be the heartless director of Alrujah's Chameleon
Soldiers—a nearly invisible army with few morals and little
conscience to speak of.

The hodge-podge collection of rough buildings still bore black scorches, a testament to the ravaging flames that had moved through the grounds, consuming the orchard of fruit trees and the expansive vegetable fields. Only the wheat fields surrounding the monastery slowed the fire and kept it from consuming the entire Cerulean Woods.

In the distance, blue-robed monks moved among the seared remains of fields and buildings. They'd fashioned new gardening tools. With their structures rebuilt, the monks had turned back to finding a way to sustain their numbers. Ironically, the burnt earth left the soil full of minerals. Already, new sprouts grew among the remains of blackened potato plants, corn stalks, and tomato vines.

"What do you think Pacha meant about the seals?" Erica asked.

Beside her, a pair of lumbering sasquatch held her parents in outstretched arms like loving parents holding sleeping children.

Ullwen ran a hand over his beard. "I've been pondering his meaning since he spoke the words. I believe, despite the evils we've already faced, a greater wickedness awaits us."

"Why do you suppose he told us to stop?"

"A clear order to stop the breaking of the seals."

"I figured as much. But where are these seals?"

"If anyone knows, it will be Dillard."

A mass of monks moved rapidly between the saplings which would, one day, become another abundant and varied orchard. Even from a distance, the front monk's skin reflected the hoary moonlight, and his eyes shone red. Dillard. Convenient.

"Lakia, Ullwen. Are you harmed?" he said.

Erica leapt off her horse and handed the reins to a young monk. "We're good." She nodded toward Norby and Breniveer. "But my parents need help, fast." The strength in her voice belied the fear boiling in her.

Dillard tilted his neck back and stared at the impossibly tall sasquatch. His brow furrowed more in confusion than fear. In his steady voice, he said to the monks beside him, "Stable their horses. Remove the armor, clean and inspect them. Re-shoe them if necessary." To those behind him, he said, "Prepare a healing room for the wounded. Bring me a full complement of bitterroot, yellow spider-leaf, and tresica leaves, purple and yellow. Also, garrunt mushrooms. Be quick and summon Eljah to the infirmary."

The robes of the men snapped about them as they rushed off to do as Dillard asked. Dillard led the others, sasquatch included, toward the small building on the western edge of the monastery grounds. Inside, several empty beds lined three of the walls. Rough-hewn harspus wood cabinets took up the fourth. The thickly-furred sasquatch handed Breniveer and Norby to Ullwen and Dillard. Erica thanked the beasts for their help, and they walked back into the forest.

Dillard and Ullwen set to work. "Remove their bandages," Dillard said as he took clean dressings and a plain brown pouch from one of the cabinets. Ullwen untied the strips of make-shift bandages Erica had torn from her dress. Both Norby and Breniveer had taken several arrows in their flight from Alrujah. In the short time it'd taken them to make it to the monastery, their wounds had started to fester. The deep crimson color morphed into a sickly yellow. Tears of pus lined the places where the skin ripped apart. They'd lost too much blood already, and if Dillard couldn't do something, she'd lose her parents. Again.

Korodeth murdered King Ribillius, who'd been like a father to Lakia as she grew up in Castle Alrujah. In North Chester, Erica's father had burned her hands over a stove before he killed her mother.

Erica never had the chance to have a family, a normal family, like everyone else, and she wasn't about to lose the last chance she had.

Dillard pulled a pinch of black powder from the pouch and sprinkled it over Norby's wounds. Ullwen did the same for Breniveer. Erica, powerless to help, sat between their beds and held their hands. "You can heal them, can't you?"

"Only Adonai can heal," Dillard said.

"You healed Sparky. Oliver's healed us before."

"Only with the power of Adonai," Ullwen said.

"Well Adonai better fix my parents," she said.

"We will do what we can to aid them," Dillard said.

The door swung open, and an older monk entered with a lantern in his hand. His salty, stubbly hair identified him as Eljah—the leader of the Monks of the Cerulean Order. Four more monks followed in after him. "How bad are they?"

"Bad," Dillard said. "I've prepared the wounds with bitterroot powder."

Eljah set the lantern on a small table near the head of the bed. He opened the glass and lit a tiny torch, about the size of a pen.

"What are you going to do?" Erica asked.

The other four monks took spots standing over Norby and Breniveer, one each at their heads, one each at their feet. Eljah moved the torch close to Norby's leg.

"Don't watch, my love," Ullwen said. He positioned himself between Erica and her parents.

"Move," Erica said, trying to push past him.

He restrained her with a gentle firmness. "Don't watch."

She stood on her toes, looked over his shoulder. A bright, hot flash of white light ignited on Norby's leg. Norby screamed a scream like Erica hadn't heard since her father held the backs of her hands over the stove flame. She broke Ullwen's grip and leapt at Eljah, but Dillard caught her. "He must do this to save them."

"How does setting them on fire save them?" she screamed. Another flash, another mind-numbing shriek. "Stop it!"

Dillard held her arms at her side until Ullwen took her from behind. The gentleness of his earlier embrace vanished, and Erica understood his strength on a more intimate level. Bruises would line her arms, but she did not stop thrashing. She kicked and shook, thrashed and stabbed his arms with her nails.

Flash. Howl. "Let me go so I can kill them!"

"It is necessary!" Ullwen cried.

"Stop burning him!"

Another shriek, this time from Breniveer. Her voice shrilled across the walls and ignited Erica's ears. "Leave her alone!" More flashes. More shrieks. "I swear to Adonai, I'll punch every last one of you!"

Dillard's arms wrapped around her like constrictors. "They will be healed, but we must burn off the infection. Burns heal; infections kill."

Erica couldn't hear him. Her ears rang with the echo of her mother's screams. At some point, she realized the voices had changed.

Her mother wasn't screaming anymore.

Erica was.

EVERY PART OF LAUREN HURT. Even her bones ached. The fangands growled and snarled. Claws clicked on asphalt. Nails screamed across the hood of the car, sending flecks of green paint fluttering like cut blades of grass in the moonlight. She backed toward a dense thicket of trees, toward the side of the road. A fangand leapt at her. Immediately, she ducked under its swiping paw and drew on the magic reserve in Oliver's staff to raise a bubble shield. When the fangand hit it, magic drained from her, but the bubble deflected the blow. She moved back, knowing she only had enough magic left to support the shield a few more moments. "Help!" she called.

The clanging of Aiden's armor across the pavement comforted her. He lowered his shoulder into his shield and ran the fangand over. It sprawled in the air, careening for yards before hitting the road and sliding back. It righted itself. Aiden leapt at it. He knocked a paw away with his shield and moved in close, driving his spiked elbow into the beast's belly. It howled for a moment before falling away.

Yarborough swung. Slower than his right hand, his left proved equally lethal with a battle hammer. He crushed the head of a fangand and spun around, waiting for more to spring from the woods, but none came. He dropped to a knee.

Lauren surveyed the woods. No more fangands. They'd killed over a dozen of the monsters, and she'd taxed her magic reserves. Amazing that she could even use them in North Chester. So, avatar *and* abilities intact. Because she'd been raptured here from Alrujah? A flimsy theory, but it seemed to make sense.

She needed to rest, but an idea tickled her brain. She'd used the staff the way Oliver had, which meant she might be able to heal Yarborough.

Placing a hand on his shoulder, her palm warmed. Her fingers moved closer to the puncture wound in his shoulder. She fingered the edge of the jagged skin, the blood running from the severed veins and arteries, the musculature, so close to human, but strange enough to be dwarvish. She closed her eyes and concentrated, thought of muscle repairing, of arteries and veins weaving together like a spider's web. She thought of skin stretching over anatomy, covering the bloody gore of his shoulder.

"By Adonai's beard," Yarborough said.

"What's going on here?" the man asked. He should be terrified; instead, irritation lined his eyes.

"Fangands," Aiden said, sounding proud to finally have the answer to something.

"Which are?"

"Werewolves, minus the sense of humor," Aiden said. Oliver had used the same description their first night in Alrujah.

Bailey Renee stood near him, her flaming sword still unsheathed. "I know it's hard to understand, but it's me. It's Bailey. And this is Lauren. I found her like I said I would."

The man put a hand against his forehead. Blood ran down the side of his face, and he leaned against his overturned car. "Concussion," he said, checking his hand. "Hallucinations feel real." He patted his breast pocket, found an unlit cigarette, and hung the soggy end on his bottom lip.

"Who is this?" Lauren asked. "You know him?"

Bailey nodded. "He's your detective. Parker. He's been working your case since you disappeared."

Stepping over a dead fangand, Lauren walked closer to Parker. "I have a case worker?"

"You don't look like Lauren," Parker whispered. Blood ran from beneath his hand. He slid down the car a bit and groaned. He took the unlit cigarette and eyed Bailey's flaming sword. "Let me see that thing." He reached the cigarette toward the blade.

Bailey sheathed it. "No way."

Aiden said, "Bro, you don't look so good. You got a gash on your forehead."

"I'm great," Parker whispered. His eyes slipped shut.

Lauren knelt next to him. She placed her hand on his forehead. The warmth of his blood burned against the cold of his skin. As she had with Yarborough, she began imagining the anatomy of the wound. More than imagine it, she understood it, as if she remembered it rather than discovered it. The knowledge of healing hovered in her head, and she reached for it now.

The wound stitched itself, but it pulled what little magic she'd been able to save. She'd wanted to heal him completely, but his wounds proved too severe. They'd require too much magic. She pulled away from him and frowned.

She had a case worker?

Yarborough stood beside Parker. "Is he ill?"

"I'll call somebody," Bailey said. She took his phone from his pocket.

Lauren grabbed her wrist. "Wait. If they find out who we are, they're going to want to talk to us."

"So?" Aiden said. "We'll have to talk to people soon enough. The minute she hangs up with 911, I'm calling home."

"Who's 911?" Yarborough asked.

Bailey dialed. "We can argue about this later. Right now, we need an ambulance here."

"We can't be here when they come," Lauren said.

"Why not?" Aiden asked again.

"They'll want us to come home. They won't let us go back."

"We're not going back," Aiden said, his voice firm.

"We have to," Lauren said. "Oliver. Erica. We can't leave them."

"They're probably already here." Aiden motioned to the trees beyond the road. "If we were pulled back, they must have been, too.

They're probably wandering around trying to find their way home. I say we go back to our houses, take a nap, get some food, and wait for Oliver and Erica to call us."

"They're not here," Lauren said. "I'd know it if they were."

Bailey Renee moved toward the tree line. She needed it quiet when she called 911. "There's been an accident," she said. "Not sure what happened, but someone's hurt. Can you send an ambulance? Piedmont Road."

"And how are we going to get Yarborough home?"

"He can stay here," Aiden said. "We'll find him a nice job somewhere."

"I need to return to Alrujah," the dwarf said. "The Hand must return as well."

"I know," Lauren said. "We'll find a way."

Aiden shook his head. "Isn't this what we were fighting for the whole time? Didn't we want to get home? And now we are, and you want to go back? I can't even believe you're suggesting it."

"And I can't believe you're thinking about staying," Lauren snapped. The shrill tone of her command, so like her mother's, startled her.

"Lauren," Aiden said, taking her hands in his. "We're home. This is North Chester. We can finally get back to normal."

Lauren closed her eyes, thought of the glorious wings on Bailey's back. "Nothing's normal," she said. "Not here in North Chester. Look at us. We don't belong here. Come on. I saw something back in the woods. Might be some sort of doorway where the fangands came from. Let's go check it out."

"Aye, m'lady," Yarborough said.

"No," Aiden said.

"Excuse me?"

"I said no. I'm not going anywhere." He took his helmet off and laid it on his shield on the pavement. "I'm staying here and waiting for help. The ambulance can take me home."

"Please don't do this," Lauren said.

"I'm staying," he said. "Stay with me." He held a hand out to her.

Lauren's eyes heated with sorrow. "You know I can't stay."

"And you know I can't go."

"Please," she said.

Aiden lowered his hand.

"We have to go now," she told Aiden.

He frowned. "Good luck."

"You must come with us," Yarborough said. "Hurry. You are the Hand of Adonai. Alrujah needs you."

"My mom needs me," he said. "And my dad."

"What about Oliver and Erica?" Lauren asked. Bailey stood next to her.

"They'll be fine without us," he said.

Lauren worked her way toward the tree line. Bailey followed her. "If she goes, I go. I'm not losing her again."

Aiden stood over Parker, shook his head. "I'll stay with him until the ambulance gets here." He waved sadly. "Look me up when you get back."

5

Tiamat took for himself a home beneath the sea. Here, he destroyed ships, swallowed sailors, forced the water of his home onto the shores of the coastal cities of Alrujah. Thus, they formed idols in his likeness and offered sacrifices to appease him and turned from Almighty Adonai.
—The Book of the Ancients

AIDEN RUBBED at his chin while Lauren vanished into the woods with Bailey and Yarborough. How surreal to see them disappear into the dark—an angel, a mage, and a dwarf. An image incongruous with the wreckage behind him, the twisted metal and shattered glass, the detective slumping to the pavement.

This was the real world, with roads and cars and policemen, with ambulances and schools, with football fields and cell phones. Alrujah had been fun, but he was home now. He needed to get to his family.

He kicked a fangand. "This is your fault," he said.

The cop behind him coughed.

"You awake, bro?"

Parker took a few breaths, slow and shallow. "You can't be here when they get here," he said. "She was right."

"What are you talking about?"

"You got no answers for the questions they'll ask. Better if you disappear a while. Lay low."

"No chance," he said. "I'm going home."

Parker took his phone and handed it to Aiden. "Call Franky. He knows more than he should. Bailey's no good at keeping secrets." Sirens split the still night air.

"I'm calling my dad," Aiden said.

"And tell him what? You're in a suit of armor, covered in blood. Get cleaned up. Let me call your folks and set up the reunion. We gotta keep this quiet until we come up with a story. Media'll be a circus."

Aiden snatched up his shield. "Don't even care, bro. Circus or no, I'll be home."

"Until my friends at the department show up and bring you down for questioning. Trust me, kid. You've been gone a while. Your bloody homecoming only makes you suspicious. If you come home and the others don't, you'll be a suspect and sit in jail until we get answers that don't involve werewolves and witches. Give me time to figure it out. Let Franky set you up someplace quiet."

Aiden deliberated before taking the phone and dialing. The sirens grew louder. "Franky," he said. "Pick me up? Piedmont Road. Couple miles north of marker 12."

Parker closed his eyes again. "Go quick, kid. They'll search the woods nearby."

Aiden handed the phone to Parker. "Get better fast." He dashed off into the woods, his armor clanging. His muscles burned, like he'd played four quarters straight without stretching. The smoldering sensation comforted him.

He was fast. He was strong. He was home.

He moved without thought. Running cleared his mind, let him shut out thoughts of Lauren, the sting of rejection. He'd loved her since before Alrujah, and right when he thought she loved him back, she chose to chase after the monk. He should have known. Oliver and Lauren spent so much time together, grew up together. Aiden had only known her for a few months. No way he'd be able to compete with Oliver's kind of friendship, with his kind of love.

The sirens grew louder, but he'd already run at least a half-mile. His feet sank in the soft soil as he dodged trees and moved with the swift, deadly skill he'd learned in Alrujah.

He'd played the dumb jock too well. Instead of asking her to tutor him, he should have been honest. Would have been simple to ask if she wanted to hang out sometime, or see a movie, or get a coffee. Of course, he'd have been terrified to talk to her, to ask her so boldly. She always had her nose in a book, either reading or writing. Why hadn't he asked her what she was reading, what she was writing? Instead, he'd played a part, a stereotype.

Girls didn't dig stereotypes.

He tried to remember Lauren in North Chester—her curly hair, the way she smiled when humor surprised her and destroyed her stoic frown. She had a wide-mouthed grin showing every perfect tooth in her brainy head. He wanted to astonish her with comedy, wanted his words to blow up any trace of self-consciousness she might have. He should have played the comic rather than the dumb jock, but, while he had skills on the field, he didn't have jokes, not like Franky.

He moved through the trees like a halfback finding a hole in the defense. He ignored the burn in his quads and pushed forward, sprinted toward an invisible end zone.

The blaring sirens quieted. Must have found Parker.

Aiden had covered more than a mile in about seven minutes. Not bad for wearing hundreds of pounds of armor.

In the distance, headlights crested a hill. Franky?

Aiden moved toward the road, waved, but the car passed without slowing. He shrugged and ran a little further, to the mile 12 marker, where he finally stopped. He put his hands on his knees, took a few deep, sharp breaths. Standing straight, he put both hands behind his head. Cold in his lungs, the air pricked his heart with a gentle chill.

He wanted Lauren with him, under his arm, wearing his letterman jacket.

More headlights, brighter this time. He waved again, and Franky's emerald Jeep slowed.

"Aiden?" he said. "Holy crap, man. You got sucked in, too, didn't you?"

The cop hadn't lied, hadn't been delusional. "Parker said I can lay low with you?"

He sighed. "Yeah. Get in."

~

IN THE LAST FEW WEEKS, Bailey Renee had been hospitalized for unexplained neurological seizures, had been pulled into a fantasy world, had grown the wings of an angel, and had fought marble statue deities bent on destruction. None of which was as strange as Lauren walking away from Aiden.

Bailey walked next to Lauren as they moved away from Piedmont Road, leaving Aiden beside the unconscious Parker. "Aiden's not wrong," she said. "We're back now. We should stay."

"Wings, hello?" Lauren said. "What are we going to do, saw them off for you? Or maybe I could eat a bunch and get fat again and forget about the fact that I can use magic. This is not our home anymore, not like this. We weren't supposed to come back like this. We don't belong, and we're not staying." Lauren quickened her steps. "We're not leaving our friends."

"What if we get back, and they're gone?" She kept her wings closed around her as they darted through trees. "We should wait for them here."

"Good lady," Yarborough said, his heavy hammer perched on his shoulder. With his shoulder healed, he moved quicker, but the girls' long strides required much of the half-dwarf's short legs. "Far be it from me to argue with one of Adonai's messengers, but I do not belong in this world. I must return to my home."

"So do we," Bailey said. Why did Lauren have to move so fast? "Do you even know how to get back?"

"The fangands got in somehow." Pine needles rustled around her booted feet. She stuck Oliver's staff in the ground and pressed forward. "Doors open both ways, right?"

"Who says a portal is a door? Are you an expert in interworld travel now?"

Lauren shrugged off the attitude in Bailey's question. "I'm trying to figure this out," she said. "We went to sleep and woke up in Alrujah in new bodies—our avatars. I wasn't fat—you had wings, Aiden was swol, Oliver was ... well, he was still Oliver, but he had mad skills with his staff. I'm thinking we haven't changed back from our avatars, even though we're in North Chester, because we got here by Rapture. The spell acts like a portal, and now we find a portal here in North Chester that apparently links back to Alrujah, 'cause we got Alrujah monsters running around in North Chester. If they got in, we should be able to get back."

Yarborough pulled a tuft of fur from the bark of a pine and inspected the black and silver hair. "They came from this direction."

"Scratch marks," Lauren said, running her finger through a deep gouge in the bark of the surrounding pines.

"The soil has been turned up here," Yarborough said, kneeling. He set his hammer down and inspected the paw-shaped craters in the soft dirt. "Warmer than the rest of the earth. Not much, but enough. They came from deeper in the forest."

Bailey followed Yarborough's gaze. Though darkness obscured the woods, her angel eyes gave her incredible vision. Something shimmered in the distance. She pointed. "There," she said. "A mile up."

"What is it?" Lauren asked.

"Some sort of portal?"

Lauren shook her head. "I never designed a spell to make portals. The closest is Rapture, but it doesn't open doorways like this."

"We must examine it," Yarborough gruffed.

"Please," Bailey said, taking Lauren's hand. "Let's not go back now.

Let's rest. Let's go home, get some sleep, and if you still want to come back tomorrow, we can."

Lauren's eyes searched the darkness for the portal. "If it's a portal or a doorway, we don't know how long it will stay open. Besides, I structured time in Alrujah to move faster than it does here. One night in North Chester is a full day in Alrujah. There's no telling what could happen to Oliver and Erica while we stand around and argue."

Bailey said, "Let's go home first and tell Mom we're okay."

Lauren walked deeper into the forest. "Go for it, but be fast, okay? I won't wait long."

"Come with me. Don't you want to see Mom again?"

"I can't." Lauren held Bailey's hands. "Seeing you is hard enough. If I saw Mom, I may not have the courage to go back."

"Then stay. Yarborough can find the doorway from here. Oliver and Erica will find their way back soon enough."

She shook her head. "I won't abandon them."

Bailey stared at her hard. "When you say 'them,' what do you mean?"

"Oliver and Erica."

"No you don't."

"I do. And my people. The people of Alrujah."

"Why do they matter to you?"

Lauren's eyes reddened. Until now, she'd kept her composure, even when she left Aiden. But here, her eyes softened. "Don't you get it? They're like my kids. Do you think Mom would ignore us if we were suffering? If we were in danger?"

"Of course not," Bailey said.

"And I won't abandon them either."

"They're not real, Lauren. It's a game."

"Said the woman with wings."

Bailey grabbed her elbow. "Alrujah's dangerous. If we go back, we may not come home again. I swore I'd bring you back, and here you are. We can be a family again. We can be normal."

"We were never normal," Lauren said. She tugged her elbow

away. "If I have to die there, so be it. I belong in Alrujah. So do you. So does he."

Yarborough lowered his head. "I do not wish to sow dissent between sisters, but I agree with Indigo."

Bailey closed her eyes and inhaled sharply. "What can I say to change your mind?"

Lauren shook her head and wiped at her eyes.

Bailey sighed and considered launching herself into the air, flying home, and hugging her mother. But if her mother saw her with angel's wings, she'd assume the worst. How would she convince her mother she wasn't dead? She'd made a promise: she'd find Lauren and bring her home. And until Lauren finished her business in Alrujah, she'd never stay in North Chester. "I'll go, but I'm not happy about it."

Lauren smiled. "I love you, Bailey Renee."

"Let's go, Princess." Bailey took Lauren's hand and led her toward the shimmering portal.

It took nearly an hour for Ullwen to calm Erica down. He held her as she screamed and clawed at his arms, rubbing the knobby bone of her shoulder. When she steadied her voice and stilled her shaking, he let her go. She knelt beside her father first and took his pallid hand in hers.

Ullwen knelt beside her.

"Put your arm around me," she said.

Before moving, Ullwen lifted an eyebrow and checked over his shoulder.

Tired of waiting, Erica took his wrist, put it on her shoulder, and leaned into him. "He'd lift me up and let me pick apples from the trees," she said, tracing the bones of her father's hand to his wrist. The fingers of her other hand rose over the mountains of his knuckles and sank into the valleys between. "I can still feel his hands under my arms, like he's lifting me up, like I'm flying. I saw my first razorbeak when I was three, an apple in my hand. Even as a kid, I knew its words but couldn't make them human."

"The name of General Norby carried a weighty authority and fear. Enemies of the crown trembled at it. Hard to imagine a man so feared as gentle as you describe him."

A flash of memory, of a conversation Norby had with his wife, a conversation she wasn't supposed to overhear. The images were fuzzy, but somehow, the words resonated in her ears now. "Mercy takes more strength than cruelty."

Ullwen nodded. "I've heard the saying in Varuth, though the Elite seldom followed the path of mercy." He put a hand on her shoulder awkwardly, as if comforting a friend who'd lost a small bet. *Easy come, easy go*, the gesture said. Ullwen was a man unaccustomed to offering comfort. She doubted "consoling" was on the job description of the Varuthian Elite.

Erica rested her head on his shoulder, took his hand, and put it on her hip. "Why won't they wake up?" she whispered.

"They will wake again."

"They better, or you're going to be in a world of hurt for holding me back when I should have been clobbering Dillard."

"Clobbering?"

She smiled. His ignorance was adorable. "Never mind." She ran her fingers up her father's hairy arm to his elbow, then brushed her mother's loose, sweaty hair from her face. "She sang me to sleep every night."

Ullwen turned but kept his hand on her hip. Deep red gashes marred his forearms.

"I'm sorry," she said. "I didn't mean to hurt you."

Ullwen checked the door then kissed Erica's forehead. "A small matter."

Erica sighed. "No, it's not. I lost my mind a bit. Never lost control like that before." She turned back to her mother, rubbing her waxy cheeks. "I can't remember the song. If I did, I'd sing it for her."

"When she wakes, she will sing it again, and you will learn it." He smelled of bark, of soil and streams. He held her for another hour, listening to her stories, reassuring her with a contagious confidence. But once the suns had set, he stood and stretched his legs. "I must go," he said. "Dillard will have a room prepared for me and a room for you as well."

"You go ahead. I need to stay here."

"I'll have Dillard bring you some bedding."

"Knock yourself out," she said. Her eyes heavied, and she rested her head against the wall.

Her father's hand twitched.

She snapped up, quiet and hopeful. "Papa?" she whispered.

He stirred a bit and grimaced. "Butterfly?"

The word rushed through her like a chill. Instantly, she was three, sitting on his knee. *Butterfly,* he'd called her.

"I'm here," Erica whispered.

Her father blinked. His fingers moved gently, slithered between hers. "Your mother?"

"Still sleeping."

He took a slow, shallow breath and smiled. "It's not a dream, is it? You're here?"

"I am, Papa." How long had she called him Papa? Until the day Korodeth took him away.

He tilted his head toward her. His breath came with great effort, as if a beresus crushed his throat. His lungs inflated, deflated in agonized gasps. White spittle dried on the corners of his mouth. "I could have died. I would have been happy. Adonai brought you back to us."

She knelt next to his bed. "Dillard and Eljah fixed you up. Don't you feel better?"

He smiled. "I feel like death." He stared hard at her. "Let me look at you, Butterfly."

Breniveer coughed. She flexed her fingers and grimaced. Her face, ashen at the cave, regained its color. Other than the heavy blue bags under her eyes, she looked nearly normal. Emaciated, but healthy. Her wounds had already begun to close and scab over. She struggled to sit up. "What hour is it?" Her voice rasped, hoarse from her screaming while Eljah ignited the bitterroot powder over her wounds.

Erica grinned, kissed her mother's forehead, and lay her back on the bed. "Take it easy, Mom. We can stay here a few days. No reason to rush your recovery."

Norby, still weakly clinging to her hand, said, "You'll stay with us, won't you? No more plans to rush off and take on Korodeth and leave us here crippled and alone?"

The light of the lamp flickered in the darkness. Orange shadows played over his face, illuminating his pallid skin in all the colors of the sunset. Her voice dimmed to a whisper. "Korodeth and I still have business. The minute I figure out how to do it, I'll slip a dagger between his ribs."

"No," Breniveer said. "I believe your father or I will have that honor."

LAUREN STOPPED inches from the shimmering silver oval, stared into it as if it were a pool of water. If she squinted hard enough, she might see the bottom of the deep end. But the rippling silver obscured everything on the other side.

Yarborough walked around it, his hammer held ready. "It is the same on this side."

"Think it matters which side we go in?" Bailey asked.

"How'd I get to be the expert on wormholes to other worlds?"

"You're the one who got us back home. You and your staff."

"That was an accident, and it's Oliver's staff," Lauren said. "I don't know how I did it. We needed to get away, and I had a feeling I had to lift the staff."

Bailey unfurled her wings, stretching them. The wheeled brace on her left wing whirred. She'd worn it since Pacha put it on her. Lauren suspected it eased her pain but did little to heal the wing. She closed them around herself again as Yarborough rejoined them.

"No tracks on the north side," he said. "They came from the

south."

"So I guess we go in the same way," Lauren said. She reached her hand toward the glimmering silver. Its eerie iridescence made her think of cold lightning. As her fingers neared the surface, she half-expected a jolt, a shock, a frigidity. Instead, the silver was warm as blood. Nothing shocked her, no electricity. It pulled her fingers, yanked them like a puppy on a rope. She stepped forward, her arm disappearing into the glistening mass. She held her breath on instinct, hoping to breathe again soon.

Her shoulder vanished. Before she screamed, the rest of her fell through.

SHE STUMBLED INTO THE FOREST. Her stomach knotted, cramped. The cool air moved over the sweat lining her skin. All the worst parts of the flu assaulted her but waned as quickly as they appeared. Steadying herself, she stood and took in her surroundings.

Tall pines stretched upward. The sky darkened in the east. Dusty motes of red and orange light spilled through the west end of the needly forest. Dusk? Hadn't it been night?

Behind her, Bailey stepped through, holding her stomach. "Worst ride ever," she said.

Yarborough stepped through, a stalwart of strength. "Did we make it?"

Lauren shook her head. "I don't know where we are."

Bailey said, "It has to be Alrujah, right?"

"We could be anywhere," Lauren said. She ran her hands over her arms for warmth. "I'm not exactly an expert on inter-world travel."

Bailey said. "This is Oliver's thing. He'd have an explanation for it."

Lauren inspected the trees.

Yarborough knelt and examined the soil.

"How about a bird's eye view?" Lauren said.

Bailey nodded and ascended through the trees.

"Smells like Yeval," Yarborough said.

"You know the smell?"

"My father brought me here once when I was very young," the halfling said. "I'll not soon forget the smell. Blood and soil and rognak roots."

"The rognak trees are extinct," Lauren said. "Have been for years."

"Give them time, Princess. They will grow again. They are a hardy tree. It takes more than a few million bugs to end their kind." He pointed to a gnarled purple root erupting form the black soil. "Behold, the birth pangs of the rognak."

Lauren smiled. Rognak trees meant Alrujah. But where in Alrujah?

Bailey descended behind them. "It's pretty much forest forever, but I saw the Dragon's Back mountains and a glimpse of water far to the north. Long way off. Miles and miles."

"Yeval," Lauren said.

"I never forget a smell," Yarborough said with a sneer. "These are the true Bleeding Grounds." He readied his hammer.

Lauren's heart tripped. "Bailey, would you say we're closer to the south of the forest?"

"Yeah."

"We go north," Lauren said.

"The Heart?" Yarborough asked.

"Can you think of a better plan?"

"We may not make it," he said.

"They won't harm us. The Council won't allow it."

"If they don't know we're coming," Yarborough said, "they may not wait to learn our names before they take our heads."

"I'm open to other ideas."

Yarborough shook his head. "Camp for an evening. Make our way out of the forest tomorrow morning."

"And go where? March for weeks on foot until we come to a town? I have a city to save, Yarborough, and I'd like to do it before I die of old age."

"I'm lost again," Bailey said.

"We'll explain on the way," Lauren said, turning north. Yarborough and Bailey followed.

FRANKY TURNED THE RADIO OFF.

Aiden turned it on. "Music's nice, bro. It's good." He kept the volume low because he still wanted to talk, but the tonality, the dissonance of Muse's distorted guitars and heavy bass riffs, soothed him. How long had it been since he'd heard rock, since he'd heard any music other than lyres and harps?

"Cool, man," Franky said. The subtle blue lights of the odometer and speedometer, of the satellite radio and temperature controls, bathed his face. His pallid blue composure made Aiden think of corpses shambling around ancient ruins, giving their body parts for the greater good of Moloch, the abomination.

Aiden closed his eyes and rubbed his temples.

"Real good to see you," Franky said.

Aiden didn't want small talk. He'd been gone so long, seen so many things, missed so much in North Chester, he wouldn't waste time with simple pleasantries. "How long have I been gone?"

"Few weeks. It was all over the news, man. Whole state's freaking out. Whole country. They chilled out a bit lately, but I'm telling you, I saw your face more in those first ten days than I have in the six months I've known you, you know?"

Aiden drummed his thumbs on his armor with the beat. Metal tapped on metal, adding an industrial flavor to Muse's blend of heavy rock and electronica. "Take me home, okay?"

Franky slowed the car, navigated around a sharp bend in the road.

"Seriously, bro. Flip it around. I want to go home."

Franky sighed. "It's kind of crazy over there right now. I don't think it's a great idea, not with you all suited up like Lancelot. I'm going to swing by my place, pick up a change of clothes for you, let you relax there." He scratched behind his ear—nervous. "Did you see Bailey when you were in Alrujah?"

"Yeah."

"Was she," he paused. "What was she like? She told me she had these intense dreams where she was an angel and had wings and flew all over this fantasy world and all."

Aiden leaned the seat back. Hard to appreciate the comfort of the seats while he wore his stiff, cold armor. The heater did little to thaw his chill-stiff chest through the metal plate. "She's an angel, bro. Full-on wings and feathers and all. Pretty mean with a blade, too."

Franky shook his head and laughed a bit. "When she told me, I didn't believe it. The whole reality being pulled into fantasy thing. No way. No one gets pulled into some video game, right? Doesn't happen. But I love her, so I believed her. And here you are, sitting in some silver armor in my Jeep. Makes my brain numb."

"Doesn't take much," Aiden said.

Franky laughed and punched Aiden in the shoulder. "Your armor's legit, man. Real silver?"

"Real."

"The blood?"

"Also real."

He shook his head. "You could sell it for like, a million dollars."

Aiden grinned. "Worth more than that, especially when you got werewolves trying to snatch your head off."

"Straight trip, man. Can't even wrap my mind around it."

"Take me home. I need to see my family."

"You show up, and the media picks up on it. You got reporters and a battalion of cops asking questions. Let's do it quiet. We'll call them, okay? They can sneak out and come over. We'll have the happy reunion at my place."

"Don't even care."

"They'll ask about the armor. Even if you show up in street clothes, they'll ask where you've been. What are you going to say?"

Aiden took a deep breath. "Seriously, bro. I'm getting irritated. I'll make something up. Get me home. I need to see my dad. I need to see my mom."

Franky turned the music down a bit and stared at Aiden. "Okay," he said. "But first, let's get you some clothes."

6

And so Abaddon ruled over those far in the north, the swamplands of Pellbred. Awed by his ferocity, they took him as their god and sacrificed animals to his name. They built idols in his likeness and set them about their city and within the swamp.
—The Book of the Ancients

THE TREES of Yeval Forest grew so tightly together, they obscured most of the natural sunlight. With stygian clouds looming overhead, it was nearly as dark as the ruins of Norgren. She'd already touched everybody's eyes, whispered over them as Langley had done shortly before they faced Moloch, the Abomination of death. The simple spell allowed them to see in the dark. Bailey walked next to her, which let them catch up on everything in North Chester. And, though she'd been in a world of her own design for weeks, Lauren still had a tough time believing Bailey moved between the worlds in some sort of sleep trance before arriving in time to battle the Seers.

A drop landed on her scalp. They didn't need rain right now. The soft soil already made hiking difficult. Add a drizzle of rain, and it'd turn into a sucking swamp. She pulled her hood up. Instead of being disappointed by the rain, she decided to be positive—at least it wasn't snowing.

Bailey stretched a wing over her head, and the other over Yarborough's, who walked beside her.

"Thank you, gentle angel," he said.

Yeval was not a vacation destination, despite its dark beauties, its sprawling spruce and sequoias. Fangands, arachands, even packs of wolves, roamed the Bleeding Grounds, which is why the Council of Yeval decided to build the Heart here. The dangers of the forest provided a natural, if unconventional, moat—a perilous span of miles surrounding the Council and the Order of the Protectorate.

A narrow path, obscured with fallen leaves and needles, carved through the dense, towering trees, and wound through the heavy foliage. The canopy of gnarled branches and green needles kept the air beneath warm. Lauren's cloak flowed behind her as she asked Yarborough, "How much longer? This place creeps me out."

"Soon," he said. "The closer we get, the taller the trees. But we must be vigilant. Danger lurks nearby. The predators of the Bleeding Grounds move in silent shadows."

"The trees get taller?" Bailey said. "I've never seen trees this big. They're like space-shuttle big."

"Sequoias," Lauren said. "Like in California. Where dad lives with what's-her-face."

With each step, the air grew thicker, tinged with the scent of wet fur and upturned soil. Her heart rattled in her chest. Her feet sank in the new mud. Each step came with a sucking sound like unclogging a toilet. So much for moving silently.

In front of her, a minuscule sound, like the shuffle of boots in dirt, or a dead animal dragged by a large predator. Some tiny echo creeping through the blackness of the trees. Fear shot through her, chilled her, slowed her pulse until her blood thickened to the consistency of mud.

"Your eyes are glowing," Bailey whispered.

"Did you hear it?" Yarborough asked.

"I heard it," Lauren whispered.

Bailey Renee said, "I see it. Some sort of giant spider woman."

The sound scuttled into the trees. Ice crusted her fingertips. Drops of rain froze around her and fell to the earth like frozen tears. "Arachand."

AIDEN CLANKED out of Franky's Jeep Wrangler and stomped toward the home of his friend. "It's weird, bro. At first, I thought Alrujah was a dream. Now, North Chester feels like the dream. Not the least bit real to me."

"No?" Franky asked. He unlocked the front door. "Parents are on a date tonight. We got hours before they're back."

Aiden touched the front door and marveled at the woodwork. The door didn't have half the detail of the finely crafted doors of Langley's home in Harland, but he appreciated the subtle charm. "This door looks like it's one-of-a-kind, but there are millions of these. Mass-production. In Alrujah, all the doors are different. Look long enough, you'll find a small notch out of place, but never in the same spot." He touched the glass in the front window and shook his head. "It's déjà vu, man. Like I've been here, but never in real life. A memory of a dream."

Franky closed the door behind him. "This is the real deal, man. Doesn't get realer than this."

Aiden had his doubts. He walked to the kitchen, took off his gauntlets, and ran his fingers over the granite counters. Strangely warm, like the rest of the house. No chill in the air, no bone-numbing Alrujahn cold.

"Hungry?"

"Starving."

Franky opened the fridge. "Mom shops tomorrow, so we're low. We got lunch meat and bread. Need a sandwich?"

"Bro, you don't know how bad I need a sandwich."

"Get changed, man. Ditch the armor in my closet. It'll be safe.

Parents never go in my room. Grab clothes from my drawers. Whatever you need."

Aiden clanked up the stairs and wrested loose the leather straps of his chest piece. He unstrapped his greaves before he'd made it to the final step. Had he ever struggled with the armor? By the time he got to Franky's room, he'd shed all his armor like a crab. He dumped the heavy, blood-spattered metal in the closet and covered it with Franky's dirty clothes. After stripping his leather tunic and wool pants off, he rummaged through the drawers, eventually settling on a black long-sleeved undershirt and a white Muse tee to go over it. Too tight in the shoulders. He'd gained a few pounds of muscle in Alrujah. At least the jeans fit, though a little loose in the waist. He pulled on a pair of black socks and Franky's slippers.

Even unkempt, Franky's bed looked appealing. He sat on it, leaned back until his head hit the pillow. Immediately, his body thanked him. Fatigue washed over him, tempted him to close his eyes and forget about dinner, but his grumbling stomach won the debate, and he hustled downstairs in slippered feet, appreciating the softness of carpet, the warmth of the wood banister. "Hope you made me two, bro."

"Three. I've seen you eat." He slid a plate across the kitchen's center island. White bread, thin-sliced oven-roasted turkey. Mayonnaise leaked from the sides. His stomach groaned. He took massive bites and polished them off in minutes. He washed them down with a cold can of root beer, savored the sweetness, and let out a low, growling belch. "Been too long since I had anything with bubbles."

He wiped his mouth. With his hunger satiated, he thought of Lauren. His heart ached for her. He should have stayed with her. If she couldn't eat like this, he shouldn't.

"Want to talk about it? Before we call your folks, I mean."

Alrujah had transformed his life. It affirmed everything he'd ever believed about God. But he had no way to explain it, no words to provide the proper context, to fully paint the miracle. Even if he did, it'd never make sense to anyone else. "Don't know what to say."

"Is Bailey Renee okay? Is Alrujah dangerous?"

Aiden laughed and finished the soda in an enormous swallow. He belched and laughed again. "Feels good."

Franky smiled. "So?"

"She's good," he said. He didn't want to tell him she'd come back and been less than ten miles from where Franky had picked him up. What good would it do? "Alrujah's dangerous, but nothing she can't handle."

"What about the others? Bailey's sister? Her friend and that Erica girl?"

"They're all there," Aiden said. He sat on the stool and stared at the drop of soda working its way around the rim of the can. "Pretty incredible people."

"You had a thing for Lauren, right?"

He grinned with half his mouth. "Still do."

"Alrujah didn't change that?"

"Made it worse," he said.

Franky nodded. "I'm still tripping on seeing you again, man. Everyone's missed you. Coach is going to lose his mind when you get back to school."

Coach? Yes, football. He'd almost forgotten about it. The championship game. "Did we win?"

Franky shook his head. "Had a bunch of college scouts out to scope you and Danny. But, without you running routes, Danny choked. Two picks, one inside our twenty."

"We lost?"

"21-17," Franky said quietly.

He should be more affected, but the news sounded far less tragic than he'd imagined it would. "Sucks for Danny."

"Sucks for all of us, man. I'm not good enough to play college ball. At least you'll have a scholarship to look forward to, especially with all your muscle. You lift weights in Alrujah?"

Aiden shook his head and frowned. "Got exercise, yeah, but no weights." He tried to imagine a Miami University Hurricane's jersey, a dream he'd had since childhood, but try as he might, the image never took shape. Hard enough to envision what it'd be like to go back to school, much less college. His stomach knotted, but not from hunger. This world, this North Chester, felt more distant than it ever had in Alrujah.

He'd readjust with time, once he got someplace a little more familiar. "Let me call my mom," he said.

BAILEY PULLED her sword from its sheath, and the hot metal ignited in flames. Bad idea. One false move might light the entire Yeval Forest on fire. Instead of the Bleeding Grounds, they'd call it the Burnt Grounds, which wouldn't be good for their chances of survival. She replaced the blade, wishing she had another weapon.

Yarborough said, "Don't let it get close." He gripped his hammer and moved closer to Bailey's back. "Don't fly. Its web runs around us. Arachands like their prey fighting."

Grounded. Fantastic. She'd have to do this the hard way. "I need a sword," she said. "Don't want the forest catching on fire because of a careless flick of my wrist."

"On it," Lauren whispered. She knelt and moved her hands over the dirt. Tiny icicles ran along the veins in the back of her hand, forming a crystallized web of frost. Beneath her hands, the mud dried out, and on top of the mud rested a sword of pure ice. "May not last long. Make it count."

Bailey snatched it up and turned her eyes toward the trembling leaves and needles of the branches above them. Raindrops froze on the ice blade and hilt.

Between the branches, the spider-woman monster moved its thick black legs. Each ended in a vicious dagger-sharp point. It used these to straddle the empty places between trees, to distribute her weight between brittle, black branches. The womanish torso leaned down, cocked her head to the side. Two massive clusters of eyes marred each side of her face. The black, segmented exoskeleton ran up her chest like armor. Four pincers split her disgustingly human lips.

Lauren's eyes shifted from a pale blue to lightning yellow, igniting the raindrops into tiny stars. Her hair crackled with electricity. "Clear!"

Bailey and Yarborough rolled behind Lauren. They shielded their faces as a lightning storm erupted from her fingertips.

The arachand howled, its pincers opening and snapping, snapping and opening, its dagger-footed legs convulsing until the massive body dropped from the trees in front of them.

"Mind the feet!" Yarborough charged the twitching monstrosity.

"And the pincers," Lauren added. Already, she lifted Oliver's staff and channeled her fear to ice. She fashioned round tips on each of the daggerish feet, rooting the monster to the muddy earth beneath.

It righted itself, pulled at its ice-cuffs until they snapped from the ground. It pinned Yarborough to the ground by the chest. He grimaced, muttered something in dwarfish.

Bailey gripped the ice handle of her blade. She took off, low enough to avoid the canopy of trees, but high enough to be eye-to-eye with the repugnant beast. She wouldn't have many shots at this, so she wanted to make it quick, to do it right.

She stared beyond the drops, through them. Her sight cleared.

Two legs swept up at her. She pulled her wings in, rolled to her left, opened her wings, and alighted back to her former position—flying straight toward the thing's face. The smell of it, all blood and decay and rot, made her want to vomit. She steeled her stomach, swallowed, lined up her shot. She cleared her mind as she did before each free throw, before each shot on the court. The mouth became the hoop, her blade the ball. She launched the delicately balanced ice blade at the creature's head.

The blade split the rain and found its mark. It pierced through the mouth and out the back of the head. The pincers snapped around the hilt, already melting from the heat of Bailey's hand. Her cold, wet palm ached, but she'd done it.

A cheer went up from Yarborough, who'd freed himself and stood, good arm raised in triumph. "Well played, Bailey Renee."

Even Lauren smiled. "That's my sister."

Nothing Lauren had ever said meant as much to Bailey.

ERICA WOKE in the same uncomfortable chair she'd fallen asleep in the night before. The bedding the monks brought her lay undisturbed at her feet. But she couldn't lie on the floor in comfort while her parents suffered. Her stiff neck protested the lifting of her head. Her spine ached. Numbness needled the soles of her feet, her calves and knees. She tried to stand, but her legs buckled under her weight. In retrospect, she should have asked for a cot.

Dillard opened the door and poked his hooded head in. "Are you awake?"

Erica nodded and rubbed the back of her neck. She grabbed her chin and the back of her head, twisting to one side. Every joint in her neck popped. "Mom and Dad are sleeping, though. Let's use our monk voices, shall we?"

Dillard didn't smile. Under his hood, his pale face grayed with shadow. "Korodeth has taken the throne. We received word moments ago."

Her numbness fled with an onslaught of rage. She stood up, opened her mouth to shout, but remembered her sleeping parents and whispered through her teeth. "He what?"

Dillard shut the door behind him and buried his hands in his sleeves. "In the absence of the heir, Korodeth has appointed himself king. It is his right, an ancient edict from the mouth of King Solous himself. The Korodeths have always been in line for the throne. He insists he will relinquish the crown upon Princess Indigo's reappearance, but we have our doubts. He will do everything in his power to ensure she does not return."

Erica shook her head. "Does he know where she is?"

"I don't believe so." He moved to Norby, gently placed his fingers beneath her father's jaw, then did the same with Breniveer. "We're not sure where she is either, but Korodeth will discover her location soon. He has his army of Chameleon soldiers."

"But Oliver's with her. He can sense them the way you can, right? He'll keep her safe." Erica knelt on the bedding on the floor next to her father, put her hand on his forehead, and whispered, "We've got to do something about Korodeth, Papa."

Moving to the cabinets of medicine, Dillard extracted a salve in a small ceramic bowl. He crumbled a brown leaf into the paste and mixed it with a mortar. "Do you recall the conversation we had in Varuth at Relina's house?"

"About the Sherpa Order or whatever?"

"The Shedoahn Order," Dillard said, mixing meticulously. "We are certain Korodeth leads the Order. He plans to break Shedoah's seals. If he accomplishes this, all we know will end. None will survive the wrath of Shedoah."

"How very end-of-the-world of him. But here's the thing: I don't care what club he started. He nearly killed my parents, and he put a dagger in the heart of the man who raised me. Korodeth will die, and I'll be the one to kill him."

Dillard took a paintbrush and walked to Norby. "I fear it won't be as easy as you believe. Korodeth's power is considerable. Remarkable, even. If you hope to defeat him, the Hand must be whole."

"Never underestimate the power of an angry daughter," Erica whispered.

Dillard nodded. "I understand. Nevertheless, it is imperative we reunite the Hand, if for no other reason than to take back the crown."

"So what do we do first? Take out the Mage Lord or go after Korodeth?"

"I believe Korodeth is the real threat. The Mage Lord has made no move toward the throne. If he were to act, he would have done it by now, when the crown is weakest."

Erica slid her hand into her papa's. "Or maybe he already did. Maybe Korodeth is the Mage Lord."

Dillard paused a moment before dipping the paintbrush in the salve. "It is possible." Gently, he slathered the pasty salve on Norby's wounds. He twitched as the brush moved over each blackened wound on his leg.

Norby squeezed her hand as the door flew open.

"Erica," Ullwen said, his breath short in his chest. "We must go. The Shedoahn Order has found Relina."

"You can't go," her father said, his voice thick with sleep and pain. "Korodeth will expect it. Varuth will be circled with guards."

"We have to do something," Erica said. Already, her palms moistened. "She's the reason we got you two out."

Dillard replaced the brush in the white salve. "I believe I have something that might be of use."

7

She will be a stranger to Alrujah, to its peoples and lands. She will carry steel, will wield it with precision and awe, and she will sing with the voice of shadows.
—The Book of Things to Come

JOSEPH PARKER TURNED off the television. Nothing good on this late at night anyway. An hour ago, he'd made the late local news. Of course, by the time the news van got to the scene, the police had cleaned up the werewolves. Dragged them out into the woods. Told the news Parker hit a grizzly. Issued a bear warning and urged people to stay inside.

Buying time. Avoiding widespread panic and public demands for answers they didn't have. Standard procedure.

Nurse Nicole walked in, eyes a deep gold. "Didn't expect to see you here," she said as she examined his chart.

He hadn't seen her since Bailey slipped out of the hospital. Felt like years ago, though it was only a few days. "Didn't expect to be here. Doctor says I'm healing up nice. Couple of days off work is all.

Couldn't even get a full week. Guess I shouldn't be surprised to see you here fixing me up."

Nicole smiled and swapped out a near-empty IV bag with one full of clear solution. Saline, and maybe a little something mixed in for the pain. He thought to ask Nicole what his doctor had put him on but decided not to. Not knowing might be better.

Nicole inspected him. "Not bad for a man attacked by a pack of fangands."

Parker furrowed his brow, and his head exploded in pain. "How'd you know?"

"I'm an angel, remember?"

Parker shook his head, reached for his unlit cigarette before he remembered Nicole taking it earlier. He needed a fake smoke now. Hard enough to swallow what happened on Piedmont Road, but to believe this nurse was an angel—it all made his brain hurt. Still, he couldn't deny what she'd done for Bailey, the wings she'd showed him days ago, only visible to those she chose to reveal them to. "So I guess you got word from on high?"

"Who do you think brought the kids back to North Chester when you were being attacked?"

"The big guy?"

"He cares about you, Joseph. He's got plans for you yet."

Parker pulled his covers up. "This conversation is getting strange. What's in the IV bag anyway?"

"No psychotropics, if that's what you're driving at." She slipped a blood pressure cuff over his right arm. "Still thinking about Bailey?"

"You could say that."

She pressed a button, and the cuff inflated as it dug into the crook of his arm. "There's a visitor in the hall."

Parker's arm and head throbbed dully. "For me?"

Nicole smiled. "She's not here for me. Came in a while back, but I wanted to give you time to rest. Up for company now?"

Someone from the department? Must be. No chance his ex would show up to wish him well—and he had no other family. Since his brother passed, he'd been the last Parker standing for three years. "I'll give it a go. Send her in."

Nicole recorded his blood pressure and took the cuff off his arm. On her way out of the room, she said, "He's ready now."

Of all the faces he'd expected to see, Becca Knowles's was the last. Still, who should walk in but the grieving mother? Had she found something?

She frowned. "A bear attack?"

Parker grinned. His face hurt. "You know momma bears."

"I know exactly." She put her hand on his wrist. "You okay?"

He closed his eyes and made a face. "Cracked my head a little. May have a slight concussion. Nothing to worry about. But you. What are you doing here? It's late."

"You were all over the eleven o'clock news."

"Don't you have work in the morning?"

"Yes, but I don't care. You're my best chance to get my girls back. Have to make sure you're back on the case quick."

Parker laughed and groaned, cradling his ribs with his hand. "Thanks for coming by. I'll stay on the case. Takes more than a bear attack to shake me."

Her playful smile vanished. "You're all I have left."

Parker frowned and touched her hand. "I'm going to get them back."

"What can I bring you? Food? I could smuggle in a burrito."

"Sure," he said. "Burrito sounds good."

SIX MONTHS AGO, Aiden's parents, Tiffany and Paul, told him they had to move to Minnesota. He'd lived in Miami his whole life, hating the thought of leaving his friends. Why would he move someplace where it snowed? But as the U-Haul traversed countless miles of macadam, the flatlands of Florida rose into hills. They moved through valleys and mountains until the trees lining the road no longer resembled those growing in Florida. The air turned sharp and crisp like an apple, a welcomed change from the muggy, damp air of Florida. He'd left a state and found another world.

Their new house looked like something out of a Christmas movie: a balcony over the front door, a two-story bay window rising like a tower to the left. A three-car garage with a room above. Even a tiny attic with a little round window above the porch. "We're going to live there?" he'd asked.

"Home sweet home," his mother said.

His father said, "I like it. Kind of like Castle Price."

He remembered all this as Franky's Jeep drove up the steep incline of his driveway, but the memory felt awkward, misplaced, as if it belonged to someone else, and he'd only borrowed it for the day. "I thought you said it was a circus over here. It's quiet."

"Guess the news guys got bored. Probably all covering Parker's crash. The bear hunt and all that."

Aiden smiled. "That's what they're calling it?"

"Story came over the television while you were changing. Guess they had to say something, right?"

"I guess." He sighed, searching for the strength to go in. He'd dreamed about this moment since he realized Alrujah wasn't a dream, but now, without his friends here, it didn't feel right. His bones ached with guilt. Lauren should be here with him.

Franky pulled into the long driveway leading up to the home on the hills. "Sure you don't want me to stick around?"

"I'm sure. But thanks."

"Remember, don't mention Alrujah. Not yet, at least."

"I can't lie to them, and you know they'll ask where I've been."

"Tell them what you told me, and they'll have you in a shrink's office faster than you can blink."

"They're not like that." He shoved his hands in his pockets. "Be cool."

"You, too."

Aiden got out of the car, and his mother raced out the front door.

She ran to him, her arms to her chest, as if she held a baby bird. Behind her, his father followed.

Aiden smiled, but his legs wouldn't move. Tears heated his eyes. His parents gathered him in their arms, their limbs shaking. He hugged them hard.

Franky drove off slowly. The chill of the night air couldn't penetrate the warmth of his parents' embrace. They stayed huddled together for minutes, hugging, his mother kissing his forehead with trembling lips, his father's goatee scratching Aiden's cheeks, before they walked back into the house.

Aiden paused at the doorway. He should feel more at home, more relaxed. The oak flooring, the wood-burning stove in the far corner, the 54-inch television mounted to the wall. They should all feel real, but they didn't. He sat on the couch, touched the coffee table tentatively, as if it might vanish.

His mother sat beside him and held his hand in hers. "Where have you been, baby? Are you okay?"

"I'm fine," he said.

"What about the others?" his father asked, kneeling in front of him and inspecting his eyes.

Aiden took a deep breath. Parker and Franky warned him. They'd want to know where he'd been, but he hadn't imagined they'd ask him so quickly, so pointedly. "They're fine," he said, his voice quiet.

"What happened?" his mother asked, her hand squeezing his.

Aiden shook his head and examined the laminated planks of oak flooring. He wanted so desperately to be there in North Chester, but he couldn't relax. Even sitting on his couch felt wrong. Comfortable, for sure, but wrong. He didn't even know what day it was.

His mother kissed his forehead. "Are you okay? Are you hurt? Do you need a doctor?"

"I'm fine, Mom." His body, bruised and achy, cried out for healing. "Nothing a little ibuprofen won't fix up." He stood and moved to the kitchen. He ran his fingers over the tile countertops. In the morning, Mom would make blueberry pancakes, then spend the morning blogging movie and television reviews. In the afternoon, she'd hike through the woods, maybe bake a cake. She'd have dinner ready by the time his father got home from working construction.

Aiden sat at the kitchen table, sat in his chair and wondered how many meals he'd missed, how many dinners.

"Hungry?" his mother asked. She moved to the refrigerator. "I'll make something."

"I'm good," he said.

"Doesn't look like you've missed many meals," his father said, taking the seat beside him. "How'd you put on so much muscle in so few weeks?"

Aiden shook his head.

"And these bruises, these scratches and scars?" his mother said. She ran her hand over his arms, his cheeks. "What happened? You have to tell us."

How could he put it into words? He swallowed three ibuprofens and washed them down with a glass of water. He stood, brought the glass to the kitchen sink. There, beside the blender, sat the chess set his father had made. He walked to it, drawn by some strange pulling. The set had a hook in him, and he brushed the dust from the sanded wood. He examined the set, picking up a pawn and twisting it under the light. His father had whittled each of the pieces from wood he'd collected on their annual family camping trips. The pawns took the shape of messenger boys. Shorter than the other pieces by inches, each boy had a wry smile, deep-set eyes, and tunics bearing the crest of some medieval city. His father had crafted one side as humans, the other elves.

"Aiden, baby," his mother said. "What's wrong? Why won't you talk to us?"

How strange to remember his father's obsession with fantasy now. Hadn't he read every fantasy novel he got his hands on? Hadn't he shelled out money for paintings of knights and princesses, of kings and wizards? Hadn't he bought two broadswords, now mounted over the fireplace?

Aiden pushed a pawn forward. It glided smoothly over the well-sanded board, but Aiden's hand trembled. "The emblem," he said, pointing to the strange two-headed bird on the chest of the pawn.

His father smiled, crossed his arms, and leaned against the

counter. "The crest of Harael. You remember those stories? Haven't told you one in years."

His father's stories? Of course. Each night before bed, up until Aiden turned eight, his father told him a story of a strange land full of knights and princesses and evil monsters.

Aiden picked up the elvish king. Tall and lanky, it looked more like a stretched human than an elf. But his father's steady hand, years and years ago, had whittled a heavy gold crown on its head, had designed the almond shaped eyes. Even the thin, brittle nose matched Aiden's memory exactly. "Neldohr," he said.

His father's ears shifted up. "You remember? I'm impressed. Didn't tell many stories about him."

How could his father know about Neldohr? About the war of elves and humans? "You've been there, too?"

"Where?" his mother asked.

Aiden steadied himself on the counter and tried not to give in to the spinning in his head. "Alrujah."

His father frowned. "Been there? No. They were dreams, that's all."

"Pops," Aiden said. "We need to talk."

DILLARD SLID a ring on Erica's finger. She recognized the tingling chill of metal, the dull golden gleam. Ma'att'tal, like her bracelets. Forged in Margwar by the dwarves and later enchanted by the elves. Oliver had given her the bracelets in the nar'esh cave, insisting they'd help her calling. And, like her bracelets, the enchantment of the ring glowed warmly, made her finger tickle. "What's it do?"

The albino monk touched each of her bracelets. "Much the same as these. They take the talents within you and magnify them. Your ability to speak with animals is only the beginning of your power. This ring will help you bond with the beasts. You will see what they see, feel what they feel, hear what they hear."

Erica ran her fingers over the metal. "Don't think the guards will stop a razorbeak from flying into the city, do you?" she asked her father.

He grinned weakly. "My girl. Already thinking like a general."

"Try it," Breniveer urged. She'd sat up in the bed, and her eyes held the same warmth Erica remembered from childhood, or more accurately, her digital childhood.

Sparky sat next to her, pushing against her leg. Without hesitation, she closed her eyes and tried to imagine the world through Sparky's eyes.

"Easy, honey," Breniveer said. She touched Erica's elbow and held it. "Working with minds is dangerous business. You must be careful. There's only room for one consciousness in each animal. If you go throwing yourself into Sparky's brain, you might damage it."

Erica opened her eyes. "Didn't work anyway."

"If it had, you might have destroyed him. You get this part from me. It's mind-witching, sure and simple. I'll have to teach you what I know when we have time. But for now, only remember, you're not controlling Sparky. You're asking him to do what you want, and you follow along for the ride. If you try to make him do what you want without asking, he'll resist, and the battle for control can rend his mind."

"Think I got it," Erica said. She closed her eyes again, ran her hands through Sparky's thick fur. *Let me see with your eyes*, she thought. *Let me hear with your ears.*

A razorbeak cawed outside. Sparky perked his ears, and Erica felt the muscles at the back of his head twitching.

His instinct burned hot in her chest. She longed to chase the bird, to snap it up in her jaws and hear its bones snap, to taste the warm blood and feathers.

Her eyes opened with new vision—a world of black and white colored with a myriad of scents—the sweat on Ullwen, the sharp iron-tinge of blood and open wounds, even wispy clouds of soap on Dillard's blue robe.

Move forward. Sparky stood up and walked toward the door. As he turned his head from side to side, Erica saw what he saw in the corner of her mind—like a television screen in the corner of her perception.

Where shall I go? He asked, though he did not use human words. As always, his will manifested in an impression of desires, of complex emotions woven together to create an idea. Erica doubted anyone understood the minds of animals the way she did.

She thanked Sparky for letting her become part of him, even for such a short time, and withdrew from his mind. "I think I've got it."

"Each animal will be different, even among the same species," Breniveer said as Dillard applied generous amounts of salve to her wounded arm. "Each human is different, too. You'll discover patterns, sure. And each experience will better prepare you for the next. Allow yourself time to adjust to the workings of their minds. Unless, of course, you mean to harm them. If you mean to defend yourself from a beast, you won't have to try hard. Leap into their consciousness and take control. If they fight you, they lose their minds."

"Wish I'd known that before that sasquatch broke me in half," Erica muttered.

8

"I have allowed myself to be chained," says the mighty Shedoah. "By my chains are my people freed. And so will come a day when I will throw off the chains and return to Alrujah to enact vengeance upon Adonai. By my power will I declare my authority and shall shelter my people from the wicked deceitfulness of Adonai."
—The Shedoahn Prophecies

AIDEN RAN his fingers over the carved wooden humans on the chess board. Though his father had used smooth white pine for the elves, he fashioned the humans out of black spruce and stained them a deep, dark red.

The detail of the pieces astounded Aiden. He'd played chess with his father, day after day, move by move, until he no longer noticed the pointy ears of the elves, the meticulously chiseled coat of arms on each knight. Now, he turned the pieces over and over in his hands, unable to put them back on the board, unwilling to cease studying them. Especially the queen on the human side of the board. Strangely enough, she was an elf. Tall, linear, almond eyes. High cheek bones. Aside from the length of the points on her ears, the elf was the very image of Indigo.

He ran his thumb over the face, the point of the ears, the thin lips. She wore a long, flowing dress. A tiara rested on her head. Aiden ran his thumbnail along the soft, sanded edge of her elbow. "Why an elf queen?"

His father, sitting at the kitchen table with a mug of coffee, tucked his left hand under his right arm. "You understand why it's hard to believe you."

His mother moved behind Aiden, rubbed his neck. Her thumbs worked over the knots. One hand slid up to his forehead.

"I don't have a fever," Aiden said. "I'm not crazy. I didn't hit my head. I woke up in Alrujah one morning. I don't know how or why, but I know what I know."

"I'm worried," his mother said. "I want to know what happened."

"I told you already." Aiden sat on the counter, picked up the fat human king. "Franky said you wouldn't believe me."

His father ran a hand over his goatee. He set his coffee down and gestured to the piece in Aiden's hand. "Ribillius married an elf to keep peace between the races. Rumors said the elves were going to rise up. They were going to find *The Book of Sealed Magic* and use it to subjugate humanity."

His mother never mocked, never scorned, but she sighed with the best of them. She used her lungs like conversation weapons. If he missed a chore, skipped out on his homework, came home five minutes late, she'd heave a sigh to make a raven weep. She preached disappointment, not disdain. It hurt more than any firm-handed spanking.

Now she aimed her sigh at Aiden's father. Probably for encouraging him in his fantasy. When she spoke, each word came out precisely measured, weighed for connotation and denotation as any good writer would. "We believe you believe what you say. But I want you to see a doctor. Just to make sure you're okay."

"I don't need a doctor or a psychotherapist or counselor. I'm not sick; I'm not hurt; I'm not crazy; I'm not brainwashed. What happened happened." He should have expected this from his all-too-rational mother, but her lack of faith stung.

"Listen," his father said, leaning in. His dark eyes locked on Aiden's. "I had dreams for years about Alrujah. I told you stories. I made this chess set. We've got fantasy paintings all around this house. I'm glad you're back, but your mother's right. These stories and paintings got mixed up in your head. You had a dream. It won't hurt to have you checked out."

"What if it was a seizure?" his mother said. "Some seizures cause hallucinations."

"Now you sound crazy," Aiden said. "This wasn't a dream or a hallucination. Look at me." He stood up, flexed his muscles. "I'm a beast, Pops. Used to be a wide receiver, and I came back a linebacker. I'm telling you, it happened." An idea hit him. He pulled his phone from his pocket and texted Franky. "Send me a pic of my armor, bro?"

Fear and concern sank his mother's cheeks and watered her eyes. "Aiden."

He put his phone down, squeezed the elf queen. He hadn't planned on missing Lauren this much, or the rest of his friends. He should be happy. He'd made it home, back to his family, but something wasn't right. The carpeting of the stairs, the wooden banister, the lingering smell of pine. These were relics, memories, phantoms, echoes of dreams.

His mother sat next to him, put her arm around his shoulder. "You know I love you, right?"

He nodded. "You want what's best for me."

His father stood by the counter. "Humor us? I'll take you to Doctor Sullivan tomorrow."

"No doctors," he said. In Alrujah, he'd followed Oliver's lead. And once he vanished, he did whatever Lauren asked. Now, he needed to think for himself, needed to make his own decisions. He needed someone to trust him, to follow him for a change.

"They were dreams," his father said. "No matter how real they were."

Aiden's phone beeped. Franky came through. He grinned and showed it to his father.

His father's rich, olive skin drained of color.

"I stashed my armor at Franky's. Didn't want to freak you guys out."

His mother snatched the phone and stared, mouth agape, at the pile of silver, bloodied armor. "What in the world?"

"I don't think you were having dreams, Pops."

"I don't believe it," his father said.

His mother looked over his father's shoulders. "You made this, didn't you? Some sort of digital manipulation? Or you found it online."

"Why would I do that, Mom? What would be the point?"

"I never talked about this armor," his father whispered. "How did you know?"

"Tomorrow," Aiden said. "I'll have Franky come over. We'll have some breakfast and talk. For now, I'm exhausted."

"No," his mother said, her voice firm with fear. She was a mother who wouldn't let her son go, who would never let him leave her sight again. "We talk tonight."

He kissed her forehead. "If I don't get some sleep, I'll need a doctor for sure. Tomorrow, Mom."

PARKER WASN'T THRILLED about the rookie cop driving him home. He didn't like depending on anyone other than himself. He'd done things on his own too long. But the kid drove fast, and he stayed quiet. Didn't mention anything about werewolves or angry bears. Smart enough to keep his mouth shut. That counted for something.

Once he got home, he thanked the rookie and pulled his phone out to call Becca. It may blur the lines of professionalism, but he refused to sit at home, even if his department ordered him to. Something happened in the forest, something strange, something entirely too sci-fi for his taste. And it happened close to Becca.

Until the werewolves jumped him, Parker assumed the key to cracking the case rested within Oliver's CPU. Now, another idea struck him.

What if he was looking in the wrong place? Was the key in the world itself? Some sort of dimensional shift? Made him wish Steven Hawking were available for police consultations.

He dialed her number; she picked up on the second ring. "Parker? You're out of the hospital already?"

Parker squinted into the sun, fumbled with his keys to unlock his door. "Listen, I know you're working now, but I was wondering if you could do me a favor."

"You're okay, then?"

The concern in her voice comforted him. It'd been a while since anyone worried over his wellbeing. Her visit to the hospital did more to expedite his recovery than any drug they'd given him. "Aside from a blistering headache, doc says I'm good. Surprised I didn't have more injuries. Called it a miracle." He remembered the weirdly warming touch of Lauren's hand on his brow, how it sent tendrils of ice and fire and electricity through him, how it hurt and healed. "Anyway, I'm home now. Rookie cop dropped me off. But I need a ride. Think you could pick me up?" He closed his front door and opened the blinds. Heated sunlight breached the window. His head throbbed, even after the pills the hospital sent him home with.

"Sure," she said.

He sensed hesitation. "If it's too much ..."

"Not at all, but why call me? I'm flattered, but I assumed you'd have someone from the force take you."

Parker opened the drawer next to his refrigerator and grabbed an unlit cigarette. He held it for a moment, rolled it between his thumb and forefinger, and grabbed a lighter. "The trip isn't exactly official police business. Shouldn't be long. I want to walk through the area where I wrecked my car last night."

"Why?"

He ignited the lighter, held it inches from the cigarette, and let the flame go out. The cigarette, still cold and dry, danced between his lips. How long had he been nicotine free? "Something's off." To pique her interest, he said, "Might be a connection to what happened to Bailey and Lauren."

Too much, he told himself, but he couldn't take it back now.

"What do you mean?"

"Detective's hunch."

Becca said nothing for a moment. Parker cradled the phone on his shoulder and pantomimed smoking. Did he really need to quit? With his luck, he'd quit and end up with cancer anyway. "You there?"

"Are you supposed to be working this soon after the accident?" Again with the concern.

He drew in a lungful of imagined smoke, closed his eyes, stilled his heart. "What if I told you it was a good excuse to see you?"

"I'd say you were behaving unprofessionally."

Smart. Way to get yourself into more trouble.

"And then I'd pick you up in thirty minutes."

He grinned. "Can't wait." He hung up, flicked the lighter, but did not touch the cigarette to the flame. He let the fire burn out and put it back in the drawer. To kill time, he decided to clean himself up, to scrub the caked blood and hospital stench from his skin. A hot shower would make his neck and back stop screaming, but it wouldn't quiet the whispering voice of guilt. He rubbed the bridge of his nose. "What am I getting myself into?"

BAILEY WOKE IN THE MORNING. Sunlight filtered through the thick canopy of the Yeval Forest. She hadn't slept well, though the hour or two she got refreshed her bones. Thankfully, Yarborough insisted they rest, otherwise Lauren would have marched them through the night, possibly to death.

The rain eased, replaced instead by a wispy mist. She thought of waking Lauren and the dwarf, but far be it from her to rob them of the little sleep they may get. Instead, she arched her back and stretched her wings. Lauren slumped over into a pile of leaves. Yarborough rested his head on his hammer.

Trees poked through the ground haphazardly. She studied them, inspecting the nascent bark and thin limbs. She tried not to think about how, hours ago, she'd been so close to home. She'd been in North Chester, less than five miles away from her mom. Now, she was right back in Alrujah. No matter how many times she'd tried to convince herself she'd made the right choice, she imagined the face of her mother, remembered her fear-cracked voice.

Yarborough yawned and sat up. His rough hand touched her wing gently. "You are missing home, I gather. I understand your pain," he said in a thick voice.

Bailey channeled her little remaining strength into her voice. "I have no home. How can you possibly understand what that's like?"

Yarborough knelt next to her. He ran his hand over the sapling. "I am the Nameless Heir."

Bailey ran through her memory of Lauren's journals. She remembered the phrase, but not its importance.

"I was born in Margwar, the great Dwarven city beneath the mountains. On the day before my naming day, my people exiled my father for his worship of Adonai. He took my mother and me with him to Harland. His hope was to finish his life quietly. But my mother died shortly after. Killed by bandits who did not believe dwarves should marry human women. My father slaughtered them all.

"The bandits sent raids after my father nearly every week for ten years, but never overwhelmed him. When I turned eleven, my father was murdered. The bandits claimed responsibility, but I recognized the work of the Shedoahn Order. They left pieces of him for me to find. They'd scrawled symbols with his blood."

Bailey's throat swelled with sorrow. "I'm so sorry."

Yarborough's lips shook. He cleared his throat and wiped his sagging eyes with the sleeve of his tunic. "I know what it is to be ripped from your home, from your family. But you have your sister still. Adonai is merciful."

How could a man who'd been through so much proclaim the mercies of Adonai? Bailey sniffed, determined not to cry.

Yarborough pushed himself up on his hammer until he stood. "There is always hope." He nodded to the sapling. "Rognak. They grew plentiful in the mountains where the dwarves lived. For centuries, Alrujah thought the tree extinct, but here they sprout from the roots of the dead trees. And so will be the line of dwarves."

Bailey wrapped her wings around herself, stared at Lauren sleeping in the leaves.

"May an old man give you some advice?"

She cleared her throat. "Sure."

"Hope is a matter of perception. If we focus on our concerns, we see only sorrow and despair. But, if we look beyond our circumstances, toward the greater good, we find hope. It will be real to us, and we can embrace it. But we must live for something more than ourselves."

Bailey nodded, following his logic, though he sounded a little like a wizened old guru sitting atop a mountain, waiting for knowledge-thirsty explorers to seek him out and ask the meaning of life. She stretched her wings. "What do you live for?"

"Adonai. In His service, I am made whole."

The branches of the pines around them bent under a stiff wind, reached down toward them like tentacles, their naked twigs like spidery appendages. She put the image out of mind. "Makes sense."

Yarborough scanned the forest again. "You wear the wings of Adonai's servant. Your name is mentioned as his emissary of war and justice. But you speak as one who does not believe."

"Not sure what I believe. I can't explain what's happened to me, to us, other than God—Adonai. But if He was real, why would He send us home only to pull us back?"

"The fangands," Lauren said, stretching and sitting. "Without us, Parker would have been torn to shreds."

Bailey smiled and helped Lauren stand. "Morning, sleepy head."

"Time for school already?" Lauren asked.

Bailey hugged her. "At least in Alrujah I don't have to ride the bus."

Lauren laughed.

"Here's what I don't get," Bailey said. "If Adonai brought us to North Chester to save Parker from the fangands, why'd he send the fangands there in the first place?"

"Who said He did?" Lauren asked. She stretched, bent over and touched her toes. "Might have been the Mage Lord's work."

"While I do not believe Adonai sent the fangands to your world, I doubt the Mage Lord has much interest in it. He is concerned only with ruling Alrujah," Yarborough said.

Lauren moved her hands in a circle, as if trying to conjure an image in a crystal ball. A sphere of fire appeared between them, grew from the size of a pea, to a pearl, to a peach. Though small, it put out a fair amount of heat and chased the cold away. "The Council of Yeval will have the information we need to find the Mage Lord and *The Book of Sealed Magic*. Perhaps they can help us get it before he unseals anymore spells. They're pretty deep into the forest, though. We'll need to start walking if we want to get there before sunsdown."

"Let us move with haste and hope the Council does not kill us before we tell them who we are."

Bailey rolled her eyes. "Not sure I like this idea."

9

And a mighty rognak will sprout from the seed of Solous. The spirit of Adonai shall rest upon him. With righteousness he shall judge the poor and rebuke the prideful and the vain. He shall rend Alrujah with the stave of his mouth, and his breath shall topple the wicked. He will wear a belt of truth, a sash of righteousness, a shield of justice.
—The Book of the Ancients

IN THE STILL EARLY morning sunlight, razorbeaks fluttered through the trees of the Cerulean Woods. The birds cawed at each other, flapped their elongated wings, sent purple feathers flitting through the trees. Erica focused on the nearest one, perched on a knobby branch above the monastery's infirmary. Honing her thoughts, she met its mind in hers—touched it gently, careful to avoid eye contact so as not to upset the savage bird. The razorbeak recoiled at first but settled down. It responded to the touch of Erica's mind and allowed her entrance into its senses.

Ullwen took Erica's hand. "Is it working?"

"It's incredible," she whispered. "I weigh about an ounce. I can feel the branch under my feet. I can fluff every feather."

"Astonishing."

"I was born to fly."

Ullwen smiled.

She saw him simultaneously through her eyes and those of the razorbeak. Strange to see him through four eyes, stranger still for the sensation to be familiar. She should be disoriented and confused, but her mind kept the images separate like a split screen for a multi-player video game.

The bird stretched its wings, leapt from the branch. Erica's breath caught. A few flaps, and the bird soared above the trees.

She felt the bird flying—the wind under its wings, the currents lifting the light hollow-boned body. Through the eyes of the razor-beak, the world appeared prismatic. Colors she never knew existed—hues of blues and greens and reds, but more radiant, more intense—screamed across the sky. More than simple mixes of other colors, these hues deserved their own names, names no human could give.

"It's so beautiful."

"Can you see the city?"

After asking permission to take full control, Erica lifted the bird's eyes, angled up to the southeast. "It's a few miles off, but yeah, I can see it."

"Be cautious."

"I always am."

The razorbeak flew faster, the wind in its face, its feet tucked under its purple fluff. The bird's close-knit feathers kept it warm despite the waning chill. Spring would be here soon, and already instinct called the bird to prepare her nest, find a decent male razor-beak, lay a few eggs. She put those thoughts from her head. Didn't want to get too close to the inner-workings of the bird's mind. To do so might break it.

The few miles it took to get to Varuth passed rapidly. With the suns on her beak, she tilted down toward the city, past the well-armed walls. "Looks like they're expecting a war."

Ullwen squeezed her hand, "Perhaps they expect only us."

"I'm sure we're scary enough to them, tiger, but they've got archers on every inch of their walls. Warships in port. Soldiers at every gate. They're expecting some sort of invasion." She leaned against the stone wall of the infirmary. The knobby stones sucked the heat from her body. Standing up straight, she folded the bird's wings and nosed down toward Relina's house near the offshoot of the bay that split the city. "A dozen Varuthian Elite on the outskirts of the woods."

"Close together?"

"Spread out."

"A fluid formation, ready to move. The invasion force is readied. Alrujah stands on the brink of war."

Erica steadied herself as the bird perched on the chimney of Relina's home. No smoke meant no fire. No fire meant no Relina. She dropped through the chimney into a soft pile of warm ash.

She took Ullwen's hand in hers. "I'm in."

"What do you see?"

"Blood on the walls. A ton of it. Table's flipped over. Chairs smashed." Her voice caught in her throat.

"Is Relina there? Her husband?" Ullwen's hand tightened around hers. "Are you okay?"

No, but she'd never admit it. She wasn't a baby anymore, not a terrified little girl standing before the stove. Fear wouldn't rule her. She wouldn't allow it. Fear would never force her to run, as she had when she abandoned her mother to her deranged father. She willed her voice to be strong. "The doors to the rooms are open. I'm going to check in there."

The bird hopped through the door to the room where Erica had stayed, where Bailey Renee had come to heal her, where Dillard had come to heal Sparky. The bed she'd slept in had been smashed in half, the straw mattress ripped wide open. No blood in this room, thankfully. She hopped to the other room, determined not to be cowed by terror. What lay in this room would be worse than the kitchen.

She was right.

The bird took in the probable scene of the massacre in its many-colored vision. The blood glowed brighter; the splinters of the bed shone deepest black; the straw shimmered dully gold and speckled yellow. On the wall, unrecognizable symbols had been painted in luminescent blood. Each took the shape of letters melted together, like wax from candles filling a mold. "Something's written on the wall."

At the monastery, Erica took a stick and recreated the symbols in the dirt. "Recognize these?"

Ullwen shook his head. "They are old, but I cannot read them."

"Get Dillard."

Ullwen moved into the infirmary. A moment later, he emerged with the albino monk. "What is it?"

Erica pointed, and Dillard knelt to inspect the symbols. "Where did you see these?"

"Inside Relina's house. What do they say?"

"They say, 'Shedoah will rise.'"

Her heart fisted in her chest. Fear bled away until only hate and anger remained.

Revenge.

She would have revenge for the murder of sweet Relina—the one who'd mixed a potion to help her breathe underwater and rescue her parents from the dungeons of Alrujah; the one who'd waddled when she walked, like the librarian at North Chester High; the one who feared retaliation from the Shedoahn Order for helping Erica and Ullwen in their service of Adonai.

She would have her revenge.

"The rooms?" Ullwen prompted.

"Relina is dead, and so is her husband."

His hand tightened.

"You're hurting me," she said.

He relaxed his grip, but his tension traveled to his jaw. He ground his teeth.

"I told her Shedoah's power couldn't touch her," Dillard whispered, still staring at the symbols. He shook his head and stood, his head bowed. "This should not have happened."

"We're going to find who did this, and we're going to kill him. Slowly."

"You don't know what you're saying," Ullwen said.

"I think I do." She thanked the bird for letting her hitch a ride and cut the connection. "I want to know where this Shedoahn Order meets. I want to know who's in it. I want to send them a message of my own."

WITH HER STOMACH GROWLING, Lauren led the way through the Yeval Forest. She'd designed it, knew how to get to the Council of Yeval, but in the dim sunslight, with leaves completely covering the ground, she found it hard to pick out the markings leading to the center. She had to rely on her sense of direction, keeping the setting suns to her left as much as possible to ensure northward movement. She wished she'd thought to put a stash of food here; a cache of delicacies in a hidden chest, a tomato vine. She'd take about anything at this point. But once they made it to the Heart, they'd have all the food they wanted.

If they lived long enough.

Bailey Renee, wings folded around herself, walked beside Lauren. She'd been quiet since they started the hike. Probably tired. Lauren didn't blame her. Even with the few hours' rest she had last night, her eyelids grew heavy with each step.

"It has been long since I last walked among these trees," Yarborough said, his voice flat with memory and pain. He held his shoulder, wet with new blood. The scab must have split last night. Her healing, though helpful, hadn't proven as effective as Oliver's. Yarborough needed medical attention, needed to clean his wounds and rest. He would do so in Yeval, the Forest City, if they allowed him to enter the protective custody. The Council allowed few audiences. Those not granted entrance were killed on the spot. This far into the Bleeding Grounds, only those options existed.

But the ruthlessness was warranted. The citizens of Yeval fought a spiritual battle, one Lauren never imagined in North Chester, one she was only beginning to understand since she'd met Adonai on Harael.

"You've been here before?" Bailey Renee asked.

"Aye, winged one. As a child. My father brought me here to meet the Council."

Lauren said, "I don't remember your father being on the Council."

"He was not. But he was in line to take the place of Oren. Unfortunately, my father did not live long enough to take the position."

Lauren froze and grabbed Yarborough's wrist.

"What's wrong? Hear something?" Bailey whispered.

Something stirred inside her, twisted and knotted, worked inward on itself until the power coursing through her vanished. "My magic is gone."

Yarborough dropped his war hammer. "Weapons away," he said, his voice steeled with command.

Bailey Renee sheathed the sword she'd used for light without question. She wouldn't drop the blade in the dirt for anyone.

A wrinkled man, stout framed and pale skinned, stepped from behind a tree and into the path in front of them. Thick as the sequoia trunk he'd stepped from behind, the dwarf had deep eye sockets which rested inches behind his nose. His bushy eyebrows were like cliff overhangs. His nose, short and fat, hid behind a steel plate descending from his helmet between his eyes. Scars ran down either side of his face. His red hair came to thick mutton-chop sideburns, each of which he'd braided down to his shoulders. On his face, only his chin lacked hair. His lips curled up. "You have entered the Hold of Yeval. You know what this means?"

If they were in the Hold, the Heart was not far. "We do," Lauren said.

"You are surrounded by the finest warriors in all of Alrujah. Drop your staff."

Lauren's pulse quickened. She considered every word. She must speak as a queen, as a follower of Adonai, or she might end up dead. "This staff is a tool of almighty Adonai."

The ugly dwarf frowned. The braided sideburns danced with the contortion. "Prove it."

Lauren raised her chin in a divinely princess way. "I am Indigo, daughter of King Ribillius and Queen Elil, who sat on the Council of Yeval until the time of her death."

"An easy lie," the ugly dwarf said. He lifted the heavy battle axe he carried from his shoulder. "I'll give you one opportunity to prove your words before I demand your head from your shoulders."

Lauren's blood ran cold. How could she prove what she said? The enchantments surrounding Yeval City were near impossible to break. The ancient magic that weaved them—a co-effort between the three primary races—elves, humans, and dwarfs—stifled any trace of magic ability from anyone within their confines. She could take a few steps backward, beyond the reach of the enchantment, but what would that prove? Her fear? And if she did, hundreds of heavily armored warriors would fall on her like an avalanche.

Bailey Renee stepped forward and spread her wings. "You may believe her. I am an angel, a messenger of hope. My name is Bailey Renee."

"Aye, your wings mark you an angel, but can angels not fall? And if that is the case, Bailey Renee, your fate will be particularly memorable."

"Is that a threat?" Yarborough asked.

Help me, Lauren prayed. Her back stiffened, and she raised her chin again. "I am a finger of Adonai. Our coming has been foretold in *The Book of Things to Come*." Her mind raced. She had the book some-where—that alone might prove it.

Bailey Renee untucked the book from under her wing and handed it to the ugly dwarf.

The dwarf's jaw swung open. "Where did you get this?"

"From Dillard, a Monk of the Cerulean Order," Lauren said. "It was given to our friend Oliver. You will know him as Vicmorn, son of Eljah Morrow, Father of the Cerulean Monastery."

"I know what is in this book, but, if you are the Hand, there should be four of you, and a fifth from within Alrujah."

Holding the staff and fueling her courage, Lauren spoke again. "It became necessary for us to separate to accomplish the will of Adonai. Though apart, each of us works toward His will." Lauren thought of Aiden, of the way he refused to return, how he gave up on Alrujah. How he gave up on her. Her heart broke a bit more, and she wondered what his abandonment meant for Alrujah.

A princess didn't doubt, she reminded herself.

The dwarf closed the book and raised his axe. "You profane the name of Adonai with your blasphemies against His prophecy!" He rushed Lauren and brought the axe down toward her.

Instinctively, she raised the staff and deflected the blow. The axe shattered. She steadied her arm, and the staff leapt from her hand high into the air, as if she'd thrown it straight up, but she hadn't.

In a burst of light, the staff transformed into a massive white bird with shimmering feathers and blazing copper eyes. With an ear-shattering shriek, it dug its talons into the shoulders of the ugly dwarf and lifted him into the air.

Bailey Renee gasped.

Yarborough fell to his knees, staring at the ground.

The bird opened its gleaming gold beak and spoke with a tongue of fire. "I am the Lord your God, Adonai. These are my servants, the protectors of my people. Do as they say, or face a wrath unseen in generations."

The ugly dwarf dangled twenty feet in the air, his face twisted in terror. The forest awoke with the sounds of armor clanging. Thirty soldiers, maybe more, emerged from the darkened trees and knelt, their faces toward the ground—adopting the same posture as Yarborough.

Lauren and Bailey Renee stared at the bird, eyes wide.

Finally, the bird released the dwarf, who hit the ground and crumpled. Struggling to right himself, he, too, knelt before the shimmering bird.

~

SUNLIGHT CRAWLED through Aiden's window and crept along gray carpet to his bare feet. He sat on the edge of the bed, holding the queen elf in his left hand. Standing, he moved to the window.

One sun.

How long had it been since only one sun came up in the morning, and why should it feel so strange now? Years of inattention muddied the few memories he had of American sunrises. He liked to sleep in, and now the memories took the hue of myth.

No such mud, no such fog of disinterest marred his memories of the Alrujahn sunrise. He'd only been there a couple weeks, but his memory, Jaurru's memories, stretched back years, to his childhood in Harland, to the early morning sparring sessions with his father wearing the green and white of his home city. The smack of sword on shield, the ringing of metal, the vibrations of impact. The need for routine burned in his muscles. He shook his head, turned away from the brilliant sun, and lay on his chest. With a carefully measured breath, he began a long volley of push-ups. He'd pressed out 120 before fatigue tired his muscles.

Sweat broke on his brow. He stopped, sat down, and crossed his legs.

By now, it'd be afternoon in Alrujah. If Lauren had made it back as she wanted, she'd have already watched the greater sun and lesser sun rise over the Dragon's Back Mountains. She'd have eaten stale bread, maybe some cheese, vegetables, and whatever fruit lasted through the last breaths of winter into the early spring.

His stomach growled, and he put on a pair of socks. He slipped on a pair of jeans that used to be loose. Now, they hugged his hips tight. The fabric of his t-shirt stretched snug across his chest and shoulders. Taking the queen elf from his desk, he slipped it in his pocket and traipsed down the stairs.

His mother, dressed in a thick red robe and matching slippers, opened the fridge. "How'd you sleep, honey?"

"Like a rock." He joined her in the kitchen as she sliced a package of bacon open with a knife and dropped six pieces into a skillet on the stove.

His mother kissed his head. "Franky's on his way." She set the carton of eggs on the counter and put her hands on his shoulder. She stared at him for a minute, her eyes searching his. "I'm still not happy about this."

"How many times did you check on me last night?"

She smiled, ran her fingers through his hair, as if she half-expected it to fall out in clumps. "Your father and I took turns, but we didn't count."

"Did you sleep at all?"

"Enough," she said, running her finger over a blackened bruise where his shoulder and neck met.

"I told you, I'm fine."

"What am I supposed to think, baby? You show up after being gone for weeks. You're cut up and bruised and scarred." Her voice cracked.

Aiden sighed and hugged her. She had enough trouble buying his story about Alrujah. He wasn't about to tell her about the fangands, the beresus, the Seers or Moloch or Belphegor. Her heart couldn't take it.

Maybe some day, if he stayed. But wasn't this what he wanted? His mother in his arms, a warm bed to sleep in, three meals a day, as much as he could eat? Isn't this why he chose to stay? He loved his mother, but that love manifested in his mind now, not in his heart, as if he didn't trust the sensation, didn't trust her to be real.

His father came out of his room, showered and dressed, and sat at the counter. "Sleep okay?"

Aiden nodded. "Better than you and Mom."

Outside, Franky's Jeep rumbled up the driveway. Aiden turned the bacon in the sizzling grease and went to help unload the armor. "Swear you won't freak out," he said as he opened the front door.

His mother wiped the corners of her eyes. "No promises."

Franky had already parked and started gathering the armor from the back. "Dude, this armor is wicked sick."

"Right?" Aiden grabbed the chest piece and both greaves. Blood flaked from the points extending above the knees and fluttered off like fall leaves in the gentle morning breeze. "Thanks for coming, bro."

"Anything to get out of school." He grinned for a minute. "Ever feel alone, man?"

"All the time," Aiden said. "What's up?"

He frowned but walked to the house. "Never mind. Not a big deal. What you got ahead of you, that's the big deal."

Aiden's father stood at the door, arms crossed over his chest. "I don't believe it."

"Let's go inside," Aiden said, pushing past him. Franky followed, and they laid out each piece of the armor across the counter.

His mother and father stared. The bacon burned. Franky turned off the heat.

"The crest of Alrujah," his father said. "The barbed armor of Ribillius's guard." He ran a hand over the cold metal. "How did you make this?"

"It was given to me," Aiden said. "Nearly a year ago, in a private ceremony attended by King Ribillius, his daughter Indigo, and Captain Korodeth."

"Korodeth is captain?" his father said. He ran a hand over his goatee. "How do you know that name? I didn't talk much about him."

"You guys aren't making any sense," his mother said. "Franky, do you understand any of this?"

Franky turned off the fire under the eggs and dished them onto plates next to the burnt bacon. "A little, yeah."

"How?" she asked, one hand on her neck. "They're speaking gibberish." More quietly, she said, "Maybe I'm the crazy one."

"You're not," Franky said, handing her a plate of breakfast. He dropped four pieces of wheat bread into the toaster. "I thought the same thing when Bailey started chattering about Alrujah."

"Bailey Knowles?" Aiden's mother asked. "Her, too?"

Aiden said, "They're all in Alrujah."

"But Alrujah doesn't exist." His father's voice seeped out in low tones. "It's a world of dreams. Of my dreams."

Franky handed Aiden's father a plate. "That's how it happened with Bailey. It started with dreams, and then one morning, she vanished."

"We got pulled in," Aiden said. "I don't know how, and I don't know why you had dreams about it so many years ago, but it's a real place. It exists and, one way or another, we got sucked in."

His mother sat down. "So this is what insanity feels like."

Already, she'd be planning on hiring a therapist for herself, for the whole family. That's how her mind worked. This wasn't how Aiden wanted it to play out, but he couldn't take it back now. "You're not crazy, Mom. It's a lot to take in." He put his hand on hers.

"How are we supposed to explain this to the police? They'll want to know where you've been, and we can't very well tell them you were abducted by elves."

"I don't know," Aiden said.

His mother shook her head and dropped the empty bacon wrapper in a plastic bag. "I'm running this out to the trash," she said. She slipped out the back door.

"She'll be back," Aiden's father said. "She needs a minute to let it all sink in." He ran a hand over the silver armor, the crest of Alrujah. "I think I need a minute, too."

Aiden took the opportunity to shovel eggs into his mouth. Burnt or not, the bacon tasted amazing.

"Know what I love about bacon?" Franky said. "It does work, you know? Fry it up, and it fills the house with bacon smell. See a movie, come home, and it still smells like bacon. It's rockstar like that."

Aiden's father scratched at his goatee. "Am I out of my mind?"

"You're not crazy, Pops."

Outside, Aiden's mother shrieked.

10

War and famine, disease and death: these shall be the birth pangs of my coming. When my chains are weakened, I shall rise again and take death captive. I will bring to my people a world without suffering, without death, without thirst or hunger. Apart from me, Alrujah cannot know peace.
    –The Shedoahn Prophecies

ERICA BURST through the door of the infirmary. Eljah Morrow oversaw two monks as they continued applying salves and creams to Norby and Breniveer's wounds. "I want to know everything about the Shedoahn Order: where they meet, who's in it. Everything."

Eljah made his face stern. "I assume the news regarding Relina is not good."

Erica's fists shook. Ullwen put a hand on her shoulder. "Relina and her husband are dead. A message was left. Shedoah will rise."

"And so he must," Dillard said. Erica hadn't seen him come in after her. He took a chair in the corner and replaced his hood over his head. "The last days are upon us. All Alrujah shall cry as a woman in labor. So says *The Book of Things to Come.*"

Erica said, "Fan-freaking-tastic, but I don't care. I'm after revenge right now. One of these little Shedoahites or whatever killed my Relina, and I want to kill them back."

Eljah said to Dillard. "It's time."

Dillard nodded. He stood. His pale skin glowed ghostly in the shadows. His red eyes stared at Erica. "The Hand must reassemble. The coming of Shedoah is imminent."

"Isn't Shedoah like the Mage Lord or something?"

"The Mage Lord is nothing," Dillard said. "He is not our concern. We must end the threat of Shedoah."

"The end of days," Breniveer mumbled.

Norby sat up. "We must do something."

"That's what I'm saying. Dillard, you know the most about this stuff. Point me in the right direction, and I'll go handle Shedoah."

"It is not so easy," Eljah said. "Certain prophecies must be fulfilled."

"The monks must go to Yeval," Dillard said. "The Hand must reassemble. The final abominations must be destroyed."

"Wait, there are more abominations? Like Belphegor?"

"Aye," Ullwen said. "Those demons who steal the worship of men and elves and dwarves."

"Three remain," Eljah said. His head snapped toward the door, as if he'd heard some imperceptible noise.

Dillard grabbed his staff. "I feel them, too, Eljah." To Ullwen and Erica, he said, "Arm yourselves." The two monks working on Norby and Breniveer moved silently but rapidly out of the room. A bell pealed through the still afternoon air. "Shedoah's grasp stretches toward us. His devoted march on us."

"Adonai be with us," Ullwen whispered. He readied his sword as Eljah tossed Erica her bow and arrows.

"Hold on. What's happening? What's going on?"

"Your quest for revenge may well be upon us," Eljah said.

Dillard moved swiftly to Norby and Breniveer and waved a hand over each of their wounds. Instantly, their tissue mended. New skin crawled over old, scarred flesh. "We'll need your skills," he said. "The Blood Monks march on us."

Erica's jaw dropped. "You healed them? Just like that?"

Dillard's eyes burned red in the shadows. "When the need arises, Adonai uses His people as He sees fit."

Breniveer threw her covers off, her face mixed between relief and fear.

Norby followed her lead. "Why would you not heal us sooner? You didn't need to burn our infections?"

Eljah Morrow opened the door of the infirmary. Already, black-robed men struck at the blue-robed monks with swords, with axes, with spears and daggers. "Later. We must defend ourselves now."

Near the edge of the woods, several of the men in black smashed clay jars on trees. Black oil ran down the bark. They lit it with torches, and the harspus trees ignited in flames.

Erica readied an arrow. Without thought or hesitation, she loosed it. It parted the sea of men in battle, rushed through boughs and leaves until, seconds later, the tip took a torch-bearing Blood Monk in the chest. He staggered back, dropped the torch. "That's for Relina. And so is this." She let another arrow fly. The tip buried itself feather-deep in the nearest black-garbed monk's chest.

Ullwen charged into the fray. Three black-robed monks descended on him. Dodging a swinging axe, Ullwen used his blade to parry another sword. The third stabbed at him. Ullwen trapped the Blood Monk's blade under his arm, twisted it out of its hand. He kicked the disarmed monk in the stomach, stabbed the axe-wielder, and elbowed the swordsman.

Eljah used his staff like Oliver. Though most the Blood Monks focused on him, he deflected, disarmed, and knocked out his adversaries.

Dillard moved beside Ullwen and made short work of the swordsman.

Erica readied another arrow, balanced it on the tip of the string. Inspiration hit her. Instead of using her eyes, she found a razorbeak overhead. Touching its mind with hers, she asked for the use of its eyes. Seconds later, she saw six other Blood Monks still half a mile off, rushing with several jars and torches. "Get your friends," she told the bird. "It's gonna get toasty fast." She knelt, drew the fletching to her ear, aimed up at a forty-five-degree angle, and loosed the arrow. The wooden shaft rocketed above the heads of the still battling monks, punctured leaves, missed branches, and found a home in the eye of a torch-bearing black-robed monk. He dropped to his knees, twitched in technicolor, and collapsed. The men beside him rushed faster.

Dark faces hid beneath the shadows of black cloaks. Each wore crimson belts around their waist and legs. Their boots stomped loudly on the leafy ground.

"How many?" Ullwen yelled as he pulled his sword from the stomach of an attacker.

"A hundred plus, easy," she said.

Norby put a hand on her shoulder. "Take out the torch bearers. Call reinforcements. These monks cannot hold off so many." He moved deliberately to the door and surveyed the battle as Erica's arrows shot past his ears. "Breniveer?"

"Minds are well guarded, love. Can't plant thoughts, can't read them."

"Emotions?"

"Impressionable, but not to fear."

"Get them angry. Hot heads don't think. Our monk friends are patient. They'll have the advantage."

Breniveer sat close to the window of the infirmary, safe from the attacks, but with a great view of the proceedings. Almost immediately, the Blood Monks nearest the infirmary rushed the monks of the Cerulean Order. But they didn't stop, they turned on each other as well, fueled with an apparently insatiable blood-lust. The blue-robed monks countered the attacks, waited for openings in defenses, and struck with lightning-fast blows.

"Still too many," Norby whispered.

"More coming," Erica said.

"The torches?"

"Dead, but trees are burning. This whole place will be lit up soon. We've got to get out of here, Dad."

"Buy us time. How many razorbeaks can you get down here?"

"I'll have a murder of them here in less than a minute."

"Keep them moving from one monk to the next. I don't want them focused on eyes. We need only distract the attackers."

Smoke burst over the tree-line. Erica wrinkled her nose. Razorbeaks came fast. She thought of calling sasquatch and fangands, but doing so would be calling them to their death. Instead, she urged them to flee.

Ullwen ducked under the blade of one Blood Monk, rolled behind another, and let the first's blade run the other through. He kicked the dead monk into the first, rushed him, and wrestled the blade from him. With a crushing elbow to the face, the first monk stilled. He tossed the blade to Norby, who caught it and dispatched an enraged Blood Monk.

"My thanks," Norby said.

"Adonai willing, it won't be in vain."

"They're blocking me out," Breniveer said. "Their minds are well guarded, as if they're all tied together."

"Hive mind," Erica said. "Like bees, and bees have queens."

"Can you find the mindwitch who guards their minds?" Norby asked.

"I'm trying," Breniveer said, holding both hands to her head and squinting. "They're fighting back, trying to get into my head."

Erica stood next to her mother as a murder of razorbeaks fell on the battle in a purple fog of feathers and claws. Erica closed her eyes. "What do I look for?"

Norby said, "Someone in the back. A mindwitch stays far from the fray of battle."

Erica touched the mind of the razorbeak nearest the back, borrowed its eyes, saw nothing, jumped to another. She did it again, and again, each time refusing to allow the explosion of colors in her mind to confuse her. Homing in on the particular black, more a navy through the eyes of the birds, and the crimson belts, she cued in on motion. A minute later, she'd found him standing statuesque in a clearing near the edge of the woods. "Got him."

Breniveer's mind touch hers, and she held the image steady. "I can't get through."

"I can," Erica said. The razorbeak turned its attention to the closed eyes of the Blood Monk mindwitch. With a terrifying shriek, it dove, beak first, to the man's face. Erica left the bird's mind.

"I'm in," Breniveer said. "I've got the link."

The Blood Monks ceased their attack. They dropped their weapons and stood around like a bunch of nerds at an eighth-grade dance. Dillard limped to the clearing near the door of the infirmary. He cradled his arm and frowned.

He'd never frowned before, nor had she ever seen anger wrinkle his temples. But, unmistakably, the albino monk was ticked. With a wave of his hand, an unearthly wind spun around him. Inexplicably, it lifted each of the blood monks and hurled them away like dolls in a tornado. The smoke, which had turned to an ashen cloud and settled over the tree-line, vanished. The flickering of flames ceased. He pounded his stave into the earth, and the Blood Monk mindwitch appeared before him, kneeling.

Dillard pulled his head back and surveyed the missing eyes. He began to whisper. Erica immediately listened in through the ears of the nearest razorbeak. "Tell Korodeth," he said, "I am displeased with his choice to attack the monastery. Remind him he is on the losing side of this battle, and his iniquity will be revisited on him for eternity."

The eyeless man grinned. "As will yours, monk." The man vanished in a burst of light. Dillard turned back to the infirmary. "The Council must know what has happened here tonight."

"I will go," Eljah said. In another flash of light, a massive black griffin appeared beside him.

Erica's breath caught. The immediate presence of the griffin, the beat of its heart, the pressing of its mind, stunned her. This griffin hadn't been anywhere nearby, not for miles. If it had been, she would have known it. A beast so majestic, so massive, couldn't hide its presence from her.

The griffin shrieked, bent low before Eljah, and folded its wings.

Well trained. Domesticated. Somehow, the idea irritated her. An animal so awesome should not be saddled, should not bear the weight of people. She touched its mind gently and found it well guarded.

Eljah straddled its neck, and the lion-bird leapt to the sky, punching through the smoke like a fist through paper.

Erica stood nose to nose with Dillard. "Start talking."

AIDEN RAN OUTSIDE. His mother stumbled backward, away from the metal trashcan on the back porch. In front of her stood a massive beresus. It snarled, its lips pulling up to reveal yellowed fangs.

If a cave troll and a gorilla had a baby and named it Ugly, this would be the child. "Inside," he said to his mother, his muscles tensing. He sprang toward the beast. It swiped the can, crushing the side like a train plowing through a car. Aiden crouched in front of it. As if on cue, it raised both fists on its freakishly long arms and brought them down. He rolled away, worked in a quick kick to its ribs. But his bare feet had little impact.

Like kicking an ox. He needed a sword, a blade or a shield, anything to help even the odds.

The beresus swung again. Aiden leapt back, narrowly escaping the watermelon-sized fists, and aligned himself with a tree to his back.

Beresus liked to swing, liked to punch.

True to form, it brought its right hand over its left shoulder and sent a terrifying backswing toward Aiden. He ducked again. Its fist cracked. The bark splintered. Behind him, someone yelled.

His father rushed toward the beast, the broadsword from above the mantle in both hands. He held it aloft in the style of the Harland

Guard, but swung with a flourish of wrists—the mark of an Alrujahn trained soldier.

Of course. Jaurru's father had been promoted from Harland guard to Alrujahn sentry when Jaurru was a child. They'd trained together in Harland and Alrujah. Because of his dreams, Aiden's dad had been there as much as Bailey had in the beginning. And now, they fought side by side.

"Give me the sword, Pops, and get inside."

"No chance," he said, leaping back from the beresus's wild swing. He countered with a quick slice across its back.

Franky shouted, "Aiden, behind!" He tossed the other sword, smaller and faster, to Aiden.

Aiden snatched it by the hilt from the air. "Thanks. Grab my shield, bro?"

"It's here," his mother said. She held the kite shield by the edges.

He took it, his face stern. "Back inside," he said.

She and Franky obeyed.

Aiden rushed the beresus, still swinging and snarling at his father. He rolled into the battle, came up with his shield above his head. The blow smashed the shield down on him but deflected enough of the force to allow him to stay poised on his toes. He came up fast, the blade slicing up, gouging a deep wound in the beast's armpit. It howled as blood ran thick as sap. Another howl. His father took the opportunity to sink his broadsword deep into its kidney.

With a broken hand, a sliced shoulder, and a sword in its back, the beresus dropped to its knees, grunting and snarling. Aiden dashed forward and sank his blade between its ribs. Warm blood sprayed his shirt.

His father, panting, pulled his broadsword from its back. He wiped his brow and struggled to catch his breath. He dropped the blade in the grass. "Kept them sharp all these years," he breathed. "Never knew why."

"A soldier cares for his weapons. It's instinct. You can't turn it off."

His father smoothed his goatee and surveyed the monster. "Why's it here?"

"Don't know. Fought a pack of fangands last night. They attacked Detective Parker's car."

His chest heaving, Aiden's father said, "Something's wrong."

Franky and Aiden's mom came outside. Franky inspected the blood-matted fur. "This thing stinks."

"Give it a few days," said Aiden's dad. "It gets worse."

His mother put her hand over her mouth and shook her head. "What is it?"

"A beresus," Aiden said.

"From Alrujah," his father said.

She stared at him. "It's real?"

Aiden said, "One hundred percent."

She stood over it and held her nose. "How did it get here?"

Aiden shrugged. "Wish I knew."

"There are more of these?" she asked.

"Creatures from Alrujah? Yes."

Franky kicked the creature. "That thing's solid, man." To Aiden's father he said, "Mad props, man. You handled that sword like a ninja."

Aiden's father stood straight and put a hand on Aiden's shoulder. "You fight well. You must have earned the armor of Ribillius's guard."

Pride swelling in his heart, Aiden grinned. "Thanks, Pops." He pulled his shirt, sticky from blood, from his chest. "Man. I loved this shirt."

"I think you should go back," his father said.

His mother said, "What?"

Eyes locked on the beresus, he said again, very quietly, "You have to go back."

11

In those days, the people of Alrujah will turn from their first love. They will burn down His house and profane His name. They will turn to strange gods. And when the days are darkest, and when pestilence and famine and death reign, Adonai will send His Hand to obliterate the evil in the land and return His people to Him.
—The Book of Things to Come

DARKNESS REPLACED the dim afternoon light as the suns set beyond the Dragon's Back Mountains. The Heart of Yeval rested among massive trees near the center of Yeval Forest. Moisture saturated the air. The Heart of Yeval made its own rain—part of several enchantments that protected the area. And despite the dampness, the blue flames of the torches lining the paths flickered on.

Lauren pulled the hood of her cloak back, stood next to Bailey, and held her hand. She still marveled at Bailey's wings. The gold contraption on the top of her left wing whirred with mechanical wheels whenever she stretched them. Now, her sister furled the wings like sails, and Yarborough walked beside her, his bad shoulder still stooped.

Borgrad, the testy little dwarf who had accosted them a few miles south, took breaths in gulps and grimaced with each step. His shoulders made Yarborough's look healthy.

Several towers and buildings—all built to resemble the natural flora and fauna of the forest—surrounded the group. Skyscrapers towered, taller than any in North Chester but no thicker than the natural pines and firs. Massive, flat leaves sprouted from the walls of the four-story armory. Bark lined wooden walls and obscured open windows and cleverly disguised staircases.

The Council of the Order of the Protectorate met outside, despite having numerous comfortable places to meet within the walls of the city. A bluish bubble encapsulated them, much like the one Langley had erected over Oliver as he prayed during the battle with Moloch. Lauren had designed the enchantment specifically—from the outside, no one could hear or see what happened inside the bubble. It would be impossible to detect by normal senses. Anyone passing by the outside, even within a few feet—if they somehow avoided the Protectorate's less-than-welcoming welcome committee—would see and hear only the forest.

Unlike a typically ornate throne room like Harael or Alrujah, the Council had arranged seven simple high-backed chairs in the center of the protective enchantment. They'd not built a dais on which to put the chairs. Their feet pressed an inch deep into the soft soil.

Only four were occupied.

Oren, the dwarf sitting in the center chair, leaned forward. He rested his clean-shaved chin on his fist as he contemplated the group standing before him. Borgrad knelt before Oren. "The Hand of Adonai, my liege."

"Your shoulders bear wounds," Oren said. His long red mustache, braided down to his chest, danced with the gruffness of his voice.

"Aye, Oren. I believe these are the marks of a manifestation of Adonai."

Lauren stood quietly, allowing the scene to play out. She'd written of the Council of the Order of the Protectorate, filled each of the thrones, but here three stood empty. She tried to suppress the unease within her, but empty chairs meant death, more often than not.

Oren wrinkled his brow, consulted with silent stares with the other three—an old human named Trieli, an ancient elf named Nyleran, and another dwarf, Dain, who, though decades younger than Oren, looked decades older. "Describe it," he told Borgrad.

Borgrad spoke slowly, cautiously. "A terrible bird, big as a horse, talons sharper than swords, wings glowing white, a beak of gold, eyes of copper, a tongue like a whip of flame."

"Did it speak?"

"Aye. It affirmed these three as the Hand of Adonai."

Trieli, a middle-aged man with a mane of gold and silver hair, stood. His sunken blue eyes moved over Lauren, Bailey, and Yarborough. "They do not fit the description provided in *The Book of Things to Come*." His voice carried a subtle fear, as if he dare not speak against Adonai. "Prophecy says nothing about a dwarf among the Hand."

"He may be the one called alongside," Nyleran said, her voice a flower on the wind. The ancient elf had more years than any of the others on the Council.

"If I may." Lauren stepped before the three. "I am of the Hand. Yarborough, our dwarf friend, is the Nameless Heir prophesied by your lips, Oren."

"The Nameless Heir? By Adonai's beard," Oren whispered. He stood, made his way to Yarborough and considered the dwarf for some time. "I am humbled to behold the work of Adonai before me."

"As am I, good Oren," Yarborough said. "My father spoke many times of your commitment to Adonai, and the stubbornness of our people in their pursuit of strange gods."

They clasped elbows. "Mine eyes are blessed for having seen you in the flesh, nameless one. As they are to see each of you. But you are not of the Hand?"

Bailey spoke this time, stepping toward the dwarf, but turning her head to each of the Council in turn. "He is a servant of Almighty

Adonai and has come alongside us in our quest to end the threat of the Mage Lord. Already, he has proved valuable in battles against the Seers and Moloch."

Nyleran shook her head. "So it is true. The Seers have fallen."

"And what of Belphegor?" Dain asked.

"Dead," Lauren said. "We killed it."

Trieli whispered, "And He shall close His Hand and crush His enemies in His fist." He stared at Bailey Renee. "This winged-one must be a messenger, the very mouth of Adonai. But what of the monk? The knight? The caller?"

Lauren dropped her eyes. "The caller has traveled to Alrujah to free the captives." Her throat clamped shut, and she forced herself to swallow. "The knight seeks Adonai's will elsewhere." She pulled Oliver's staff to her chest, held it tight, wished its power would warm her and affirm Oliver's well-being. "The monk fell in our battle against the Seers."

"Then all hope is lost," Dain said.

A brilliant explosion of light erupted overhead. Borgrad fell on his back, and the Council fell to their seats. A white heat pushed Lauren back, pressed Yarborough and Bailey to their knees. Lauren held her hand to the light, shielded her eyes, searched the brightness. A shape solidified—the same shape that punctured Borgrad's shoulders and lifted him into the air.

The brightness dimmed, and the glowing white bird spread its wings, shadowing the entire Heart of Yeval. Folding its wings, it landed soundlessly before Oren.

"My Lord," the dwarf said, and fell to his knees. "I'm unworthy. Have mercy on my soul."

"Arise, Oren," the bird said with the voice of an erupting volcano. "You have served Me faithfully since birth. You've spoken My words, guarded My people, defended My honor. Your reward is nigh. Truly I tell you; today your eyes will see paradise."

Lauren's breath froze in her lungs. Borgrad, the dwarf, trembled. Yarborough put his fist before his heart. The massive bird sucked whatever bravery, whatever sorrow or pride indwelled them, and replaced it with an irrepressible joy and fear.

Here was Adonai. What could stand against Him? What could clip His wings?

"You others must remain. The enemy stirs. Already, he schemes against My will. He will do what he can to sabotage the redemption of Alrujah. You must move against him, against his devout. You must strike him down with a mighty Hand."

"You speak, and we do," Trieli whispered. "What is Your will?"

"You will know. Your Council may no longer hide in the safety of Yeval. Your seven must go into Alrujah and wipe the blackness from its face."

"Seven, my lord?" Nyleran asked. "We are but four."

"I have called four to complete your number." With a flash, Eljah Morrow appeared on the back of a black griffin. The beast sat back on its haunches and shrieked.

Eljah moved his head from side to side, inspecting the forest, disoriented.

Langley of Erul appeared in an empty chair. His initial confusion vanished behind the guise of an arrogant leader.

Another flash, and Lauren sat in an empty chair. Beside her, Yarborough filled the empty seat, confusion clear on his face.

Oren, still kneeling before the massive bird, realized Eljah stood before Oren's seat, the griffin shrieking at his side. "But my Lord."

"You will come with Me, Oren. Your work is complete." He turned to each of the seven on the chairs. He breathed on each in turn until, at last, he came to Lauren. His copper eyes pierced hers. Without moving its beak, Adonai spoke. "You have questions, daughter. I will answer what I will. I gave you your vision of Alrujah, your heart for adventure, your love for the knight. I have called you here because I love Alrujah as I love Earth, both of which were created by My words, not yours. You are needed here in a way Earth will never understand. Find *The Book of Sealed Magic*. Topple evil under my Name. Wrap the innocent in my banner. Restore peace to this land as I shape it into something new."

"I will," Lauren said.

"Blessed are you among women. My plans for you reach beyond the coming war." The bird breathed on her, and her sense of magic nearly erupted from her fingertips, her eyes, her mouth. The power within her threatened to burst from every pore to the point of pain. Her neck snapped back, and she screamed, but no sound came out. Her eyes, wrenched wide, filled with tears, and she gnashed her teeth until, at last, she found something quiet within her, a simple peace that swallowed up the power. She took fast breaths, forced herself to release her rock-crushing grip on the staff resting over the arms of the chair.

Seconds after she regained her senses, Oren leapt on the back of the massive bird. With two gale-inducing flaps of its wings, the bird vanished into a shimmering rift in the sky.

DILLARD'S heavy blue cotton robe pulled against him in the breeze as he moved from monk to monk, laying his hands on them and whispering prayers in the ancient language. Only those monks with the worst wounds, those clearly dead, lay untouched. Ullwen moved behind him, offering sips of harspus tree sap and mushrooms wrapped in yellow spider leaf. Erica stood next to her parents, hugging them each in turn, keeping her eyes from the blood-stained soil, the writhing bodies of wounded Monks of the Cerulean Order.

The murder of razorbeaks dispersed, each earnestly searching for Lauren, Aiden, Oliver. She drew strength from her parents, from their very real arms around her, their very real tear-stained cheeks on hers.

"The catacombs are beneath," Dillard said, opening a cellar door. "We have several dead. Will you call friends to aid in their burial?"

Erica stared at his pale face, clenched her teeth and fisted her hands. "I'm not helping you until you answer my questions."

"I'm not one to question the monks, but my daughter is correct. Your behavior does give concern," Norby said.

Dillard hid his hands in his sleeves and came closer to Erica.

"Very well." To another monk, he said, "Palloth, please see to the wounded." The monk dipped his head low and continued working with the injured monks. Dillard hoisted the limp body of a dead monk on his shoulders and began to carry him toward the cellar door. "Please, come with me."

Ullwen came alongside her and followed her and her parents toward the cellar. They moved in silence, each overcome with the horror of the outcome of the battle. Erica held Ullwen's hand and followed the flowing blue robe of Dillard.

"As you know, I am a student. I've spent my life studying *The Book of the Ancients* and *The Book of Things to Come*. In that time, I've unlocked several mysteries no one else has been able to decipher." He descended several rough-hewn steps, turned a corner, lit a torch, and proceeded down a deeper staircase. Chiseled from the deep stonework of the rocky soil, no step had been hewn evenly. A hasty masonry job. Shoddy workmanship by monks' standards, but, when pressed by a man as evil as Korodeth, compromises had to be made, she supposed.

Dillard continued. "Both books speak of a coming battle that will break Alrujah as we know it. These days will be recognized by several signs, most of which have occurred in these last weeks."

He moved gracefully, even with the dead body flopped over his shoulders. Erica took each step with care, holding on to Ullwen for balance.

"You speak of the end of days," Norby said.

"And the coming of Shedoah," Breniveer said.

"The famine and the rise of the ancient evils were the first signs. Then the droughtworm, the coming of the Hand, the outcry of rebellion, the fall of ancient evils. We've seen these things. The famine began last year. Varuth rose against Alrujah, as do Harland and Port Smalth. Belphegor has manifested himself, as did Moloch and the Seers."

"I wouldn't say Belphegor did it," Erica said. "The Mage Lord was the one who brought the stupid thing here."

Dillard proceeded on, as if she hadn't spoken. "No matter how we toil, our crops yield only enough food for ten people. Other cities face the same problem. Food is running short everywhere except Pellbred."

"The swamps?" Norby said.

The staircase opened into an expansive room, lined with several hollows in the walls. The cold, damp air and low light creeped Erica out. She wrinkled her nose with the smell and hoped she'd grow accustomed to it soon. Dillard moved from wall to wall, lighting torches along the way with the one he held.

"Another ancient evil," he said. "Abaddon has taken a body. His power has grown with the worship of the devoted in Pellbred." He continued working his way toward the back. The catacombs grew darker, colder, damper. "These signs mean the inevitable is upon us."

"The rise of Shedoah," Ullwen whispered.

"Only five can stand against him," Dillard continued.

"So all of this is about the Hand facing down Shedoah? Whatever happened to the Mage Lord? I thought he was the bad guy," Erica said.

Dillard deposited the body about a hundred yards deep into the catacomb in an empty hollow near the ceiling. "Compared to Shedoah, the Mage Lord is nothing."

"He's something alright," Erica said. "He snaps his fingers and Belphegor appears? Doesn't sound like 'nothing' to me. Besides, he's got the book, right? Don't we need that to beat this Shedoah guy?"

"Even with the book, Shedoah's power is greater," Dillard said.

Erica swallowed a wave of nausea.

Couldn't have this chat outside? Had to do it a football field deep into the dead. "You're totally off topic. What I want to know is how you healed my parents all of a sudden, and how you were able to wave your hands and put out the fires. You've got some crazy powers you never bothered telling us about."

"The will of Adonai," Dillard said. "I was a willing vassal for his power."

"I don't buy it. You're not telling us something."

A hand on her shoulder—Norby?

"Please. Do not question the will of Adonai."

"I don't," Erica snapped. "I question this guy. Slipping on a blue robe doesn't make him any holier than you or me."

"You're right," Dillard said. "My actions speak for themselves." He raised his staff, and Alrujah blinked out in a flash of white.

12

And this will be a sign to all Alrujah: when the broken angel spreads her wings, when she speaks with the voice of Adonai, when she foretells wars and disease, then Alrujah shall know that war is nigh.
—The Book of Things to Come

THE BIRD HAD VANISHED LESS than a minute ago, and already the Council fell into chaos.

Lauren's pulse thumped in her temples. Langley had no business here. Why would Adonai choose one like him to sit on the Council?

Yarborough had similar thoughts. He raised his axe toward the elf. "Explain yourself, Langley."

Eljah's griffin calmed after Adonai departed. It found a small, quiet patch of soil and lay down, rubbing its paws over its beak.

The monk lifted a hand to the half-dwarf. "Peace, Yarborough."

"Peace?" Lauren sneered. "Last time we saw him, he tried to kill us."

Trieli folded his arms. "What's this?"

Axe still raised, Yarborough said, "Your actions demand explanation."

"If we are to have peace among our number, we must have honesty and truth," Nyleran said. "Langley of Harael, is what they say true?"

Langley pulled his long black hair behind his pointed ears. "If I'd wanted them dead, they'd be sleeping with their ancestors now. I moved slowly. I gave them time to react to the spells I'd conjured."

"Why?" Lauren asked, still adjusting to Yeval, to the new power living within her. With the flick of a wrist, she could set the smug elf on fire.

Langley pulled the Blood Sword from his hip. "This is the most powerful blade in Alrujah, and even it cannot secure the throne of Harael. The elves are a people who respect power, who disdain humans. I needed to demonstrate my strength and my loyalty to my people. How else will they accept me as king?"

"So you pressed us into service as your political tools?" Yarborough gruffed. "Your beams of light and water spouts were only for show?"

"How long have you known me?" Langley asked the dwarf. "The elves respect politics; my display of strength had to be enough to wrest and hold a contested throne. Neldohr's son already schemes against me, even with the Blood Sword on my hip."

Yarborough raised his voice. "I care nothing about the politics of your people. You nearly killed us!"

Nyleran stood from her chair. "Neldohr is dead? How long? Do the elves still suffer?"

"I killed Neldohr days ago," Langley said. "It was necessary."

"Killed him? Are you a common assassin?" Trieli said.

Langley replaced the Blood Sword in its hip sheath. "My actions were necessary to end the misery of my people and restore peaceful relations between elves and humans."

"Launching beams of light at us is a strange way to make peace," Lauren said.

"I've answered your accusations, Princess. Either accept it or don't, but do not badger me like some low-level senator."

"And what have you done to end the grief of Torap and Uhesdey?" Nyleran asked.

Langley folded his hands. "Droughtworm has made its way even into Harael. Most of my people starve, while those in political positions live extravagant lives. This is an inequity initiated by Neldohr to secure political power. I will remedy the mistake immediately. Already, in the few days of my reign, I've put laws into place to protect the right of the lower classes to work and earn respectable livings."

"They need healers. They need leaders who are not too proud to trade with outlying cities," Lauren said.

"Enough," Dain said. The dwarf, though standing, only came up to Langley's hip. "Adonai saw fit to seat you among our number, yet you hold a cursed blade. What are your intentions, Langley of Harael?"

His brow furrowed, and he scowled, as if, inside him, the old brash Langley, the devoted worshiper of Torap, warred with the new Langley, the half-elf king that'd pledged himself to the service of Adonai. "My intentions are to better my people. To restore the elves to the proud kingdom they once were, and to re-establish a peace between humans and elves. This is the charge Adonai has left me with."

"The proud kingdom you speak of subjugated humans to slavery, worked us nearly to extinction. This is the kingdom you believe Adonai wants you to restore?"

"It is the charge He left me with shortly before He carried Oren away."

"He spoke to you, too?" Lauren asked.

"To all of us, assuredly," Yarborough said. "He charged me with the same. I'm to oversee the emergence of the dwarves."

"And I am to assist," Dain said. He clasped Yarborough's elbow. "By the name of almighty Adonai, I pledge my service to you, Yarborough, the Nameless Heir, as has been prophesied by Oren and confirmed by Adonai himself."

"But what of the Mage Lord?" Lauren asked. "We must hunt him down.

Nyleran spoke softly. "*The Book of Sealed Magic* is already in his hands."

The griffin squawked and stretched its wings.

Eljah's voice came softly, nearly a whisper. "*The Book of Things to Come* says plainly, the Hand of Adonai cannot come without the power of *The Book of Sealed Magic.*"

Lauren should know. She'd written the book, but she hadn't included anything about the Hand of Adonai coming from another world. She'd studied *The Book of Things to Come* in its strange language nightly, pored over the symbols, wracked her brain for the understanding of a language she'd created years ago. And though she'd developed a skill in the language, pinpointing an exact meaning proved near impossible. It was written in poems, in riddles, in symbols and vague language.

Dain took up the conversation in his raspy, age-worn voice. "The book that summons them shall spell their salvation. And shall come the four, and then the five. By his power shall they come and go. His Hand upon *The Book of Sealed Magic* shall bring the salvation of Alrujah."

Trieli retook his seat. "The Hand moves in and out of Alrujah by the power of the Mage Lord. And that power can only come from *The Book of Sealed Magic.*"

"I thought 'his' meant Adonai," Yarborough said.

Eljah said, "The translation is unclear. Until recently, I believed the same. But, after speaking with Dillard, I believe I better understand. He has devoted his life to the study of *The Book of Things to Come*. He knows more of ancient texts than anyone alive. More than the dwarves or the elves, or the humans, all of whom have turned from their allegiance to Adonai and fallen to the worship of strange gods."

"I must get *The Book of Sealed Magic*," Lauren said. "Each of you has a task trusted to you by Adonai. But we all need sleep before we embark on our journeys."

"Aye," Yarborough said. "We depart at sunsup. For now, let us find rest among the trees of Yeval. And rest well, for tomorrow we may die."

"Before we sleep, I have news the Council must hear," Langley said. "The Seers have fallen, as have Moloch and Belphegor. But I have word from my ambassadors in Pellbred and Sylvonya. The strange gods of the humans have now manifested themselves."

"Abaddon and Tiamat," Eljah said. "I have words from the devoted about persecution in those cities at the hands of sycophants of their demonic gods."

Trieli folded his arms and sat. "Even here, on the outskirts of Yeval, the peoples fall to the worship of Legion."

Eljah continued. "The Cerulean Monastery was, only yesterday, attacked by Blood Monks."

Nyleran's lilting voice cut in. "We've not had word of Blood Monks for decades. Their emergence and bold attack must be a sign of weakening among Shedoah's bonds."

"There's more," Eljah said, his legs crossed. "Captain Korodeth has ascended the throne of Alrujah."

"What?" Lauren's temper flared. Power crackled through her chest and arms, through her legs. Her eyes burned with fury.

"Korodeth sent word to Harael about his reluctant acceptance of the crown after the assassination of King Ribillius," Langley said, taking his seat.

"Ribillius is dead?" Yarborough asked, both fearful and crestfallen.

"So begin the birth pangs," Nyleran said. "Disease and death will follow, and then war. Abaddon flies in Pellbred. Tiamat swims the deeps near Sylvonya. And Legion amasses power here in Yeval."

"My father is dead?" Lauren whispered.

"Aye, lass," Dain said. "The news is indeed sad."

"It was Korodeth. He killed him. It had to be. With me gone, he'd be next in line to assume the throne. Who else would be so foolish as to kill the king?"

"It makes sense," Langley said. He explored the arm rests of his chair with his fingertips. "Korodeth is no lover of elves. He'd not want a half-elf on the throne of men."

Dain furrowed his brow. He asked, "Where is the angel?"

Bailey? Lauren snapped her head around. Where was she? "Bailey?" she said. Then, "Bailey!"

ERICA SPUN AROUND. The dank musty air of the catacombs vanished, replaced instead by the crispness of a late winter's warming. Behind her, sprawling trees, pines and firs—in front of her, Douglas Street.

North Chester.

Without Ullwen, without her parents.

"No," she whispered. "Please God, no. Don't bring me back here." She ran her hands over her body. She still wore her purple dress, the dragon-winged opal tiara. Her hair, rough cut and short, tickled her ears and the top of her neck. The jagged scar on her left arm ached to her bone. She was still Lakia, but how?

Fear gripped her as she thought of her hands, so ruined in North Chester, so perfect in Alrujah. She peeled the backs of her gloves from her hands. It made her sick to imagine what she might find, but a morbid, terrified curiosity compelled her.

No burns. But the memory was there—unrecognizable flesh, red and white and swollen and ugly and nauseating—and the imagined pain in her hands might as well have been real.

Whoever brought her here, Adonai or Dillard or the Mage Lord or whoever, was completely empty of justice. To bring her from a world where she was loved, a world she loved, and to dump her into a world she hated? That was a new kind of low.

Clasping her hands together, she concentrated on slowing her breathing, beating back the burning behind her eyes. This wasn't her home. Not now, not anymore. It never was. Alrujah—that was her home, where she belonged, where her family lived.

Here, she had nothing. A drunk foster mother, a crazy father, a dead mother.

Tears heated her eyes; she clamped them shut. She added Dillard's name to her "to kill" list.

Think. There had to be a way back. The woods? Douglas Street ran to North Chester High and beyond, up to the slummy apartments where she'd spent the last year. No way she'd go back there. She couldn't. She wasn't Erica anymore.

She ran to the woods, ran with a fear that dwarfed the terror she'd felt in the nar'esh cave, or facing Belphegor, or even the king-killing Korodeth. Her real enemies lived here: a hollow life, hopelessness, fear, loneliness.

Her feet leapt over roots, dodged uneven ground, found purchase in solid soil and propelled her deeper into the woods. Trees grew denser, trunks thicker, canopies darker, until the sun became a series of diamonds twinkling among pine needles. Already, the souls of the animals glowed around her. Beavers near the river, chipmunks in the trees, deer bounding toward the street, and wolves, glorious wolves. She ran faster until something—a massive, angry life-force—appeared in front of her.

Black Bear.

She stopped short as the bear pressed through the trees in front of her. It stared at her, its roar echoing off the mountains behind it.

"Easy, girl," she said. "Up a bit early from your nap, aren't you?"

No response. Only anger. She had new cubs, this one, and they were close.

"I'm not going to hurt you," Erica whispered. "I'm not going to hurt them."

No dice. The bear would have none of it. It swiped at her with a paw the size of a boulder. Erica rolled, narrowly escaping the mauling. Using the ring Dillard gave her, she stretched out, touched the bear's mind, gently at first, to calm it, soothe it. But the rage of the bear burned hot. She wanted blood. She wanted death.

Erica scrambled to her feet and ran. She squeezed the bear's mind, pressuring, pressing, wrestling for control. The bear resisted, chasing her on foot and fleeing from the pressure of her mind. Erica slipped between trees, the closer the better. The bear slipped through the grasp of Erica's mind.

Think and run. Run and think.

The bear's heavy footsteps echoed inches behind her; its hot breath tingled across the back of Erica's neck. She leapt over a root bank, punched with her mind—punched hard, a single determined thought: your body belongs to me.

The bear stumbled, crashed behind her. It tried to stand, but its legs shook. Its growl diminished to a whimper. Lying on its back, the bear's legs twitched. Erica had seized its mind, but little remained after the struggle. It'd been broken, as Breniveer had said it would. She tested the legs, the arms, the jaws. Nothing moved, not on her commands or the bear's. Paralyzed, but worse. Whatever emotion ran so hot in the bear moments ago vanished. In the woods, a body without a mind meant death.

The bear gave its life defending its cubs, like Erica's mother had given her life protecting her. Erica remembered the crack of the broom over her father's head as he held Erica's hands over the fire. He'd let go then, turned on Erica's mother with his blistered hands.

Erica ran—terror choking her. Halfway down her block, she heard her mother's screams.

She should have gone back, should have grabbed the busted broom and put the sharp side through her father's chest. She should have protected her mother, should have been her mother's momma bear.

Kneeling next to the bear, she touched its head. "You're a good momma," she said. "I'm sorry."

She closed the bear's eyes, rested her head on its chest, fought to think of something other than her father, other than the smell of charred flesh and singed hair.

Move. Act.

She got up, started running without direction, wound through trees, hurdled bushes. Sweat burned cold on her forehead in the chilling wind. The air dampened; the soil moistened. Rain loomed.

She didn't care. Let it come. Let it wash the filth from the earth.

Bring another flood, for all she cared. The trees thinned ahead. Another road, one she didn't recognize.

A hundred yards down, a green sign stood beside the road. She ran toward it, curious and desperate for anything to take her mind from the bear, from her father, from her utter failure as a daughter. The sign didn't help. In bold white letters, it read: *Twin Lakes Correctional Mental Health Facility, six miles.*

Okay then. She'd handle this justice thing herself.

SECONDS AFTER THE MASSIVE, gleaming white bird lifted from the ground, Bailey Renee's wings stretched and flapped with a power she'd never known. They moved as of themselves, without her conscious thought. She flew, a marionette caught up in the strings of the master, dancing with a delicate precision. She set her sights on the bird, on the squat dwarf clinging to its neck. The bird pulled her, no doubt, and when she matched her will with its, she flew with an unfamiliar speed and strength.

The trees beneath her shrank, became saplings, roots, seeds, until the entire Yeval forest stretched out like a field of new grass. Mountains and mesas played over the landscape like marbles. The suns inflated—glowing white balloons bursting with plasmatic helium and hydrogen. She thought to ask where they were going, but she already knew.

The sky split before them, as if unzipped, and behind the brilliant blue sang a golden light burning neither hot nor cold. Beyond the rift, a city splayed out before her, teeming with mansions, with rivers and waterfalls, with streets gleaming in gold.

They passed through the rift. The cold, thin air of the Alrujahn atmosphere vanished into something warm, heavy with moisture and oxygen, almost like swimming. Angling down, she followed the bird and the dwarf through the streets of the strange city, weaving through the mansions, the gardens, over the rivers, beyond the waterfalls.

Men and women, children, elves and dwarves waved. Ahead, a castle as large as a city itself broke from the ground.

Constructed from some mix of pearl and marble and opal, the walls gleamed, a sparkling luminescence, blinking blue and wandering to white. Diamond windows sat recessed in gold panes. Three towers dominated the center of the intricate castle, and around each a staircase spiraled up toward the tip. Here, she inexplicably knew, angelic beings conducted the business of heaven. She felt it in her, felt the call to assume her duties within the pearl walls. Instinct pulled on the feathery part of her, her spirit, her core. It guided her now, an irrefutable imperative, a compulsion driving her beyond reason.

She was a created being. She had a purpose, and she'd see her purpose accomplished.

The bird before her transfigured, the body reshaping to a human likeness, but the wings remained. Touching one glowing foot to the golden streets, Adonai set Oren down. The dwarf fell to his knees in worship again.

Words bubbled in her stomach, rumbled up to her lips, and she spoke in two voices, one distinctly hers, the same she'd used in North Chester and Alrujah, one an octave lower—the voice of a man, of a beast. "Holy, holy, holy, is the Lord your God. Adonai is His name, and worthy is He of your worship."

Her knees buckled, and she bowed, in reverence, in fear, in awe.

Adonai inexplicably tucked his wings into his back and assumed the form of a man. Rather than a face, Adonai wore a mask of light, one she knew hid a brighter radiance, a blinding, fatal luminescence. No mortal could look upon His face and live, not even angels.

"Well done, good and faithful servant," Adonai whispered to Oren, his voice an avalanche.

A familiar spirit approached the dwarf.

Adonai said, "Pacha el Nai will show you to your new home, Oren."

Of course. She hadn't recognized him. She remembered Pacha el Nai as a fearsome angel of war. He carried a flaming sword, towered over elves and humans, had the physique of an Olympic bodybuilder. Here, he had no wings. He could be a human—a very well-muscled human. Only his spirit, the impression of who he was beyond his physical appearance, remained.

And she understood in the form of memory. Pacha el Nai died.

Angels could die.

And when they did, they took different forms. She'd grown up believing it to be the opposite—that humans became angels after death. Quite different in reality. And though her heart mourned for Pacha, she understood his physical death led only to a new physical form, and that his role of angelic herald of war became one of peace. Retirement, really. Now, he had only to worry about showing new residents to their mansions.

Pacha led the dwarf through the gate in the castle walls, and Adonai turned from Bailey.

She followed Him, compelled beyond words, into the castle. He weaved through the rooms, blessing each angel as they broke knee to Him. Most, like her, had two wings and the body of a human. The others took the shape of winged elves, dwarves, and a dozen other races Bailey couldn't pinpoint, though all felt strangely familiar.

They moved through countless rooms, each ornately furnished with gold, with jasper and emeralds, with pearls and opals, sapphires and rubies. Here, creation vibrated near its creator, filled her ears with a humming melody of adoration and praise. Even the stones, the gems, the metals and woods, sang together with the voice of the earth.

When, at last, Adonai ascended his throne—a massive prism of light—a host of angels bent knee before him, their faces to the golden floor. Bailey knelt with them. She had to. She wanted to.

"Bailey Renee," He said.

She stood, approached him with eyes dropped.

He spoke again, though only to her. His voice, which shook walls, resonated in her ears only. "I am well pleased with you. You have served me faithfully. You have spoken my words. You have defended my people. But your work is unfinished. You will succeed Pacha el Nai's role as Herald of War."

"My sister?"

"Your sister is well guarded."

Bailey nodded. "You alone are worthy of praise."

In his hands, a staff formed from light. It glowed and shimmered until it took on a luster, a wooden sheen. The staff was composed of three different woods, all braided together. He handed it to her, then touched her forehead. Her back twitched, the skin opened. Bone formed beneath her skin; sinews and muscles gathered, split, stretched. Two new wings sprouted from beneath the first two. Her arms, her chest, tingled with power. Her entire body stretched, until she stood seven feet tall. The sword on her hip grew heavy in its sheath.

Bailey Renee, Herald of War, stretched all four of her wings, the mechanical brace whirring in harmony with the vibrations of the gems and metals and wood around her. She breathed deep, pulling heavenly air into her crackling chest and flew toward the rift Adonai opened in the sky.

13

Shedoah sought to throw Adonai from his throne. Using a deceptive, forked tongue, he rallied a third of the angels in the heavens. They followed him, thirsty for power and for war, for blood and destruction. But Adonai's army stood against them, and Adonai threw them to Alrujah below.
—The Book of the Ancients

SWALLOWING HIS SURPRISE, Aiden asked his father, "Are you for real right now?"

He didn't take his eyes off the monster lying in his back yard.

His mother took a few steps back and leaned against the wall. "He's not going back."

His father held his arms out, still bathed in beresus blood. "He has to. Whatever is happening in Alrujah is spilling over into North Chester. This time, it's a beresus. Next time, it may be Shedoah himself."

She put a hand on her forehead. Though the morning air was mild, sweat beaded on her skin. She cleared her throat and spoke through tears. "I don't want to lose him again."

Aiden checked his father's eyes. Had he hit his head fighting the beresus? A concussion, then. Why else would he suggest Aiden go back?

"He's not going back," his mother said. "He's staying with us."

Aiden's throat tightened. He'd already considered returning to Alrujah, had made up his mind, but had no clue how to tell his folks. How could he break their hearts?

But the pit of his stomach never lied: he had to return. "Mom."

She moved inside, her shoulders quaking in sorrow.

They followed her. His father helped her sit down. "He'll be fine. God will bring him back to us again."

Aiden wasn't sure.

"That thing," she said between gulps of air, pointing to the beresus outside. "It almost killed me. And there are more of them out there?"

His father knelt beside her, his hand on her knee.

Aiden scratched his neck. "Not exactly like them, but yeah. Other monsters from Alrujah."

"Wicked thought, man." Franky whispered to Aiden, "Should I go?"

Aiden shook his head. He sat on the coffee table in front of his mother. He wanted to assure her he'd stay, wanted to say anything to steady her nerves, but he wouldn't lie to her. He had to get back to Alrujah, had to get back to Lauren. "I'll be fine, Mom. I'll come right back as soon as I figure out what's going on. Okay?"

"But for how long?"

Aiden frowned. He didn't know if she meant how long he'd be gone, or how long he'd stay in North Chester if he returned again.

"For good," his father said.

She shook her head. "I won't let him go."

"He's not ours to keep or to send. It's God's call. He took Aiden once and brought him back. He'll do it again."

"God?" Franky asked.

"How else would you explain what happened to him?" Aiden's father asked.

"Still think I'm crazy, Mom?" Aiden asked quietly.

"If anyone here is crazy, it's me." She touched his cheek, kissed his forehead. "Baby, I love you so much."

"I know, Mom. I love you, too."

"You fight so strong and fast." Wonder and fear lined her voice.

His father pointed to the beresus outside. "That isn't okay. It doesn't belong here. Neither do the other things, whatever they are. Something very wrong is happening, and God wants you to fix it."

"What if it's not God doing it?" Franky asked.

"Even more of a reason for him to go back," Aiden's father said. "If for no other reason than to find the other kids." He stood and scratched his goatee. "The other kids are gone. Lauren and her friend Oliver, that Erica kid, and Bailey." He cleared his throat. "If he can get them back, don't you think he should try? If he can fix the whole 'monsters in North Chester' thing, shouldn't he try? We can't be selfish about this."

His mother stood and hugged him. "I love you with my whole heart, baby. I won't lose you again."

Aiden held her and closed his eyes. "Pops."

"Enough," she said, her voice suddenly firm, lined with steel. "I don't want to hear another word about it. You're not leaving. You're staying here."

His father said, "I'll go with him."

"No," she said. "Neither one of you are going. End of discussion."

"You can't come, Pops. You gotta stay here and protect Mom in case another beresus stumbles by."

She shook her head. "Aiden Price, I forbid you to go. I don't want to hear about it anymore."

"Forbid?" Aiden asked. The word should have weight to it, but it felt hollow, like an empty aluminum can. It wrenched his heart to think of disobeying his mother, but he knew what he had to do, no matter the cost. He had to play his cards right, had to leave in such a way that his mother wouldn't resent his father. "I have to go, Mom, and I'd like to do it with your support."

"Too bad," she said, sorrow cracking her resolve. "I've made up my mind."

"And so have I."

"Maybe I should head back home," Franky said.

"Stay," Aiden said. "I'll need your help."

"Aiden needs to go," his father said.

His mother's arm pulled back and cracked across his father's face. The slap echoed in the living room.

Franky walked backward toward the front door.

"This is your fault!" She pulled her arm back again.

Aiden caught her wrist. He'd never imagined a scenario where he'd yell at his mother, but when his voice broke from his throat, it came with the steel timbre of Jaurru. "It's my fault," he said. "My decision. It was a mistake to come home, but I had to see you and Dad again. I never should have left Alrujah, but I did, and now I have to go back, no matter what you say. Please don't make this any harder, Mom."

Her arm shook. "You're hurting me," she said, pulling back from him. She looked at him as if considering a stranger in her home. Fear leaked from the corners of her eyes.

He'd gone too far. "I'm sorry," he said, but he struggled to feel the regret. He couldn't deny the instinct within him urging him back to Alrujah. This was the right call, and if it meant angering his mother so that she didn't hate his father, so be it.

Franky opened the front door quietly.

"Bro, stay. You're not going anywhere." He took a breath, considered the fear in his parents' eyes. His heart broke. "Doesn't matter what you or Pops say, I have to go back. What can I do to get you to understand? To support me?"

His mother crossed her arms over her chest.

His father walked toward her, but she backed away from him. "Babe," he said.

"This is God's plan," Aiden said. "You taught me that, right? Listen to the still small voice of God. Right now, He's whispering. My friends need me, even more than you and Dad."

His father handed the sword to Aiden. "We support your decision, but it's hard to let you go after you've been away so long."

"Don't you dare speak for me," his mother said.

This was a battle he couldn't win, and every minute he spent fighting it was another minute his friends were in peril. "I'm dragging the beresus into the woods before anyone sees it. Last thing you and Dad need is another media circus."

"And then what?" his father asked.

"And then I go back."

Bailey Renee, bearing the newly crafted braided staff pushed through the watery rift into a world with a red sky the texture of oatmeal. Clouds hummed orange; trees stretched out with light green leaves. Beneath her, jungle covered the land. Far off to the west and east, green seas undulated. The warmth and humidity reminded her of summer.

She'd never been to this world, but she knew it: Myrassa. Since Adonai had transformed her, she'd become a new creation. And in the same way He'd added wings to her body, stretched her muscles and bone, illuminated her eyes, imbued her with power, He'd also built on her mind.

Adonai had given her this knowledge without speaking. Here, He had a different name: Izanji.

She folded her four wings behind her, the supernatural, mechanical brace on her top left wing whirring. Wind rushed past her face, tickled her nose with the scent of salt air and rich soil. Boats with black sails, with blue sails, with white sails, trolled the waters pulling fish in nets and squabbling over invisible lines. Myrassa: a world of murderous land disputes, unceasing schemes for power both within and without their clans. All men were born with murder in their hearts, lust in their loins, dishonesty on their lips.

Shedoah had a stranglehold on this world. His bonds weakened with each passing day.

Her memories of North Chester remained, as did her love for her sister. Her memories of Alrujah, her experiences fighting the Seers, even the pain of her once broken wing, all remained. But he'd added to her knowledge. What she'd studied in high school seemed laughable now. Chemistry. Biology. Physics.

Human understanding was so limited.

But, like Adonai, she admired their tenacity.

She stretched her wings and soared through the moist, briny air.

When had she come to think of humans as "them"?

Few would argue she was human any longer, but a part of her held to her humanity, despite the power of her heavenly body.

Miles off, the sea beat against the shore in a tireless assault. Trees and vines shrank to green-gold carpeting covering the eastern continent beneath her. Patches of blue shone through the canopy of thick jungle leaves.

Silistrus flowers grew near the base of tree trunks and near the banks of small pools of golden water. The blue of their leaves reminded her of Oliver's robe. Not unlike hibiscus flowers, these had petals as blue as its leaves, and a red stamen jutting out from the centers. Of course, these were far larger than any flowers she'd seen in North Chester or in Alrujah. Their diameters would be measured in feet, not in inches. She tightened her grip on the staff.

Already, she detected Oliver's presence in Myrassa. A relief to know he survived the battle with the Seers. He made his way toward the Utahemi women's camp with the assassin. He'd be there in an hour, but by then, she'd be gone.

Better for him not to see her, not like this. He had enough on his mind.

A tingling in her feathers pointed her down. She folded her wings and descended. Near a pool, she spread all four of her wings and alighted along the bank. She twisted the staff in her hands and tucked it under her arm as she made her way toward the camp of Utahemi women.

Dark shadows ran over the assorted foliage, the red yullian flower, the yellow markaada plant. She knew the names, understood their physiology, could diagram the root structures.

She steadied her heart, preparing it for what lay ahead—women bearing deep scars, missing eyes, broken limbs not properly set. Still, they would work, under threat of their lives, cultivating a difficult jungle, hunting what animals escaped the eyes of the men.

A short walk brought her to the compound. Ten huts in a circle, thatched roofs in disrepair, termite-eaten lumber comprising leaning walls. Women, old and young, made their way through camp, carrying water, sweeping huts, gathering roots for food. The youngest still smiled. A miracle of Adonai. The older women had suffered much, something Adonai sought to change soon.

The women busied themselves with cleaning, repairing fallen roofs. The smallest girls, the children, walked close to their mothers and helped gather berries and fruits.

Slowly, one by one, they turned their heads toward her. Their faces wore a mix of fear and hope, as if she'd come to kill them, to end their long suffering.

Bailey said, "I come not to harm you, but to bring you a deliverer."

An old woman with streaked, gray hair walked toward Bailey. Age had bent her shoulders, and wrinkles mapped her remarkably unscarred face. Her eyes had gone white with cataracts. Blind, she kept a hand on a younger woman's shoulder. "Your voice," she said. "Izanji's shadow."

The prophecy, she meant. The others in the camp called the woman Mother Eider. She'd led a life of suffering, of incredible loss and resilience. Before they'd gone blind, her eyes studied the few books the camp had. They were few and far between, but whenever a daughter returned with a stolen book, Mother Eider had been the first to know of it, to read it. She kept them in a small hole she'd dug under her mat. Her devotion to the ancient texts warmed Adonai's heart, which is why He chose to bless her with the news of a deliverer.

Bailey furled her wings and approached the old woman. She

stretched out her hand, let what power she had flow into Mother Eider.

Her eyes unclouded, and Mother Eider fell to her knees. "Izanji's shadow! I am unworthy."

Bailey's heart broke.

"I am as you say," Bailey said. "And I bring you news of a deliverer. Before the sun sets, before the close of day, he will come. His robe will be as a silistrus flower, and his name will be Oliver."

"Shadow Singer?" Mother Eider asked, her voice trembling and wet.

"So shall she return as well."

Mother Eider turned her head up with fear marring her renewed eyes. "The Blood Bolts?"

"Soon," Bailey said, her heart heavy with knowledge of the future, "will come the breaking." She held the staff, the one Adonai had given her, toward the kneeling woman. The stave had been fashioned of three woods braided together: oak from North Chester, harspus from Alrujah, and jissa from Myrassa. The smallest portion of Adonai's power radiated in it. "He will have need of this."

Mother Eider took it, tentative and trembling. "I will see he gets it."

"Do so, and he will bring you to a new home."

Mother Eider smiled despite her tears. "Thank you," she whispered.

Despite her new physicality, Bailey found her heart broke the same way it had when she had been human. Her wings tingled; her feathers twitched. "I must go." She unsheathed her flaming sword, cut a wide swath in the air before her, and stepped through the glowing wound left in the world's weave of space-time. Sometimes, her job awed her.

LAUREN HADN'T SLEPT SO WELL in her life. Upon awaking in the plush bed—mattress and actual sheets, light linen blankets for the first time in months—she considered keeping her eyes shut, imagining the walls of her room around her, the nagging beep of an alarm clock, the crowded halls of North Chester High.

She cracked her eyes open to the dimness of the sunslight filtering through pine needles, the crisp mountain air tinged with the scent of damp soil wafting through the glassless windows of the bark-lined buildings of the Heart of Yeval. She reluctantly pulled the covers off and put on the dress the Council selected for her—a white, form-fitting top accented with a flowing white skirt, divided for riding. Purple and gold embroidery ran up the sides in braided vines. And while the dress lacked sleeves, her arms wouldn't want for warmth. Two elegant satin gloves ran from fingertips to biceps, each terminating in a thick gold band which kept the gloves from sliding down. She pulled on the pair of ruby-studded steel armored boots and marveled at how light and comfortable they were on her sore feet. Enchantments did incredible things. Lastly, she strapped on steel shoulder armor and a wispy chiffon cape with matching gold and purple embroidery.

She adjusted the golden tiara on her head, pinning it to her wispy blonde hair, and the magical power within her amplified. While it did not increase her magic reserves as her gloves and dress did, the enchanted gold intensified her empathic magical abilities. The boots would increase her speed, and the shoulder armor helped resist magical attacks. This is how she designed them in the game, but putting them on felt like leveling up. She half expected to see a graphic of the stat boosts they provided: Magic +50%, Spirit +25%.

Someone knocked on her door. Lucky for her, Yarborough hadn't put his helmet on yet. If he had, she'd never have recognized him. He'd done away with the armor he'd worn to battle the Seers in favor of something a little lighter, a little stronger, and a lot more flexible. Steel-scaled plate armor covered his torso and shoulders, the backs of his arms, his legs and feet. Beneath it, steel mail provided enough of a cushion to grant some comfort. Each piece had been painted red.

Stylized dragon heads stood in gold relief against the crimson metal. Like her dress, his armor came with strong enchantments as well— resistance to physical and magical attacks, increased speed and strength, which he'd need to wield his new weapon—a double-headed, diamond-edged steel battle axe. At two-and-a-half-hands, the blade must weigh a ton, but he lifted it like a stick, inspected the gold dragon inlays near the middle. Slipping the weapon on his back, he flashed a smile brighter than his armor. "Being on the Council has its advantages."

She smiled and tried not to think about how much she missed Aiden and Bailey, Erica and Oliver. "We've got a long road in front of us."

"Let us go, then. Today, we face our destiny." The half-dwarf offered her his arm.

She took it, allowed herself, for a moment, to enjoy his friendship, his trust. "Ready to decide the fate of Alrujah?"

"Not in the least." He led her to the circular stairs running from floor to floor inside of the massive tree structure. He took the steps quickly, walking like a man newly healed. His breath came easy. The healers of Yeval had worked a miracle on his shoulder—something she'd tried to do with Oliver's staff and failed. Now, however, with the mass of magic swelling in her, she wondered if she'd be able to work a similar marvel. A short walk later, they arrived in the Heart of Yeval, a soft rain still falling.

The rest of the Council had already assembled. Langley sat in his chair, posture perfectly erect with all the pride requisite of an arrogant elf-king. Behind his haughty mask, Lauren recognized the lines of stress in his forehead, the creases only the weighty concern for one's people can fold. Dain, his gray sideburns braided for war, drummed his fingers on the arm of his chair. Nyleran, the elf, wore her customary brown dress. The tips of her pointed ears pierced her silvery braided hair like rocks splitting river rapids. Trieli's smooth, human face marked him as the youngest of the old Council. His hair retained its youthful blond luster, though the hoary hair of the aged flanked his ears and temples. He'd come a long way since serving as a

Chameleon Soldier before proclaiming Adonai as his God. He wore the clothes of an Alrujahn noble, though he had no noble blood. Gold trimmed his purple vest and ran down the seams of his pressed black pants. He left his white shirt unlaced in the front, perhaps an homage to his humble heritage. He, least of all, looked prepared for war.

Yarborough, his white beard braided in a complex weave, took his seat beside Dain.

In the center chair, still in his blue robe, Eljah Morrow rested his prayer staff across his knees, holding each end with his hands. "Your seat awaits, Indigo, Daughter Queen of Alrujah."

The formal title shivered Lauren. Princess was the customary term. Daughter Queen was only used if a princess took the throne after the murder of her father—something that'd happened only twice before in Alrujahn history. She'd never expected to be the third.

She nodded. "Of course," she said, adopting a formal tone. She took her seat and stood Oliver's rognak staff next to her. Posture straight, she reminded herself. She was a monarch now and must act like it. She turned her gaze to Langley and said coldly, "I believe you were telling us why we should trust you, Langley half-elf."

Langley said, "My title is king. Please use it. Trust is a commodity we have little of, Daughter Queen. You spring from the line of Solous, the man who nearly eradicated my entire race."

Eljah stood and tapped his staff twice. "Enough. Adonai put us on our seats. If He trusted us, we must also trust each other."

A name came to Lauren's mind: Judas. Hadn't Jesus picked him as one of His disciples? And hadn't he been the one to betray Him? If any on the Council were a Judas, it'd be Langley.

The half-elf king stood for a moment and considered Lauren. "I understand your concern, but we must focus our attention on what truly matters now—the fate of Alrujah. Korodeth has assumed the throne of Alrujah illegally. Your throne, Daughter Queen, and he must be dealt with. His actions have split the cities of Alrujah further. War is coming. He must be punished."

"Korodeth is no simple soldier," Trieli said. "When first I joined the Chameleon Soldiers, I took pride in my work. But as Korodeth gained power, he began to make unusual requests. We rarely followed the orders of Ribillius, but instead followed his commands. He seeks *The Book of Sealed Magic*. All Chameleon Soldiers have standing orders to report any news about it to him directly and immediately. I have no doubt he will use the power within the book to practice the sealed magic. He may even summon Shedoah himself."

"The magic itself is not evil," Dain said. "The power within the book helped establish the throne of men, the reign of Adonai, and establish the Council. Have you forgotten these things?"

Lauren said, "In the hands of the Mage Lord, the magic is black. Already, he's summoned Belphegor, Moloch, and the Seers. Other than Korodeth, who else in Alrujah would want such abominations in our land? He's a known follower of Shedoah. He must be the Mage Lord."

Nyleran spoke in her lofty, queenly voice. "To summon such abominations, he would need the book and need it unsealed. Yet he sends Chameleon Soldiers to spy on monasteries, and recently, sent Blood Monks to attack the Cerulean Order. This suggests he lacks either the book or the power to unseal the spells. I do not believe he is the Mage Lord."

"I can handle Korodeth," Lauren said, her loneliness eclipsed by seething hatred.

"He is no easy quarry. He controls Alrujah," Dain said.

"Alrujah belongs to me," Lauren said.

Trieli said, "The peoples of the cities circle rumors of dissension among their rulers. Rebellion is a distinct possibility. Dalova seems to be the most dissatisfied with Korodeth. Viceroy Gerald may crown himself and make a play for the throne."

"Viceroy Gerald?" Yarborough asked. "He has no royal blood. He is a mercenary."

"Was," Nyleran said. "Ribillius raised him to noble shortly after he saved Indigo's life when she was a child."

"Korodeth killed my father," Lauren said, her gums hurting

beneath the bite of her teeth. "It's the only thing that makes sense. Who else would kill my father, but him who stands to wear the crown? Why are we even talking about this? I should be on my way to Alrujah now avenging the death of my father."

"Rebellion is already in the air," Yarborough said. "Any action now may ruin what chance we have of retaking the throne and reestablishing the church of Adonai."

Langley said, "Upon my return to Harael, I will raise the army of the elves. We will march on Alrujah in two weeks' time."

Lauren leapt up. "Not a chance, pointy-ears. Alrujah's mine!"

Eljah tapped the butt of his staff on his chair again. "We are the Council of the Order of the Protectorate. We've been put here by Almighty Adonai himself. Langley's plan is sound. Korodeth will not release the throne without a show of force. We must gather allies as we can."

"And what about the Mage Lord?" Trieli said.

Eljah said, "We're no closer to knowing who he is now than we were months ago. For now, we must move ahead and trust Adonai's instructions. We return to our people and prepare them for war. We can only overcome Korodeth with the might of the elves and dwarves behind us."

Lauren's neck bristled. Her hands fisted and fire bit her palm. "You keep your filthy elves out of my kingdom."

Langley pointed to her ears, the nubs of points hidden by her hair. "My filthy elves are your people, too, Daughter Queen. Retake the throne in two weeks' time, and you'll not need to worry about our people marching on your kingdom. But so long as Korodeth is on the throne, he is our enemy, and we will treat him as such."

"We cannot repeat the mistakes of the War of the Suns," Nyleran said, her voice soft but strong, a mother's voice observing a simple fact her children overlooked.

"This is not the War of the Suns," Eljah said. "It is a war of gods."

"I'm leaving," Lauren said. "And when I finish with Korodeth, I'll find the Mage Lord."

"You cannot go alone," Nyleran said.

"Come with me if you like." She turned and left the Heart of Yeval, turned her toes toward the griffin stables in Yeval city. Alrujah was only three day's flight from Yeval. She would destroy Korodeth, establish her throne, and set about finding the Mage Lord. And once she'd secured her kingdom, she'd find out how to get Aiden back from North Chester.

14

Tiamat took for himself a body of horror and made his home in the depths of the Alrujahn Sea. He spread his wings and rose from the deep and terrorized the water people with fire and strength, with impenetrable scales and the voice of many seas.
—The Book of the Ancients

AS HE EXPECTED, Aiden and Franky didn't run into anyone on the hiking trails. At this hour of the morning on a Wednesday, most people would be at work or school. Franky would be too, if he hadn't come over to bring Aiden his armor. The mid-week hikers who frequented this part of the woods came out in the early morning or late afternoons. No one sat beside the lake, feeding the ducks or taking an early spring swim.

North Chester High. Had he ever believed he could return to normal life? How could he go back to football after slaying a nine-foot minotaur and half-decomposed corpses? Somehow, the importance of algebra and essays waned. Had he ever been concerned with such things?

Still, as he cut the cord binding the beresus to the riding mower, he checked over his shoulder. Paranoia ran strong in Alrujah's guard. Survival instinct.

Franky drove the mower, lawn blades up, carefully through the trees. It hadn't been designed to pull heavy loads, but it had more horsepower than Franky and Aiden combined.

"Serious stench, man. Like cat pee and pickles," Franky said, curling his lip at the dead monster.

Nearly seven feet tall, this one dwarfed the first beresus Aidan had battled in Alrujah so long ago, but it used an almost identical attack pattern.

The first encounter had left him broken. If not for Oliver's healing magic, Aiden's back would still be busted. How easily he'd turned his back on Oliver, forgotten about him. The thought of how quickly he chose to stay in North Chester shamed him. "Ready to head home?"

"Not yet, man." Franky leaned forward, elbows on the wheel.

"What's up, bro?"

"I want to go with you. To Alrujah."

Aiden folded his arms and leaned against a tree. "Why?"

"I don't belong here, either, man." He paused for a minute, stared at the tracks the beresus had made in the dirt and leaves. "Parents are getting divorced."

"Serious?"

"Didn't want to tell you last night and ruin your triumphant return. I guess the beresus did a good enough job of spoiling your homecoming, so might as well pile it on, right?" He picked at the bark on the tree. "Truth? I don't even think I'm gonna walk."

"Grades that bad?"

"Hardly made it through first semester, and this one's worse."

"Come on, bro. You can pull your grades up. You've got plenty of time."

"Sure, if Bailey were still around to help me. Without her, I don't stand a chance."

"Bailey. That's why you want to go with?"

"Part of it, for sure, but not all of it." He sighed. "Nothing here for me anymore. My best friend's running around stabbing gorilla-trolls. My girlfriend's flying around like an angel. My parents don't talk unless they're screaming. Hardly notice me. Brother and sister are in Texas worried about college, and I can't even get the grades to get out of high school."

Aiden scratched his back on the bark of the tree. "I thought you said your parents were out on a date last night when you picked me up."

"Not with each other."

Aiden grimaced. "Ouch."

"Right?"

Wind rattled branches like brittle bones and stirred the leaves near the beresus. The sudden chill cut through his shirt, and he shivered. When it passed, Aiden stood straight, cracked his back. "That's why you got all jumpy when my parents got into it?"

"Like déjà vu, man. I was counting on a scholarship to get me into college, but after we were eliminated in state, the scouts stopped calling. I needed a big game in the championship. I needed you. Without you," Franky said, "it got ugly."

Aiden scratched the back of his neck and stared at the ground for a moment. "Sorry about that."

"Not your fault."

He sighed and met Franky's stern gaze. "Feels like it, bro. Let's get back to my house. We can talk on the way."

"You're not going to talk me out of it." Franky started the mower. "Like it or not, I'm following you back to Alrujah."

Aiden didn't doubt it. Franky had always been good at sticking to his plans, no matter how poorly thought out they might be. "If you're set on it, you'll have to help me find a way back. Right now, I'm clueless."

"We'll figure it out," Franky said. "God will show us."

Aiden scowled. Had he heard him right? Franky, though a classy, character guy, never expressed any interest in religion. Maybe seeing his best friend slay a monster from a different world awakened the faith in a reluctant believer. Either way, Aiden decided not to push it, but to accept it gently, and to encourage that line of thinking. His faith needed a little bolstering. "I'm sure He will."

BAILEY RENEE ROCKETED from the rift in the sky, a meteor on a collision course with Port Smalth, the city by the sea. She folded her four wings back, soared over the water, lungs filled with air heavy with salinity. Even from this height, she smelled fish, octopus, and squid. Sea gulls parted for her like cars pulling over for an ambulance. Wind pressed her face hard.

The suns erupted brightness above her. Her shadow darkened the docks where fisherman unloaded dhows of their early morning haul. The wound cord of their nets strained against the mass of fish, dying, but fighting. The fishermen bent their necks, hands shading their eyes from the brilliance of the twin suns.

She soared past them so fast, the triangular sails, caught up in her wake, pulled after her. Each muscle worked together with precise, fluid movements. She'd never been this fast, and wished, for a moment, she'd been seven feet tall in North Chester. She'd have dominated the courts. But her purpose lay in Alrujah now, and her impressive size demanded a higher purpose than stuffing balls through hoops.

Ahead, a massive wooden bell tower dominated the center of the city. The rough grain and reddish-brown coloring marked it as having been constructed entirely of rognak. An expensive undertaking, but Port Smalth's booming economy accommodated such extravagances. What Port Smalth lacked in size, it made up for in economic strength through trade with outlying countries. Adonai had blessed the people here, had honored their devotion to him. While Sylvonya, a port city to the north, adopted the worship of Tiamat, Port Smalth remained true to their God. And while the fishing industry struggled in Sylvonya, forcing its residents to turn to piracy, to smuggling, to thievery and other nefarious occupations, the sea near Port Smalth teemed with fish. What taxes Sylvonya's viceroy wrested from the tight fists of his subjects, as well as the money sent to the city from Alrujah, went to its army.

Bailey Renee touched down on the top of the bell tower and surveyed the city. The people below stared at her, eyes wide, mouths unhinged. In the alleys, dead bodies lay huddled along walls, a crimson smudge staining the cobblestones and the base of the walls.

Droughtworm. The touch of Shedoah grew stronger. Bailey's heart stirred, not with sorrow, but with righteous anger.

Alighting near the bell, she unsheathed her heavy, gleaming sword and smashed the hilt into the bronze bell. The resounding gong arrested the attention of the denizens. "Hear me!" she said, her voice piercing the gong of the bell like an arrow through straw. "War is upon you! Sylvonya marches from the north! Tiamat stirs in the deep!"

The populace of Port Smalth trembled at her voice, her words.

She leapt from the side of the tower, cruised south about a quarter mile, and touched down inside the walls of the castle. The pale-faced archers let her pass. She worried about them. If she struck this much fear in their hearts, how would they steel themselves to face Tiamat?

She made her way through the castle, weaving through halls and corridors, through banquet halls and foyers until, at last, near the rear of the castle, she came to the throne room on the third floor. The windows on the back wall looked out over the sea. Instead of the musty, stale castle air she'd experienced in the other rooms, this room smelled of the sea, of the bazaar surrounding the bell tower, of the lilacs in bloom and the pollen of the spider-leaf fichus. Under any other circumstances, the lighting of the room and the pleasant damp air would put her at ease. It'd be a great place to kick up her feet and get some homework done. But those days were behind her now.

Viceroy Delvyn, a massive man with a chest as broad as an ox, sat on a chair upholstered in blue fabric. His thick red beard identified him as a former mercenary. For him, fear must be a strangely unfamiliar emotion, and yet, his knees trembled as he stumbled forward out of his chair and fell before her. "I am a man of blood," he said. "I am unfit to stand before you."

"Be not afraid, Delvyn. Your city needs you." Bailey Renee extended her hand and helped him to his feet. The man had to be six and a half feet tall. How odd to tower over him, to have to look down to meet his eyes. "Sylvonya marches from the north. Tiamat stirs in the deep."

"We are unprepared for war," he said. "My people are prosperous, but droughtworm has thinned our numbers. Those who remain are merchants and fishers, not warriors."

"There can be no room for fear in your heart. Adonai has placed you on the throne for this purpose. Your courage is needed now. Your battle prowess is needed. Your leadership is needed. Evacuate those who cannot defend the city. Recruit those who can wield weapons to defend their homes and families and shops."

"We have no army. How can I train one in a matter of days?"

"Adonai will provide. Speak what you need."

"Soldiers. Warriors. A general."

"You will have it." She unsheathed her sword again, flashed the gleaming blade, and cut a swath through the air as if she'd slashed a tunic on a laundry line. The air opened in a gleaming radiance before him, and through it walked three people. "Viceroy Delvyn, Adonai wishes you to meet Ullwen of Varuth, Norby of Alrujah, and Breniveer of Sylvonya."

Delvyn lifted his hands toward her, palms out; a gesture of surrender, a humble request for mercy. "You summon legends. Much have I heard of their battles."

"This is a portion of what Adonai can do. Truly, I tell you, you shall see a finger of the Hand of Adonai. She will come with another, equally as vital to your cause."

"When shall we look for her?"

"She will come in her time. Until then, you must prepare your city." Bailey Renee stepped through the rift she'd opened with her blade and vanished into light.

AFTER HE'D GATHERED his armor and shield and a duffel bag of snacks, Aiden's mother hugged him as if he were joining the Army and going off to war. Apparently, in the time it'd taken him to haul off the beresus carcass, she'd settled down. His father had always been good about talking her off ledges, and it looked like he'd done it again.

"I love you, precious boy," she said, her voice tight with tears.

He wouldn't cry. Not with Franky here. "I love you, too, Mom."

She steadied her voice, pressing her hand on his chest. "When you were a baby, I promised God I'd give you to Him. We had you dedicated in the church and everything. I never imagined He'd ask you to go to another world."

Aiden didn't know if he should smile or frown.

When his mother released him, his father took him in his arms. Pops held him hard, and surprised Aiden by kissing his forehead—something he hadn't done since Aiden was a child. His father's goatee tickled his skin, a familiar feeling, though one long lost in the stream of distant memory.

It broke the dam of emotions Aiden had walled up. Despite his best efforts, he cried, shook in his father's arms like he was eight years old again.

"It's alright, son," his father said. "God's hand is in this. He won't forsake you."

Aiden shook harder. God's hand. The Hand of Adonai.

This would be the last time he saw his mother or father. He couldn't say how he knew it, but he did. They must know it, too.

He hated God for taking him from his family, for throwing him into a distant world with a sword and shield, for upsetting the normalcy of his life. But God had never promised him normalcy.

He took a deep breath, clutched the back of his father's shirt, and tried to regain his composure, an act as simple as slaying a sasquatch while unarmed.

God's hand was in this, and Aiden was in God's hands.

He was the Hand of Adonai.

And to hear Oliver talk about it, Adonai and God were one and the same. One creator, multiple worlds.

The dampness of his cheeks slicked his father's shirt, and Aiden pulled away. He blinked, wiped his eyes with the cuff of his sweatshirt, and slung his athletic bag holding his armor over his shoulder. He examined the house once more before he met Franky at the door.

"You ready, man?" Franky asked.

"Not even close, bro. Let's go."

BECCA DROVE SLOWLY toward Piedmont Road, and Parker wished she'd step on it. She hadn't said anything the whole trip, aside from a flippant disregard for his thanks for picking him up. Did she resent him for asking this favor? He thought to say something to her, maybe crack wise to lighten the mood, but he didn't know many jokes, so he cleared his throat and shifted in his seat.

The sun split the sky with rays of white. Gentle shadows of millions of pine needles played over the street. Two more minutes and they'd be back at the scene of the accident. Memories flashed in his mind, free-falling from neuron to neuron. Fur and claws, teeth and blood—glass shattering, metal twisting. He closed his eyes and pinched his nose.

"You okay?" she asked.

He tried to play down his shock at hearing her voice. He'd assumed she'd remain silent the entire trip. "We're getting close."

She pulled over near the shattered glass strewn across Piedmont Road and locked the doors.

Parker turned in his seat. "Something wrong?"

She twisted her hands over the steering wheel. "On the news this morning. I heard it on the radio on my way to get you. Some hikers found something. A pack of werewolves or something, they say."

Parker's throat tightened. Hadn't the department cleaned them up? Had they missed some? "You don't say."

She turned in her seat to face him. "You didn't hit a bear last night, did you?"

Leave it to a woman to ask a question with no good answer. If he told her the truth, she'd accuse him of lying. If he lied, he'd be lying. "It was dark," he said.

"Stop it," she snapped. "You're as bad as my ex."

She sounded like his, but he at least had the good sense not to say it. "What do you want me to say?"

"How about the truth?"

"I'm a cop. There are things I can't say."

"Don't play the cop card." She touched his shoulder. "Not while my daughters are missing."

He reached for a cigarette and slipped it in his mouth. It danced as he spoke. "It wasn't a bear."

"I knew it." She sighed and stared back out the windshield. "I know what they are. They're not from here."

"Got the sense they were out-of-towners myself." He eyed the cigarette lighter in the center console. Did it still work?

"They're called fangands," she said.

Parker took the cigarette from his mouth. "You read Lauren's journal?"

She shook her head. "Can I trust you, Joseph? I want to tell you something, but I'm afraid you'll think I'm crazy."

He took another imaginary puff. "You understand you're talking to a man who emptied a couple clips into a pack of mythical creatures last night. How crazy are you going to sound?"

"Can I trust you?" she said again.

Her beauty stunned him. *Keep it professional.* "'Course you can."

Her hands fiddled with the keys.

He said, "Stop. You're making me nervous."

She pulled her purse onto her lap and opened and closed the clasp. "I used to have these dreams. When I was young."

Parker waited patiently for her to continue. His back ached. After a thorough examination, the ER doctor prescribed ibuprofen for his pain. "Bumps and bruises," the doctor had said. "You're lucky not to have head trauma after an accident like that. Not sure how you escaped a car so wrecked."

When he closed his eyes, a phantom of Lauren's touch warmed his forehead, poured heat over his freezing skin. The pain had moved under her touch, perceptibly, marching like ants toward her fingers. And then, it vanished.

"In my dreams, I was a queen. An elf queen, actually, but married to a human. Anyway, there were these creatures in this world I dreamed about called fangands."

Parker unbuckled. He took another imaginary drag and tucked the damp cigarette behind his ear. How strange to hear the words of Alrujah on her lips. He wanted to press her for more information, but, judging by her distant stare, deep, possibly repressed memories locked up her conscious. "Yeah?"

"Stopped having the dreams years ago, when Lauren was born. I miss them."

Parker took Lauren's journal from the inside breast pocket of his coat. He opened the pages, flipping through until he found a sketch of the elf queen. "Your husband?" he said.

"Never told him about the dreams. He'd say they were silly. He didn't like that kind of thing. Besides, he'd have gotten jealous if I told him I was dreaming of another man. How's that for irony? The jealous one runs away with the bimbo in California."

"The one in the dream. Was it King Ribillius?"

She closed the clasp on her purse. Fear eclipsed the distant wonder in her voice. "How'd you know?"

Parker showed her the journal. "I think it's time you read through these," he said.

"No. Lauren was very protective of those. She never let me look at them."

"Considering the circumstances, I'm sure she'd understand." Parker took a deep breath and launched into a very brief, very thorough outline of what the journals contained.

Becca worked the clasp on her purse.

"Now the clasp's making me nervous," he said.

"She had the dreams, too?"

"More than dreams," Parker said. "I think Alrujah is real, and I think Lauren and Bailey are there right now."

"Now you sound crazy."

"Believe me, I know. Been thinking about seeing a shrink for days now. But I've got a few reasons to think that's the case. The most obvious is the fangands in the forest. If Alrujah is here, North Chester must be there." He sighed and slipped the cigarette back in his mouth. He'd come this far, why not go all the way? "Listen, Becca. I need to tell you this."

She put her purse down. "I'm listening."

Parker frowned and rubbed the bridge of his nose. "Last night, they came out of the forest and saved me. Lauren and Bailey and a dwarf. They turned around and went back." He thought about adding Aiden's name to the mix but hearing that he had stayed while her daughters went back might undo her. Better not to reveal that now.

"My God," she whispered.

"You believe me?"

She clasped her purse. "Why would they go back?"

15

And the hope of salvation shall spring forth from the mighty Hand of Adonai. He shall raise a golden scepter and rule with justice. The nations will turn from their wickedness and bless his name.
—The Book of Things to Come

ERICA TRIED to ignore the biting cold, her freezing arms, the throbbing in her scarred shoulder. The backs of her hands constricted, ached as they had every winter since she was seven. Remembered pain only, she told herself. Still, she checked beneath her gloves to assure herself.

Still fine.

But she would pay her father back for killing her mother, for searing her hands. Now, she had a chance to do what she should have done at seven. She would do what the momma bear did to her, only this trip would not break her mind. She'd be stronger than the bear.

Her heart, her whole chest, tightened, compressing her lungs. Breath came in heavy gasps as she ran down the road. Footsteps joined hers; hundreds of animals careened through the forest on her heels. They followed her. She'd not deliberately called them. Instead, they fed on her anger, her fear, her anticipation. Some came to join in her planned violence, others because they didn't want to miss the show.

Behind her, six cougars matched her steps, as did four bobcats, a gray lynx, fourteen timber wolves, three beavers, a half-dozen raccoons, a bear—too much like momma for her taste—and a bison, wherever he'd come from. Hawks circled overhead, and several owls woke up early to accompany her.

She didn't ask questions.

She moved toward the red brick building in the slanting gray rain. Two stories high, the prison looked more like a college dorm.

She'd lived in fear of his escape too long. No more. She'd walk into the maximum-security facility unchallenged. She'd find him and pummel him.

Few cars remained in the parking lot. Probably staffers. Visiting hours ended an hour ago and few came to visit their crazy relatives. What guards patrolled the prison all had high-powered rifles, best she could tell, but the trees gave her the cover she needed.

How would Ullwen handle this?

Touching the minds of the beasts near her, she coordinated her attack. Birds and bats swooped in droves on the tower guards. Those on the ground were overwhelmed by the wolves who'd crept up on them silently.

She raced toward the entrance with her menagerie behind her. The bison lowered its head and charged the door, busting its hinges. The foyer exploded in chaos. Guards reached for weapons as 150-pound timber wolves leapt on their chests, knocking them back and snarling at their throats. The macabre petting zoo circled around her, chomping and chirping, growling and snapping.

"Here it is, people," Erica said. "I need Robert Hall. Keep your weapons holstered and my friends will keep their teeth muzzled. Make it quick, and me and my menagerie will be out of your hair before you can say dandruff."

A man in a crisp blue suit and red tie stood up. His black hair had

"Just for Men" written all over it. He kept a neat goatee, trimmed close to his lips. "Am I to assume you can control these animals?"

"And the ones surrounding the building," she said, voice as cold as the rain. She wiped her brow, tried to keep terror from cracking her voice.

His olive skin paled, but he spoke with patience, like every shrink she'd ever had. The man reeked of psychotherapist. "We have visiting hours, young lady. We're a minimum-security prison."

"Shut up and bring me Robert Hall."

"Why do you want him?"

"Because Momma Bear is angry."

"And if he isn't fit for visitors?"

"I don't care what he's fit to do. You can walk me to him or bring him here. If you refuse, things get messy."

The man placed a hand on a young woman in medical scrubs. "Can you promise none of my employees will be hurt?"

"As long as they don't play hero." Her heart hammered her chest. If she didn't do this right, she'd end up in a cell next to her father.

"I can't take you back to him. It would compromise security and endanger the lives of too many of my staff. Let my guards come back with us, and I'll bring Robert out to you myself."

Wolves snarled and snapped. The bear roared. The bison bellowed. Raccoons scurried over the felled guards. Hawks perched on lamp fixtures, squawked at the warden. Bobcats crouched low to the floor, their bellies barely touching the broken glass from the shattered front door.

Erica stared at the man, her anger melting into fear.

What was she doing?

"Bring Robert first. Then you get the guards." She'd never imagined a situation where she'd end up taking hostages, but she had. These men had families, like the bear. How many people would she have to hurt to get her revenge? To get some long overdue answers? She put her brave face on, tried to show the psychotherapist she meant business. "Bring him quick."

BEFORE OPENING HIS DOOR, Parker waited for the media van to pass by. Further up, a group of people had gathered, parking along Piedmont Road, scouring the forest for a possible glimpse at the werewolves. They'd be disappointed. The department probably had most of it cleaned up already. But it wouldn't stop dim-witted enthusiasts from skulking about the woods hoping to find other mythical creatures— Big Foot hunters and unicorn trackers and every other imaginable whacko looking for proof of their sanity.

He opened the door and double-checked the magazine in his Beretta. "You should stay in the car," he told her.

"Fat chance." Becca slammed her door and armed her alarm. "My daughters are out there somewhere, and you think I'm going to sit in the car playing with my iPhone?"

"We killed some fangands, but it doesn't mean there won't be more."

The sun shone behind her head. Sunlight tangled in her blonde hair. He wanted to sketch her, to preserve her image in charcoal shadows and cotton fiber sunlight.

"Besides," she said, her frustration and fear abetting. "I'll be safe with you, right?"

Pride and confidence swelled within him, but he tried to keep it from showing. Instead, he shrugged. "I can't guarantee your safety."

"I'm not sitting this out," she said.

Parker nodded. "Stay close."

"I was planning on it." She walked beside him, her feet shuffling through dead pine needles.

Parker kept his gun aimed at the ground, and his arms tensed, ready to spring and shoot if necessary. He settled his nerves by telling himself the fangands were dead. Anything he heard out here in the woods, anything he saw, would be other idiots scavenging the woods for memorabilia and a place in the weird-o hall of fame. Had to be.

They weaved their way deeper into the woods. Parker had no idea where to go, had no sense of north or south, east or west. He did his best to follow upturned soil, hair in the bark of trees, and other signs of animals, but he wasn't a hunter. For all he knew about tracking, bears may have made the prints, may have scored the tree bark.

Not his greatest idea, having Becca come along.

"Are we close?" she asked.

Parker shrugged. "They were out here." He hoped his bravado concealed his doubt.

The shuffle of feet in needles startled him. In the span of a second, he switched his safety off and leveled his gun at the sound.

Becca moved behind him, put a hand on his shoulder. "What is it?"

FRANKY DIDN'T TAKE NEARLY AS LONG at his house. His parents were gone. He'd run inside, packed a bag of clothes with a few bottles of water and protein bars, left a note, and locked the door. In all, the trip took no more than six minutes.

"What'd you say to them?" Aiden asked.

"Said I was going on a road trip. Told them I'd check in with them when I could."

Aiden shook his head. "You should call them."

"So they can tell me not to go? No chance, man. Besides, they wouldn't care. I think they're meeting with the lawyers today. Going to hammer out who gets the house, who gets the car, and who gets me. Least I can do is make that decision easier for them." He turned the key and drove away from the house.

Aiden turned the radio down and shifted in his seat to better face Franky. "I get you're not happy here, but there's no guarantee you'll be happy in Alrujah either, bro. I don't know if we'll be able to find the others. You may not see Bailey again."

"If I stay here, I'll for sure never see her again. There's a chance, small as it is, that I can find her in Alrujah, so I'm going. Where are we headed?"

Aiden shrugged. "The accident scene. Lauren seemed to think there was something there."

Franky turned toward Piedmont Road. "Sounds about right. Think we should stop by Bailey's house? Let Ms. Knowles know what we're up to? Tell her the girls are okay? I think she might need some encouragement."

"Nice thought, bro, but we better get going. Whatever was there last night might be gone already."

Franky frowned. "You sure?"

"If we're going to do this thing, we better do it. Hard enough to leave my family. We stay much longer, I may change my mind again." Inside his pocket, the elf queen chess piece pressed into his thigh. It reminded him too much of Lauren to leave it. It helped to hold it, to remind himself why he had to leave his mother and father, why he had to find Lauren. In his bones, an inexplicable fear of her danger tolled like a church bell. Probably guilt for staying back, but thinking that didn't alleviate his nagging worry.

Franky cranked the wheel, turned onto Piedmont Road, and slowed. A silver sedan sat parked along the shoulder near the crash site from the night before. He turned the radio off. "Dude. That's Ms. Knowles's car."

"For sure?"

"No lie. What do you want to do?"

Aiden cracked his knuckles and rolled his neck from side to side. He wanted to get out of the comfortable, confining car. He never imagined longing to ride a horse, but he found himself doing so now. "Park behind her. We'll see what she's up to. It's on our way, anyway."

Franky pulled behind the sedan and cut the engine. "This is weird, right—seeing her car out here and all?"

"Sure isn't normal." Aiden slipped out of the Jeep and shut the door behind him. He considered the duffel bag of clothes and snacks, of his armor and shield. The sword he'd used to kill the beresus hid beneath the back seat. Hard to put that in a bag. "Think we should bring our stuff?"

"Might look kind of strange." Franky locked the car and shoved his hands in his pockets. "Got media crawling around the woods. Guess news of the fangands broke this morning. Where do you think Ms. Knowles is?"

Aiden walked to the car. Ahead, broken glass glittered across the pavement and shoulder. He examined the loose soil of the shoulder. "Couple sets of footprints here." He pointed to small ridges raised up like miniature mountain ranges. Stooping lower, he inspected them closely, something Ullwen had taught him to do before he took off with Erica. "This set is deeper, bigger. Probably a man. A little heavier than me. See how these ridges pull a bit? Think he's limping."

"Look at you, all Sherlock Holmes now."

Aiden shrugged. "Live in Alrujah long enough, you pick these things up." He followed the trail, eyes searching the soil and disrupted pine needles carpeting the forest floor. He lacked Ullwen's tracking skills, so he took it slow, checked and rechecked to ensure they stayed on the right trail. Didn't want to wander off and find some nut case searching for Big Foot. But, the further they got into the forest, the easier it became to track them. They quickened their pace, moving as quietly as possible. Aiden halted and put out a hand. Franky shuffled to a stop.

"I hear them," Franky whispered.

"About 200 yards up." Aiden pointed. "Who's she with? Can't tell from here."

Franky frowned. "Parker."

16

"When the Blood Bolt flashes seven times, I shall free myself," says almighty Shedoah. "I shall rend the chains of my bondage and break the very worlds that hold me. Then will I punish Adonai for his deceit and evil."
—The Shedoahn Prophecies

ELIJAH FOLLOWED at Lauren's heels, his breath sounding heavy in his chest. "Lauren, wait."

She moved through the pine needles covering the dirt. She'd not unfisted her hands since she left the Heart of Yeval. She passed through the training grounds, past elves and dwarves working together, forging and enchanting, enchanting and forging. Several humans trained with swords and shields. Mages tossed fireballs and raised ice shields. None compared to the power surging through her, through Oliver's staff. As an empath mage, her magic wasn't restricted to one discipline or element. Instead, what she felt became her spell. Right now, with hot anger and searing loneliness boiling inside her, she could raze Yeval City.

The griffin stables lay on the outskirts of the forest city, where the trees grew thick and tall and dense. They liked to perch high in the dark branches and watch over Alrujah as silent sentinels, but they rarely involved themselves in war.

Lauren didn't slow down when she spoke. "Wait for what? For Langley to launch an attack on my kingdom? For his stupid power play to crumble my city walls? I helped him take Harael from Neldohr and the Seers, and he thanks me by trying to kill me and endangering my people? Do you know how many people would die if the elves march against Alrujah?"

Eljah fell in step with her. His long stride compensated for her quick steps. Their staffs thwipped in the soft soil in perfect rhythm. "No more than will die at the hands of Korodeth when he turns Alrujah to the worship of Shedoah."

"My people are not stupid," Lauren said. "They'll never turn from Adonai."

"Did the people of Sylvonya not turn to Tiamat? Did the dwarves not turn to Belphegor? Did the elves not turn to Torap and Uhesdey? Did the people of Pellbred not turn to Abaddon? And have not the people of Orensdale themselves turned to Legion?"

He had a point, but no way she'd concede it now. "Alrujah is smarter."

"As the ruler goes, so go the people," Eljah said. "History has shown us this. Turmoil and fear move people to desperate measures. Droughtworm ravages cities. Famine devours our crops. Cities prepare for war. Alrujah is ripe for an insidious revival."

The path between the buildings stretched further toward the stables. The buildings became fewer, more scattered. The griffin stables lay beyond the industry district of Yeval. They'd be there soon. The ringing of metal on metal, the rush of heat and chill, of electricity in the air subsided. The forest itself seemed to breathe. For a moment, she imagined a world not on the brink of war. Something like North Chester, where she concerned herself with simple problems; seeing the latest movie or worrying whether or not Aiden liked her.

She tried to put him out of her mind but failed. He should be here with her. Why hadn't he come back to Alrujah with her? She thought he loved her.

She swept her self-pity away. What was the love of one man when she had the fate of a city, of an entire world, in her hands? Alrujah demanded more of her.

But she needed Aiden, needed his love.

She cleared her throat and wiped her eyes with her gloved fingers. "I am the leader of my people," she said, the chill in her chest frosting each word.

"Do your people know this?"

"They will," she said.

How long had she been walking? She didn't remember the griffin stables being so far off. She almost asked Eljah but refused to show any weakness. If she had to walk to the center of the forest, she'd do so as if she meant to.

Eljah moved beside her, craned his neck up and back, around to the sides as if Chameleon Soldiers crept through the branches. "Where are the stables?"

"Ahead." She did not slow.

Before them, nestled into a small thicket of trees, pale wood ran together to form tall walls. Above them, the eagle-like heads of griffins peered through the shadows. Had they been wild, these griffins would have shrieked like death wails and charged Eljah and Lauren. But these magnificent creatures had gentle spirits. A dozen dwarves had been charged by Oren himself to rear these from hatchlings to fledglings to full-grown griffins. Though the original griffins had been tough to tame, these had been born in Yeval, and they knew the hands of the dozen as they knew the wings of their mothers.

"They're beautiful," Lauren said. Somehow, the steady gaze of the golden-eyed animals soothed her. She'd always loved griffins.

"Don't go alone," Eljah said.

"Come with me."

"I must stay here in the Heart and oversee the matters of the Order, the running of the city, and the business of the Council."

Lauren smiled at a dwarfling. "I'll need a griffin saddled and readied to ride. Quick as you can."

"Of course, Daughter Queen," the dwarfling said. He couldn't be more than twelve years old, and only up to her knee. But he'd be familiar with the griffins, would know how to saddle them, even if he hardly reached their bellies.

Lauren ran a hand over the black griffin's beak. "It's a three-day's flight to Alrujah. I'd like some company."

"Stay. At least for an hour and let us find you a companion to travel with you."

Didn't matter who they found. She wanted Aiden. But Eljah's words made sense. Even with all the power bubbling in her, she'd need an extra pair of eyes at night, if nothing else. "I'm not going back to the Heart. If I can help it, I don't want to see Langley again unless it's in battle."

"You mean on the same side, of course," he said.

"Of course."

The griffin touched its beak to her shoulder and pushed gently. A sign of affection. Lauren ran her fingers along the feathered head, down its neck until feathers fanned out to a thick furry coat of ebony.

"I'll wait one hour, and I'll trust you find someone worthy to fly beside me."

Eljah nodded. "Consider it done, Daughter Queen."

For a minute, Erica wondered if the psychotherapist would come back at all. He took so long returning, she touched the minds of the birds outside, had them scan the area for a suit running to a car. They found nothing unusual.

The guards squirmed uncomfortably. Erica wiped her forehead with the back of her arm, wondering how a building could be so hot and stuffy at the end of winter with spring a good week away.

How long before the police showed up with a SWAT team? The

sparrows didn't see anything for miles, but that didn't mean they weren't on their way.

The wolves howled impatiently, hungry to snap necks, to taste the warm, fresh blood of a good kill. She worked hard to keep them all under control. At first, drawn by her insatiable anger and blood lust, she hardly thought about controlling the swarm of animals plodding along at her heels. They'd been caught up in eleven years of her burning hate.

With every tick of the clock, her anger waned, and her fear grew. But the bond between animal and caller flowed in two directions. Rather than wrestling to keep them in line, she deliberately touched the mind of the wolves, let their thirst for the hunt fuel her rage, replace her fear. She drew the calm of the hawks, perched in the rafters, staring down at a scene that might as well have been a television pilot—a spectacle, but little worth their concern. She weaved the varying emotions of her posse, threaded her own feelings into the tapestry. Fear succumbed to anger, poise guided fury. The complex juggling required intense concentration—allowed no time to give in to her childish anxieties.

When the suit finally returned, he pushed a terminally thin man with graying hair in a wheelchair. Metal cuffs chained his hands and ankles to the chair. Thick padding surrounded the shackles. He rocked back and forth in the chair, rubbing his hands together. This wasn't the man she remembered from childhood—the aloof veterinarian too busy to be bothered by a child. He'd been fit and athletic, strong, with a head full of dark brown hair. The man in the chair was a scarecrow, made of straw, a Halloween decoration.

"This is Robert," the suit said. "I'm going to open the door, now. Once my guards are on this side safely, and all your animals on your side, I'll wheel him out myself. Deal?"

The calm of the hawks, the howl of the wolves. "Try anything funny, and I'll knock the door down."

"I believe you." From behind bulletproof glass, he pressed a buzzer, and a heavy lock unlatched. He pushed Robert to the door separating the visiting area and the foyer.

"Let them up, guys."

The wolves snarled and snapped, but they moved off the guards. "Keep your hands on your heads, boys. I'd hate for momma bear to think you were making a move for your guns."

The men complied and slinked past the snorting bison to the door. Once they'd passed, the suit asked, "What are you going to do with Robert?"

"None of your business."

The suit nodded. He wheeled Robert out but stayed beside the chair. He closed the door behind him.

Robert rocked and rocked, rubbed and rubbed. "Fifty stars, thirteen stripes," he mumbled.

The gray lynx hissed at the suit. The bear sniffed Robert's face. He didn't flinch. Bobcats circled both men, their purrs rumbling like thunder.

Erica swallowed the lump in her throat, pulling the thrill of the hunt from the wolves. With the low, threatening growl of a bobcat, Erica said, "What's wrong with him?"

"Endost Syndrome. A degenerative disorder. On initial onset, the symptoms present much like paranoid schizophrenia—simple confusion, delusions, difficulty separating reality and fantasy." He continued patiently, as if Erica had asked. "Advanced cases are more complicated, identifiable by a violent psychotic break." He kept his eyes on Erica's, ignoring the bear, the bobcats and wolves, the lynx and raccoons. "You're Erica, aren't you?"

Wolves howled. Raccoons nipped at the suit's loafers.

"Fifty stars, thirteen stripes."

"Forgive me," the suit said. "I've become very familiar with Robert's file. I assume you came here for revenge?"

"You don't know me," she rumbled with the voice of the bison.

"I know what anger can do to a person. What your father did—it wasn't his fault. He's sick. You can't be mad at someone for getting cancer."

The alpha wolf leapt at the suit, knocked him over, and landed on his chest. It howled and snapped. The suit screamed, flung his arms over his face, shook under the alpha's heavy paws. The wolf wanted this man's blood, wanted to rip his throat out, wanted to shake the corpse until the neck snapped.

Or was it Erica who wanted that?

Robert's neck bent back, his head tilting up toward hers. His hollow, sunken eyes blinked in Morse code. His hands snapped up and reached for her throat. The shackles caught around his wrists, but still he strained. Beneath the pads, his wrists showed deep scarring. He'd done this annoyingly often when Erica was young, on the few times her first foster mother dragged her to the asylum to visit him. She was all about forgiveness, that woman...

The alpha snarled like a buzz saw. The bear exploded in a roar, knocked Robert's chair over. It stood over him with all the wanton blood lust of the wolves, with all Erica's blinding anger. All fear vanished.

This man wasn't her father. He was her mother's murderer. And if the state of Minnesota couldn't give her justice, by Adonai, she'd wreak her own vengeance, administer justice between the jaws of a four-hundred-and-fifty-pound black bear.

"Fifty stars, thirteen stripes."

Erica's lip curled. She bared her teeth, a badger ready to attack. "Kill him!"

White light flashed brilliantly.

FAR OFF, two men walked toward them. Young. Early twenties? Younger? Hard to tell from this distance. Parker replaced his weapon. "See them?"

"Who are they?"

"I'll find out." He took his badge from his pocket and took several confident steps toward the young men. "Need something, gentlemen?"

"What are you guys doing out here?" the shorter one said. His voice sounded familiar. Aiden?

Parker took a few more steps, Becca on his heels. Without his armor, Aiden looked smaller, but his build, his nose, the timbre of his voice marked him as the same kid Parker talked to last night after the fangand attack, the one who'd helped save his life, the one who'd killed three monsters with a shield and pointy-jointed armor. "I could ask you the same thing," he said.

"Does she know?" the taller one said. Parker squinted. Much as he hated to admit it, he needed to calendar an appointment with an optometrist.

Franky.

"A little, yes," Parker said. "I told her."

"Everything?" Franky asked. They came within a few trees of each other.

Parker stuck a thumb to the two teens. "Becca, meet Aiden. I think you already know Franky."

"Aiden?" she said, her voice a birdish chirp. "You've been there, too, haven't you? You know where Lauren and Bailey are?"

"I think so," Aiden said, sliding his hand into his pocket. He pulled out the tiny carved chess piece. Aiden studied it then stared at Becca. He shoved it back in his pocket. "Came out here to try to find them."

"Us, too," Parker said. He slipped a damp cigarette in his mouth. It danced with his words. "Any idea how to get back to Alrujah?"

"No clue. You planning on going with us?"

"Yes," Becca said.

Aiden moved his eyes over her. "Not sure Alrujah's the right place for you," he said. "Too dangerous."

Parker said, "He's right."

Becca spoke with a sudden assurance and authority. "You need me."

"Why?" Franky asked.

"Because I know Alrujah."

"So do I," Aiden said.

"Not like I do." She elevated her chin.

Parker hadn't seen this side of her, this confidence, this command.

Somehow, she'd turned from a weepy, worried mother to a regal queen.

"I know it well enough to stay alive."

With a sudden confidence, she said, "You cannot know Alrujah like her queen knows it."

17

And for a time, the world will go dark. Shedoah will come in his power, and the world will break beneath him.
—The Book of Things to Come

AFTER BAILEY RENEE'S miraculous transformation, Alrujah felt smaller, scaled down to the size of a Hollywood model. She burst through the opening in the sky with a rippling surge of power, folded her four wings behind her, and dove headlong at meteor speed toward Pellbred, the swamp city. The nascent spring air burned cold against her skin as she sped toward the brown marshlands. Seconds before landing, she opened her wings and slowed herself at a rate that would tear a human apart.

But she was no human. Not here, not anymore.

Unwilling to sully her armored boots, she arrested her fall inches above the mucky swampland. She ignored the stench—some woeful mix of sewage and cabbage—and moved through the grimy outskirts, marked by homes with rotting wood walls and thatched roofs thick with filth. Old wood bridges traversed the marshy causeways splitting the city yet linking shops and homes. Dark hemlocks, gnarled oaks, and sycamores claimed the few spots of solid ground to be found. Their roots stretched out like boys' fingers digging in mud, as if they'd unearth at any moment a haul of worms to gross out the girls.

She used her wings in alternating pairs to push forward without touching the earth. Villagers, upon sight of her, raced back to their homes and slammed their doors and their shutters, rusty hinges squealing like frightened mice.

The heart of the city had been constructed on dry land, as opposed to the much of swamp surrounding it. The stone walls of the castle dominated the rest of the swamp with their shadows. Brown muck ran up the walls, making it look as if they'd been dipped in expired paint. Toward the top, they glistened pristine and white, lined with turrets for the archers. A torch lit each turret against the persistent obscurity from swamp gasses and thick foliage. A tangible darkness settled on the city like a bearskin. The air smelled like old gym socks.

She launched herself over the sparsely guarded walls, a small feat for her new powerful body. She hadn't expected much in the way of resistance. South of the Dragon's Back Mountains, Pellbred sat so far north, its people had little concern for the politics of the southern cities of the kingdom. They were determined, proud in their own way. While few would choose to live in the swamp, the families who worked the outlying farms, the blacksmiths and carpenters, took a special pride in their work, in Pellbred's role as Alrujah's first line of defense. Their soldiers were few, but the warriors of Pellbred made up for their lack of numbers with an intense training regimen.

But the people had been led astray, like so many others in Alrujah.

She leapt from the top of the wall, flapped twice, and set herself near the center of the city, at the doors of the temple of Abaddon. She'd find the viceroy here, offering his afternoon sacrifice of rotten vegetables and spoiled meat.

What perverse worship.

Now, she'd face down the viceroy and deliver the message Adonai had charged her with. Funny how, only a few weeks ago, she flew alongside Pacha el Nai, learning the ropes of being an angel and delivering messages. Now, she flew alone, with a keen, powerful lesson learned; angels can die.

She pressed the doors of the temple gently, but they flew open beneath her hands, nearly pulling the hinges from the wall. As she anticipated, Viceroy Herater knelt before a crudely carved wooden statue—some sort of demon with bat wings and nails like claws. He wore a flowing black robe with red trim—the customary garb of the priests of Abaddon. The gaudy gold ring on his left hand marked him as an Alrujahn political official.

Ribillius's predecessor had elevated Herater from ambassador to viceroy. He'd served faithfully in his new authority until Ribillius took the throne. After, Herater became a priest of Abaddon and outlawed the worship of Adonai. Ribillius should have stripped him of the ring, but the lack of political interests went both ways. Ribillius had no need for swampland. So he concerned himself with other things—the elimination of droughtworm, the thinning of the church of Adonai, the famine ravaging Alrujah.

Now, these things fell to the worry of Korodeth, a man misguided by ambition and blind devotion. Such men were dangerous.

Herater was no such man. Like many men, he wanted only wealth and power, something Abaddon promised him. But the promises of Abaddon could not be trusted.

At the sight of Bailey Renee, Herater raised his hands to his face, as if she'd threatened him. "Don't hurt me," he said.

"You know from Whom I come," she said.

"Don't kill me, please," the old man mumbled, cowering like a child before an angry father. The pasty white skin of his hands and face reflected the light emanating from Bailey Renee, from her armor and her sheathed sword.

It would be easy to end him here, to take his head from his shoulders, but Adonai had called her to be a protector, not a murderer.

Words bubbled up her throat. She spoke the words of Adonai.

"Viceroy Gerald of Dalova has set a crown upon his head and rejected the kingship of Korodeth, who sits on the throne of Alrujah."

Eyes toward the floor, Herater said, "He'll never stand against Alrujah."

"Viceroy Burkoth of Weileighn has pledged fealty to the crown of Dalova. Armies will march on Pellbred with a new weapon of war. She will crush your resistance and put your people to the sword. She will claim Pellbred as her own."

"You speak of treason. They cannot stand against the might of Korodeth. Korodeth will protect us."

"Brave words from a cowardly man."

Herater lifted his eyes to Bailey's. Whatever fear lined his face earlier vanished in a puff of smugness. "Abaddon will protect us."

"Your worship of Abaddon is a stench in Adonai's nostrils. He shall turn his Hand against you, and Abaddon will fall. The pangs of birth are on Alrujah." She unsheathed her sword and smashed the wooden idol to splinters. Exiting the building, she cut a large diagonal swath in the air. The fabric of space and time ripped before her. She stepped through the rift and sealed it with the palm of her hand.

ALRUJAH, again.

Her father with her, still shackled to a fallen wheelchair. His arms reaching for her throat. His lips pulled back in a frown. Fingers scarred by scorching flame.

No bear or bison, no hawks or bobcats, no raccoons or lynx, no wolves.

She was the only animal here in this empty street market.

She leapt at him, shrieked with the voice of a griffin, her voice a shrill siren.

Her fingers wrapped around his neck.

He didn't struggle to free himself but reached toward her throat still, arms shaking under the binding of his shackles. His voice, a pinched whisper beneath her trembling fingers. "Fifty stars, thirteen stripes."

Harder. Squeeze harder.

His face reddened, sunken eyes bulged.

She gasped, pulled breaths in gulps, shrieked and howled and squeezed.

Something hit her, knocked her back. A body, a person.

She swiped at his face with her claws, snapped at him with her teeth.

"Erica!" it said. It grabbed her wrists.

She kicked, tried to free her paws.

"Erica! It's me!" Voice like waters, like streams.

She blinked, her chest slowed. Breathe.

Beard, hair long and black. Scent of cedarwood, of damp earth. Ullwen.

"Erica!"

Yes, Erica. She was Erica.

His hands held her wrists tight, protecting his face from her nails. She didn't speak, too embarrassed to say anything. Instead, she sat up, pressed her lips hard against his.

He kissed her, hands still on her wrists, with a terror lined passion, and with each second his lips pressed hers, she became more Erica and less animal. He loosed her wrists, an act of trust and of love. She wrapped her arms around him, buried her head in the crook between his shoulder and neck, and wept.

"I've got you," he said, standing and lifting her with him.

"I missed you," she cried. "I missed you so much."

Behind her, a presence, an animal, a huge wolf. She dropped to her knees and spread her arms wide as Sparky bounded over to her, toppling her and licking her face. She laughed and hugged him. She didn't recognize the city streets, but she understood—she was home.

Ullwen helped her up again, keeping his arm around her. "We must get out of the streets."

Erica took in the scene around her—canopied tables, weathered wood signs, cobbled streets. This had to be a market of some sort, a bazaar, Alrujah's answer to a mall. But, even with the flickering enchanted street lights, no vendors manned their tables. All the goods had been packed up for the night. "Why?"

"The curfew. Come, we're staying in the chapel." He took her hand and pointed to a large building behind them. Unlike most of the buildings in Alrujah, this one had windows—circular stained-glass buildings depicting scenes of nature, mainly the sea.

He set Robert up and marveled at the wheelchair. He ran his fingers over it, ignoring the man in the shackles trying to strangle him. "Fifty stars, thirteen stripes!"

"The construction is admirable. Simple metal frame, thick leather to form the seat. "I've never seen leather dyed this color."

"Yeah, it's a miracle. Can we go?"

He grasped the handles, and Robert calmed, went back to rubbing his hands. "Amazing! What composition of material is this?"

"The handles? They're rubber, dear. Don't bother trying to wrap your head around it right now. Push him into the sea, and I'll explain it while he floats away."

"The wagon chair floats?"

"No. Come on, Ullwen, let's go."

"We should bring this man to the monks. He is injured and ill. They may be able to heal him."

Erica shook her head, put her hand on Sparky, let his realness reassure her. "I don't want him healed. I want him dead."

"Is he your enemy?"

"He killed my mother."

"Breniveer? She is fine, my love. She sleeps in the castle."

Breniveer, Norby. Her parents—the ones who loved her and protected her. "Bring me to them," she said.

Shock should have dropped Aiden's jaw, but Becca Knowles's revelation didn't slow him in the least. In fact, he found it surprisingly easy to swallow, given what he'd learned about his father's trips to Alrujah.

Wouldn't it stand to reason that the other kids' parents had similar experiences?

"Queen?" Franky asked.

"Yes," Becca said. "I am the Queen of Alrujah."

"Hold up. How's that possible?"

It had to be true, but something concerned Aiden. As a child in Harland, he'd heard the news: the queen had been murdered. Shortly after, Ribillius had called for the services of Aiden's father. But they had never found a body. "They said you died," he said.

"I'm very much alive." Becca's voice was too much like Lauren's for Aiden's taste.

Somewhere behind Becca and Parker, a shimmer caught his eye. Something like water, like a waterfall in mid-air, but silver, and gold near the edges. His heart froze in his chest. "Am I the only one seeing this?" He pointed.

Franky followed his gaze. "I see something but don't know what it is."

"Stay here," Parker said. He replaced the cigarette behind his ear, drew his weapon, and moved toward the shimmer cautiously. "You say it's down this way? Where, and what, is it exactly?"

"You can't see it?"

"Vision isn't what it used to be." He replaced his badge in his inside coat pocket and steadied his weapon with his left hand. "What are we talking here? Monster?"

"A shimmer," Becca said.

The golden-edged ripple beyond the trees vanished. Aiden shook his head. "We missed it," he said.

Parker asked, "Missed what?"

"A gateway," Franky said. "That's what it looked like. Some sort of portal."

"You sure?" He loosened his grip on the handgun.

"Nope," Franky said. "But don't know what else it'd be. Let's check it out."

"Hang on," Aiden said. "If we're going, lemme grab my gear." He raced back to the car, grabbed his duffel bag and sword, and returned.

Becca eyed the blade. "That's not Alrujahn."

"My sword didn't make the return trip." He pulled the shield from the bag. "Better?"

She shook her head, a hand over her open mouth. "It's been so long."

"Let's go," Parker said. They moved forward, Parker in the lead, his trained steps coming slowly, surely. He kept the weapon trained at the spot Aiden had pointed out, arms straight, taut under his overcoat.

Franky moved behind Parker, walking beside Ms. Knowles. Franky whispered something in her ear, and she smiled.

Already, fangands had attacked Parker, and a beresus had found its way to Aiden's house. What other monsters might traipse through this gate? The nar'esh? An abomination like Belphegor or the Seers? Aiden slung his duffel over his back like a backpack and held his sword and shield in front of him. He moved past Parker. "Better let me lead."

He rolled his shoulders; the muscles of his back tensed and relaxed. Aiden motioned Parker down a bit, and they spread out. But as they moved toward the spot where the gate had appeared, as they moved through the soft soil and ducked between thick trunks of evergreen trees, they found no tracks, no sign of anything Alrujahn coming into North Chester.

Until something cawed.

The bird's voice came deep and throaty like a raven's with a shrill echo.

"Razorbeaks," Becca said. "I don't believe it."

Aiden counted fourteen of the purple birds and immediately thought of Erica. How long had it been since he'd seen her? He wished she were there, to talk to them, to communicate, to send them back to Alrujah to find the others.

"Don't look them in the eye," Aiden said.

"Why not?" Franky asked.

"They'll peck your eyes out," Becca said, wonder thick in her voice.

Parker kept his eyes low and knelt in the soil. Aiden moved back toward him. The soil near Parker's feet had been turned to glass. "That's new," he said.

Aiden shook his head. "We missed it."

With a violent cawing, the razorbeaks lifted from the branches and flew off toward the west.

"Where are they going?" Franky asked.

"Could be anywhere," Aiden said.

"No," Becca said. "See how they all fly together? They know something."

"What do they know?" Parker asked.

"There," Franky said, pointing toward a cliff. "Isn't that your house, Ms. Knowles?"

The echo of the birds' caws rang off the cliff face as they flew over the town below. Seconds before flying directly into the rock face, they shifted up, and vanished through a shimmer.

"Well how about that," Franky said.

"What happened?" Parker asked.

"Get in the car," Becca said. "We have to go. Now."

18

Famine and disease, poverty and death; these are the signs of his coming.
The elf and the dwarf, the man and the woman, will call out for the
mountains to fall on them, to bring them to a swift end.
—The Book of Things to Come

IT TOOK Erica a moment to readjust to being in Alrujah. She'd never heard of Port Smalth, but Ullwen told her it was a coastal city responsible for the majority of Alrujah's importing and exporting with the eastern islands. The damp air sagged with the weight of salt and the scent of fish. Builders had fashioned the walls and buildings with brick or stone, and, in some unfortunate cases, both. And while the bell tower near the center of the town loomed over everything else, even over the lighthouse on the eastern edge of town, she found the empty streets far more imposing. Aside from her and Ullwen, and their well-armored escorts, no one walked the streets. The rest, Ullwen told her, had made their ways home or out of town.

The armies of Sylvonya were on the march. Because armies moved much slower than a few bandits on horseback, the town had a few days to prepare, but little more. Already, several hours had passed since the angel brought news of the coming attack. She'd apparently brought Ullwen, Breniveer, and Norby here as well. If Erica ever got a chance to talk to this angel, she'd give her a piece of her mind. How dare she bring her parents here in the midst of a war. They should be resting at the monastery with Dillard.

But then, Dillard was a bit sketchy himself. And if more Blood Monks marched on the monastery, it may be as dangerous as Port Smalth.

The docks and market behind them, Ullwen led her west, toward the center of the city, using the six-story bell tower as a guide. The castle, only three stories, had been built south of it. Ullwen mentioned something about the builders of the city starting with the tower and working out concentrically. Not only did it serve to keep the city on the tight schedules a shipping town demanded, but it doubled as a type of crow's nest, a way of surveying the entire city, scanning for trouble within the walls and without.

"This place is a kinda creepy," she said.

"A sign of the times. A week ago, you'd not say so. You would see the good people of Port Smalth, their devotion to Adonai, their friendly and welcoming spirit. Port Smalth is a home for several different races, different people groups, from the eastern islands and beyond. They do not care where you come from. They simply open their arms, their doors, and share their meals with you."

"You sound pretty fond of the place."

"My grandparents came to Alrujah from West Eukara Island. They arrived in Sylvonya but found the place distasteful—overrun with smugglers and pirates and all sorts of evil. When they traveled south, here to Port Smalth, they found a very different type of people indeed. They lived here until the day they died, nearly six years ago."

"I'm sorry to hear they passed," Erica said. She kept her hand in his—it kept her connected to something real, to someone who loved her, to someone she loved. It kept her mind human.

The guards opened the gates of the walls surrounding the castle, then the doors into the stone building itself. The ceiling of the foyer reached up all three stories, and various staircases ran along the walls to balconies positioned at different heights. Thick square columns, strangely lined with shelves of books, jutted up from ground to ceiling. How anyone reached the books on the top shelf, mere inches from the top, baffled her.

"What are my parents doing?"

"General Norby is overseeing the training of the army. He locked himself in a room with several of the commanding officers shortly after the angel left. I've not seen him since. Breniveer keeps herself busy visiting soldiers, using her gifts to grant courage and calm."

"And what about you?"

He paused, as did the guard pushing Robert Hall.

"Fifty stars, thirteen stripes."

"Aside from treating soldiers with droughtworm? Viceroy Delvyn has tasked me with training several of his more unconventional soldiers."

She grinned. "So you get to train the special forces?"

He did not smile. "Warfare in Varuth is a type of art. My days in the Infiltrators and Elite have taught me many things. But every hour of every day, our commanders hammered one truth into us: men who die quickly cannot rally their troops."

"Got it," she said. "Kill the head and the body dies."

His voice carried an edge of unease. "Kill one to save the many."

She changed the subject to spare him any further discomfort. "So where are they?"

"We should not interfere with your father's planning. His gift for strategy may save the city. We will find your mother near the training gardens in the back of the castle."

"Lead the way."

True to his word, Breniveer, dressed in a lustrous blue dress with orange hems, moved through the troops as they practiced swordplay and shield defense. The entire courtyard rang with the sound of metal on metal, with men grunting and shouting. It sounded as if the battle had already started.

Breniveer didn't speak. She simply moved through the courtyard, her hands moving on her wrists as if she traced the ebb and flow of the Alrujahn Ocean. The soldiers nearest her doubled their efforts. They moved as if they didn't see her, didn't know she walked immediately behind them. Sword hit shield, armor deflected glancing blows.

The soldiers had been well trained, but they had too few swords. Erica had no idea how big a city Sylvonya was, but she'd bet a box of Cracker Jacks they'd be facing an army at least twice as large.

"She looks peaceful," Erica said. "I hate to call her away from what she's doing."

"She'll want to see you," Ullwen said. He called to Breniveer, who turned at the sound of his voice.

Her eyes widened, and she gathered up her dress to run to Erica.

Erica smiled; her chest expanded with air and pride, with the overwhelming breadth of unconditional love. "Momma," she said.

"Lakia! Child, I've missed you so!" Breniveer stopped, her eyes locked on Robert. Instantly, her smile melted into a menacing, twisted frown.

Robert rocked, rubbing his scarred fingers. "Fifty stars, thirteen stripes."

"You," she said, furious.

"Wait. What?" Erica said.

"You know this man?" Ullwen asked.

Holding Erica tight by the shoulders, Breniveer whispered, "This man must be killed."

Erica grinned at Ullwen. "Told you."

WITHIN THE HOUR, after the dwarfling saddled the black griffin, Eljah returned with Borgrad.

Lauren rolled her eyes. "Of all the people to choose to go with me, you pick him?"

"Borgrad is a well-respected warrior. Few equal him in skill with the axe or morning star."

Lauren shook her head. "You understand he nearly ordered our deaths."

"Forgive me, Daughter Queen," Borgrad gruffed. He stood tall, his back straight, his shoulders pulled back, his chin lifted with arrogance. "I only did so out of my loyalty to the Council, to Adonai Himself." On his back, he wore a long-handled axe.

"He has guarded the Council faithfully for years," Eljah said. "He is also well skilled in defensive magic."

Lauren thought of Aiden. "The best defense is a good offense. I don't plan on retreating or hiding any time soon."

"You cannot foresee the future," Eljah said. He motioned to the dwarfling. "A saddled griffin for the honorable Borgrad."

The dwarfling waddled off, and Borgrad put a fist to his chest and dipped his head. "You are on the Council. It is my sworn duty to protect you. I offer my apologies for not trusting you earlier."

Lauren crossed her arms. This might be interesting. "If he slows me down, you'll have to send out a search party for him."

Borgrad smiled broadly, his braided mutton chops lifting from his shoulders. "You will be well pleased with my service, I'm sure, Daughter Queen."

She mounted the black griffin as the dwarfling ascended a short ladder and flopped a saddle on a white and black griffin beside her. It lowered its head, allowing the dwarfling to insert the bit in its beak.

On the griffin, Lauren felt eight feet tall, powerful. Between the majestic animal she rode and the power Adonai had awakened in her, she was invincible. Korodeth would cower at her feet, and she'd see him dead.

Eljah moved from the stables and lifted a hand toward her and Borgrad. "Go in peace, I pray you. May Adonai shelter you with mercy and love. May He guide your steps and your thoughts."

Lauren grinned with half her mouth. "Thank you, Eljah. May Adonai richly bless you."

She guided the griffin from the stable, and with a quick kick of her heels, the griffin flapped its wings. The muscles in its back lifted her, and she felt, for a moment, as if she were on a carousel, holding tight to a pole as her carved wooden animal rose and fell and spun. Soon, Borgrad's peppered griffin caught hers. They flew together, through the canopy of trees, until the leaves split and the brilliant blue sky of Alrujah burst into view. The suns hung high, and her stomach dropped. She rode, weightless, on the back of an animal she'd dreamed of since childhood.

"Magnificent, isn't it?" Borgrad asked. His wrinkly, scarred face had a certain charm, now that he didn't hold an axe to her throat. The wind wove through his bushy eyebrows, made them flutter like feathers.

"Why did you come?" she asked. She spoke as a queen, loud and forceful, from her diaphragm. She did not shout as Borgrad did, but her voice carried over the rush of air and the beating of massive wings.

"You are the Hand," Borgrad said, as if it were answer enough.

He smiled, yes, but at what? Riding a griffin? Being close to a queen, or a member of the Council? He didn't care for her, didn't love her as Aiden did. To him, she was only a crown, only a finger.

But that must be good enough for now.

19

"Be not troubled," says Almighty Adonai. "War will come and break the nations. Death will swallow kings. But for those who love Me, I will stretch out my Hand to protect them."
—The Book of Things to Come

BECCA LEAPT FROM HER CAR, engine still running, and sprinted toward the cliff. "I told you!" she shouted to Parker, two steps behind her. "I told you there was something about this cliff!"

"Slow down!" he called back. He caught her by the elbow inches from the precipice. "You can't go jumping off cliffs."

"Let me go!" She struggled to pull away, but Parker only tightened his grip.

He wouldn't let her leap off a cliff, no matter how much she believed there was a gateway on the other side. He admired her belief, her faith, but desperation fueled it; a dangerous combination.

Behind them, Franky's Jeep came to a fast halt. He and Aiden rushed to Parker's side. "Hold on," Franky said. "Let's make sure it's safe first."

Aiden kicked a rock over the side. They all leaned carefully over to get a good view of it.

Thirty feet down, it vanished.

"See?" Becca said. She tried again to pull herself from his grasp, but Parker held on tight.

"You have no idea where it leads. Even if it does go to Alrujah, the gate may be three hundred feet in the air instead of thirty."

"He's right," Franky said.

"It leads to Alrujah," she said with a terrifying serenity. With a final, violent pull, she wrested her elbow from his hand. She backed to the cliff, her heels hanging from the edge. "We have to go before it vanishes."

Parker swallowed. He took two quick breaths. The air warmed his lungs, and the scent of spring sprang through the leaves. His heart broke for her. He knew exactly how much she wanted her daughters back, knew she would gladly trade her life for theirs. He chose his words carefully. "What good will you be to them dead?"

"I won't be dead," she said.

"How do you know?" Aiden asked. "This is the second portal we've seen, Ms. Knowles, which means there's probably more. Let's find a safer one, okay?"

She shook her head. "I'm not waiting anymore."

Franky put his hand out to her. "Ms. Knowles, please."

Turning, she leapt.

Before Parker could reach her, before he could grab her, Aiden pushed past him. Becca and Aiden fell over together. Weightlessness moved in Parker's stomach, as if an elevator cable had snapped and sent him into free-fall instead of them.

"Aiden!" Franky said. He, too, leapt.

Parker dropped to his knees, bent over the cliff. The gateway shimmered menacingly. He expected sounds of cracking branches, of voices crying out in agony and fear. He heard only the breeze, only the distant hum of tires on pavement. He had no words, nothing to say, and no one to say it to.

He hadn't convinced himself he was in his right mind. And now, as he reviewed his options, he wondered if his decision came from the same insanity that plagued him since the four teenagers disappeared, or if he'd hit a new kind of crazy.

"Right," he whispered, slipping the damp end of his cigarette back in his mouth. He swung his feet over the edge and pushed himself off the cliff.

VICEROY DELVYN's disheveled red hair and long beard did not present a stately appearance. He looked more like a commoner than a governor, but the dark circles under his eyes and the weight of stress on his stooped shoulders marked him as a man in charge of a city on the brink of disaster. Instead of velvet or satin or whatever rulers wore, he bore the armor of a soldier, still stained with blood. He clanked when he walked and sat down with a heavy clang.

Breniveer, Erica, and Ullwen inclined their heads, fisted hands over their hearts. "What's with the bloody armor?" Erica whispered.

"Viceroy Delvyn used to be a Red Beard. He renounced his affiliation when Ribillius appointed him viceroy, but he maintains their battle customs."

"Clear as mud," she muttered.

A man in a brown robe stood beside the throne, his head down, hands in his sleeves. Another monk?

"My city prepares for war, and you bring me a broken-mind on which to pass judgment? Were you anyone else, Ullwen of Varuth, I would have you thrown from the Bell Tower. Your reputation and battle prowess alone stay my hand from your execution. And you, Breniveer the mind-witch, you of all people should understand the weightiness of this offense."

Breniveer nodded. "I do, Viceroy, and you have my apologies. If it were not an issue of city security, I would have dealt with it myself. But I do not have the power to pass judgment, nor the authority to order executions."

"Fifty stars, thirteen stripes."

Breniveer pointed to the man rocking in the wheelchair. "This man is a traitor of Adonai, an obsessed worshiper of Tiamat—the very evil we prepare to face in the coming days. His presence here jeopardizes the safety of the city."

Delvyn stood and approached Robert Hall. He inspected him closely, ran his fingers over the handles of the wheelchair, the aluminum frame, the wheels and spokes. "What contraption do you bind him to?"

Ullwen shifted his weight from one foot to the other—a nervous sign. "We found him this way, Viceroy."

"Found him?"

"He appeared with me," Erica said, holding her voice firm. If Ullwen worried before rulers, she didn't. She'd been through too much. The disapproval of a viceroy, even of a king, didn't much matter to her. Even if he ordered her thrown from the Bell Tower, she'd have a sasquatch catch her. If he attacked her, he'd have to fend off the thousands of bats she'd call to her aid, not to mention one very angry wolf. She scratched Sparky behind his ear.

"Viceroy," Breniveer said, her voice pinched with sorrow. "This man's crimes extend beyond the worship of Tiamat. He kidnapped my daughter."

"What was that?" Erica said.

"Must have been ten or eleven years ago," she said, struggling to keep her voice even. "He came to Port Smalth from Sylvonya. He whispered things, things no sane person would say. He was brought to me, to heal his mind. He spoke of traveling between Alrujah and another world. I tried to fix his mind, but before I could, he'd seen my daughter. My Lakia. She was six. He called to her. I told him to sit down, to calm down. But he chased after her, said she was *his* daughter. My husband wasn't home, you see. He was overseeing the city guard at the time.

"He grabbed her," Breniveer continued. "My daughter screamed. I had to protect her, you see. He ran from my door with her. I reached inside his mind, tried to make him drop her, but he resisted."

"You broke his mind," Erica whispered, her eyes wide.

"I had to, Viceroy. The man is evil. I felt something in his mind, something menacing and dark."

"Explain," Delvyn said, standing over Robert.

Robert's hands opened, wrists straining against the leather straps. "Fifty stars, thirteen stripes."

Breniveer continued. "It was another mind."

"He was already mind-witched?" Ullwen asked. "He cannot be held responsible for his actions."

"No," Breniveer said. "Not a human voice. Not a human mind."

"What are you saying?" Erica asked.

"I believe," she stammered, "it was the voice of Tiamat himself."

"Possession?" Delvyn roared.

"Tiamat was in his mind," Breniveer shouted. "He may still be. We must destroy this man, or Tiamat will come for him."

Ullwen stepped forward. "Viceroy, assuredly Tiamat is already coming. We must heal this man's mind and discover what he knows of Tiamat. He may prove a valuable weapon in the coming war."

"It's too dangerous," Breniveer said.

Erica's mind struggled to keep up.

Her father traveled between worlds? What had he said when he held her hands over the fire? She'd spent so many years trying to forget, the memory had faded to a distant haze. She remembered only the pain and the screaming. But he'd said something to her.

The man in the brown robe whispered something to the viceroy.

Erica clasped her hands over her ears and slammed her eyes shut. What did he say?

After school. Television on. He nearly breaks the door down when he comes in, the stench of blood and animal hot on his scrubs. He should be at work, elbow deep in an ailing Collie. He grabs her hard—his hands cold on her wrists. He squeezes so hard she screams.

It's not real. Only a memory.

Instinct kicks in. "I'm sorry!" she shouts to appease his wrath, though she'd done nothing wrong.

He ignites the gas burners on the stove.

Her mother's voice. "Stop it! Let her go, Robert! What are you doing?"

Does he hit her?

Yes. One hand comes free, cracks across her cheek. His hand comes back to her wrist fast, blood ridging his knuckles. He shoves her hands over the fire.

Pain erupts. The world blurs. Her tears spatter and steam through the flames. Her screams ring in her ears, but his voice circles the edges of consciousness, a boat caught in a whirlpool.

How it hurts! Her hands shake, and she shrieks and kicks, and he holds her with a crushing grip.

He says something. Yes, his voice pulls from the ether, from the sinking undertow. "Call for help!"

It's not real.

"I know you can call them! And if you can call them, you can call him!"

"He knew," she whispered.

"Can you fix him?" Delvyn asked the brown-robed man.

He'd taken his hands from his sleeves and put them on Robert's head. "Not alone. I would need the mind-witch."

So he can speak. As a rule, Erica didn't trust men standing behind kings and whispering in their ears. But the monastic robes lent him a little credibility, so long as they weren't black.

Robert's hands strained against the shackles, straining for the monk's throat. "Fifty stars, thirteen stripes."

"What's he saying?" Delvyn asked.

"Our flag," Erica said, "has fifty stars and thirteen stripes."

"Your flag?" Breniveer said. "You are from his world?"

Erica steeled her nerves and pulled her mind from childhood to Alrujah. "Momma, I have to tell you something."

Lauren and Borgrad soared for hours over the Yeval Forest, and hours more over the expansive plains north of Harland. From this height, Alrujah played out beneath her like a living map. Far to the east, the water of the Alrujah River sparkled under the waning light of the suns. The shimmering pencil line, as they flew, grew thicker and closer, widening to the stroke of a paintbrush, to a hand's width, to a highway.

They rode quietly, listening to the soundtrack of Alrujah—birds cawing from the sparse trees in the plains, frogs croaking their love songs near the bank of the river, bugs zipping past her ears, their wings buzzing, the gentle swoosh of griffin's wings pressing. Up and down. Her legs grew sore as she guided the massive animal as it rose and sunk, bobbing like a buoy at sea.

As the suns sank behind the Dragon's Back Mountains, she motioned to Borgrad to land near the river.

The heavily-armed dwarf nodded, his pale skin reflecting the sunslight. The griffins descended, galloping along the shoreline as they slowed themselves and stopped. Lauren slid off her mount and stroked its beak. "You're incredible," she said.

It nuzzled her shoulder and exhaled gently, its hot breath pouring from its nostrils.

"Does it have a name?" she asked Borgrad.

"Wind Dancer," Borgrad gruffed. "And mine's is Steel Beak."

She grinned. She'd named these griffins years ago. English class, if she remembered correctly. Each griffin had two-word names, as opposed to horses, which generally had one-word names. Her heart swelled from standing so close to the beasts. She'd never imagined such magnificence, such nobility and pride and beauty. She'd dreamed of riding them, hoping the digital experience might somehow give her a glimpse as to what it'd be like to ride one in real life. Now, she no longer had to imagine. She pulled raw bear meat from an enchanted saddlebag. Droughtworm had nearly driven the small packs of cattle and swine into extinction. The impact reached as far as the Heart of Yeval. They made do with the little meat they found.

Wind Dancer snatched it in its beak and swallowed it whole. Griffins weren't picky. Meat was meat, be it beef or pork or chicken or rabbit. In the wild, though, griffins hunted beresus and the occasional sasquatch.

Borgrad fed Steel Beak a slab of bear meat before hefting his axe and heading toward a nearby tree. "I'll return soon, Daughter Queen, with wood for a fire."

"Don't call me that."

"Why not?"

Lauren sighed and shifted her weight to her left foot while she pulled bread from the saddle bag. "Every time you say it, it reminds me my father is dead."

Borgrad twirled his axe. "As you wish. What would you have me call you?"

She shrugged. "Lauren, I guess."

"But is your name not Indigo?"

"That's fine, too."

Borgrad pulled at his braided sideburns. "I shall call you Indigo, then." He paused, mouth open, a question or statement barred by his thick tongue.

She waited, staring at him as she pulled a chunk of bread from the loaf and slipped it in her mouth. "Yes?"

He closed his mouth and frowned. His eyebrows danced as he spoke. "I'll return shortly."

20

And so Adonai threw Shedoah into the pit and sealed the pit with seven
seals. But Shedoah's taint weakened the bonds, and his chains groaned in
weary resistance.
—The Book of the Ancients

TRUE TO HIS WORD, Borgrad returned shortly, his axe on his back and arms full of cut wood. His chopping had echoed over the river and kept Lauren company as she marveled at the griffins. Wind Dancer lay close to Steel Beak. Lauren added river water to the pot of bear meat and vegetables and spices—carrots and onion, sage and oregano, potato and thyme. The water would add a hint of fish to the mix, but she didn't mind. Better than nothing. If she let it boil long enough, it'd thicken up to a nice stew instead of a soup.

Borgrad dropped the wood in a pile. Kneeling, he built a circle of stones and put pine needles beneath a tent of thin sticks. He banged two rocks together, grunting when the spark didn't take. His side-burns danced with his scarred cheeks.

Wrinkles did not groove his face, but scars; countless crisscrossed canyons and ridges, white valleys and pink berms. How many battles had this old dwarf weathered and lived to tell the tale? "Need a light?"

Borgrad nodded. "If it please you, fair Indigo."

She let heat line her fingertips and snapped. A flame consumed the needles, igniting a fire six feet high. It burned fast and hot, and eventually died down to embers. The tent of sticks collapsed in on itself, and the campfire came to life. Lauren hung the pot over the flames and sat on a saddlebag. She crossed her arms and shivered. She'd been quiet too long. Out of patience for awkward silences, Lauren spoke. "How long have you lived in Yeval?"

Borgrad warmed his hands by the fire. The flames cast a quivering orange hue on his pallid forehead. He frowned, and his bushy eyebrows lifted. "All my life. Sixty-six years." He waved the steam from the pot to his flat nose. "Delightful."

"Thanks."

The moon rose high overhead.

"So, your parents had you in Yeval?"

Borgrad nodded. "My mother, aye. My father died fighting the nar'esh."

Lauren stared at her boots. "I'm sorry."

Borgrad shrugged. "His sacrifice allowed my mother to escape."

"Do you miss him?"

"Hard to miss what you never had," he said.

Right. Stupid question. "You know I come from a different world, right?"

Borgrad nodded and stirred the soup.

"My home, where I come from, my father left me when I was six. So I kinda grew up without a dad, too."

"He was slain?"

She shook her head. How could she explain this to a dwarf—a race fiercely loyal to family? "Where I come from, men can be fickle. He ran away with another woman and left my mom to raise me and my sister."

"If he were a dwarf, he would pay for his infidelity with his head."

"Wouldn't that be nice?" she said.

Steel Beak yawned. His red tongue whipped out and curled back into his beak. The soup began to boil.

The salty scent cramped her belly. "Ribillius is my father here. And Korodeth took him from me. I mean to see him dead."

Borgrad tugged at his braided sideburns. "I mean to help, if I can. No child should ever be without a father."

Lauren rubbed the back of her neck and sighed. Power burned in her, and she longed to use it. She let the heat in her fuel the fire. Steam billowed from the pot, mixed with smoke. Sticks burned to cinders.

Borgrad took a step back. "I've not seen fire so hot. It needs more wood already."

"Save the wood," Lauren said. "I've got this."

Erica kept her explanation as simple as possible, avoiding unnecessary details whenever possible. They had little time, and she had few answers for the inevitable questions.

Robert knew.

Like her, he'd been pulled from his home and thrust into a strange and unfamiliar world, a world of magic and love. Or had it been different for him? Had he been born in Alrujah? Either way, the strain of two worlds had snapped his mind.

"How do you move from world to world? What magic do you use?" Delvyn asked her.

She blinked. Her eyes moved in flitting motions, from the burn scars on Robert's hands, to the bonds on his wrists, the dull aluminum of the wheelchair, to the viceroy's pale face. "I didn't do it. It just happened."

"Rapture," the brown-robed monk said. "Old magic, sealed by King Solous." He turned to Erica. "Where is this Oliver?" His whisper transformed into a voice of wonder. He pulled his hood back and stared at her like she had a disease, like he was any other jock at North Chester High, any other prom queen like Sarah Skeleton, afraid to stand too close, as if they'd contract some terminal social illness. He looked like them, too, with all his perfect black hair and pale perfect skin and piercing blue eyes.

"I don't know. After we kicked Belphegor's butt, I took off to rescue my parents."

The monk spoke softly. "You say he's a Monk of the Cerulean Order?"

"Yeah."

"The Hand of Adonai," Viceroy Delvyn whispered, a grin curling the edges of his lips. To the monk, he said, "The Hand is among us. Assuredly this means a coming victory."

Ullwen spoke, his voice firm. "Do not count victories before the final sword is swung. Adonai is with us, yes. But men may still die. We must do what we can to protect those who protect the city. This man may have knowledge that will help. We must heal him."

Breniveer steeled her voice and fisted her hands. "We must kill him quickly, Viceroy. He's dangerous. Healing will only make him more so."

Viceroy Delvyn took his place on the throne, set his hand on the hilt of the battle axe resting against the orange upholstered chair. "What do you say, world traveler?"

She didn't need this, didn't want this. This shouldn't be her decision, because she'd make the wrong one. No matter what she chose, it would end badly, and they would blame her. She wanted him dead. The burn scars on his fingers reminded her of those on the backs of her North Chester hands. She hadn't checked her hands since she'd been back in Alrujah, hadn't been strong enough.

"Fifty stars, thirteen stripes." His hands strained toward the monk, his wrists scarred in shiny pink skin like thick bracelets.

He'd taken everything from her. Murdered her mother. Burned her hands. Doomed her to a life of social exile, of awkward stares and laughter, a life of lazy foster parents more worried about state checks than the child they were supposed to care for, supposed to love. She'd never known love, not since she was six, not until she came here to Alrujah, and it was this man's fault.

He must die, but she wanted him to know she was the one killing him. She wanted him to see her, to remember, and to know, but he couldn't with a broken mind.

Delvyn stood, hefted the heavy axe on his shoulder. "Should you choose to have him executed, I'll do so immediately. If you say he is to be healed, the mind-witch and the monk will begin the process immediately."

"Be strong, dear," Breniveer said. She kissed Erica's forehead. "I will love you no matter what choice you make. You're far from defenseless now. But I still think he should pay."

"Me, too," Erica said. Her heart tightened in her chest, and her breath came in tight, fast gasps.

Instead of Robert's hands and wrists, instead of his shackled ankles, Erica stared at his eyes. She recognized the blank, motionless stare—she'd seen it on the bear whose mind she broke.

She understood then: Robert was a wounded animal. No matter how much she wanted him dead, no matter how much she wanted revenge for her mother and for the last lousy eleven years of her life, she wouldn't murder an injured beast.

Erica sighed. "If Adonai wants him dead, He'll have to do it himself. Let's heal him. I want him to see my face before he dies."

FREEFALL. Weightless.

Parker was a child again, leaping from the high dive at the public pool near his apartments. How long had it been since he felt this young, this terrified, half-expecting to die, half-expecting to yellow the pool?

Thin with warmth, the air snapped to a chill as it grabbed his overcoat and threw it over his head, the fabric pulling at his shoulders. *God help me. God help us all.* Seconds later, he dropped through the shimmer.

He expected to feel something, like plunging into cold, dark waters, the sting of impact reddening his skin. His muscles tensed, and he drew in his breath, holding it tight in his lungs, expecting a splash, expecting a bone-crushing landing.

Instead, in a puff of white, he dropped into several feet of snow.

As a kid, he'd made angels in the snow, his arms and legs stiff and frigid, cold pinking his face.

The impact knocked the wind from his lungs. He tried to groan, but his chest seized. He blinked twice, marveling at the shimmer hovering feet above him.

He should be dead. What were the chances the dumb portal-thing opened above snow this deep?

His breath came back to him and he stood, brushing the crystalline snow from his sleeves and slacks. "Didn't expect this," he mumbled. Instinctively, he patted his pockets, then checked behind his ear.

No cigarette.

He swallowed, hoping to quell the fear in his gut. He scanned the white snow. There, a few feet away, lay his sole cigarette. He grabbed it, slipped it between his lips. The damp end froze. Like sucking on a nicotine icicle. He'd switch to gum, but it'd be too hard to keep between his lips. He scanned the area for Becca, for Franky and Aiden, but the thick, swirling snow made it near impossible. The world around him ran white, only turning to grayish shadows beyond his limited eyesight. "Becca!"

"I'm here." The voice came from the left, but the echo made it hard to track.

"Where?" he said.

"Over here," Aiden said.

Parker squinted. Three silvery shadows walked toward him. "You guys good to go?"

"Nothing broken," Becca said as she limped through the knee-deep snow drift. "Twisted my knee, I think. And I'm cold."

"So where are we?" Franky asked.

"Dragon's Back Mountains," Becca said. She leaned on Parker's shoulder, and he put an arm around her waist.

Aiden walked forward. "Stay with me. We need to get off this mountain and find someplace warm."

"How far's the walk?" Parker asked.

Becca leaned on him heavily. "Depends on where we are in the mountains. We're on the Alrujah side. We can head straight down."

Behind the haze of snow and clouds, two bright lights diffused into silver disks. Two suns? He'd read about that in Lauren's journal, but seeing it was something far different.

Thank God they wouldn't have to climb. Parker doubted his legs had it in them. Walking in snow this deep was tough enough. Climbing higher might prove fatal.

Franky held Aiden's sword while Aiden donned his armor.

"Sure you want to do that?" Parker asked. "It'll slow you down, and I'm guessing the metal's pretty cold. Might throw yourself into hypothermia."

Aiden didn't slow. Instead, he pointed. "Ms. Knowles, take them down. I'll catch up in a minute. Think I caught a glimpse of Pellbred."

"I saw it, too," she said. "Greenish light, to the east."

"Follow it. The swamps sit in a valley, should be warmer. We can rest for the night and get whatever supplies we need."

It'd happened faster than Parker expected—Aiden took charge. In North Chester, Aiden respected Parker's badge, listened to him. Here, Aiden held the authority. His confident voice belied his age. Franky deferred to him, even Becca, who, by her own admission, used to be the queen of this place. But his directions made sense, and Parker couldn't think of a better plan, so he moved forward with a cautious urgency—enough to keep Becca moving and warm, but not so fast as to leave her behind.

They'd only made it about twenty yards downhill before Aiden, complete in his shining armor, walked alongside them. "Enchanted," he said, answering Parker's earlier question. "Keeps me warm in the cold."

"Must be nice," Parker said. He pulled his jacket tighter around him. The snow pressed against his legs. His shins went numb. His feet tingled. He wiggled his toes with each step, hoping the additional blood flow would keep them warm. He had no desire to deal with frostbite.

Becca shivered.

They walked for an hour. Parker stamped, rather than stepped. The snow had gone from knee-deep to ankle deep, and they made better time. Trees split the snow, and the foot of the mountain finally came into view. Greenish lights shimmered in the distance as if underwater. Parker clenched his teeth to keep them from chattering.

"Almost there," Aiden said.

"Good thing, too," Franky said. "Can't feel my toes."

"Can't feel anything," Becca said. "Not sure I can go much further."

"Sure you can," Parker said. He picked her up, knees in one arm, shoulders in the other.

She laughed and brushed the snow from his shoulders. "This isn't what I expected," she said.

"I don't think anyone expected it," Franky said.

"Another hour, tops," Aiden said. "Then we can rest."

"Dude, we're not all crazy conditioned knights. I can't even catch my breath."

"Want me to carry you, bro?"

"Can't we stop for a bit? Build a fire or something?"

"You got a lighter?" Aiden asked Parker.

"I wish," he said.

"You got smokes, but no light?"

"Long story," Becca said.

"Seriously, bro, let me carry you."

"Not going to happen."

"Wait a minute," Parker said. He turned to Franky. "Know how to snowboard?"

Franky grinned. "Dude. I live in North Chester."

"Don't call me 'dude,'" Parker said. "Or 'bro.'" He eyed Aiden's shield. "Why not put that thing to work?"

21

"From my Hand," says Almighty Adonai, "I will bring rest to the weary,
peace to the troubled, health to the sick, and life to the dead."
—The Book of Things to Come

LAUREN TRIED NOT to think of Korodeth, but her mind returned to the oily-haired usurper every few minutes. The peaceful currents of the Alrujah River didn't soothe her. Neither did the gentle breeze, the rustling of the woods to the west, nor the quiet squawking yawns of the griffins or their playful pawing.

Borgrad shivered. "Spring comes, but here it is cold," he said.

Lauren's fault. Her chilled blood cooled the air like an open freezer, but her anger stoked the flames of the campfire. Already, a few short hours after sunsdown, they'd burned through the wood Borgrad collected, enough to last through the night if her anger hadn't heated the flames. The stew tasted good, but even the broth turned her mind to the famine spreading through the land, to the proliferation of droughtworm among her people. And what did Korodeth do to help?

He killed the king, her father, the one man who might have been able to do some good.

She stood up and marched toward the woods.

"Where are you going, Indigo?"

"To get more wood," she said.

"If I may, I will accompany you."

"You should stay here with the camp in case bandits show up or something."

"I've neither seen nor heard any evidence to suggest the coming of bandits, and we have the griffins beside. Steel Beak and Wind Dancer are fully capable of defending our camp."

Borgrad may be a wrinkly old dwarf who'd threatened her, but he knew what it meant to grow up without a father. Even if she didn't want him along, he wanted to go. His company may take her mind off Korodeth. "Okay. Let's go."

Borgrad leapt up and fastened his axe to his back. He moved quickly despite his short legs. He slung his braided sideburns over his shoulders and walked beside her. "I must apologize. I should not have questioned you in the Heart."

Lauren shrugged. "Kind of your job."

"If I had known *The Book of Things to Come* better, I would have known."

"Maybe." This far outside of Yeval, no rognak or harspus trees grew. Instead, oaks and maple, chestnut and cedar, made up the woods near Orensdale. Rather than a sharp scent of pine, these woods smelled like a school yard, like harvest festivals at Oliver's church. Strange, to remember Halloween now. How many heads would she turn at a party dressed like this, and to show up with a dwarf? They'd win best costume for sure. The idea stilled her nerves, and she smiled at Borgrad. "Smells like Halloween," she said.

"Halloween?" the dwarf asked, his boots swishing through grass.

"An old tradition in North Chester." She ducked a branch—something Borgrad seldom worried about. "Once a year, we dress up in scary costumes and give out sweets."

"In whose honor? Was Halloween a respected warrior or a political leader?"

Lauren shook her head. Ridges lined the bark of the branches like stretch marks, as if each tree were a proud mother. "Neither. It's silly. Don't even know why we do it, but we do. A lot of our holidays are like that."

Borgrad stooped to tie his boot. "My mother spoke to me of dwarven holidays. The Feast of the Eagle, which we celebrate in the spring with roast boar and fruit wine. It honors Adonai's coming to Solous. Shortly after, there is the Feast of the Suns, to honor Solous's establishment of the throne of men. Degnar's rout of Togan is honored with an evening of silence in the autumn. Karan's victory over his older brother Rilin is honored by the planting of a rognak. And we honor the blessed mother Coilana, mother of dwarves, with a day of prayers."

Though the wind stilled, the branches trembled. Lauren stopped. Twigs twitched.

Nothing. Must be a trick of the light. "Christmas is the day we honor Jesus's birth. We chop down a tree and decorate it and sing songs and exchange gifts."

"Why decorate a dead tree? Was this Jesus a woodsman?"

Lauren smiled as she walked further into the woods. "No, but I see your point. It does feel a little silly." She stopped. Something between the trees caught her attention, some sort of shadowy orb. The basketball shape rested atop a stick. She moved forward and flashed a ball of flame in her hand to cut through the blackness. She intensified the flame until the image became clear.

Stuck on a stick sharpened at both ends, the head of a beresus lolled to one side. Loose bloodied flesh dangled from the neck, as if a sasquatch had ripped it from the body.

What animal would post the head on a stick? Not a sasquatch. Not the nar'esh. Only humans would do something so profane.

Or an elf or dwarf.

"What is it?" Borgrad asked.

Her blood ran cold, and the air frosted. Her breath came out in billows of silvery steam. She moved closer, fighting back waves of nausea as the acrid smell of decomposing flesh hit her nostrils.

"What is it?" Borgrad asked again, his axe poised at the ready.

"Evil," Lauren said. Oliver's staff shook in her hand.

She'd felt this before, moments before they fought Belphegor, and again before Moloch and the Seers.

A tall man in a white robe stepped from behind the trees.

Lauren's blood iced. She didn't wait for him to speak. Though he held *The Book of Sealed Magic*, Lauren thought she might be able to best him as long as she held Oliver's staff. She lifted her hand to smother him in a white-hot beam of pure light, but the Mage Lord absorbed the attack with his obsidian-tipped partisan.

"I am not your enemy," he said. "These things must be done, and you must do them."

"I'm not doing anything you want me to do," she said.

Borgrad raised his axe. "Shall I cut him for you, Daughter Queen?"

"He won't be here long enough," Lauren said.

The Mage Lord's eyes glowed gold from behind his black mask. "Like you, I serve Adonai."

"You're nothing like me."

Flies circled the head, buzzed in and out of the ears, crawled over the yellowed fangs. The skin of the nostrils peeled back from the bone of the nose. Instead of eyes, two glowing coals sat in empty sockets.

"Soon, you will have the answers you seek. I will send for you when I am ready."

"Don't expect me to come running."

The Mage Lord lifted his partisan, and he blinked away in a shimmer of silver light.

The beresus head smiled. "Daughter Queen of Alrujah," it said. "Borgrad son of Horin. You have no place in my woods."

"Your woods?" The heat of indignation eclipsed Lauren's chill of fear. "These are my woods. I'm the Queen of Alrujah."

"So you are, but we are Legion, and all Orensdale is mine. The head twisted on the stick. The coal eyes surveyed the trees around it. Its lips peeled back in a sickening grin. "You are in our home, without an invitation."

A small blue light rose from the patchy fur of the head, floated to a nearby tree.

The tree groaned and wrested its roots from the ground. Its branches twisted and stretched, clutching at Lauren.

LONG BEFORE THEY reached the city walls, Aiden spotted the dilapidated homes on the outskirts of Pellbred swamp. Their damp, wooden walls rotted near the corners. Entire slats fell like soggy cardboard to the rocky crags rising from the brownish watery causeways. Even here, hundreds of feet off, the air thickened with a greenish, damp tint.

Rickety wooden bridges ran between the homes, built on edges of rocks, on stilts, around rotting trees. Murky green waters ran under the wooden platforms. The thick, greenish air held more warmth than the side of the mountains had. Already, Parker and Becca looked better, warmer, stronger. He'd worried about them more than he had Franky, but even Franky, toward the end, had started to shiver and slow, like he might drop over from the cold.

"Is that Pellbred?" Franky asked, pointing to the stone walls rising from the brownish muck of swamp water near the center of the homes and small shops on the outskirts of the town.

"Yes," Becca said. She leaned on Parker and favored her left knee. "We'll be lucky if they let us in. Pellbred likes its privacy."

"Does it always smell like this?" Parker asked.

Aiden hadn't realized it until Parker mentioned it, but the thickening air carried a pungency like the dead beresus—like vinegar and rotten fruit. His eyes watered, and each breath made his throat itchy.

"You get used to it," Aiden said. "Eventually."

Franky pulled his shirt over his nose. "At least it's not a million degrees below zero here."

Parker wrinkled his nose. "Don't suppose there's a Hilton around? I could go for a hot shower and shave."

"There's an inn, yes," Becca said. "At least there was when I was here last."

"The Griffin's Paw," Aiden said. "Tiny little thing. A few rooms, but they're probably open. Pellbred doesn't get many visitors."

Franky said, "If they've got someplace to sit and a fireplace, I'm for it."

They moved further along, through dark hemlocks and oaks, ancient gnarled trees. Aiden blinked back tears, but he didn't hold his breath. Already, though they moved further into the outlying town, the smell lessened. Another few minutes and they'd no longer notice it, but what a grueling few minutes it would be.

Stepping over roots that weaved in and out of loose, damp soil, he pointed to a rickety two-story building with a thatch roof. It'd been built on rock, but a massive hemlock supported the second story. More of a treehouse than a tavern. "There." He stepped onto the ramshackle wooden bridge spanning the muddy waters. Cicadas called to each other. Mosquitoes darted over the stagnant water. Dragonflies roamed lazily over the swamp, to the trees and back again. Frogs croaked. Somewhere, a dog barked.

The wooden bridge bowed under his weight. By the quality of the boards, Aiden judged several planks had been replaced recently. Others hadn't, but they'd likely need to be in a few more days. Repair work kept many in Pellbred working. "Watch your step," he said. "Stick to the new planks best you can. Don't want to fish any of you out of the muck."

Parker walked behind him, Becca leaning heavily on him. Her knee must be worse off than she let on. Aiden would check it out once they got inside. A few weeks ago, he wouldn't have had to worry about a twisted knee. Oliver healed all sorts of pains, but with him gone, every bump, every bruise would linger and fester. He sighed as they walked up to the Griffin's Paw. "Stay here," he said. "Until we can get you some appropriate clothes, it's best you stay out of sight as much as possible."

"What's wrong with my clothes? I paid good money for these," Franky said.

"Not exactly fitting in," Parker said.

"So, clothes first?" Franky said.

"Becca needs to get off her knee," Aiden said.

"And we all need to rest," Parker said.

Aiden moved inside.

The innkeeper, a vapid young woman with stringy black hair, leaned both elbows on a desk in bad need of good repair and eyed him suspiciously. "More soldiers? Hardly have room for the ones King Korodeth already sent." The girl straightened, blinked twice in rapid succession, a trait most Pellbreders shared. "Would be nice if he told us where to put you all. As it is, I've got too many bodies in this shack. You'll have to go someplace else."

Before he could stop himself, Aiden asked, "King Korodeth?" He had missed too much. How long had he been gone? What happened to Ribillius? Whatever had transpired in his absence, it wasn't good. They were all in danger, though he didn't know the exact type of danger. He needed to think, to figure this out, to find a way to get to his friends, but he had no idea how to find them or contact them. "Where else can we go?"

His voice must have been softer, because she smiled. "Why can't you go back to camp, soldier?"

If he didn't know any better, he'd think she was flirting with him. He put it out of mind and searched instead for a good excuse, a good reason. He returned her smile, hoping the friendly gesture might persuade her. "I have need of supplies. They work us hard at the camp, and I thought I might rest here for the night."

Her smile broadened. She pulled her fibrous hair over her knobby shoulder. "Why not gather those supplies, soldier. I'll see if I can't find you a room."

"Your kindness is appreciated." He thought about leaving, but a familiar sparkle of hope gleamed in her eye.

Lauren had the same sparkle in North Chester, whenever they talked about his essay. She sparkled in Alrujah, too. At least she had, when they first started talking. Somewhere along the line, maybe in the nar'esh cave, she'd stopped. He hadn't realized, until now, how much he missed it.

His smile pulled into a serious stare. "I'll have some dignitaries with me," he said. "Will there be room for all of us?"

Her smile vanished. "How many?"

"Three more."

"Cute as you?" she asked.

He grinned. "One is of an age with you, and cuter than me."

She blinked twice. Her lips bent into a wry grin. "I'll have a room ready for you within the hour."

ERICA CROSSED her arms and held her elbows. She rested her head on Ullwen's broad shoulders. Breniveer sat in front of Robert.

His arms reached for her. "Fifty stars, thirteen stripes."

The monk took up a staff and pulled his hood over his face. He stretched out his arm toward Robert, gripped the staff in the other hand, and muttered something in a language Erica didn't understand. Aside from the robe being brown, his posture, his voice, reminded her of Oliver. She missed him, missed his affection and affirmation. She had liked him, the awkward little nerd. For a while, she figured she would end up with him, if he'd take her. But she doubted he'd ever have loved her. No one had, not since her mother died. Eventually, he would've grown tired of her sarcasm and insecurities and left her.

But Ullwen stood next to her now, in all his woodsy-smelling manliness. His arm around her—something even the most daring couples in Alrujah didn't do—told her something; he'd stick around. He'd already seen the worst of her, her biting wit, her condescension, her insecurities. He had stayed by her bed while she healed from near fatal wounds.

But none of that compared to the simple fact that he came with her. She'd hardly asked, and he had packed for both of them. Sure, Oliver offered to go with her, but he didn't fight for the honor.

No matter how cutting her jibes toward Ullwen, no matter how hairy her legs were or how bad her pits smelled, the man stood next to her and never commented once about her overgrown eyebrows. He protected her, shielded her, healed her, lifted her up.

He had never said he loved her. He showed her.

What was it about men so lethal that got her heart racing?

"Tiamat's hold is strong," the monk said.

Finally, some English. Or Alrujahn, or whatever you called it here.

Robert's normally passive, mundane voice jumped an octave. "Fifty stars, thirteen stripes!"

Whatever the monk did, it worked.

Breniveer closed her eyes and took slow, measured breaths. She touched Erica's mind, impressed a thought. *This is a bad idea.*

I know, Momma.

"Don't fear," Ullwen said.

"I'm not. I figure if he tries anything, he's got to get through you before he gets to me, right?"

"Right."

Robert's rocking turned violent. He shook, as if a seizure gripped him.

"What's happening?" Delvyn asked, rising from his throne.

"Tiamat resists," the monk said, his voice strained. He tapped the staff on the ground three times and prayed louder.

Erica picked out two words: Tiamat and Adonai. He said them over and over again, split by two or three other words she didn't recognize. Each time he said Adonai, Robert shook harder.

"I can see him," Breniveer said. "Tiamat's hold is weakening. Keep at it."

"Fifty stars! Fifty stars!"

The monk dropped to a knee, then rose weakly, his legs shaking beneath his robe. "You have no power here, Tiamat! His soul belongs to Adonai!"

Robert shrieked and lashed out. The shackles on his wrists snapped. He leapt toward Breniveer, but Ullwen moved faster, tackling the man, flipping the chair, still shackled to his ankles.

Robert's mouth opened, and he roared. His hands found Ullwen's neck and squeezed.

"Kill him!" Erica said, kicking her father in the ribs. "Let Ullwen go!"

Ullwen grabbed Robert's wrists in opposite hands, twisted them from his neck and pinned them to the ground.

Robert flailed, but Ullwen proved too strong.

"Got him!" Breniveer said.

The monk collapsed, breathless. He wheezed. "Tiamat's hold has been broken."

Robert ceased thrashing and stared up at Ullwen blankly.

"Is he resisting?" Erica asked.

"No," Breniveer said with disappointment. "He's cooperating."

"How bad is the damage?" Delvyn asked.

Breniveer squinted. "His mind is unlike anything I've seen. It's arranged differently. Give me a moment."

A roar shook the castle walls.

Norby's voice sailed through the glassless windows of the castle. "Steady, men! Shields and arrows! Arm the catapults!"

The door to the throne room burst open. A young boy, breathless, called to Delvyn. "Sylvonya attacks!"

A massive animal, the largest she'd felt in Alrujah or North Chester, pulled on Erica's mind. It swam deep, but the presence moved with alarming speed toward the surface of the water.

A new voice spoke, one so soft Erica didn't recognize it at first. "He's here," Robert said.

22

"I will wipe the taint of Adonai from Alrujah. I will break the worlds and reform my creation from the ashes of the usurper Adonai," says Shedoah the Mighty. "From its death I will bring forth life."
—The Shedoahn Prophecies

THE TREE GRABBED for Lauren with its twisted, gnarled branches.

No freaking way.

Lauren rolled away from the creaking branches. They might sound arthritic, but they moved more like leopards than zombies.

Borgrad leapt from another tree, also made animate by a glowing sphere from Legion. Several more swam into the surrounding trees. The whole wood uprooted itself and chased after them. Borgrad deflected attacks with his axe.

She needed Oliver. He'd have erected some sort of shield by now. He'd have done something.

Borgrad moved swiftly, chopping branches like a lumberjack on speed. She understood why Yarborough had been so terrified when entering the Heart. If he'd wanted to, Borgrad could have cut through her, Bailey, and Yarborough by himself.

How his axe never dulled baffled her. She rolled under a sweeping branch.

Roots snaked up from the soil and grabbed her like angry tentacles, trying to pull her under the dirt.

"Hold on," Borgrad shouted, swinging his axe through a cedar.

Lauren reached within her, found a tremor, not of fear, but of anger. She opened her palms, and the ground shook. Their roots released her and whipped underground, but they could not support the weight of the walking tree. It collapsed and fell like timber before her.

Borgrad flung his axe in a hemlock and grabbed the maple branch closest to him. He shouted a word she didn't recognize, something long and guttural, and the brown bark of the tree hardened to pale granite. A chestnut twirled, its branches shattering on the stone tree.

Impressive, but it may not be enough to hold off the number of trees attacking them. She pulled power from Oliver's staff, struggling to formulate an attack plan.

Trees lumbered toward her, their branches creaking and reaching. She leapt over a gnarled oak limb. The trunk roared at her, its knots reshaping into eyes. The bark somehow transformed into a type of skin. Fire rumbled up her throat. Her fingertips burned like blisters. She readied a massive fireball but thought better of it. Hard enough to avoid swipes from swinging branches; dodging flaming limbs might be impossible. Electricity would have little effect, and ice would take too long. "Little help!"

Borgrad heeded her call, chopping his way toward her. He turned another tree to stone, and another. "I have little power left."

She needed time. Maybe attacking wasn't the right strategy now. Rolling under a smashing attack, she set up a blue shield over her and the dwarf. Oliver had done the same when they fought Moloch, but now, as the trees righted themselves and punched for them, she understood the amount of power it required.

Angry birches splintered their limbs on the blue shield, but the enchantment held. The shield bought them time, but little else. Each blow weakened the shield and drained her magic.

The staff shook in her hand. It took too much power, even with the new reserves she'd received from Adonai "We've got like twelve seconds in here," she said.

Borgrad gripped the staff. Immediately, whatever power he possessed strengthened the shield. "We cannot hold long," he said. "We need a plan."

Lauren focused on the sneering face of the beresus head, the glowing coals for eyes. Its decomposing lips twisted into a sinister grin as blue orbs possessed the woods.

Souls, she realized, like the Seers.

"If we smash the head, the rest should die, right?"

Borgrad's braids trailed behind him as he rolled out of the shield toward the head.

Legion sneered as Borgrad pulled his axe from the fallen hemlock. "Little dwarf, how do you think to approach me?"

Two cedars fell before him. The impact shook the ground, and Borgrad rolled away.

Lauren let the shield fall. She needed another strategy.

The staff trembled in her hand. Amidst the sharp shrieks of branches creaking, of trees wailing, of trembling stones and shifting soil, the still, calm voice of Adonai touched her ears.

Pull.

Yes. She would pull.

She lifted the staff, reached inside her for the little power she had left, and pulled at the orbs. Three of the glowing spheres rocketed into the staff.

She pulled again, and several more orbs stretched from the head, turning from spheres to ovals to eggs, to tentacles, to tendrils of blue smoke. They screamed as they entered the staff.

Whatever dark magic Legion wielded, he used it now to hold the orbs away from Oliver's staff.

"Keep at it!" Borgrad said, smashing the limbs rushing toward her.

The souls rattled in the staff. Their power and anger shook the wood. She touched it, and her magic reserves replenished. She did not want to think where the orbs came from, who they'd been before they'd died, before they'd been tortured by the forced removal of their souls.

She pulled.

Legion wailed.

"How many does he have?" Borgrad shouted.

"Thousands," she said.

"Can you get them all?"

"Before or after they kill us?"

She extended a hand toward Borgrad and let the power of the souls extend to him.

The dwarf wasted no time in changing trees to granite. By the end of this fight, this place would be called the stone forest.

"We are many," Legion buzzed. It opened its mouth, and a thousand orbs spewed out like a swarm of lightning bugs.

She had little chance of pulling so many, but she grabbed all she could. The remaining orbs disappeared into a pack of dark shadows in the night sky.

Shrieks split the sky, low and guttural, rumbling like a panther's purr. A pride of griffins, and all possessed by Legion. As they dropped from the sky, angry shrills like trains braking on wet tracks, she saw them in the middle. The black fur and the gray, the orange beak and the white. Wind Dancer and Steel Beak.

A SHOWER OF COLD, of numbness, froze Erica.

"Tell us how to beat it," Ullwen shouted.

Robert blinked fast. His eyes circled the room. "Where am I?"

Delvyn knocked Ullwen off Robert, grabbed the thin man by the neck, and lifted him with a growl. He brought his axe back and stared at the man, whose feet dangled inches above the stone floor. "Tell us or I'll throw you from the Bell Tower!"

Robert, holding the thick wrist of Delvyn, gasped. His eyes met Erica's, and his face fell. "Not you," he whispered.

"Better believe it's me." Fury filled her voice. "I could have killed you."

Fire erupted outside the castle walls. Battle sounds assaulted the castle; thin rings of steel on armor, thick bodies falling on cobbled streets. Tiamat's roars echoed across the Alrujahn Sea.

"Which one are you?" he asked.

Breniveer, her mind now disconnected from his, balled her hands up in fists. "The same one you tried to steal from me eleven years ago!"

Erica said, "Doesn't matter. You scarred us both."

Robert gripped Delvyn's wrists. His legs kicked. "You called him, didn't you? I knew you could."

Erica said, "I was six, Robert."

"He's here. Oh, God! We're dead. We're all dead."

"You die first!" Delvyn rumbled. He brought the axe toward Robert, but Ullwen deflected the blow with his sword.

Ullwen pressed toward Robert, his bearded face inches from Robert's purpling cheeks. "What do you know about Tiamat? You studied it, worshiped it. You must know its weakness."

"He's unstoppable," Robert said. "When he rises from the water, your axes will prove a mercy compared to his jaws."

Delvyn dropped him, and Robert crumpled to his knees. "Stay with him," Delvyn told the monk. "If he thinks of something, notify me immediately."

"Where are you going?" Breniveer asked.

"To aid my men. Finish quickly. We'll need each of you on the battlefield." He raced from the door, bellowing for his guards to follow.

Robert gasped and choked, holding his neck. "Forgive me," he spluttered. "I didn't mean to. He had my mind. He made me do it. He wanted to find a way into Earth."

Erica's fingertips tingled. She wanted to kick the man, to hit and scream and scratch and bite. She took a breath and focused on the problem. "Figure out a way to kill Tiamat. Then maybe I can forgive you."

Robert's shoulders sank. "His scales are impenetrable. He breathes fire, he swims like water dragons, and flies like griffins. Nothing can hurt him, not swords or axes or arrows, nothing made of steel or iron."

"Is he telling the truth?" Ullwen asked Breniveer.

"Yes. I told you we should have killed him."

"Maybe in North Chester. Maybe a tank, or a bomb." Robert closed his eyes for a moment, before he opened them and looked at Erica. "My daughter. My only child. How old are you now?" He reached toward Erica, but Breniveer smacked his arm away.

"Don't ever touch her, monster. She is my child, not yours. She was never your child!"

"How does it breathe fire?" Ullwen asked.

His cheek still glowing red, Robert said, "I hardly think it matters."

"Tell us."

"He has two glands, one on either side of his throat. They each produce a biochemical. When the two mix, they ignite. But they're buried deep in his throat, beneath his impenetrable scales."

"What if I were inside its mouth?" Ullwen asked.

Robert leaned against the stone wall. "You mean, let him swallow you?" His frown broke, his eyes shifting from floor to ceiling, from wall to wall. "He would not swallow you." With his eyes on Erica, he said. "But he would swallow me."

THE ROOM in the Griffin's Paw smelled mildly better than the swamp outside. Oil lanterns burned dimly on a warped bedside table. Parker stood next to it, breathing in the smoke. The perfumed oil made it sweet, like pipe tobacco. He'd not smoked a pipe in ten years. Cigarettes had consumed his tobacco funds for more than the last decade. Sweet or not, the smoke settled his nerves and his stomach. He wasn't a huge vanilla fan, but any scent was better than the stench outside.

Becca sat on the bed, her hand in his. Strangely, he didn't pull it away. In this world, professional distance didn't hold the same importance.

Franky stood in the corner and opened the door for Aiden, who backed in, arms full of armor and weaponry. Swords and shields. "Let's have you try this gear on before we turn in for the night," Aiden said. "In a pinch, you'll need to know how to get it on quick."

Parker had worn Kevlar body armor, never steel. "Looks too heavy. I'll stick with the villager clothes. Easier to grab my Beretta."

"Bad idea, bro. You only got fifteen rounds. It'd take four or five to drop anything bigger than a razorbeak."

Parker needed a cigarette. "Call me Parker?"

"You need the armor," Aiden said.

He squeezed Becca's hand. She'd back him up on this, wouldn't she?

She shrugged. "It can get pretty scary at night," she said.

"Fine," he said. He picked up a sword, twisted it in the lantern light. The orange and blue flames flickered off the steel. Four feet long and less than four pounds. He arched an eyebrow. "Figured these things would be heavier."

Aiden sorted through the pile while Franky peered over his shoulder. "Broadswords are, but you want a one-hand sword, something quick to parry attacks and allow you to use a shield. Swing it fast enough, that blade will cut through almost anything."

"It ain't quicker than a bullet."

Aiden shook his head. "Save your bullets. You never know when you'll need them."

"I've never even held anything like this. How'm I supposed to swing it?"

Aiden said, "You swing a bat? Play Frisbee? Golf? It's all in the wrist."

Becca said, "Besides, we don't need all the attention a gun would bring. We want to blend in, make our way to Alrujah, and find my daughters."

Franky grabbed a breastplate and examined his warped reflection. "Don't know about that, Ms. Knowles. Darcy said Alrujah's splitting up or something. Some sort of civil war."

"Darcy?" Parker twisted a knob and lengthened the fabric wick of the oil lamp. The smoke came heavier.

"The innkeeper," Franky said. "Black hair. Funny grin. Blinks a lot. You know."

Parker said, "Didn't know her name. You talked to her for a while."

"Yeah." Franky lifted a shield and examined the leather straps on the back. "Anyway, the death of Ribillius turned things all upside down. A lot of the cities don't trust Korodeth. She said something about Dalova naming itself the new capital or something."

"Not while I'm alive," Aiden said. He helped Franky strap on the breast plate. "We head to Alrujah. That's where Erica was going when she split off from the group. We'll find her and Ullwen. When we do, she can send out a razorbeak to find the others."

Parker strapped steel greaves to his shins. Surprisingly, it only weighed a few pounds. Still, he felt ridiculous, like he was going to some renaissance faire or a bad costume party. "Tell me we don't have to walk all the way there."

Aiden handed Becca a small brown bag. "Ginger root," he said. "Should help with the knee."

Becca took it, bit off a piece and chewed. She gestured to her armor with the half-gnawed root. "Last time I wore something like that, I was a queen. And an elf."

Aiden nodded toward the window. "Should be a ferryman a couple miles west. We can catch a ride there, take it all the way down to Alrujah."

Franky slipped his helmet on and shook his head. "Dalova has control of the Alrujah and Fellian Rivers. They're not letting anyone pass."

"How much did Darcy tell you?" Parker asked.

Franky grinned. "More than she should have."

"How'd you get her to talk?" Aiden asked, helping Parker strap on his breastplate.

Franky blushed and scratched the stubble on his throat. "I sang to her. She likes my voice."

"I knew you had it in you," Aiden said. It wouldn't have been easy for Franky when he was so hung up on Bailey still, but Aiden thought the move would help them get the information they needed. Besides, if Franky wanted to make a home in Alrujah, he'd need to make Alrujahn friends.

"Whatever helps us find my daughters," Becca said, her voice steel strong. Even with a sore knee, she carried herself with a regal confidence.

Parker liked the change, appreciating the mettle in her voice. "So we're back to walking?"

"Not necessarily," Franky said. "We can catch a ride on a supply wagon. They run from the camp to Alrujah almost daily. The route is secured by Alrujah."

Aiden smiled as he unfastened the breastplate from Franky. "You can't pass Econ, but you remember all that from a ten-minute conversation with Blinky? That voice of yours may be your best weapon."

Franky's eyes sparkled. "Like you said; use what I got."

23

There is one coming who will remake the worlds, who will fashion a new
Alrujah. He will conquer the evil with a scepter of peace.
—The Book of Things to Come

AIDEN STRUGGLED TO SLEEP. He sat on the floor in the corner of the small room of the Griffin's Paw. He'd shed his armor and, though the inn was far warmer than the Dragon's Back Mountains had been, the mild chill still challenged his sleep. Eyes closed, he rubbed his arms for warmth until he smelled smoke. Not the delicately scented perfume of the oil lantern, but something sharp and acrid—charred wood and swamp gas.

His throat burned, and his eyes watered. Did everyone else smell this, too?

Darcy's shriek punched through the room. Aiden leapt up and grabbed his sword. Franky, who slept in the opposite corner, also moved to action.

"What was that?" Becca asked from the bed.

Parker put his hand on her shoulder and took his gun from his holster. "Stay here," he said. "I'll check it out."

"Put the gun down," Aiden said as he moved to the door, Franky beside him.

Becca hobbled to the window, where the smoke poured in. "The city walls are burning."

"Weileighn is here," Franky said.

Aiden sped down the stairs, Franky on his heels. The smoke grew thicker. He coughed, and his lungs tightened like crumpled rags. He blinked, squinting to see past the billowing black cloud. The front door buckled under the force of something. It beat like a heart, the wood expanding with each blow, until finally, the wooden lock-bar shattered, and the door crashed in, its hinges shooting across the room like bullets. Splintered fragments of the door sailed past his ears and shoulders. He should have brought his shield, should have put his armor back on.

Soldiers poured in. Their burnished iron armor bore two crossed red daggers on a field of white.

Franky was right. Weileighn, which meant *swordcrafters*, likely as not. Mages trained in the art of swordplay. This would not go well for Pellbred.

The nearest soldier unsheathed his sword and pointed it at Darcy. "Do you house soldiers?" he demanded.

Aiden put his arm out, barring Franky from leaping down the stairs. They receded up, kept themselves from the view of the distracted soldiers.

Darcy's voice came out in a pinch. "No."

"If you are lying, it will be your life."

Aiden pushed Franky upstairs. Parker's head stuck out the door.

"Hide the armor and weapons," Franky said, taking the remaining stairs two at a time.

Parker disappeared into the room, and Aiden and Franky followed suit.

Moments before the door crashed in, Aiden stashed his sword and the final breastplate under the bed.

Two Weileighn swordcrafters, weapons drawn, marched into the tiny room. "Identify yourselves," one barked.

"Peddlers," Aiden said. "Buying wares." He kept his eyes low.

"Your face is familiar," one said. "What's your name?"

Aiden froze.

"Are you daft?" Becca hung each vowel with a lilt. She'd adopted a pitch-perfect Varuthian accent. "Of course he's familiar! This is Troa, son of Asomac."

Aiden didn't recognize the names, and judging by the confusion on the soldiers' faces, they didn't either, but she spoke with such authority, such mock outrage and derision, neither soldier wanted to admit their ignorance.

"Of course," he said, nodding. "Sorry I missed it." To the other soldier, he said, "The other rooms, quickly."

Once the soldiers vanished, Franky asked Becca, "Who are Troa and Asomac?"

She shrugged. "Sounded Varuthian to me. I gambled."

"Remind me to take you to Vegas when we get back," Parker murmured. He kept his hand on his weapon—a cop habit. But firing it, even brandishing it, might have fatal repercussions.

Aiden said, "Seriously, Parker. Keep it hidden. I don't want questions. You shoot that thing, they'll have us standing before whatever viceroy is closest, probably before Korodeth himself."

Becca whispered tightly. "Korodeth is a murderous snake. I knew he was. Going on and on about Shedoah the deceiver like he was the savior of all mankind. The snake of a man called me a paranoid elf. Said I didn't trust humans and that I wanted to kill the king. But my Ribillius was too smart. He wouldn't listen."

Her Ribillius? What a strange way for her to speak, as if she were still the queen.

Another crash. The soldiers had made their way into the other room. "Alrujahn soldiers!" they cried, before ringing metal cut off their voices.

"Darcy," Franky said. He pulled his sword from beneath the bed and bounded to the stairs.

She shrieked.

Aiden grabbed his shield and raced down the stairs.

"Leave her alone!" Franky screamed. Then, "Whoa!"

Aiden rounded the bottom of the stairs, shield raised. The soldier had turned his attention from Darcy, who cowered in the corner, her hand fisted in her hair, to Franky, who leapt back from a lethal blade.

Aiden interposed himself between the soldier and Franky. "Watch the stairs!" he said. To the soldier, as he hoisted his shield to deflect another blow. "Don't make me kill you, bro."

The swordcrafter soldier fought all the harder, flicking his wrist and igniting his blade in flames before bringing it down toward Aiden's head.

Aiden side-stepped, grabbed the man's wrist, and twisted. Immediately, he dropped the blade and struggled to free his arm. The flames smoked out before it hit the floor.

Aiden put his foot in the man's back and pushed him to the wall, then pulled his wrist hard. "If you want to keep your arm attached, you'll let us walk out this door with Darcy. She's not a soldier, and you have no right to kill her."

"She lied to the crown of Weileighn! She is a traitor!"

"Last I checked, Alrujah was still in charge of Pellbred, which makes you the traitor far as I can see."

The man grimaced, his face flat against the wall.

Franky helped Darcy to her feet. She trembled in his arms. "Let's go," he said.

Parker and Becca raced down the stairs with the two Alrujahn soldiers. Clearly, they'd won the skirmish in the upper room. "Ranks are forming outside the city walls," one said. "Don your armor and meet us there."

"On our way," Franky said.

They disappeared out the door.

"We're going into battle?" Becca asked.

"Not a chance," Aiden said. "Not until we know which side to join."

"You'll all be tried for treason!" the Weileighn soldier yelled.

Franky sighed and brought a crushing right hook to the side of the man's head. He slumped, unconscious. "Dude was getting on my nerves," he said.

Darcy stood and ran to Franky. She shook in his arms, as he hummed to her.

Outside, an incredible roar shook the walls of the Griffin's Paw.

"What in Alrujah was that?" Becca asked.

"Abaddon," Darcy said, clutching Franky's shirt. "He'll be the death of us all."

ERICA'S EARS HURT—TOO much noise. Steel swords on steel shields, iron maces crushing iron helmets. Men screamed like mice with their tails caught. She pushed Robert along in his chair, hoping a stray arrow might find its way into his heart. But she banished the thought from her mind—he was her father, at least in North Chester, no matter how much he made her skin crawl. More importantly, he might be her only chance for survival.

Robert's hand tightened around the handle of the knife. He moved it from hand to hand, his eyes on the gleaming blade. "This is a bad idea."

They'd met up with Viceroy Delvyn shortly after Robert's epiphany. Now, Delvyn ran in front of them, cutting a wide swath with the broad arc of his axe. He moved with a violent grace, a terrifying beauty, a frightening fluidity. Delvyn's was a macabre dance of death.

Behind her, Ullwen and Norby dispatched whatever Sylvonyan soldiers thought to attack her flank.

Tiamat circled overhead, spraying fire in explosive bursts across the city. The bell tower burned like a funeral pyre.

Beneath Tiamat, in a tiny boat floating on concussive waves, a man in a white robe stood. His obsidian-tipped partisan glimmered in the nascent sunrise, and those eyes glowed gold from behind a black mask. She'd seen this dude before.

The Mage Lord, moments before he summoned Belphegor.

Did he bring Tiamat here as well? Must have.

She fisted her hands, and the gold ring Dillard gave her bit into her palm. She stretched out for the mind of a parial-barbed vi-fish, anything to bring the Mage Lord down, but she found nothing, and the Mage Lord blinked away in a shimmery pool of silver light.

She made a mental note—find the Mage Lord and make him hurt.

Breniveer ran beside her, shielding the small group from the consciousness of the nearby combatants, from the seadragon Tiamat.

Ullwen shouted, "There's too many!"

"Cavalry's coming," Erica shrieked. Already, she touched the minds of the hundreds of bats racing from their caves toward the city. She'd organized a pack of fangands to ward the Sylvonyan attackers from the gate. Beresus pulled down the siege ladders, and arachands wove webs between buildings, snatching up Sylvonyan soldiers like bugs.

Tiamat twisted back to the sea and dove beneath the surface with a splash.

Norby grunted and dropped to his knees.

Erica turned Robert's chair so fast, it nearly overturned. She kicked it hard at the Sylvonyan soldier standing over Norby. It crashed into the steel-clad knight, knocking him to his back. She leapt on top of him and twisted his helmet around. The man growled, and as he spun it right, Sparky tore out his throat.

She helped her father up.

"He was quick. Got my cheek," Norby said.

Erica said, "Have to keep moving." Ignore the gore, the blood, the bits of neck stuck between Sparky's teeth. It should sicken her, but instead, her stomach rumbled in hunger.

She had to go.

She grabbed Robert's chair and raced it over the blood-slicked cobbled streets, the rubber wheels squeaking. She maneuvered it around bodies, around unclaimed shields, swords in the dismembered hands of dead soldiers.

"He's coming," Robert mumbled. "He's coming for me."

"Kind of the plan," Erica said. "Hide the knife."

Robert crossed his arms over his chest, tucked the blade under his armpit, and rocked. "This isn't what I wanted."

"Revenge, Robert. Be a big boy and think about how good it will feel to get rid of him at last. You'll have a quiet mind again."

Ullwen kicked a soldier back and came alongside Erica. In the distance, a dark shadow rose from the Alrujahn Sea. The impact of the overwhelming life force slammed against Erica. She understood what the bug feels like to meet the windshield. When she regained her breath, Erica pressed on toward the lumbering beast.

The creature split the water, silvery scales catching the moonlight. Water ran from its wide wings, from its gaping maw. The serpentine neck stretched toward them, the twisted horns jutting backward. A single, long dorsal fin ran from forehead to tail, a journey of over thirty yards. Tiamat flexed the webbed fingers of his hind claws. It shot up from the water and took to the air.

No. Not flying. The beast's scaly wings lacked the strength required to keep a body so thickly muscled aloft for long. It glided like a flying fish, shifting directions, contorting its body, twisting back toward its tail.

It stared down at them, jagged teeth splitting through its lips. It opened its mouth and let forth a stream of flame.

Erica dropped to her knees and covered her face. Pain ignited the backs of her hands. She buried them in her stomach, shrieked with the voice of a murder of razorbeaks.

Ullwen lifted her. "Move."

How hadn't he been burned?

She checked her hands.

Ruined. Her skin bubbled like overcooked chili. Flames snapped up the wooden walls of the buildings around her with whip-cracking embers. "Not again," she said. "Please, God. No."

"Move," Ullwen said again. He grabbed the rubber handles of the wheelchair and pushed Robert forward while Norby dispatched the soldiers who made it past Delvyn's wide swath of death.

Erica ran with them, cradling her hands, trying to blink back the tears, trying to keep her dinner down.

Tiamat, after circling the city, igniting homes and shops, dove back into the deep.

Screams shook the air; terrified, agonized shrieks and wails echoed.

She tried to shut the sounds out, tried to ignore them, to think of anything other than stoves and flames and hands, but with each pop of every damp wooden wall, new wails assaulted her.

She ran faster, reached deep within her chest and let out a volley of punctuated sharp sounds, resonant caws. Murders of razorbeaks responded. They blotted out the waning moon. They dove at the soldiers, cleared paths for the few families still trying to evacuate.

"He's coming again," Robert said, his voice fearful, a child confessing to a father.

Anger eclipsed her fear. Tiamat had taken her hands twice now, in one way or the other. The end result was the same. She would see the dragon dead, and she'd sing when it died. "Get us to the water!"

The razorbeaks swarmed around her and Ullwen, around Breniveer and Viceroy Delvyn. She ran faster. The wall of Tiamat's life-force pulled at her like gravity.

"Don't make me do this," Robert said. "I've changed my mind."

"This was your idea. You're not getting out of this, cold feet or not," Erica said.

"You're our only chance," Breniveer said. "No one else knows how to do it."

The surface of the water broke. Tiamat's massive body arose again. The beast pulled its neck back, preparing to belch another stream of fire, until its eyes saw through the razorbeaks, until it locked eyes on Robert. Tiamat looped back toward the docks.

Robert whispered, "Oh God."

Ullwen pushed him hard. The wheelchair hit a loose plank, and Robert spilled onto the wood.

He scrambled away from the water's edge, the chair dragging behind him. His fingers clawed at the bloodied wooden dock.

Delvyn brought his axe down hard on the remaining ankle shackles and leapt toward land.

"Now," Erica said, as if her mother needed the command. By now, Erica planted the one-word message in Tiamat's mind.

Sacrifice.

Breniveer touched Robert's mind, stirred his courage, and subdued his fear. She would keep her connection to him when he was in the dark of the maw.

Tiamat's streamlined body, silvery scales sparkling in the light of the moon, opened its maw, and swallowed Robert, the chair, and Viceroy Delvyn's ankle.

Delvyn, hundreds of yards above the sea, managed to plunge his axe into Tiamat's eye. The beast howled with pain and dropped Delvyn, who spiraled down toward the sea.

Ullwen leapt after him.

By now, Robert should be in the back of Tiamat's throat. He should be shredding the glands with the knife. The mixing of the biochemical secretions should blow Tiamat's head off. That was the hope. He'd have to do it all by feel, since there'd be no light. The plan, in hindsight, seemed far-fetched, but all their hopes rode on it now.

"Come on," Erica said.

Breniveer said, "He's alive, but confused. Very dark."

Ullwen, masterfully, pulled Delvyn to the surface. How he'd found him so quickly, pulled him so nimbly, baffled Erica.

"He's got something!" Breniveer said. "He's found them!"

The massive dragon glided across the blackened sky on sparkling wet wings. It writhed, shaking its neck back and forth like a tail swatting a bee.

The light hit her eyes first, then the sound, the concussive heat.

Tiamat's head burst into a ball of fire. The rest of its body plummeted toward the sea, but before it splashed into the ocean, a massive black cloud brewed above the falling abomination. In a brilliant flash of red lightning, the abomination vanished.

"What was that?" Breniveer asked.

Exactly like Belphegor, Erica thought, though she had no idea what it was or what it meant. Likely, it didn't matter. Not now, not anymore, because her father, like Tiamat, was dead, and they were alive.

THE PACK of griffins spiraled down toward Lauren. Five white griffins followed Wind Dancer and Steel Beak in the pouncing plunge.

Lauren's heart broke. She wouldn't fight griffins, wouldn't hurt such majestic animals. But they'd been bred for war, and if she didn't fight, she'd die.

She rolled away, used Oliver's staff to deflect a swiping paw. In the spare second she had to compose her thoughts, she ran through a list of her spells:

Quake: useless against flying enemies. Fire: too harmful, might catch the trees on fire and burn her in turn. Ice: took too long. Poison: hadn't used it much. Might take too long and might inadvertently kill Wind Dancer. Lightning. She'd use enough to slow them, not enough to kill.

She let a volley of blue electricity dance through the pride, and they plummeted into the marching trees below.

Borgrad rushed through the saplings and ancient roots toward Legion, but before he made it within twenty yards of the head, a flash of red light knocked him backward.

Lauren dug deep into her core and found a sense of light. Extending her hand, an intense beam of white-hot light stabbed toward the head. Legion screamed, and the blue orbs burst into tendrils of smoke.

The griffins surrounded her.

Behind the pack, ancient roots lumbered toward her.

In the distance, fangands howled. Before long, Legion would possess every beast between Orensdale and Harland. She had to end it fast.

Borgrad righted himself and dashed through the griffins, swiping at their beaks with his axe.

"Don't hurt them!" she shouted.

"If we do not kill them, they will kill us!"

There had to be a better way.

Beaks cracking open at the jaws, the griffins howled at her, at Borgrad, their twisted voices some cross between an ear-splitting shriek and the low bass of a lion's roar. Their eyes, so beautiful when she'd drawn them in her journal back home, had been transformed into something diabolical, something evil. Instead of a clear blue, the irises of the beasts shone black, like luminescent tar.

She needed Aiden.

She needed Oliver, or Bailey, or Yarborough, or Erica, or Ullwen, or Eljah. She'd even take Langley's help right now.

She shot another beam of light, as Langley had done in the Ruins of Norgren. It cut a swath between the pack, sent them scattering, and burned straight through an old oak. The beam finally found Legion, and he howled again.

She followed behind the beam, ran through the wake of its destruction, racing toward the beresus head. If she could kill it, she might have a chance, but she'd have to get closer, set it on fire or encase it in ice.

Trees smashed limbs in front of her, behind her. She leapt over them, throwing a volley of fireballs at the griffins to keep them at bay.

Legion laughed, his lips pulling up in gruesome decay. Yellowed teeth hung loose from his gums. Flies swarmed the decaying flesh at the neck and near the blood-soaked eye sockets, coals still gleaming. Her fireballs washed over the head and did little more than scatter the flies.

She'd used most of her magic. She needed more orbs. Emptiness ate at her core.

Each spell would have to count. She shifted to electricity, which also proved ineffectual. She dug deep, planting her heels in the earth, spun away from the swipe of a griffin, and loosed a final blast of light.

Legion opened his mouth and swallowed the light as if it were an early morning cup of coffee.

"We are ancient," Legion said. "We understand your magic now, the magic of the empath mages. It is sweet."

Hot tears burned her eyes. If her magic couldn't touch the abomination, how would they win?

Blue orbs swarmed in the air, buzzed with some sort of electricity, some sort of power. Thousands of blue lights like bees.

She hated bees.

Her magic flickered away. Lethargy washed over her and buckled her knees.

It wasn't supposed to end like this. Hadn't Adonai promised great things to come from her? But here she knelt, completely powerless, completely drained of strength, before the twisted half-decayed face of an abomination. It sickened her. Hate simmered in her stomach.

A griffin pounced on her. She fell on her back. It pinned her shoulders to the ground with its front paws, reared its head back and snapped its beak at her face. Somehow, she managed to avoid the attack. If she'd had her magic, she'd ice the beak together.

Its claws dug into her shoulder, and she shrieked. She remembered the touch of the nar'esh, the slimy pain that poisoned her, that killed her. Her shoulder burned again as the claws pierced her flesh. "Please don't," she whispered. "Adonai, please help."

A low, dwarven growl distracted the griffin. It snapped its head up.

Borgrad stood over her, his eyes white hot. He struck the griffin with the butt of his axe. It reared up, and Borgrad twisted the axe head under it, chopping off its front paws.

The griffin lifted into the air, but two more swooped in from opposite sides.

Borgrad drove the butt of his axe into the earth, and two columns of rock shot up, punching each griffin in the chest. They spiraled out of control, smashing into the lumbering ancient roots. "Pull," he said.

Lauren knelt. With head bowed, she pulled with the wispy air of power left in her. It wasn't much, but enough to capture an orb.

Strength.

She harnessed the power to pull again, and two orbs rushed into the staff.

Fangands howled.

Legion screamed. "Enough!"

Pull. Four orbs.

Borgrad's breath came heavy. He bled from his back and shoulders, from his left leg.

Eight orbs. One hand touched Borgrad, healing his wounds.

The other hand gripped the staff tightly, raising it into the air and yanking sixteen orbs into the rognak wood.

The wounds from the claws of the griffin mended themselves. The emptiness within her filled with might. Her magic blinked back, and Oliver's staff hummed with power.

"Adonai has judged you, Legion. Your corruption is over."

The head sneered. Orbs shot from its mouth, its eyes, its ears, poured from the bloody stump of a neck. The woods came alive with the sounds of griffins and fangands, arachands and beresus.

"We cannot defeat so many," Borgrad said.

"I will crush the Hand of Adonai. And you, little finger, I will break first."

"I disagree," Lauren said. She took Oliver's staff in both hands and set it gently on the soil. Behind her, a silvery pool opened in the air.

24

Adonai brought him from a dangerous world of war to one of peace. His service there pleased Adonai, and Adonai swore to him, so shall he see the Hand, and the Hand cannot come unless they come by his call.
—The Book of Things to Come

IT TOOK a moment for the weight of the situation to hit Erica.

Her father was dead.

It happened so fast, she hardly had time to think. Isn't this what she wanted? Hadn't she been ready to kill him hours ago?

She should have turned away, hid her eyes.

His hands had shaken on the armrest of the wheelchair as Tiamat circled over him. His voice trickled out thick with terror.

No one deserved to be swallowed whole. But he'd chosen to do it, chosen to give his life for hers, hadn't he? It was his plan, conceived within Delvyn's chambers. It was only natural for him to have second thoughts when fear set in.

It wasn't her fault, she told herself, though she had trouble believing it.

"Your hands, dear," Breniveer said.

Erica blinked back the tears. "I know."

"We need to get you to a healer."

"Help!" Ullwen cried from the water. He pushed the viceroy toward them.

Standing at the base of the ruined dock, Norby reached out and grabbed Delvyn's arm. Breniveer grabbed the other, and together, they pulled the massive Red Beard to what remained of the splintery wooden dock. The sight of his mangled ankle, slicked with blood and seaweed, nauseated her. His ruddy cheeks paled. He'd lost too much blood already and would lose more if they didn't do something fast.

"The monk," Ullwen gasped.

Of course. If Oliver could heal, other monks would be able to as well. And didn't Delvyn have a brown-robed monk adviser? "Mom?"

"He's on his way, dear," Breniveer said. "The viceroy's in a fit of pain. I'm blocking most of it, as I am yours, but Tiamat's teeth are lined with poison. Got that from Robert before he found the glands."

Ullwen pulled himself from the water and stripped off his leather tunic, then tied it tight above Delvyn's macabre ankle. Water matted the hair on his well-sculpted chest.

Erica swallowed.

He pulled his sword and headed toward the battle.

"Where do you think you're going, sweetie?" Erica asked.

"To cut a path for the monk."

"You're not going into battle without a shirt. Leave the path to me." She neighed, and the armored horses of Sylvonya's soldiers reared up, kicking their riders to the ground. They rushed to her like frightened children to their mothers. "Grab the black one. The others will ride with you to get the monk.

Ever stoic, Ullwen leapt on the black horse. Shirtless, with a gleaming chest, Ullwen grinned. He could have been the cover of a cheesy romance novel.

"The soldiers' minds are clear," Breniveer said.

"How many can you control?" Norby asked. His voice blew over her like fresh wind. She'd almost forgotten he was there.

"Not many," she said, folding her arms. "Five or six. Shall I send them to get the monk?"

"No. Have them attack the other Sylvonyan soldiers. With luck, they'll all turn against each other." He stepped forward, deflected a soldier's attack, and hit the soldier hard in the helmet with the butt of his sword hilt. The soldier stumbled back and collapsed. "The battle is coming to us. When they see the viceroy, they will attack without mercy."

"We killed their god," Erica said. "I imagine they'd be pretty upset."

Delvyn gritted his teeth and tried to sit up. Erica held his shoulders down with her elbows. "Easy. Your job is to get better, so you can run this place once we give Sylvonya's army a black eye."

The horses cut a wide path through the soldiers, leaving disoriented bodies in their wake, but the soldiers righted themselves and attacked soon enough. Erica needed more firepower.

If her hands would work, she'd put a few arrows in eyeballs. Sylvonyan soldiers met the animals she'd summoned to help in the battle—fangands, sasquatch, beresus, arachands—at the gates and walls, kept them from entering the city to help. None would make it to them in time. With the ocean at her back, and very few animals left in the city, she had woefully few options.

"To the north docks," Norby said.

"The boats are all smashed," Breniveer said.

"Not all," Norby said.

"We'd be at the mercy of the Sylvonyan navy."

"I can handle them," Erica said, sensing the beating of hearts beneath the ocean. Water dragons, vi-fish, massive serpentine beasts ready to crush and capsize. They'd do little to help on land, but, with Tiamat out of the picture, the sea might be their rescue.

"How will Ullwen find us?" Breniveer said.

Norby said, "If we don't move soon, he'll find our corpses."

"The boathouse," Delvyn said. "They'll have small ships we can take."

"We shouldn't move him," Erica said, her elbows still on the viceroy's shoulders. The soldiers pressed in. In less than a minute, they'd be on them. "We have to jump. We have to swim."

Norby's eyes searched the city street. The shipwright was too far. He leapt in, dragging Delvyn with him. Erica and Breniveer splashed in a second later.

Even with Breniveer blocking most of the pain from her hands, the cold water on her blistered skin agonized her. She didn't have the option to not use her hands now. Had to play through pain.

The soldiers crowded the docks. They would follow them in. Erica had to put distance between her family and the army bearing down on them.

She stretched out with her mind, found the biggest thing she could—a water dragon. If it had wings like Tiamat, it might carry them from the sea to safety. Instead, it would have to pull them under to the relative safety of the dark waters. She touched its mind gently, with a single, urgent plea: *help.*

It responded and rushed up from the deep. Its back split the surface, reflecting the moon with wet scales. "Grab on," she said.

The dragon's back, long and lined with sharp fins, provided enough dangerous hand-holds for each of them. She looped an arm around a spike rising from its back, held to it with her elbow. Norby held Delvyn under the arm, keeping the viceroy's head above water. His breaths came in heavy gasps. Even in the water, the Red Beard was heavy. His thick muscular body must have been like holding a filled bookcase. She did her best to help, using her free hand to grasp the viceroy's knees. If they didn't make it to a boat soon, they might drop him.

Several soldiers stripped off their outer armor and leapt into the sea in their tunics. They carried knives and swords in their teeth. Archers drew their bows.

"Hold your breath!" Erica shouted. At the same time, she touched the water dragon's mind. *Dive.*

Water and panic swallowed her. She couldn't hold her breath long. She couldn't even hold on long. She thought of Ullwen, of his kiss beneath the Alrujahn Sea as they swam from Varuth to Alrujah to rescue her parents. Her heart longed for Relina's proper accent, for the way she waddled across the kitchen while she spooned up a bowl of soup, for her potions that had kept them warm in icy waters.

Here, she had no potion, only the will to live. Each moment holding her breath contradicted her desire. She wanted to live, to breathe, but here, murky waters submerged her, threatened to take the very life they now protected from the archers.

They'd shoot the moment they surfaced, and they'd have to surface soon. The shadow of Breniveer flailed. Norby kicked fluidly, but his eyes showed his strain. She had to do something. Most of her razorbeaks had been slaughtered. The bats, too.

But the other water dragons might serve as distractions. They'd have to be fast. Coordinating several animals at once proved difficult, but Erica wanted to breathe. Her lungs burned; her chest ached. She released a few bubbles of air and commanded three water dragons to show themselves near the surface in three different areas, one at a time. They did, and arrows split the waters near them. Three volleys meant the first row of archers would be reloading. Now, they had three targets. She prodded the mind of the water dragon towing them toward the boat. It surfaced long enough for them to grab breaths, then it plunged back under.

More arrows split the waters near them, but nothing close enough to concern her. Soon, they'd be out of bowshot. She repeated the process, bought them enough time to surface on the other side of the boat. Latching on to the side, she sent the water dragons out to the few Sylvonyan ships still at sea.

She pulled herself onto the lone Smalthan ship, gulping in air. With throbbing hands, she helped pull Breniveer in. Once on board safely, they helped pull Delvyn to the deck. Norby, gasping and sputtering, followed close after. They lay flat on the deck while arrows from the nearby Sylvonyan ships flew overhead.

The Sylvonyans didn't last long.

With a terrifying roar, the four water dragons assaulted the ships. They lurched, and the archers lost their footing. Several fell overboard, and the water dragons and parial-barbed vi-fish made short work of them.

Erica reached out with her mind to find the sasquatch and the fangands. They'd brought friends to the party. Once the pack smelled the blood in the air, caught scent of the flesh to tear, they came roaring from the woods and lay waste to the Sylvonyan soldiers at the gates.

"The wall is safe," Breniveer said between short gasps. "Ullwen's bringing troops to the docks. The Sylvonyan lines have broken."

The crew of the ship cheered.

"We've won," Norby said, his slim chest heaving with heavy gulps of air.

Erica inspected the deep, jagged wound on Delvyn's ankle. Cut down to the bone. "We have to get him back. He needs a healer, or he may not make it."

25

And with his wicked deceit and treachery, Adonai subverted my power and took a portion of it for himself. But my power is limitless, and my heart is good. I will retake the seat of power. I will assert myself over Alrujah and rule with a scepter of peace.
—The Shedoahn Prophecies

OLIVER STEPPED through the shimmer and half expected to emerge at the bottom of the ocean. The rippling air chilled him, making his skin and limbs slick, wet, cold. Instead, he emerged into a forest. Massive hickories and elms bent branches toward the ground, as if bowing in a great wind. Others lay prostrate, uprooted, like the two trees he'd felled before crossing the river. Brambles of tangled roots hung heavy with upturned soil. Fangands moved through the trees, swarming the women from the camp, pouncing on the Nochiko warriors. Arachands spun webs between animate and stone trees. Beresus grunted and pounded fists into the soil.

Between them all, hovering and spinning and surging through the chaos, blue glowing orbs teemed like fish.

The souls of the living.

Somehow, they'd been pulled from their human bodies and sent into the wildlife of the forest. Even the trees, those that hadn't mysteriously been turned to stone, moved like lumbering trolls.

He'd delivered the camp and the Nochiko warriors into the jaws of death.

Rumbling shrieks carried through uneasy air. The battle cry of griffins. Thank Adonai—The Council of Yeval must be battling whatever evil possessed the forest.

But the noble beasts he'd programmed months ago were not aiding the cause of Adonai, and these were not the trees of Yeval. Instead, the griffins stretched for the Nochiko warriors with thick-pawed limbs and razor-sharp beaks.

In the dim shadows of the moon, Oliver leapt forward, nimbly avoiding the swipe of a fangand. It howled at him. Thicker in chest than those he'd faced in the Cerulean Woods so many weeks ago, this fangand's eyes glowed black.

It had been possessed.

Something in its eyes caused Oliver to pause. He'd expected rage, a primal anger, a violent blood-thirst. Instead, fear illuminated the fangand's eyes. "You come in His name," the fangand said, his words twisted by savage teeth and a too-long tongue.

Oliver lifted his staff to the fangand's chest. "In the name of Adonai, come out of the beast."

The orb moved from the fangand's chest to Oliver's staff, and the beast fell. "Don't hurt them," Oliver told Shigani.

Too late. Already, the Nochiko warriors had slaughtered dozens of fangands. Arachands fell in droves. The Nochiko moved with a maddening speed, a wholly terrifying aggression, as if the blood of the beasts would somehow erase the last few days and restore things to the way they should be.

Even the Utahemi women joined in the fight. They used pots and pans, bags and walking sticks. Mother Eider, though old, moved with the fluidity of a bird.

Shadow Singer moved from shadow to shadow, slicing branches

from trees with her enchanted blade and staving off griffins with savage strikes.

"Pull!"

Lauren's voice? Was she here?

Oliver gripped his staff and pulled at the blue orbs indwelling the trees and beasts. As he wrested them from the beresus and arachands, the bodies crumpled. Not dead, but not a threat. He directed his pulling toward the voice, and beasts toppled by the dozens. Shigani fought behind him, and Shadow Singer cut a wide swath beside him. With those two around, he had little fear of tree or limb or root or claw.

The chaos cleared, and Lauren stood before him, dressed like a warrior princess, all flowing white cape, purple clasps, gloves and boots, and, on her forehead, her pearl tiara.

A peaceful wrath twisted her face, and she extended her arms, holding his rognak staff beside her. Blue orbs plummeted into it.

Since when had she learned to use his staff?

Beside her, a dwarf with braided red sideburns swung a wicked axe in a wide arch. Borgrad? What was he doing here? He should be guarding the Heart of Yeval.

In the dwarf's arm, he cradled a pile of a girl with melting black hair and bronze skin.

Lily.

"Shigani, help the short man. Bring as many warriors as you need."

"As you say, Baikada." He vanished through brambles of fallen roots.

Behind him, a griffin shrieked. Shadow Singer melted from the shadows and kicked its paws away from him. "This would be easier if you'd allow me to kill them," she rasped.

"Lily's with the dwarf," he said.

"I know." She vanished deep into the shadows.

Oliver raced toward Lauren and the dwarf, making good use of his new braided staff to fend off attacks from beast and branch alike.

An arachand dropped in front of him and opened its pincers in a wide vertical smile.

Two Nochiko warriors made short work of its legs, and the spider-woman collapsed onto her abdomen. When she stopped convulsing, they turned their swords on the beresus closing in on them. In a flash of war-hardened brilliance, they used the severed legs of the spider-woman as spears, launching them through the bellies of the gorilla-like monsters.

Oliver gathered his strength and stilled the piston of his heart. He sprinted. When he reached Lauren, he erected a blue shield. "Situation?"

"Abomination. Legion. The head on the stick. Using souls to possess the trees and creatures."

"Got that much," Oliver said. "Where are the others?"

"Just me and Borgrad," she said, staring at the head before her. For every blue orb she pulled from its mouth, two more flew into it. "Glad you're alive."

"Same. Look, we're not going to beat it like that," Oliver said.

"Ideas?"

"Let me handle the souls. I can pull faster than you. Think you can make its life difficult for a bit?"

"I've got a few tricks left."

OUTSIDE THE GRIFFIN'S PAW, Parker took two steps back. His heels pressed up against the ragged boards of the bridge running toward the city walls.

Soldiers pressed against soldiers. Swords clanged on shields. Maces twirled overhead. Spearmen rode in the midst of the battle atop armored steeds. They sank their pole-arms into the joints of the armor of the opposing side—the neck, the shoulders, the backs of the knees.

Blades lit in flames or glowed in ice or crackled with electricity.

He couldn't keep the soldiers straight, even with the city

emblems emblazoned on every chest, every shield: here a silhou-
etted tree in front of a blue moon, there the Razorbeak with a sun
above either wing, there crossed red daggers. He'd ascribed the
names of the city to the logos—Dalova, Alrujah, Weileighn. He'd
heard their names, understood Alrujah was at war with the other
two. But the bodies in the armor, the faces twisted in strife and
agony, the contortion of pain, blended into a muddy swamp of
soldiers.

"Where do we go?" Franky asked, holding hard to Darcy.

"Away," Aiden said. "We use the distraction to slip off. Steer clear
of the fighting. You're not ready for war. You're not even ready for a
skirmish."

Parker had his gun, but it wouldn't do much against so many.
Would his bullets even pierce their armor? "Lead the way. I'll bring
up the back."

"Stay away from the walls," Becca said, adopting her formal
queen's tone. It amazed him how seamlessly she'd adopted a new
role, how confidence flooded her voice and eclipsed any worry or
concern, any panic-induced anxiety. She was hardly the same trembling woman he hugged near the edge of the cliff outside her home
in North Chester. Iron forged the woman who had been so fragile in
North Chester.

She was in Alrujah, and her daughters were a stone's throw away.
This burning city, this war-torn land was the single greatest hope she
had of finding what she'd lost, of reclaiming her daughters.

In North Chester, she was a grieving, hopeless mother.

In Alrujah, she was an avenging queen.

If things went bad, she'd be able to handle herself. She wore her
regal confidence well.

They moved over the rickety bridges toward the edge of town.
They'd have to avoid the roads; too many soldiers. They hurried,
dodging from shadowy hemlock to gnarled oak. Aiden moved as if he
had a GPS stashed somewhere in his shiny armor. Conviction
marked his movements, and Parker followed him willingly, his hand
on his holstered Beretta.

Beyond the tree lines, an ear-splitting sound stormed from the bowels of the land.

Parker turned. The attacking soldiers set fire to the gates of the city. An unearthly moan, a rumble of rock and stone, a buzzing of feedback and flies.

"What in the world is that?" Franky asked. He pointed above the city to a massive beast hovering over the walls.

Parker squinted and willed his eyes to focus beyond the black smoke and greenish swamp gasses. The lights of the city burned, the flames of the gates licked the filthy walls.

"It's him," Darcy whispered, clinging to Franky. "Abaddon."

A demon glided over the carnage. No other word would describe it. Black bones weaved with gray muscle tissue. An exoskeleton? A scratched bone plate covered most of its face, the forehead, the eyes, the nose, or at least where those things should have been. Below it, sickly green-gray fleshy lips strained against sharpened teeth. On its head, six horns twisted up. Two from the forehead, two from where his ears should be, and two from the back of its neck. From its back, two skeletal wings stretched. Thickly muscled, its body defied gravity. It must weigh close to four hundred pounds, maybe more. How did it fly?

"What is it?" Aiden asked. He finally relented from his measured pace.

Darcy said, "He's death and destruction. He pulls life from the land."

"An abomination," Aiden said.

Got that right. "What do we do?" Parker asked. "We can't fight it."

Aiden cracked his neck. "I can."

"Dude, there's like, a million soldiers over there," Franky said. "Let them handle it. We gotta get moving. We have to find Bailey and Lauren."

Aiden drew his sword. "I'm not leaving these men to die. I don't care which side they're fighting for. That thing stinks to Adonai, and I'm not about to let it live."

Franky said. "It's massive, smells like death, and I'm willing to bet it knows how to fight. Let the soldiers deal with it. It's not our problem."

"It's my fault," Darcy whispered. "I prayed to him. I sacrificed to him."

"You what?" Becca asked.

Her voice trembled like the ground beneath them. "We had to. The viceroy made us. I had to, to keep the inn, I had to sacrifice."

"Sounds like the viceroy's to blame," Franky said. He put a gentle hand on her shoulder. "Not your fault."

Aiden cracked his knuckles. "This is why I came back," he said.

"I thought you wanted to find Lauren," Franky said.

"I'm the Hand of Adonai. This is why he brought us here. To kill that thing. Stay here."

"Fat chance," Parker said. "We're moving. I'm taking them to the river. We'll move south. Catch up with us when you're done playing hero."

"Take Darcy," Franky said.

"You're not coming?" Parker asked.

"I can help," Becca said. She snapped her fingers, and a flame appeared between her thumb and forefinger.

"Gonna need more than a candle."

"I've got more," she said. Cupping her hands, the flame grew to an intense ball of heat. She extended her arms to the monster, and light leapt from her palms in a column of crackling flame.

DELVYN SAT UNCOMFORTABLY on his throne, his ankle extended before him, elevated on a wooden footstool. The jagged lacerations from Tiamat's serrated teeth bled in puddles down the finely-sanded and lacquered hickory. The color ran from his face, as if it, too, emptied through the deep gashes.

The skin around the wounds yellowed, and the red hair on his legs matted and fell out in clumps.

No question, infection had set in, and Erica knew how monks dealt with infection.

She turned her back as the brown-robed monk poured the black powder in the open wounds.

Would Delvyn scream the way her parents had? Would his voice twist into a pinched yelp?

The backs of her hands burned. She'd had enough fire to last her a lifetime.

Through the chaotic din of the castle—soldiers clamoring through the stone halls, bringing the injured to the infirmaries downstairs, organizing rebuilding efforts, planning for possible follow up attacks, putting down the final few Sylvonyan soldiers who resisted—Erica almost didn't hear the sizzle of flame touching powder. But it came all the same, swirling with the acrid smell of sulfur and singed hair.

She wanted to scrub the inside of her lungs.

To his credit, Delvyn did not scream. Either he had a very high pain tolerance, or he was blacking out.

When the sizzle died down, Erica checked the ankle. The seeping yellow flesh blistered black. But the infection wouldn't spread. He wouldn't be walking for a while, but he'd live.

The monk knelt and mumbled in a language she didn't understand. He sounded exactly like Oliver.

She missed him, missed his awkward nerdy confidence, his goofy grin, the absurdly thin sideburns. She was comfortable around him. She'd given her heart to Ullwen and didn't regret it, but there'd always be a spot there for the techno-geek from North Chester.

"How do you feel, Viceroy?" Ullwen asked.

Delvyn blinked. Color tested his cheeks, like a child dipping his toes in a cold pool. "Embarrassed."

Norby, standing beside Erica, said, "You bear no dishonor, Viceroy."

"Had I set my feet properly, I'd have had a perfect opportunity to take Tiamat's head."

Breniveer sat on the steps leading to the dais. Her dress torn, her face smudged with smoke and sweat, she set her elbows on her knees and put her hands behind her head.

"What's wrong, Momma?" Erica asked, sitting beside her.

"So much emptiness," she whispered. "So much death."

Erica wrapped her arms around herself and shivered.

"I think," Breniveer said, her voice thick with memory, "Robert loved you."

Erica stood up. "So?"

Breniveer frowned. "While he was in the mouth, he thought of you. He was sorry, for what it's worth."

"Well, I'm sorry, too."

"I wanted him dead as much as you," Breniveer said. "But his sorrow, his regret. I've seldom felt anything as crippling."

"Why would you tell me this?" Erica asked, her eyes hot.

"You were right to have us heal him. If you hadn't, we might not be here. He saved us."

Erica put her arms to her sides. "Let's not make him a hero. He paid a debt, that's all."

Breniveer stood, wiped her cheeks with the sleeve of her dress. "He wanted your forgiveness, love." She took two bandages, wet with a healing salve, and began to wrap Erica's hands.

The chill of the salve shocked her, and pain needled the backs of her hands and wrists. "Little late for that now, isn't it?" Erica asked.

"It's never too late to forgive," Ullwen said.

Erica's mouth twisted into a frown. "Forgiveness isn't my thing. I won't forgive Korodeth for having you thrown in the dungeon, and I won't forgive Robert for killing my mother—my North Chester mother. You can't earn forgiveness for those kinds of sins."

Norby hugged Erica. She let him take her in his arms and hold her. He smelled like blood and salt. "Butterfly," he said. "You forgive. Let me avenge."

"We have more important matters," Delvyn said.

Outside, soldiers chanted. They'd formed a snaking line through the streets and down to the sea. They passed massive wooden buckets of sea water down the line toward the bell tower. It'd been constructed from rognak, so it would survive the fire, if they put it out fast enough.

The monk draped a wet cloth over Delvyn's ankle, and the viceroy sat straight in his throne, his hand still on his axe beside him. "I'm indebted to you all. How may Port Smalth repay you?"

"We need no repayment other than rest," Norby said.

"Our city has wealth. I will give you each a letter with my name. Find what you need from any of our shops and show them my seal. They know I will repay them for whatever you choose."

"Blank check?" Erica said, happy for the change of conversation. "Makes me want to go shopping."

Ullwen grinned, a boyish gesture for a man so handsome, but Erica liked it. He looked mischievous. She didn't see his playful side often. Made her want to work at making him happy. "Thank you, Viceroy. If you are agreeable to it, I believe my companions and I would like to stay here for the night."

"Stay as long as you wish. You are the saviors of Port Smalth, and so it will say in my letter."

Through the window, Erica considered the soldiers working to repair the city. There would be little shopping opportunities tomorrow, thanks to Tiamat. But Delvyn's praise felt unfounded. They'd done very little, comparatively. Without Robert, they'd be dead. She didn't know how she ended up back in North Chester, or returned to Alrujah at the right time. Too many coincidences not to be fate. Someone, or something, wanted her to bring her father back. "Pretty sure Adonai did the saving. He brought Robert here. We'd never have beaten Tiamat without him."

"I didn't think you believed in Adonai," Ullwen said without a trace of condemnation in his voice.

"Getting harder not to believe." She could still trace the path of the massive beast, feel its gravity push against her. In her mind, she retraced its flight from where it surfaced, to where it snatched Robert from the dock, to where its head exploded over the ocean. Such a spectacular eruption.

And what would the people back in North Chester think? What

kind of manhunt would they mount to find Robert, to find Erica? If she'd ever wanted to go home, she couldn't now. She would be a felon, and she'd end up living out her days in a prison like Robert had before her.

She had what she wanted; her father was dead. He'd paid for his sins, but she didn't feel any better. Some wounds must not heal, not with revenge, not with justice, not with time. She sighed, walked next to Ullwen, and put her head on his shoulder.

"Perhaps we will stay," Norby said, taking Breniveer into his arms. "Your men fought bravely. I can mold such men into formidable soldiers. Your numbers are small, but they fight with their hearts. And they can handle boats. We may be able to use them to launch a flanking attack on Alrujah when Dalova marches."

"I'd thought the same thing," Delvyn said. He smiled broadly. "We will wrest Korodeth the Usurper from the throne in the name of Adonai." To his monk, he said, "See to the girl's hands. Then, have rooms prepared for our guests. Warm linens, fresh candles, laundered sleep wear. Tomorrow, we begin work."

WITH OLIVER BESIDE HER, furiously pulling orbs into his new staff, and the weird samurai guys running around cutting up the trees, Lauren decided she had time to put her power to work. Holding Oliver's staff, she closed her eyes, trusting Borgrad and the others to keep the beasts far enough away from her to make this work.

She cleared her mind, pulled heat from her core to her skin. She sizzled in the night. Using a trickle of her power, she heated the air around her and chilled the air beyond it. Wind circled her feet. Remembering how she'd floated the first day she awoke in Alrujah, she sought the same lightness. Instantly, her feet lifted from the ground. Thrusting her arms out to her sides, she spread her chiffon cape, which caught the currents of wind and lifted her into the air.

Heat seared the back of her right eye. Her left eyelid crusted with ice. Electricity crackled between each strand of hair.

"A triune mage," Borgrad's voice gruffed through the tumultuous battle.

Better. She was an empath mage, capable of duplicating any spell, of creating new spells based on her emotions.

The trees, which until recently had been closing in on them, stepped back, as if to reform their plan of assault.

Aiden left her.

Korodeth killed her father.

Bailey Renee vanished.

Her life spun wildly out of control.

She wouldn't let it, not anymore. She refused to be a victim, refused to let things simply happen to her. From here on out, she called the shots. She made her decisions and followed through. No stupid beresus head, no ancient animated forest would stand in her way.

Fire seared her palms. Two flame whips dangled from her hands.

"We are the Hand of Adonai," she said, staring directly at the beresus head. "You cannot overcome us."

The wind twisted her. She spun, arms stretched out, whips twirling around her. Sparks and flames leapt from the tendrils of the whips. They sliced through the reaching branches of the oaks and ashes, of cedars and hickories. Smoke filled the air, making the forest smell like a backyard barbecue.

Something hard smashed into her side, and she fell. Keeping a clear head, she slowed her descent. Once on the ground, she found the offending tree. Seconds later, a massive ice spike shot out of the ground and ripped the tree apart from inside out. It howled with the voice of the wind.

Borgrad smashed the butt of his axe into the earth, and a wide chasm split beneath a pack of fangands. It toppled trees into lumbering beresus and threw arachands from their perches in the stickly branches of the trees.

Oliver knelt, mumbling something in the ancient language. His staff drew orbs to itself, pulling them into oblong ovals. They clung to the trees with spectral fingers, stretched out like power lines. His face paled. Sweat dampened his robe.

The trees, once the spirits had been extracted, collapsed as if a lumberjack had felled them.

"We are many," the beresus head said. It opened its mouth, and hundreds of orbs spewed out. She lashed her whips, swinging them with violent precision. Orbs scattered like marbles. The cottony spirits twisted in the spiraling wind and lifted up with furious abandon, rocketing up beyond the tree people to the now light sky.

Floating fifty feet above the ground, Lauren turned her attentions to the griffins circling the forest. She cracked the whips, taking the magnificent killing machines in the wings, near the back. They shrieked and plummeted. They'd survive but wouldn't fly any time soon. As they fell, she sent a tendril of magic into the staff and pulled. The orbs sprang free from the beasts. With any luck, they'd help fight the other beasts. New orbs replaced the ones she'd pulled from Legion and dashed her scant hopes.

Oliver couldn't pull the orbs fast enough, and for every soul he reclaimed, Legion sent two more.

Lauren pulled again, hard. The orbs strained against her, clung to the bark of the oaks and hickories. Hundreds inched toward her. The magic in the staff drained, but Lauren pulled harder. They were closer, and Oliver's troops held the beasts back. Harder, she pulled, and the orbs obeyed the call of Adonai.

They entered the staff. Lauren exhaled, wiped sweat from her forehead. The chill of the air surrounded her. Legion released more orbs, but Lauren pulled those, too. Unattached to trees or griffins, the orbs came easier, rushed faster. With the souls trapped in the staff, Lauren allowed herself to drop back to the ground. Hundreds of trees lay strewn about, as if knocked over by bulldozers. The earth and soil, turned up by loose roots, lay scattered in clumps and mounds.

"This isn't working," Oliver said. "We could pull for weeks and he'd still be spitting out souls."

"I agree," Lauren said, cracking her flame whips toward a particularly bold arachand.

"Try pushing," Borgrad said. He kicked a bleeding beresus and retreated closer to Oliver.

They'd been fighting for hours, and Borgrad's exertion marred his haggard face.

A pit of emptiness gnawed at Lauren. She could only replenish so much power, and she refused to take the full energy of the souls. It seemed wrong.

"Of course," Oliver said, rushing headlong toward Legion.

The lips of the abomination peeled back. "Stay back, monk."

"What are you talking about?" Lauren called, steps behind him.

Every beast, every tree, turned its attention to Oliver. Whatever he planned to do, Legion didn't want him to succeed, which meant she needed to help him.

Red light shone forth, but Oliver collected the energy in his staff. Whatever enchantment had protected Legion from Borgrad's earlier attack had no effect on Oliver. The head was powerless compared to the power of Adonai's chosen.

She reached deep and found a sense of light. Extending both hands, she cut a path in front of Oliver, cutting trees in half and igniting fangands in hot bursts of flame.

Oliver stretched his staff out and touched the tip to Legion's forehead.

The abomination frowned. Its glowing coal eyes dimmed. "No, please."

Yes, the pieces coming together. He pushes; I pull.

"Ready?" Oliver asked.

Lauren grinned. She'd had enough of this stupid talking head. "Ready."

Oliver closed his eyes, pushed the staff into the socket of Legion's eye and shouted, "Adonai!"

In a burst of blinding sound and deafening light, thousands of orbs exploded from the head, shattering the skull and ripping the decomposing flesh.

Lauren pulled.

So many souls.

They rushed at her like bullets, and her legs failed. She slumped to the earth while the orbs smashed themselves into her staff.

Oliver knelt, blue orbs bulleting into his staff.

Her breath caught.

Way too many.

Above, stygian clouds billowed together from nowhere. Finally. They'd fought long enough, hard enough, and now the blessed red lightning would take the rest of the filthy abomination, and, hopefully, the glowing souls rattling her staff.

"No," one of the men said.

Sparks flashed, like a cigarette lighter, like flint and tender, all orange and yellow, but the bolt would come in a fascinating ruby.

And when it came, it branched out like the roots of a tree, each tendril snapping up a soul in its deadly garnet embrace. Lauren dropped the staff a half-second before the bolt came, and it echoed as it cracked through her staff and Oliver's. He'd dropped his, too. Still the bolt came so close it knocked them both back, stole their breath, and crackled their hair with wisps of electricity.

"Indigo!" Borgrad said. He rushed to her, his chest filling with heavy gulps of air. In his left arm, a black-haired girl clung to his neck. "Are you harmed?"

The orbs slowed and thinned. She retrieved her staff. It trembled in her hand with a violent relief. She tried to stand but found herself too dizzy. "I'm fine," she said, reaching her free hand out to find something to steady herself.

A black-haired woman took it. What a violent beauty this woman had. Her sea green eyes narrowed, and she'd veiled her face with a black cloth. "You are unwell." Her voice sounded wrecked, irreparably broken. "Your song decrescendos."

What language did she speak? It sounded like English, but the last word had to be foreign. The Ancient Language?

"The blood bolt," the man said.

She put her hand to her forehead and sat. "I need to rest, I think."

"Yes," Borgrad said, kneeling behind her. "We all do."

"Oliver," she said as her eyes slipped shut.

He said, "I'm here."

~

AIDEN RACED TOWARD THE ABOMINATION; his heart sprinted in his chest. He had no chance alone. Even with all three armies fighting with him, they'd never topple Abaddon. It had to be seven feet tall, maybe bigger. The size of a sasquatch and lined with some sort of bone-mail.

Through the chaos of armies skirmishing, in the thin moonlight, a flash of white caught Aiden's eye. There, in the city, near the walls, a tall man in a white robe with black symbols embroidered up and down the sleeves and hoods.

Aiden shouted, "You brought this thing here, didn't you?"

The Mage Lord's eyes shone gold behind his black mask. He lifted his obsidian-tipped partisan, and the black blade flashed in the green, swampish gas billowing up from the air. In a voice as loud as a shout, but quiet as a whisper, the Mage Lord said, "This must be accomplished. I am not your enemy."

Aiden rushed him, sword high in the air. He moved through the distracted soldiers of Dalova and Weileighn and Alrujah. "You bring abominations to Alrujah and say you're not the enemy of Adonai?"

"Our time is near," the Mage Lord said in his paradoxical voice. He touched *The Book of Sealed Magic* and blinked out in a misty shimmer.

Like the portals.

Abaddon roared and lifted seven soldiers up with an invisible power. They withered from thickly-muscled soldiers into decrepit seventy-pound octogenarians. Some sort of life-drain power. Aiden steadied his heart and cracked his knuckles. He'd worry about the Mage Lord later. For now, he had an abomination to kill.

He'd have to bring it down to the ground if he wanted any shot of beating it. Could the archers distract him long enough for the mages to get him to the ground? He could get in close before it had a chance to drain his life, could get his sword under the bone plate over its face. It had to have a weakness.

"To me!" he shouted as he raced through the cluster of Alrujahn soldiers. They followed him. To the soldiers from Dalova and Weileighn, he called, "Hold the assault! Archers, take aim!" Remarkably, they heeded his orders. Even the captains deferred to him. He spoke with authority, and the soldiers responded. They must recognize his battle armor, recognize his authority. Must be so afraid, they'd follow anyone showing any courage in the face of certain death. Or, perhaps, they recognized him as the Hand of Adonai.

Abaddon opened his mouth, and a cloud of flies sprang forth. It moved like a missile toward Aiden. He ducked and raised his shield, but the swarm buzzed around him. Fat flies swarmed together and obscured his vision. They landed on him, crawled up his skin, weighed down his armor.

Torture. The buzz was the stuff of nightmares, a vision of hell.

He flung his shield around wildly, hoping to dislodge the insects, but they clung to him like honey.

A burst of heat flashed over him, and the bugs fell. Beside him, Becca crafted a fireball in her palms. She launched it toward the Abomination, and it howled. Swarms of flies dissipated and fell.

"You can throw fire?"

"There are other mages," she said. "They're not far off, about a half mile south. Can Franky get them?"

Of course. It'd keep him out of the fighting. "Franky! Take Parker and Darcy. Head south until you find the mages. Form them into lines about a hundred yards back. Have them hit Abaddon with everything they got. Don't hold back. Get him on the ground."

"On it!"

Beneath Abaddon, hundreds of black-robed monks poured from the church built to honor the abomination. While the monk robes encouraged him, the blackness of them didn't. "Who are they?"

"Blood Monks," a soldier said. His shield bore the Dalovan tree and moon.

A memory came to him. Men in inky robes marching from

Harland. They'd been put out of the city when Jaurru was only six. His father had helped them out, with a blade to their backs. They'd murdered several citizens and practiced Blood Magic, which had been forbidden within the tiered walls of the city.

"Archers," he shouted. "Form up!"

Immediately, archers from all three cities lined themselves up.

Becca extended her hands and shards of glowing ice shot from her fingertips. They crackled with electricity as they rocketed toward Abaddon.

The beast roared and turned toward her.

Aiden raised his sword. "Light up! Row one, target the abomination!"

They did.

"Loose!"

Hundreds of flaming arrows split the sky, and while plenty struck Abaddon, none stuck.

Better focus on a target they can hurt. "Second row! Target the monks! Loose!"

Men shrieked. Flames engulfed robes. Those uninjured rushed the line of archers.

He needed a horse. This would take a coordinated effort between the three armies, but the Blood Monks interposed themselves between the soldiers. "Ms. Knowles, slip them up?"

She grinned. "I've missed this." She flattened her palms toward the ground, and a layer of ice formed beneath their feet. The monks slipped and fell together in a huddle.

Aiden ran to the south shouting, "Archers! Form up!" He found a soldier bearing the plumed helm of a Dalovan captain. "Get them in lines. Keep the soldiers back. Keep the arrows on the monks. I'm going to find a way to clip Abaddon's wings. When I do, we pounce."

The captain nodded and took over shouting commands.

Aiden made his way to the mages. Franky had them lined up. No telling how he and Parker convinced them to follow orders, but he suspected it had something to do with their fear. "Good job."

"Thanks," Franky said.

Darcy stood between him and Parker, trembling in fear. "You can't stop him."

"Won't keep me from trying." To the mages, he said, "All you skilled in ice, block Abaddon in. I want it to weigh him down. Use whatever tricks you have to get him on the ground. I can take it from there."

A skeletal voice echoed over the gathered troops. "Slayer of Moloch and the Seers. Slayer of Belphegor. Where are your friends? Where is the Hand? You cannot stand before me." Each word rang with an unearthly feedback.

"Dude," Franky said. "I think he's talking to you."

Aiden grinned. "Funny. He sounds a lot like the last four guys I killed."

The massive horror touched down and swung its club-like arm toward the archers. The front row of the eastern archers scattered, but three moved too slowly. With the force of Abaddon's blow, the three archers flew backward for fifteen yards before smashing back into the earth. Abaddon swung again, completely disbanding the rows Aiden had worked so hard to form.

The Dalovan captain ordered his archers to loose. The arrows bounced from the bony armor. What a waste of arrows. He wished he'd rethought his plan, but he had no time to second guess.

The ground shook beneath Abaddon's steps. He moved intently toward Aiden. With him on the ground, Aiden had a chance. He sprang forward, no definite plan in mind, only instinct, hope, a vision of his sword wresting the bony plate from the monster's face.

If nothing else, his charge may give the other soldiers a chance to rally together and form an assault. Hopefully someone had war hammers. Those would be useful. Of course, only dwarves carried hammers.

Mere feet from Abaddon, Aiden leapt, twisted in the air seconds before Abaddon could crush him with his bony elbow. Righting himself, Aiden hacked at the demon's spine. His attacks only irritated the abomination.

Abaddon spun.

Aiden raised his shield and hoped. The force of Abaddon's blow knocked Aiden to his back.

Abaddon grabbed him and raised him to the sky. He lifted back into the air with a flit of his bony wings.

So, this is what death felt like—a crushing grip, immeasurable pressure cracking his ribs, his very life pulling from him. He felt nauseous and sick; his head throbbed with a devastating headache. Abaddon had struck him with some sort of pestilence, some unspeakable disease threatening to kill him from the inside out.

He thought of his mother, how crushed she'd been when he left. He couldn't die like this, not this easy. "Help," he shouted, but the word came out as a strangled whisper.

"Where is your God now, oh valiant knight? Where is your Adonai?"

Aiden prayed for his life. A simple, selfish prayer.

"Where is your Savior?"

An explosion rang out over the sounds of battle. Black bone blasted past Aiden's cheek. He tried to focus through the pain, tried to discern what happened.

Abaddon released his grip on Aiden and turned to Parker.

The detective stood between two mages, his gun leveled at the demon. He squeezed off a few more rounds, each chipping the black exoskeleton. With each shot, the demon moaned. He opened his mouth, sent out another cloud of flies. Two fire mages launched a quick blast of heat, and the flies fell dead.

Aiden tried to stand, but his head spun with pain, his abdomen fisted, and he thought he might throw up. A hand touched his shoulder. Darcy. How had she made it here from the line of mages?

Never mind. Not important.

She offered him a vial.

He didn't bother asking what it was, didn't have to. He bit down on the cork, pulled it from the mouth of the glass vial, and swallowed the purple liquid. It tasted, strangely, like grape Kool-Aid. It settled his stomach and eased the throbbing of his head. The sounds of battle lessened, and the burning behind his eyes vanished.

"I have little Berktarp sap left," she said. "Franky is bringing more to the others."

He needed Oliver to heal him. He needed Lauren's clever use of magic. He needed Erica to call down a murder of razorbeaks. Ullwen would find a weakness on this thing.

What he wouldn't give to have his friends, to have Bailey Renee here with her flaming sword.

"God," he whispered. "We need you now."

26

Solous will reign over Alrujah for all time. The crown shall not depart from him. The hearts of the people will follow after his commands.
—The Book of the Ancients

OLIVER LEANED AGAINST A FALLEN TREE, his muscles still tensed in anticipation of attack. Legion had fallen, but his body refused to believe they'd won. Beside him, Lauren lay in a charred pile of leaves. Uprooted trees lay burnt, their roots tangled together like neurons. Toppled stone trees sank into the soft soil. Entire packs of fangands limped away, while beresus grunted and lumbered off. The griffins, so ominous, so beautiful in their savagery, lifted into the air and made their way back to the Dragon's Back Mountains or Yeval Forest. Arachands lay dissected and dismembered, littered across the forest. Smoke rose from smoldering leaves and blackened branches and animals like incense.

The whole area looked like a bomb had gone off.

"Baikada," Shigani said. "What you did was evil."

"Excuse me?" he said.

"The Nochiko are worried. The Blood Bolt has terrified them."

Oliver reached for his staff. Mother Eider had explained the Blood Bolts to him, the prophecy foretold. He'd seen it represented on the chests of the Utahemi men when they gathered the women from the camp. What was it Mother Eider said about it? "And seven times shall mark the breaking of the worlds."

Of course—how could he have missed it?

"We must not let it strike seven times. The breaking of the worlds will be the death of Myrassa and Alrujah," Shigani said.

Oliver shook his head. "If that were true, we'd know it. It'd be in our *Book of Things to Come* or *The Book of the Ancients*. Or *The Book of Sealed Magic*. But there's nothing in those books."

"These are the birth pangs," Mother Eider said, appearing from behind a fallen tree with a bloody pan in each hand.

Oliver thought for a moment, reviewing the code he'd compiled so long ago. But the game had changed so much. It wasn't even a game, was it? These worlds were real. "Wait," he said. "There is something. In *The Book of Sealed Magic*. A spell that summons red lightning."

A hand touched his shoulder, and Oliver clenched his staff.

"Your song is discordant. You must relax. The threat is over, and we must move on," Shadow Singer said.

"If what Shigani says is true, it means the Mage Lord seeks to break the worlds. Don't you see? He has *The Book of Sealed Magic*. He is our enemy, not our friend. He was there when we battled Belphegor. Once we defeated the abomination, there was a flash of red, just like this."

"Two strikes," Shigani said.

"Three," Oliver said. "After Moloch. And the Seers. Lauren and Aiden likely defeated them. If they fell, there must have been another blood bolt."

"Four, then," Shadow Singer said. "We must stop the others."

He exhaled, forced his back to unclench. Steadying himself with his staff, he stood. The burden of leadership lay on his shoulders, and no matter how much he wanted to call it a day and kick his feet up, he couldn't stay here.

Oliver didn't know what to think. Nothing made sense any more. "If we want to stop the other Blood Bolts, we'd have to protect the abominations. Doesn't seem right. Their very presence corrupts Alrujah, sickens it. If we allow them to live, Alrujah will fall into chaos and disarray."

"The world will still stand," Shigani said. "Sick, but alive."

Oliver sighed. If nothing else, he should find the other abominations. Maybe, rather than killing them, he could find a way to get some answers. Better yet, he could find Dillard. If anyone knew about this world breaking prophecy, it would be him.

But they needed to move away, someplace safe, someplace quiet. They needed to regroup, to rest before they hatched any plans to save the worlds.

But how many would be moving? How many had died in the battle?

He ran a finger over Lauren's placid cheek. She'd exhausted herself, probably to the point of a comatose sleep. No telling how long she'd be out or how bad off the others were. Borgrad, the dwarf, weathered the battle well. He entertained Lily as he knelt next to Lauren.

"How did we fare, Shigani?"

The Nochiko warrior couldn't be much older than Oliver, but war had aged his face. "The numbers of enemies slain outnumber our warriors who have fallen."

Oliver's stomach clenched. It had been foolish to imagine coming out of a battle like this unscathed. He asked the question but feared the answer. "How many?"

"Twelve breathe no more, and eight bear the wound of the warriors."

He decoded the unfamiliar comment by context. Twelve dead, eight mortally wounded. He didn't even know where they were in Alrujah, how far from a city, how far from a monastery. Lauren would know, but she wouldn't be talking any time soon.

"Borgrad," Oliver said.

Lily yanked at the dwarf's braided sideburns. "Your face is hairy."

Borgrad smiled. "Someday, when you are older, perhaps your face will be as hairy as mine."

"Borgrad," Oliver said again. "Where are we?"

The dwarf stood and dipped his head in reverence. "The woods west of the Alrujah River. A day's walk from Orensdale."

Probably a few miles or more from the river. Not a long walk on most days, but with a group of wounded warriors and a comatose princess, the journey would take hours. Once at the river, they could lay the Nochiko to rest. They'd died under his leadership, and Oliver would honor their sacrifice, even if it meant carrying dead bodies.

What he wouldn't give for some horses now. What he wouldn't give to see Erica again.

"Prepare the bodies," he told Shigani. We march to the river. We will honor our dead and rest for a day."

"And after?" Mother Eider asked.

"I'll figure it out tomorrow." Already, the moon began to sink in the sky, and the thin line of light illuminated the horizon. Before long, the suns would be up, and day would be on them. But none of them were in condition to march. He stooped beside Lauren. With a deep breath, he picked her up, and walked toward the edge of the smoldering woods.

She weighed less here than she did in North Chester. How long had it been since he'd given her a piggy-back ride from the cliff's edge to her house?

"You feel for her," Shadow Singer said.

"She's my friend."

"You worry for her health."

"I worry for all of my friends."

"The other," Shadow Singer said. "The caller. Your heart sings for her."

Erica. He missed her. He needed her humor now, a well-timed barb, a droll joke to lighten the mood. He'd loved her once, and while his heart still cared for her, the romantic infatuation had waned since she left for Alrujah.

He shifted Lauren slightly, favoring his left leg. He was too weak, too injured to carry her for miles, but he'd try it nonetheless. "I worry about her, yes."

"You speak of Adonai. Will Adonai not protect them?" Mother Eider asked. She walked beside him, and Lily followed beside Shadow Singer.

He said, "I hope so."

SIX ROUNDS DOWN. He'd have to make his last nine shots count. He didn't know if the bullets helped or not, but they at least distracted the thing long enough to give Aiden a chance. And, moving between the mages and archers, the rows of mounted soldiers and infantry-men, Parker made himself nearly invisible. He ignored the soldiers' wonder and fear, reverence and awe. He ignored their burning, unspoken question: "What is that thing?"

"Stay with me," he told Becca, falling back behind the mages. They lifted a volley of fireballs toward the black-robed monks, but each fizzled before reaching their targets.

None of this made sense. Whatever happened to good old-fash-ioned shoot outs and car chases? He'd take a good freeway chase over a maniacal demon and crazy cultists any day.

Becca lifted her thin arm and lightning danced from her finger-tips. The blue light crackled, sizzled toward the hulking black demon all covered in bone.

"We have to get to Aiden," Becca said. "He's hurting still."

"Darcy's on it," Parker assured her. "All we have to do is stay alive. We should be running, not fighting. This whole thing is crazy." He leveled his gun at the monster, steadied his aim, and squeezed off another round. It hit its shoulder. In the murky darkness, a shadow blasted from the contact spot. Must have chipped some of his bone armor.

Seven down, eight to go. "Let's move."

Through the noxious cloud covering the city, a glimmer of light erupted overhead like a lone star, shining before the rise of the moon, like a monstrous firefly. But the sound that came with it, as if the inner dome of heaven had shattered, said it was something bigger, something powerful. A meteor? Maybe it'd fall on Abaddon and end this whole mess.

A cop could hope, right?

"What was that?" Franky asked, fear hot in his voice.

"I don't know," Becca said. "But it's heading for us."

Parker said, "Great. Another abomination?"

"No," Franky said. "Bailey."

The creature falling toward them—some four-winged angel, didn't look like Bailey. "Way too big," Parker said.

"Trust me," Franky said.

Becca said, "He's right."

And then he saw it, saw her, the burning eyes, the narrow face of determination, the massive flaming sword at her hip. The ground trembled under their feet as she landed, rocketing up mud and dust and the bodies of dead soldiers and monks.

She unsheathed her sword and struck at Abaddon, but the abomination didn't flinch as it punctured his shoulder. He struck back at her, sending out a cloud of beetles.

"I don't think so," Becca said, and sent fire hurtling toward her. The pillar of flame somehow twisted around Bailey's head. "Get your filthy hands off my daughter!"

"I think he should be more worried about her," Franky said. "Kick his butt, baby!"

Between archers, Parker leveled his weapon at Abaddon again, but couldn't get a clear shot around so many people. Bailey and Abaddon struggled, and Aiden stood between him and the abomination. Parker moved again, but the haze was too much.

His stomach knotted, cramped. He was going to puke. Waves of nausea weakened his knees, and he slumped to the ground.

"Parker?" Becca asked.

He tried to speak, to tell her he'd be fine, but when his mouth opened, his lunch came out.

~

IN A BRILLIANT FLASH OF LIGHT, Bailey Renee rocketed from the shimmering rift in space time. She folded her four wings behind her and plummeted through the thin, crisp air of Alrujah's upper atmosphere. The suns rose, but their rays didn't penetrate the stink of Abaddon hovering over Pellbred.

She'd heralded the coming wars, warned the worm Herater of the armies descending upon him, and still he worshiped the abomination.

Now, she'd put her strength to use.

The chill in the air pressed against her skin like a million needles. The city grew rapidly as she fell meteoric from the sky.

She pulled her flaming sword from its sheath on her belt. In moments, she'd fallen to within a hundred feet of the center of the city, where Abaddon stalked forward. She landed immediately in front of him. Even with her new height, Abaddon stood two heads taller than her. She folded her wings behind her and held the sword in front of her. "Adonai has spoken. You are a stench before His throne. Your evil ends here."

"Little angel," it screamed through thin lips. "I do not remember you. Where is Pacha el Nai? Has he fallen asleep in his vigil?"

Bailey's blood ran cold. The heat from her blade pressed against her chest. Abaddon sickened her—his reach of pestilence surrounded her.

"I was hoping to kill him this night," the abomination said. "But I guess your blood will have to do."

Bailey struck. Her blade surged forward and twisted into Abaddon's shoulder. He stepped back but made no noise. He grabbed her wrist and opened his mouth.

Millions of beetles poured out, buzzed around her face.

She closed her eyes and pulled away from him, but his grip

proved too tight. This wasn't supposed to happen. What about her strength? Her power? Where had it gone?

Blasts of fire cleared the air and singed her hair. She gasped and coughed, tugged and pulled, but his grip only tightened.

"You came to rescue the people?" Abaddon whispered in his squealing voice. "What can you do?"

Seven people rose in the air, circled around his head, and withered before her eyes. He yanked the blade from his shoulder, and the wound sealed shut. The seven people swirling around him collapsed.

Herater. He must be behind this, practicing his dark magic. His worship of Abaddon strengthened the abomination.

Black-robed monks circled the temple of Abaddon. The armies of Weileighn and Dalova rained arrows on them. Rows of mages hurled fireballs, but the magic did not touch them. And while the archers felled many, in the dark of Abaddon's stench, their aim left much to be desired.

She would have to do this herself. She kicked his chest hard and pulled at the same time. The extra force provided the torque she needed to free herself. She'd have to think about how to handle him. She'd not anticipated him being this large, this strong. He bore little resemblance to the angel who helped King Solous overthrow the elves. She thought of Pacha in heaven.

Even angels can die.

Adonai had assured her Aiden would be here, somewhere, but she hadn't seen him yet.

A sound blasted above the racket of battle. It sounded exactly like a gunshot.

She leapt into the air, surveying the battlefield. Near the city walls and surrounded by soldiers and mages, Parker leveled his gun at the demon.

How did he get here? And who stood behind him, with the golden hair and the steel eyes? If she didn't know better, she'd have thought it was her mother.

Abaddon lifted himself into the air after her. He flew much faster than she thought capable. She spun, her flaming sword at the ready.

Rather than stabbing at him again, as she had last time, she used it to parry his attacks, to swipe at his hands, the sharp, bony processes on each knuckle.

"You cannot defeat me," he said. "I'll suck the life from the very land itself. I am immortal."

Water pulled into the soil, but not enough to keep it moist. The roots of the trees withered, turned brittle, and cracked. If Pellbred was sick before, it was dying now.

She ascended higher, hoping to draw him farther from the land than his pestilence reached. But no matter how high he flew, the very life force poured into him, drained from the land, from the people.

She needed help. She had to bring him back to the city, where the mages and archers would distract him.

Barreling past him, she touched down in the center of the city. The archers and mages had assembled themselves in ranks and stood at the ready, though their twisted bodies and pale skin made them look fluish, as if they might collapse at any moment. If she hoped to win this battle, it wouldn't be as an angel of fury. The best offense here was a good defense.

Abaddon landed in front of her and smiled. "When I have drained your life, I will drain the life of Adonai's Hand, and Alrujah will bend its knee to me."

Behind him, the black-robed monks continued their chanting.

She reached deep within her memory, a world and a lifetime away, and found what she needed.

Basketball.

Abaddon was nothing more than a big, ugly center, and she a fast, nimble point guard. Behind him, the hoop. She faked left, and Abaddon struck at her.

She swiped his clubbish hand aside, pivoted on her foot, and spun around him.

Abaddon roared, but she'd already lunged to the circle of monks. With a broad sweep of her blade, she cut them down.

Something hit her hard in the back. Bone knives? She crumpled.

She smiled, swallowing her nausea. "I know how this battle ends," she said. "With your death."

"Bailey?" Aiden said from behind her.

She recognized his voice immediately and turned to him. "You are the Finger of Adonai," she said. "This battle belongs to you. Take my strength."

The wound in her back spread up her spine, to her shoulders, to her neck. Pain stabbed her bones. She collapsed before Abaddon, her mouth unhinged in pain.

WHATEVER POTION DARCY had given Aiden did little to steady his legs or return his strength. He wobbled as he walked toward Abaddon. Confronting him now would be suicide. Abaddon's power to drain life seemed to be tied to those black-robed monks. He had the wrong target.

A pop rippled in the sky, distant, but came shrieking down in a winking flash of light. Did a plane explode?

The hazy air thickened and rippled with a burst of clean air as a four-winged angel landed in front of Abaddon.

The ground shook with the force of her landing, and Aiden's shaky legs crumpled.

He wouldn't die like this. He was the Hand of Adonai. He'd come back to save his friends, not to die before he found them again.

Think of Lauren.

He remembered her, the gentle slope of her nose, the menace in her eyes when mad, the subtle smile when self-conscious.

The angel in front of him, lunging at Abaddon, striking and moving, looked like Lauren.

Bailey? Couldn't be. She wasn't even 5'8", and this four-winged monstrosity stood near to seven feet tall. But the litheness of limbs, the movement, the graceful dance of her sword; it had to be her.

Shots exploded from the row of archers.

Mages ineffectively hurled fireballs at the Blood Monks.

The people fought a losing battle. Their strength, Aiden's strength, waned with each passing second.

He wouldn't die like this, kneeling in the mud, too weak to lift his shield or his sword. And what good would a blade do against an enemy armored in bone? He needed a mace.

Didn't the army of Dalova have a regiment of mace men? A horse would be good, too. But his legs were too weak to stand, let alone ride.

He reached within himself, willed himself to stand, willed his legs to hold his weight.

Unsteadily, he stood, using his shield for balance.

The ground shook again. The angel fell, collapsed before Abaddon, her face tilted up toward the lightening sky.

Yes. How did he not see it earlier? "Bailey?" he said.

"You are the Hand of Adonai. This battle belongs to you. Take my strength."

The weakness in his legs vanished. His stomach, once twisted into knots, loosened. A strange, surging power traveled up his arms to his shoulders, then down through his back. He stood, shield at the ready. "You okay?"

Bailey collapsed. A wound on her back grew black and gangrenous. Yellow pus leaked from the wound.

"Bailey!" Becca shouted.

Abaddon swung at Aiden. He had enough time to raise his shield. The force of the blow knocked him back, but he kept his feet. Earlier, the force of Abaddon's blow almost destroyed him. Now, he was on an equal footing. "You better hope you didn't hurt Bailey for good."

"The little angel will die moments before you. But I will let you live long enough to see her perish."

An otherworldly power surged through him, a righteous anger burning meteor hot in his heart. "I am the Hand of Adonai," he said. He stood before the abomination as a dwarf stands before an elf. He raised his shield and declared, "Attack!"

Volleys of arrows darkened the hazy air. Fireballs launched. Blocks of ice crystallized around Abaddon's feet. Lightning split the air, charged the stench with static electricity. The cavalry rushed in, and Abaddon knocked them back. He belched billions of beetles into the air.

Aiden grabbed a mace from a fallen Dalovan and walked to Abaddon. "I am war."

"You are nothing," Abaddon said as he crushed a horse under his foot. He lifted his arm and brought it smashing down toward Aiden.

Aiden deflected the blow and followed with a crushing swing of the mace. The steel spiked ball crunched into the abomination's left shoulder. Its bone armor chipped. Beneath it, the ball sank into stringy, soft flesh. "I am wrath."

Abaddon swung again, and Aiden deflected the blow easily. The power in him was a new aliveness, a new sense of being, an overwhelming sense of righteous power.

Gun shots. The bullets chipped the bone, and Aiden targeted the chinks in the bone armor. He brought the mace down with a cruel strength.

Bone gave way to steel. The flesh beneath surrendered easily. This was no abomination. This was a bug, a cockroach, and Aiden was the boot. "You hurt my friend," he said.

"The angel was nothing."

Minutes ago, the fear in Abaddon's pinched voice would have surprised him. Now, it made sense. "I am judgment." He swung the mace at Abaddon's head. The abomination blocked the blow with his left forearm. It snapped under the force of the blow, and the monstrosity bellowed.

Aiden swung again, and this time, the mace split the bone visor.

Aiden displaced himself, forced himself to ignore the smell, the bubbling flesh, the crunching of broken bones. He was a child, smashing rotted pumpkins with a baseball bat. He was hitting rotten apples off a tee.

Blood Monks rushed him, but all fell before they got close, with arrows or with flames or with bullets.

Smash.

Abaddon didn't move, but Aiden pressed on, fueled by a deep, burning hate. He knew, as he brutally crushed Abaddon's lifeless body, the wound on Bailey's back would not heal.

He crushed Abaddon's head, because it was all he could do. It was all so sad—returning to Alrujah, leaving his parents, only to see his love's sister die before her mother.

"I am vengeance." With a deep, animalistic growl, Aiden crushed Abaddon's head beneath his armored boot.

The suffocating stink coalesced into a dark, swelling cloud, into a tidal wave of ink, until, at last, a rippling peal of thunder shook the ground, and a glowing garnet bolt flashed from the cloud, completely destroying Abaddon, each shard of bone and the tangled flesh, even the stink of the beast.

Aiden's muscles shook, with rage, with relief, with a baffling, unsettling fear.

He'd seen this bolt before, with Belphegor, the Seers, with Moloch, and now with Abaddon. He didn't like the stench the bolt left. Something was wrong.

27

War and strife will mark his coming, and Alrujah will cry out against him. But his root will not wither. His tree will bloom, and a new kingdom will be established in his branches.
—The Book of Things to Come

WHEN SHE WOKE, Lauren's head was in Oliver's lap. She blinked. Her body hurt from scalp to toes. An otherworldly fatigue paralyzed her muscles. Bruises and cuts burned. She didn't even remember getting these wounds, and yet they burned. She gathered the little strength left in her and spoke. "Oliver?"

He ran a finger along her cheek. "Easy. You're in a stasis hold."

Of course. A stasis hold would hurry her healing. "How bad?"

"You'll live. Be back to normal in a bit, I'm sure. You exhausted yourself out there. Overextended."

"And you didn't?"

Oliver shook his head. "Someone had to save the day."

She smiled. "When do we move?"

"Tomorrow. Today, we rest and heal."

She took a breath and worked her energy into words. "We're going to Alrujah."

"About that," Oliver said. He slid a saddle bag beneath her head and stood up. Leaning on his staff, he continued. "Remember the red lightning? The crimson bolts we saw after we beat Belphegor and Moloch? Turns out Myrassa has some sort of prophecy about those things. Mother Eider, the leader of the Utahemi Women, was telling me they herald the breaking of the worlds."

Lauren's head spun. Her body ached, but she hated lying still. "Worlds?"

"Right? Plural. My guess is Alrujah and Myrassa, but I worry about Earth, too. They're all connected somehow. You were raptured back to North Chester, you said, and then came here from North Chester through a portal. We've already been to Myrassa and back through similar portals. Have you found anything in *The Book of Things to Come* about it?"

"Not the lightning," she said. "Let me get up? I'm feeling better." She wasn't, but she was already tired of lying down. She wanted to stretch. "If Earth is in danger, we have to stop the bolts. Aiden is back there."

Oliver waved a hand over her, and the stasis field vanished. Immediately, she wished she'd been more patient. Pain appeared as quickly as the field disappeared. The bumps and bruises, scratches and scrapes, made themselves apparent. She worked to ignore them, to steady her legs and stand, but the shaking in her legs and hands told her sitting was a better idea.

She clasped her hands together to keep them from trembling. "So you think the lightning is going to break our worlds?"

Oliver shrugged. "Feels like we'd know about it, if it were, you know? Like, if Adonai wanted us not to kill the abominations, he'd have said, 'Hey, how about you don't kill them?'"

"Maybe the worlds are supposed to break."

Oliver slid his hands in his long sleeves. "Can't see why we'd want them to."

Where was Bailey Renee? Aiden? Erica? She missed her friends so much her heart hurt.

Oliver sighed. "Flip through the book again, see if you can find something."

"What are you going to do?"

He folded his arms. "I have bodies to bury."

As he left, the shadows of trees coagulated into a body. The woman in black, the woman Oliver brought back with him, walked toward her.

Maybe Lauren had taken a hit to the head. If she didn't know better, she'd have sworn the woman was shadow.

She knelt in front of Lauren. "You are awake now. Good."

"Who are you?"

"I am Shadow Singer," she said, her voice a pinched whisper.

"You're from Myrassa?"

"I am." A black cloth hung from her ears—the veil she'd donned before slaughtering hundreds of fangands and beresus.

Lauren wanted to ask her about the red lightning, about how she'd gotten to Alrujah, but it hurt too much to talk, took too much energy. She lay back down, put the back of her hand on her forehead. She needed water. Her throat felt like beef jerky.

Maybe Aiden was right. Maybe she should have stayed in North Chester. She was there, blocks away from home, from her bed, from a hot shower, from her couch and television and Xbox. She could have stayed and been happy.

Until the world broke. "The red lightning," Lauren said.

"Is a bad sign. Seven times it strikes, and then the worlds break."

Seriously. What happened to this girl's voice? Had she been punched in the throat? "What worlds?"

"All of them."

"How do you know?"

"The words of the prophecy are clear. Even the women know the prophecy."

"If it has to do with the end of the world, Korodeth must be involved in it somehow."

"Oliver will send the bodies to the sea soon. Will you come?"

Lauren shook her head. "Too tired, and they're not my people."

Shadow Singer tucked her feet beneath herself. "This is your world. By extension, they are your people."

"But they're not from Alrujah."

"Nor are you. Your bones sing of another world but carry a subtle Alrujahn melody."

The little girl, Lily, Oliver had called her, sat beside the woman and rested her head on Shadow Singer. "What are you guys talking about?"

"Nothing," Lauren said.

"About the ceremony," Shadow Singer said. She held the young girl like a mother holds a daughter. The gentle gesture contradicted the savagery she'd shown in battle. At one point, Shadow Singer had savagely torn two limbs from an attacking oak, melted into shadows, and emerged behind a fangand, beheading it before she vanished and appeared in the limbs of an old hickory long enough to plunge her blade into the distended black abdomen of an arachand. She was a woman of brutal grace, of vicious beauty. No wonder Oliver stared at her with affection and fear and wonder. He looked at her as if he'd never loved Erica, which saddened Lauren in a way. If he could fall out of love with Erica, how much easier could Aiden fall out of love with her?

"You and Oliver?" Lauren asked.

"We are friends," the woman said. The girl put her hand on her mother's knee. "In Myrassa, a woman does not pick a man. But if I could, I would spend my days with him. His song is unbroken, its melodies haunting and evocative."

"When are we going?" the girl asked.

"Soon," Shadow Singer said. To Lauren, she whispered in her wreck of a voice, "He speaks of you. The monk. He names you friend. He was worried when I took him. He insisted you needed him. But he needs you more."

Lauren arched an eyebrow. "What do you mean?"

"His song is different when you are near. He loves you. Not as a man loves a woman, but as a sister loves a sister."

"You mean a brother?"

"In Myrassa, women do not have brothers. Only sisters."

"Sounds like an interesting place."

On the other side of the river, a deer nibbled grass only feet from the bloody remains of a fangand.

"You are a queen?" the girl said.

Lauren nodded.

"In Myrassa, women do not have power. I think I like Alrujah."

Lauren smiled sadly. "Me, too."

WEEKS AGO, or was it months, Bailey Renee broke her mother's heart. She'd stood in the threshold of her front door while her mother forbade her to leave the house. Bailey left anyway.

She'd had to find Lauren.

How long had her mother cried that night?

And now, she had to break her mother's heart again, and Franky's, too.

The wound on her back spread up her spine. The corruption of Abaddon crawled through her flesh like worms through soil. Already, it spread through her nerves—a tar-like taint blackening the veins of a leaf.

This was the end. This was how she died.

The stink of Pellbred dimmed. The gaseous brown haze hovering over the swamp city lifted, but the light in the world faded. Sounds swirled together like food coloring in water. It took all of her strength to remain awake, to stare back into Aiden's terrified eyes. He spoke, but the words ran together, and Bailey found herself thinking about Franky, about Lauren, about her mother.

"Bailey?" The high-pitched voice must be her mother's.

She drew in breath, tried to put the raging infection down. She needed a minute of lucidity, sixty seconds of clarity, for her to say goodbye. Offering a silent prayer to Adonai, she inhaled deeply.

Water near her elbows. No. Blood. And mud. The cobblestones beneath her back. Bodies in black robes. Soldiers in heavy armor. Cavalry in mail. And in the middle of the chaos, her mother. She thought to ask how, but she already knew—Adonai. He'd brought her mother, and, inexplicably, even Parker and Franky. "Mom."

Her mother knelt beside her and ran a panicked hand over Bailey's cheek. "Honey, what happened? You're sick. What do I do?"

"Find Lauren," Bailey said. "Shedoah will come. She must stop him."

"Bailey?" Franky's voice, like a harp.

Her chest rose with each slow breath. Inside her, the infection burned, and the air cooled the searing pain.

He, too, collapsed beside her. He grabbed her hand. Tears cut clean streaks through the mud on his face. His skin glistened in the nascent sunlight.

"Don't cry." Each word seeped from her like air from a balloon. "I love you."

"I love you, too, baby. Hang on, okay?"

Her mother pleaded to Aiden. "Do something."

"I can't. Don't you have a spell or something?"

She shook her head. "Baby, don't leave me, okay?"

The light in Alrujah dimmed. Bailey closed her eyes.

Oliver would have healed her, if he was there, or at least he'd have tried, but the infection must be beyond his limitations. Still, he was brilliant. He'd have found a way. He'd have come up with something to save her. Or maybe he wouldn't, and when she died, she'd see him again in heaven. They'd have family dinners again, Oliver sitting beside Lauren, her mother worried about work.

But those times had passed. Her spirit slipped. A few more minutes, and she'd be back with Adonai, with Pacha el Nai. She'd have a mansion right next to his.

~

SHIGANI TOOK great care to describe the processional in detail. Like he had with each of his instructor's lectures back in North Chester, Oliver committed Shigani's words to memory. He made connections between the ritual burial. It wasn't far from other ancient burial rites he'd studied when creating Alrujah, but water played a more prominent role.

Reverently, he anointed the forehead of each of the fallen with river water. Hip deep in the piercing cold current, he let each body sink into the Alrujah River.

The current would pull the bodies of the fallen downstream, probably as far as the bay, where the water dragons and vi-fish would feast on the bloated flesh.

Red lines flowed in the river like ribbons in wind.

Shigani stood on one side, Mother Eider on the other.

Oliver performed the same ritual for the women as he did the men—something they'd never have done in Myrassa, but Shigani insisted, and Mother Eider eventually relented. In all, they returned twenty-seven Nochiko and thirteen women to the sea. Over each body, he spoke Myrassan words of peace. He even had Shigani translate a simple phrase for him. "May you find your way beneath Adonai's wings."

His heart broke each time the water swelled over their faces, and their bodies sank, carried downstream in the frigid current. The water washed away the blood, made them appear healthy, but the lack of bubbles chilled him, erased any thought of their well-being.

Lauren sat near the camp beside Borgrad. Shadow Singer sat next to her. They whispered together, Lily on Shadow Singer's lap.

He made his way out of the river and patted himself dry with an old tunic. The wind bit at his wet skin with icy teeth. He pulled his robe back over his head and folded his arms.

Shigani put a hand on his shoulder. "You have done well, Baikada."

Oliver thanked him and grabbed his braided staff. He knelt in front of Lauren. "What are you two talking about?"

"None of your business," Lauren said. She smiled.

Her coy answer confirmed his suspicion. They'd been talking about him. How much had Shadow Singer told her? It didn't matter. The work before them outweighed any of the numerous, embarrassing stories either of them might tell the other.

Before the ceremony, on their walk from the woods to the campsite beside the river, he'd tried to explain what'd happened to him since Harael—how he'd woken up to Shadow Singer, sailed into another world, taken over the Nochiko clan, rescued the Utahemi women from the breeding camp, and found his way back to Alrujah. It was a lot to summarize, and he left out plenty of irrelevant details —mainly about Shadow Singer's forthrightness, the kissing and the like.

In turn, she told him about the battle with the Seers, how Langley flipped out, how they ended up in North Chester and came back, all but Aiden. She told him how Bailey vanished, how Yarborough and Langley and Eljah ended up on the Council, and how she'd left the Heart in a haze of anger. Borgrad, the dwarf, insisted he go along to protect her.

She'd asked if he was interested in Shadow Singer, and Oliver dodged the question each time it came up. But his well of excuses had run dry. If she asked again, he'd be forced to tell her.

"So no word from Erica?" he asked.

Lauren shook her head. "Still in Alrujah, I'm guessing. I'll find out when we get there in a few days."

Oliver scratched the end of his staff in the loose dirt near the bank of the river. "We can't simply walk into Alrujah. You know how dangerous Korodeth can be."

"He's no Mage Lord, and I'm pretty sure I can handle him."

Shadow Singer said, "I admire your confidence, but assassinations require more subtlety."

"I'm not going to assassinate him. I'm going to take my throne back."

Borgrad said, "A contested throne is not an easy throne to sit. You must remove anyone with claim to the seat you hope to hold."

"Or we could wait," Oliver said. "I don't like Korodeth either. And he'll pay for what he's done. But we have to be smart about it."

"You sound like the Council," Lauren said. "I didn't come back to Alrujah to sit around while Korodeth ruins my world."

"We have more important things to worry about," he said.

From behind him, Shigani spoke. "The Blood Bolts must be our priority. If we cannot stop them, you will have no world left to rule."

"Come with us," Oliver said. "We've been apart too long. Don't go to Alrujah by yourself."

Borgrad slammed the butt of his axe into the earth. "I say we go to the Council. If any know of these Blood Bolts, it will be them."

Lauren arched an eyebrow. She stood and brushed the grass from her dress. "If they knew of them, wouldn't they have told us?"

"Borgrad says you left in a bit of a hurry," Oliver said gently. He had no will to stir Lauren's anger. "What if they know, but didn't have a chance to tell you?"

Lauren rolled her eyes. "Pretty weak argument."

"Please," Oliver said. "When I was in Myrassa, I saw the blood bolt stitched to the men of the Utahemi. Shigani spoke to me of it. I knew it then, and I know it now—the Blood Bolts will be the end of all Alrujah."

"If we go to Alrujah," she said, "you could see Erica."

Oliver shook his head. "This is bigger than me. It's bigger than Erica. Don't you get it? The end of the worlds. That means North Chester, too. We are all connected."

Lauren's eyes glowed blue. She wasn't happy, but she was listening.

"A good queen listens to her advisors," she said. "Very well. We will go to the Council to see what they know."

ERICA WOKE LATE. The suns hovered high in the sky. Must be close to noon, but she'd gone to bed late, and even with the mattress and sheets—something she'd not had in forever—she couldn't sleep.

Each time she closed her eyes, she saw Tiamat swallowing Robert, heard his scream cut short as the abomination's jaws snapped shut, its grisly teeth poking out the sides of its mouth.

Each time she breathed, the backs of her hands ignited in searing pain.

Phantom pains—the monk had healed the hands—though the scarring remained, and now Lakia bore the same disfigurement that Erica had. Sleep did not come easily.

Shortly before the suns rose, her imagination gave up. Her eyes slipped shut, and no images of burning buildings, of wrecked wheelchairs, plagued her.

She woke slowly, blinking crusted eyelids and yawning. She rolled out of bed, stretched, and bent over to touch her toes. Her muscles ached, and her back protested. But she stretched every morning, no matter how tired or sore. She needed to be limber now, needed the relief of well-maintained muscles.

Delvyn had a new dress delivered to her room, and she put it on now. This one better suited her. Sleeveless, the black fabric was stitched with gold thread. Though it was a bit long for her taste, she appreciated the simple, flowing design. She'd end up tripping on it a half dozen times at least.

Oliver should have programmed a sewing machine into this silly game. If he had, she'd make herself some gloves. For now, she'd have to find a pair in town.

She sighed and opened the wooden shutters of the window.

Outside, birds chirped as they alighted on blackened timber. Tiamat's flames had decimated the city, but the wildlife tweeted on.

People lined the streets, most in simple brown clothing, sleeves rolled up as they brought in new timber. Men worked with axes, attacking the charred bones of walls that refused to fall. Women worked to prepare meals and bring whatever the men asked.

Chauvinists. She bet half the women were as good with an axe as they were with a needle. Some of them had enough meat on their bones to easily outswing the men. Instead, they quietly gathered food and scrapped together stews for lunch.

The smell of salt and spices and smoke did little to mask the sour stench of death.

Erica wrinkled her nose and turned away from the pile of bodies. Tiamat had quite the body count, but he hadn't killed so many. Droughtworm. Among the fallen soldiers, piles of old men, of women and children, lay interspersed.

Delvyn had said something about droughtworm, and bodies had piled up even before Tiamat arrived. She didn't know what the sickness was or how it killed, but Ullwen said it was quick and ruthless. Mere hours marked the time between infection and death.

Men walked by with wheelbarrows of the dead. They wore cloths over their noses and mouths like surgical masks. Probably more for the smell than for safety. Somehow, she doubted they had the medical knowledge to know how to prevent the spread of disease. Alrujah needed some basic health knowledge, and maybe some anti-bacterial soap.

She turned from the window, her stomach knotting.

For all the talk of Adonai, Erica wondered why He would allow such suffering. Same problem on Earth: AIDS, cancer, war, famine, death, tornadoes and typhoons. What kind of God would allow such suffering?

She knelt and rubbed Sparky's head. "You ready to go? Big day of shopping ahead of us."

Sparky pressed against her leg and licked her hand.

They made their way out the door and wound their way through the castle. When they reached the foyer, Ullwen joined her. A new sword at his hip, he walked with a posture which belied the stiffness and fatigue that must rack his body. If he was half as sore as her, he'd be limping, or his shoulders would be slumped, or he'd be grimacing. Instead, he carried himself like he could go another few rounds with Tiamat. "You're entirely too happy this morning."

"We are alive," he said. "Is that not reason to be content?"

She frowned. "We're alive, sure. But the streets are lined with bodies. I kinda don't even want to go shopping." Her eyes dropped to the leather sheath on his left hip, the black belt circling his waist, the golden buckle holding it up. "Guess you already went."

"A gift," he said, his fingers contemplating the hilt with gentle caresses. "Delvyn gave it to me this sunsup."

"Sunsup?" she said. "That's about when I fell asleep."

"You did not sleep well?"

"I slept late," she said.

Sparky growled.

Erica took Ullwen's elbow. "Hold on," she said. "Something's out there."

Ullwen inspected the castle gate. "The city, yes."

"No. Sparky's spooked. Something magical."

"Indigo?" he asked, his voice hopeful.

She sighed. "No. I don't think he's friendly."

Ullwen unsheathed his sword and nodded to the guards. They opened the gate, and a man in a white robe stood at the entrance. Black runes lined his sleeves, and he held an obsidian-tipped partisan.

Ullwen raised his sword at the ready.

Sparky snarled and snapped.

Erica's heart seized. "You brought Tiamat here. I saw you on the boat."

"I did," the man said, his voice resonant. "But your weapons are unnecessary. I'm not here to harm you."

"But maybe we'll harm you," Erica snarled. She made fists of her ruined hands and reached inside her to find the minds of every beast within twenty miles of the city.

The Mage Lord put up a hand. The world around him, around Ullwen and Erica, halted. Even Sparky's snarling face froze, lips up, teeth barred.

"What'd you do?" Erica asked.

"Our conversation need not be heard by those around us."

"This is a dark magic," Ullwen said. "A sealed spell."

"Indeed," the man said from behind his mask. With deliberately slow motions, the Mage Lord pulled his hood back and unstrapped his mask. His skin, milky and smooth, stretched across a hairless scalp. His eyes glowed red.

An albino.

A tall albino.

"Dillard?"

He smiled. "Your friends await you."

28

In the darkness, men will fall on their swords, dwarves on their axes, elves on their spears. They will weep for their very lives and cry out in anguish for a savior.
—The Book of Things to Come

THE STENCH of dead bodies and rotting insect carcasses stung Parker's nose. He stood close to Becca, gun hot in his hands, as if he didn't trust the black-robed monks to stay dead, nor the abomination. His heart raced, strained by twenty plus years of smoking. His chest heaved in the acrid haze of Pellbred.

Becca took a step toward Bailey, her hand stretched out to the four-winged angel, as if, by willing it, she could turn Bailey back to Becca's beloved teenage girl or heal her on the power of faith alone.

And why couldn't she? Moments ago, she hurled fireballs from her palms, seared men in black robes with a piercing white light. She'd called ice from the air, lightning from clouds.

But her power could only destroy.

Becca ran to Bailey, knelt beside her, took her hand.

Too much blood. It pooled from her back, soaked the damp soil beneath her.

This angel wasn't the overly mature, desperately determined four-teen-year-old girl who'd hid in Franky's house for days. She wasn't the one who sat in his office and told him her sister had been sucked into a video game. Couldn't be. Too tall, muscles too long, too lean. The color of the eyes was wrong, too. They were gold, not blue. But the cheeks, pale and sunken, the sloped oval-shape of her eyes, the slant of her nose, the lips so like Cindy's, so like Becca's.

Blackness crept through her skin, like ink under tracing paper, stretching out with twisted, knotted fingers.

He cleared his throat, slipped a cigarette in his mouth, and stepped over a fallen monk. He stood near her feet praying—something he'd never done before. *God, Adonai, whoever you are. Whatever you are. Don't let it end like this. Not in front of Becca.*

And not in front of him.

Franky slumped to the ground next to Bailey, his face crushed in grief, his knees broken in sorrow. He shook from shoulders to hands when he took hers in his.

Aiden stood over her, tall and imposing, the bloody mace slung over his shoulder.

Bailey's brilliantly white wings twitched beneath her. Mud and blood sullied the scaly white feathers. "Mom," she said.

Trees, dried and cracked, moistened. Roots plunged back into damp soil. The sour stench softened, replaced instead by a thick earthy odor, the smell of the swamp, the smell of life teeming in overly-wet soil.

Someone stood next to Parker, a young woman. Darcy. Blinky, he thought of her now.

"You gave Aiden something, some sort of potion. You have more?" he asked.

She shook her head, folded her arms, and cupped her elbows in each of her hands. "The soldiers took what I had left."

Parker holstered his gun. Whatever battle was about to go down between the three cities was over. No one won, and he doubted any would push to fight it now. Illness crippled most of the armored soldiers and knights, the mages and swordcrafters.

Parker's stomach turned. A little healing potion would do him well, too.

"Honey, what happened? You're sick. What do I do?" Becca said to Bailey.

Bailey drew in a deep breath. The inky fingers tightened around her ribs. "Find Lauren," Bailey said. "Shedoah will come. She must stop him."

Franky steadied his sobs long enough to say "Bailey." The word came out as a song.

"Don't cry," she said. "I love you."

"Hang on, okay?"

Parker's throat tightened. What he wouldn't give for a lighter about now. He stashed the cigarette behind his ear and cleared his throat.

Becca said, "Do something."

"I can't," Aiden said. "Don't you have a spell or something?"

She shook her head. "Don't leave me."

Bailey's eyes closed.

Parker's nails bit into his palms. Tears burned hot behind his eyes. This shouldn't be happening. He was used to dealing with bad guys in the real world, people who had the decency to die or give up when you put a few bullets in them. He was used to rescuing kids, bringing them to the hospital, watching them heal.

Evil this big was above his pay grade. He didn't belong here. None of them did. He wanted to snatch up the massive angel and leap through the next shimmering portal he saw.

He put his hands on Becca's trembling shoulders. So much for prayer. Where was God when you needed Him? Where was Adonai?

Behind him, a warm light rippled over them.

He turned. Someone tall stepped from a blazingly bright rift. He wore a white robe with black runes.

Hadn't this guy led the Blood Monks out of the church of Abaddon? Parker pulled his gun from his holster and leveled it at the man's chest. How many rounds did he have left? One? Two?

Didn't matter. So long as he had one, he'd make it count. "Freeze," Parker said.

The man stopped moving forward.

Ice crystals formed on the barrel of Parker's gun. Cute.

"I can save her," the man said, his voice low but strong.

"Says the man who tried to get us killed," Aiden said. He sprang forward, mace raised high over his head.

The man stepped out of the way, and Aiden's mace smashed into the cobblestones. Bits of rock and mud sprayed up two stories high.

Parker holstered his gun and walked toward the man. He may not be in great shape, but he threw a mean right hook.

But his feet stopped moving. Something held them down. Ice.

"Please," Becca said. "Let him help, if he can."

"What if he's trying to hurt her?" Franky said.

"She'll die if he can't help!"

Franky fisted his hands but relented.

Parker kicked out of the ice blocks. Toes numb, he stepped aside.

The man stood over Bailey Renee. "I know you don't trust me," he said to Aiden, "but we must work together."

"Save Bailey, and we can talk."

The man pulled his hood back and removed the black and gold mask he'd worn. Parker expected something gruesome, some sort of disfigurement or Hannibal Lecter face. But the man looked startlingly normal, save for the ashen white skin and red eyes. An albino?

This place got weirder and weirder.

The man lifted his staff, and the world blinked out in brightness.

LAUREN RAN her fingers along the side of her neck. Her mother used to do the same thing when nervous. When had Lauren picked up the habit?

Around her, Nochiko warriors busied themselves by gathering their supplies while others fished in the river with their swords and arrows. The Utahemi women gathered wood for fires and prepared soups for the camp. Borgrad walked beside Oliver, speaking to him in reverent tones. Shigani shouted orders in a language she didn't understand.

Lauren stood beside her griffin and ran her hand along its feathered head. It'd be easy for her to fly back to the Council. Oliver could ride the other griffin, and Borgrad could march the Nochiko to Yeval —a week's march for a group this size, easy.

But when she suggested it to him, Oliver declined. He needed to stay with the Utahemi and the Nochiko. Of course, she was pretty sure Oliver only wanted to stay with Shadow Singer. She followed a step behind him, unless she was beside him, her hand in his. And always at her heels, the little girl with the black hair.

Lily, Shadow Singer had called her.

So Shadow Singer had a daughter, but no husband. Lauren didn't know how things worked on Myrassa, but she knew in North Chester or in Alrujah, a girl of her age, unwed, with a child? Sketchy. She'd have been put out of her house here in Alrujah and left to earn a living for her daughter by prostitution. It wasn't a pretty side of Alrujah, but no less true.

Of course, when she sat on the throne, she'd change all that.

Oliver had the right idea. Instead of judging her, Lauren should be thinking about how to help.

The griffin purred—a sensation which rose rumbling from its belly until it squeaked out the beak.

Every muscle in her body ached, but her mind filled with images of straddling the saddle and flying off to Alrujah, the conquering queen.

What she wouldn't give to fly again, to feel the press of wings, the knotting of muscles beneath her, the press of wind against her face, the lift and lull, like a patient, enduring tide.

The motion had made her a little sick at first, but once she grew accustomed to it, put it in the frame of a merry-go-round, her stomach steadied.

"You're a good girl," she told the griffin. "No one else to talk to, but you've got ears, right?"

It pressed its head against her shoulder. She leaned into it, let the beak rub some of the stiffness from her shoulder. "Everyone wants to talk to Oliver. It's like I'm not even here, like I'm back in North Chester."

The griffin squawked and flit its wings.

"I know. I miss Aiden, too." For a moment, she wondered if she should have stayed in North Chester. Of course, if she had, she'd have no chance to stop the Blood Bolts, or to kill Korodeth.

But she'd be back with her mom. Bailey would have stayed, too.

She wouldn't think about it, wouldn't dwell on it. She'd made the right choice. They didn't belong in North Chester anymore. And while that might be good for her, it wasn't good for Aiden or Oliver or Bailey. They all had something to go back to—a loving family, popularity at school, college scholarships for football or academics. She had only a prickly, work-weary mother.

But she would have changed, right? Her mother would be happy to see Lauren again, would love her again, would forgive her for the terrible things she'd said before she vanished.

"You want to fly, don't you?"

The griffin pawed at the ground.

She smiled. "Me, too."

She slipped a booted foot into the stirrup and kicked her other leg over the saddle. The suns, now high, heated the oiled leather. For the first time in a long time, the suns warmed her skin. No goose bumps today, no shivering or chattering teeth. Tonight, maybe. For now, she'd enjoy the early spring weather and fly.

She'd let Wind Dancer lift her, soothe her, ease her knotted, aching muscles.

The majestic animal leapt toward Oliver, flapped its brilliant wings once, and landed beside the monk.

Oliver and Borgrad ceased their conversation. Lily pulled on his robe, and he lifted her. "Leaving?"

"For a bit," she said. "You have things under control here. It's been too long since I relaxed."

Oliver smiled. "Nothing quite like the flight of a griffin to clear the head. When should we expect you back?"

"Before dusk."

"Be safe," he said.

Shadow Singer lowered the mask covering her face. "Where will you go?"

Lauren shrugged. "Wherever the wind takes me. Queen's prerogative."

"You should tell us where you go, in case you do not return when you say you will."

Was that worry on her face? Strange to see such a savage woman, a ruthlessly efficient assassin, capable of concern. Still, she had a point. "West, I think. Maybe north. I'll scout the road to Yeval. Might as well make it a worthwhile trip."

"Shall I ride with you?" Borgrad asked, his axe slung over his shoulder.

Lauren shook her head. "You're talking. I'd hate to take you away from such an interesting conversation."

"She wants to be alone," Oliver said.

How well he knew her, and she loved him for it.

Wind Dancer squawked when Lauren dug her heels into its flanks. He dipped his shoulders low and pounced into the air. With a powerful beat of its wings, the griffin lurched upward and upward. Like a horse galloping through water.

With each beat, Lauren's apprehension lessened. She cleared her mind of Korodeth, the usurping snake, of Oliver's taking control of the group and making decisions. Mostly, she worked to put Aiden out of mind.

Instead, she focused on the land spilling out beneath her. Colors, like ink, ran together in blotches. Trees became green splotches. Lakes and rivers became rivulets of water on paper. The forest where she'd battled Legion rose like a pale pink scar. A smattering of black marked the spot the Blood Bolt struck.

She'd made this land. At least, she believed she had, until Adonai told her differently. Still, pride swelled in her. She'd known this land, loved it, long before she woke up in Alrujah Castle. And she'd love it long after she died.

At this height, her life felt smaller, less significant. Wind Dancer didn't care that she was the Daughter Queen, didn't care about Korodeth or Aiden or Bailey Renee. It knew only the wind under its wings, knew only the fingers of warm air currents pressing like fingers through its fur.

Time was hard to measure at this height, hard to follow at this altitude. When the suns lowered, she reasoned her time atop Wind Dancer had come to a close. She leaned left and brought the black griffin around, steered it back toward the scar of the woods, toward the dots scurrying around camp fires.

Wind Dancer spun downward, circling the people hustling around Oliver. The old woman, Mother Eider, and the man with the wrecked nose stood beside Oliver. And who was he talking to? Another monk, judging by the cloak.

No. The cloak was white, and the man wore a mask—black and gold and scary all over.

The Mage Lord.

He'd pay for bringing Legion into Alrujah.

Lauren leaned forward, and Wind Dancer shrieked, claws outstretched toward the man. Lauren would end it here, even if it killed her.

But as Wind Dancer swiped at the Mage Lord, its paws sailed straight through the man. Wind Dancer galloped across the camp to slow itself after its attack plunge.

Lauren didn't wait for it to double back. She leapt from its back and sent a blast of electricity through the air toward the white cloaked man, but he absorbed the magic into his obsidian tipped partisan. "I am not your enemy."

"You tried to kill me and my friends. You brought the abominations here." Her muscles tensed, and magic surged through her. She readied herself to leap out of the way of some fireball or lightning bolt or ice shards. Who knew what he'd throw at her. Probably something ten times more dangerous.

Instead, he said, "I've taken a vow not to harm people."

"Only monks take that vow," Oliver said. Why didn't he sound terrified? Instead, he sounded as if he were watching the news back home. Always in control. How irritating.

The Mage Lord drew back his hood and removed his mask. Beneath the black and gold, pale skin stretched across a knobby, bald face. Red eyes gleamed, no trick of the mask, but of genetics. An albino.

The albino.

Dillard.

"You?" Lauren said.

"Our Myrassan friend is correct about the Blood Bolts," Dillard said, his voice returning to its normal timbre. "And, if we do not act fast, the final bolt will strike."

"There's another abomination?"

"No. Before he died, Pacha el Nai passed his seal to Bailey Renee," Dillard said.

"If you've hurt her," Lauren said.

"She is hurt, but not by my hand. I must return quickly, before her life fails completely."

"Take me with you," Lauren said.

"I will take you all with me," he said as he lifted his partisan.

Alrujah blinked out.

OLIVER BLINKED.

Trees the size of skyscrapers. Thick foliage. Fir and pine.

Yeval. The Heart.

Before him, in a half-circle, seven chairs sat empty. Oliver's stomach roiled and lurched, as if he were carsick. He swallowed, willed his head and stomach to stop spinning. Once they stilled, he turned, searching for Shadow Singer.

Instead, *she* stood still, hair as black as pavement and a dress to match.

Erica, as beautiful as ever.

His heart lurched, and guilt twisted his intestines. Why? They weren't married. They weren't even dating. Still, Shadow Singer's kiss haunted his mind.

"Good to see you, too," she said.

Oliver struggled for a word. "Hi."

She grinned, and Ullwen took her hand. Had he been there the whole time?

She ran her fingers between Ullwen's and squeezed.

Guilt left him. He exhaled and smiled. "Missed you."

"Us, too," she said. Behind her, two thin, gray-haired adults stood. "My parents," she said, "but you already knew that."

"Glad they're okay." He wanted to hug her, shake her hand, something. But nothing felt right.

"Who's the girl?" Erica asked.

Oliver grinned shyly. "Shadow Singer," he said.

Shadow Singer lowered her veil and smiled. "You are Erica, the caller. Your bones sing a lovely, sad song."

"Excuse me?"

"Later," Oliver said. He pointed to the silver-armored knight and the teenage boy standing next to him. They stood with two other people. A larger man with a cigarette behind his ear and a tall, lithe woman? A very familiar woman.

"Ms. Knowles? How'd you get here?"

Ms. Knowles bent over the body of a massive four-winged angel near the center of the circle. "Help her," she whispered to Dillard.

Dillard frowned. "I have done what I can, but she has little time. When she dies, Shedoah will be freed."

"I knew it," Erica seethed, her hands fisted into tight balls. "You were working for Korodeth this whole time."

"No," Oliver said. Already, his mind pieced together the sketchy information they had. "She is the final seal, and if she dies, the final Blood Bolt will wreck the worlds."

Dillard took the middle seat—Eljah's chair. "Shedoah's touch has weakened her beyond our ability to heal her. She will die soon, and Shedoah will be freed."

"Dillard?" Mother Eider asked. She walked toward him, one trembling hand outstretched.

The albino monk lowered his head. "It is good to see you again, Kachaan."

Oliver furrowed his brow. "Wait. What?"

"You've been gone so long. Have you been here this whole time?"

Dillard nodded. "By the will of Izanji, the will of Adonai."

"Am I the only one who's confused?" Erica asked, Sparky leaning against her leg. "What's happening here?"

"No clue," Aiden said.

"You are the boy?" Shadow Singer asked. "I've heard tales. Now, your plan makes sense to me. You wanted to rescue the women from Myrassa. You wanted me to protect Oliver so he could bring them here."

"I had other tasks that required my attention here," Dillard said.

"What tasks?" Aiden said. "You summoned the abominations here to Alrujah from God knows where. You wanted us to kill them, didn't you? To break the seals and free Shedoah."

Dillard shook his head. "The seals—the abominations—had been tainted by the touch of Shedoah. Only Pacha el Nai resisted the taint. The bonds, little as they were, weakened with each day." He held *The Book of Sealed Magic* up. "My studies of ancient texts led me to believe I would see the coming of the Hand, and the rupture and renewal of the seals. However, I'm not certain that holds true now. Already, I feel the power of Shedoah swelling. It's far more than I imagined it to be. If the final seal ruptures, we may not be able to stop him."

Erica folded her arms. Oliver recognized her face—she'd figured it out. "You brought us here." She turned her head, considering Ms. Knowles weeping over the angel. "And our parents."

"My dad's dreams," Aiden said.

"I sought the Hand, yes. I called your fathers here, your mothers, through their dreams. I thought I'd found the Hand, but they were not the Hand."

"And you pulled Bailey here, too? With her dreams?" Becca asked.

He shook his head. "Bailey was brought here by Adonai himself."

"Why?" Oliver asked.

"Adonai's ways are his own," Dillard said.

"You were wrong about the abominations, maybe you're wrong about Bailey being the last seal," Lauren said, her voice hardly above a whisper. She knelt beside her sister and slipped an arm around her mother.

"He's not," Oliver said. "Those black lines are the touch of Shedoah, and Shedoah can only touch this world through his seals."

"That's what Abaddon did to her," Aiden said.

"The wound, yes," Dillard said. "The transformation to a herald of war was the work of Adonai, at which time, he transferred the seal from Pacha el Nai to Bailey Renee."

"How do you know?" The teenage kid next to Aiden asked. Franky? How'd he get here?

"He's right," Oliver said. "I can feel the taint and the seal. Monks can do that."

"I don't care about any of this," Ms. Knowles said. "I want my daughters back. I want to take them and go home."

"We can't go," Lauren said. "We have to stay. If we go back, how are we going to stop Shedoah?"

"The final Blood Bolt will rend your world as it will ours," Shigani said.

"Who asked you?" Ms. Knowles snapped.

The man said, "I'm not sure I get all this seal and doom and gloom and Armageddon talk. I've got a job to do, so I'm going to take these girls and get them home."

"How exactly are you going to do that?" Oliver said. "We don't have a lot of power here. The way I see it, we've got to find a way to keep Bailey alive." Of course, they had to plan to defend Alrujah if she died, but he didn't want to think about it. Not Bailey.

"That you talking, or the girl?" Erica asked. Sparky sat, impatient with all the chatter.

Shadow Singer replaced her veil. "I speak for myself, caller. His words are his alone."

"What happens to Bailey," Ms. Knowles said as she stood, her face splotchy and red, "if we break the seal? Will she get better?"

Of course. Why hadn't he thought of that? The touch of Shedoah was killing Bailey, but he could only reach her through the seal. And if that connection were severed, Shedoah's taint would wane.

"Would she get better?" Lauren asked again.

"Long enough for the worlds to explode," Oliver said. "What we need to do is find a way to transfer the seal to someone else."

"None are strong enough to hold it," Dillard said. "Adonai's transformation of Bailey was to ensure she would survive bearing the seal. If any of us were to take the seal ourselves, we would die, and Shedoah would be freed."

"So break the seal," Ms. Knowles said. "You owe her that much."

Ullwen said, "We cannot. To do so would be to end our worlds. We must find someone strong enough to hold the seal."

"He's right," Oliver said. He didn't like the way Ms. Knowles studied Bailey Renee.

"Don't," he said, as if she could, as if she knew the ancient, sealed spell to destroy the bonds of Shedoah. She couldn't know it. He doubted if Dillard, with all his ancient knowledge and prophecy, even with *The Book of Sealed Magic*, could do something so powerful, which is why he had the Hand destroy the abominations. "Give us time," he pleaded. "Let's find someone."

"She's dying," Becca said. "I won't wait. I won't watch her die."

Like Lauren, Ms. Knowles would be an empath mage—able to wield powerful spells they'd never cast as long as they'd seen them worked. And if a Blood Bolt had struck, it meant the spell had been unsealed from *The Book of Sealed Magic*, which meant that Ms. Knowles could conceivably break the seal.

And, if Bailey was the final seal, Ms. Knowles may have seen a Blood Bolt.

Ms. Knowles closed her eyes and lifted her chin.

Oliver's braided staff shook in his hands. The hair on his arms stood up.

She couldn't, wouldn't. "Ms. Knowles?" he said, touching her shoulder gently. His fingertips brushed her skin, and an impact like dynamite punched him back.

The air above Bailey Renee rippled in silver pools of water.

"What's she doing?" Erica asked.

"Please don't," Oliver said. "Give us a chance to find another way. Maybe we can forge new seals before this one ruptures."

"Mom?" Lauren asked.

Ullwen said, "Not yet. We aren't ready!"

"Protect the seal." Dillard stood, stretched out his partisan toward her. White hot light erupted from the tip, but, with a wave of her hand, Lauren dissipated the radiant blaze.

"How dare you attack my mother?" she said.

Shigani unsheathed his sword and leapt toward Ms. Knowles, but Lauren knocked him back, too. "Have you lost your minds?"

"Lauren," Oliver said. "Don't let her. We need time."

"Bailey doesn't have time," Lauren whispered. "If this is what it takes to save Bailey, we've got to do it now."

A brilliant crimson bolt flashed fission-hot from the silvery waters down to the ragged, blackened wound across Bailey's back.

She shrieked like a griffin, like metal twisting and tearing.

The ground growled and groaned, shifting beneath Oliver's feet.

And the world broke beneath him.

**PLEASE ENJOY THIS SAMPLE OF
ANOTHER BRIMSTONE FICTION TITLE**

Crossing Into the Mystic

By DL Koontz
PART I
Valley of the Shadow

CHAPTER 1

All of it became mine that day: the hefty trust fund, my mother's red SUV, and my stepfather's ancestral estate isolated amidst the caverns of the Blue Ridge Mountains. I was embarking on a 500-mile journey to make solo use of all three.

As long as I remained in Boston, I would continue to live my life backward—dwelling on the past and longing for the parents and sister who were dead. Buried. Gone. There was no way I could have known that by turning away from death I would be running into it.

That day seemed like the perfect time to launch my escape. The rising sun shot beguiling streaks of crimson through the divisions of the massive brownstones on Boston's Beacon Hill, teasing away any threat of "Red sky at morning, sailor take warning."

In the stillness of the morning, I heard a house door latch, then a husky voice grumble. "Ouch ... ouch ... dang!"

My cousin, Michael, barefoot and clad only in gym trunks and a T-shirt, pranced between stones as he hurried up the steep three-block incline toward me. He was carrying travel snacks, but what I hoped he was bringing me was reassurance of our individual escapes.

"Grace, go! Go! Go! Click your heels and get the Sam Hill out of Oz before she changes her mind!"

Though Michael's words echoed my resolve, I laughed. He was four inches taller and eight years older, but a million times more sociable and often reminded me of an oversized little boy.

"Auck, Dorothy." He reached my car, glanced back toward our house, and handed me a zip-locked bag stuffed with trail mix. "You're too late. You'll never get to Kansas now."

I turned to see the subject of his wicked witch allusion exit through the oversized front door of our ivy-covered brownstone and begin her march up the sidewalk with Uncle Phil dawdling behind. Aunt Tish wasn't toting a flying broom, but she was storming along, face scowling, hands fisted.

Michael grinned. "I guess she's saving the flying monkeys for me."

"Maybe. She wasn't very happy about you leaving tonight for Chile. You sure you're tough enough to stand up to her?" I elbowed him, knowing he wouldn't feel the jab. Despite his baby face and wire-rimmed glasses, he had the abs of a bodybuilder.

"No problem. She can't control me anymore. It's you who better leave quickly."

"I'm going. Don't worry about that." I tossed the trail mix on the back seat. From the front, my dog, Tramp, watched it land and turned back to the front window, more excited about going somewhere than the goodies. He barked twice. Let's go.

"Good. It will be two years before you'll get another chance," Michael warned in a whisper. "I won't be here this summer to save you like I have before."

"Which is exactly why I'm leaving today. Thanks for coming home to see me off. She's not that bad you know." Maybe voicing such hope would make it so.

Eyes wide, he said, "What? She's an unstable, soul-sucking—"

"Shush." I stifled laughter. "She'll hear you."

He sobered and leaned against my car, crossing his arms. "You're sure about this?"

"The trip? Of course."

He shook his head. "The house. It sounds ... weird. Like Norman Bates lives there."

I looked at him, startled. Michael was generally carefree and titillated by the unknown. He loved the notion that people held secrets within themselves.

"That's crazy," I affirmed, lest his uncharacteristic concern unnerve me.

"Is it? Jack was so close-mouthed about the place."

"Michael, stop it! It's only a house. Jack was there three years ago. How bad could it be?"

"Remember. I'm only a phone call away. You have to live there what—three months?"

"That's what the will says. Then it's mine to do what I want. Including selling it. And, of course, that's exactly what Aunt Tish expects me to do."

"We'll work that out later. Stick with this charade that you're fixing it for your senior project, then selling it and moving back to Boston. By the end of summer, my new company will transfer me back to the states, and you can live with me. Just don't come back here."

"I know, I know."

"And keep Tramp close by."

I shook my head to indicate his concern was unnecessary. But inside, I couldn't

help but wonder if Tramp would be able to stop all threats that I might encounter.

After stopping to assess her own vehicle and bark orders at my Uncle Phil to take it to the car wash, Aunt Tish reached us. As her eyes scanned my car, Uncle Phil plodded up behind.

Beside me, Michael murmured, "Shoulda' tied garlic around our necks," then he donned a Cheshire grin and bellowed, "Good morning, Mother dearest."

"Nice of you to grace us with your company, darling," Aunt Tish clucked with saccharin sarcasm and crossed her arms. Her face was stern, her eyes leveled. "If I didn't know better, I'd think you were trying to sleep your way through the day until your flight leaves."

"Got in late, Mom."

She arched a skeptical brow. "If you're turning right around and leaving for that ridiculous job in Chile, why did you even bother coming home? You could have been working at MacGruder's, you know. They are the most prestigious firm in Boston."

"Yeah, Mom, I know."

"They certainly would have paid better. Must be nice to have no concerns about money."

"I haven't cost you a cent since I turned twenty-one. And if you're so worried about money, why do you live in this pretentious place? How can you afford it anyway?" He clicked his thumb and middle finger. "Oh, that's right. You used Grace's education fund."

She exhaled into a pout. "You kids are so disrespectful. Why do you do these things to me? Haven't I suffered enough?"

"Here we go." Michael rubbed his forehead.

"And look at you. Go put on some clothes. What will the neighbors think?" Her eyes darted to the windows of the lofty brownstones shadowing the street.

"Yeah, Mom. They'll probably think I feed nails to little children since I don't wear shoes." He turned his back to her and smiled at me, then withdrew to the back of the car and shook my bike as though to make sure it was tethered securely. I could see his grin from the corner of my eye.

"We'll talk later about you arriving home one day just to leave the next."

She turned to me, swapping irritation with sadness as easily as if she'd replaced a straw hat with a ball cap. Wiping at invisible tears, she sniffled and brushed back a lock of frizzled hair, causing her peace sign earrings to sway to and fro. With characteristic dramatic flourish, she took one of my hands and pressed an object into my palm.

"Your keys. Why your mother insisted you keep this atrocious gas-guzzler, I'll never know. I never did understand her."

I wrapped my fingers around the keys, feeling the shape of independence. "Thank you."

It was expected of me to treat this as a heart-rending gesture on her part, even though she had readily agreed to the trip because she wanted the house to be sold as quickly as possible, thereby placing more money into my accounts, to which she had access.

Aunt Tish pouted. "You selfish kids are breaking my heart with these trips."

I kept quiet. Best not to acknowledge her fabricated sadness or her varnished insult.

Receiving no response from her selfish kids, she turned to my uncle. "Philip, I must be crazy. I'm going to be thrown in jail for letting a 16-year-old live by herself ... in some creepy house in a ... a ... redneck wilderness."

From the back of the car, Michael groaned.

"Aunt Tish—" I began.

Uncle Phil cleared his throat and stood tall, looking for a moment more like the commanding professor he was when teaching Chaucer at Boston College than the ventriloquist's dummy he played at home for his formidable wife. "Tish, she'll be fine. It's only for the summer."

"But it's so far away from Beacon Hill and civilized society, for bloody sake," she responded stiffly. "She won't be around our kind. Those people are so provincial. What will my friends think? And that house ..."

Uncle Phil sighed. "The house is fine. The management company said so."

"Yeah, Mom," Michael scolded from his retreat, "just because the place is old doesn't make it creepy. Heck, our house is old."

Uncle Phil shot his son a quelling look. "Jack loved the place. He spent a lot of time there. It must be in good shape. And if it's not, then Grace will fix it up. That's the whole point of this trip anyway." He frowned. "Besides, by the time you were sixteen, you had already been arrested for disturbing the peace and indecent exposure."

"Oh gawd, Pops." Michael cringed and reached up to rub his temples. "Too much information."

Uncle Phil continued. "You already set up a bank account for her. She has a credit card. She's got everything she needs. If anyone can take care of herself, it's Grace."

"Yeah, Mom," Michael chimed from behind the car. "Crimeny, she's been taking care of you for the past three years."

Aunt Tish pushed her tangled hair behind her ears and huffed. "Fine. Obviously no one cares what I think. Just go, Grace. But stay out of trouble. I don't want any calls from the police."

I mouthed a "thank you," to Uncle Phil, shoved my backpack on the heap of boxes lining my back seat, and shut the door. Tramp sat waiting on the passenger seat. On the floor, my cat Chubbs crouched in his carrier, obviously annoyed. On the console sat an envelope containing $5,000 in cash, covered with road maps graphing my way from Massachusetts to West Virginia.

"Aunt Tish, I'll be fine." I pulled her into a sideways embrace as I rounded to the driver's side and opened the door. She was my only aunt and despite her opinions of me, I wanted to believe her capable of feeling genuine concern. "I promise to call every day."

"Be careful. If something goes wrong, it's a reflection on me." As she pulled away, she flicked at my hair. "And for pity's sake, Grace, do something with that ridiculous hair while you're there."

I ignored her. "Remember your dentist appointment tomorrow. I left a note on the fridge."

She waved that away with a Yes, yes, I know all this dismissal, but I knew she would forget.

Then, because I felt it was expected of me, I looked back toward the house and lied, "I'll miss this place."

I voiced some inane comment about what I'd miss, but my thoughts were on the excitement of being me, rather than a dead couple's orphaned child or Tish Rosenburg's ungrateful niece.

The goodbyes complete, I climbed into my car and pulled away. I could see Michael standing behind my aunt and uncle, flailing his arms in a dramatic don'tstop-keep-going wave.

"Call your Grandma Sadie, she's not doing so well," was the last thing I heard Aunt Tish bark as I descended the hill and rounded the corner onto Beacon Street, took a final glance at Boston Common, and headed toward I-95 South.

The trip underway, I exhaled deeply. I'd loved to have driven into the future without looking back, to have fast-forwarded to summer's end when Michael and I could plant roots somewhere together. But, there was no shortcut to that time, and I felt dread press in on me as if each accumulated mile were adding a hole to the safety net I hadn't yet hung in place.

OTHER BOOKS BY AARON GANSKY:

The Bargain

Who is Harrison Sawyer

Heart Song

Firsts in Fiction

ABOUT THE AUTHOR

Aaron Gansky is an award-winning novelist, teacher, and frequent speaker at national writing conventions. He earned his MFA from the prestigious Antioch University of Los Angeles. He's also a bit of a nerd--a comic book fan, a lover of games (board, video, and card). Mostly, he's a father and a husband. He's pretty proud of that.

 facebook.com/adgansky

 twitter.com/adgansky

 instagram.com/aarongansky